SOLDIER

SLDIER

NEW YORK TIMES BESTSELLING AUTHOR
JULIE KAGAWA

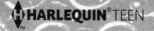 **HARLEQUIN**®TEEN

ISBN-13: 978-0-373-21160-9

Soldier

Printed in U.S.A.

To Nick

PART I

RECONNAISSANCE

GARRET

The world was on fire.

Flames surrounded him, crackling in his ears, filling the air with heat and smoke. Coughing, the boy huddled in a corner the fire hadn't reached yet, tears streaming painfully down his cheeks, burning his eyes. He couldn't breathe. Everything was so hot; sweat poured off his small body and drenched his clothes. Gasping, he crawled toward an open closet on the far wall, wanting only to escape, to hide in the beckoning darkness and hope it all went away.

"Garret!"

A blurry form moved across his field of vision, and someone swept him off the floor. Instantly, he relaxed, burying his face in her neck as she clutched him tight. He was safe now. As long as she was here, he was safe.

"Hold on, baby," she whispered above him, and he squeezed his eyes shut as she began to run. Heat pressed against his back and arms and scalded his bare legs, but he wasn't afraid anymore. Somewhere close, he heard shouting and gunfire, but he didn't care about that. Now that she had found him, everything would be okay.

A cool breeze hit his skin, and he peeked up from her shoulder.

They had left the building; he could see it burning behind him, orange-and-red tongues of fire snapping overhead. The shooting and screaming got closer, and a couple people went rushing past them, toward the noise and the chaos. A deafening boom rocked the earth behind them, and he flinched.

"It's okay," she murmured, stroking his hair. He could feel her heartbeat, thudding rapidly against his chest as she staggered down the road. "It's okay, Garret, we're okay. We just have to find Daddy and—"

There was a roar above them. He looked up just as something huge and terrifying swooped down on black leathery wings, and the world cut out like a light.

★ ★ ★

"Ladies and gentlemen, at this time we're beginning our descent into Heathrow Airport. Please return to your seats and make sure your seat belts are securely fastened."

As the captain's voice drifted over the intercom, I opened my eyes and blinked as the plane came into focus. The aisle was dim, with only a few reading lights shining here and there. Outside the window, a faint pink glow had crept over the distant horizon, staining the clouds below it red. Most everyone was asleep, including the elderly woman in the seat beside mine. The engines droned in my ears as I yawned and shook my head. Had I dozed off? That wasn't like me, even on a ten-hour flight over the Atlantic Ocean.

The remnants of a dream lingered in my mind, familiar and disturbing at the same time. Heat and smoke, fire and gunshots, a woman carrying me to safety, the roar of a dragon in my ears. I'd had this nightmare before; for years my sleep had been plagued with death and flames and, above all, dragons.

The frequency of the nightmares had faded with time, but every so often, I'd be right back in that burning room as a four-year-old, a woman I no longer remembered carrying me to safety, the screams of dying men echoing all around us.

And my first glimpse of the monster I'd soon dedicate my whole life to fighting, descending on us with a roar. That was where the dream, and the memory, ended. How I'd escaped certain fiery death, no one really knew. The Order had told me I'd repressed that memory; that it wasn't uncommon in children who'd experienced something traumatic. They'd said I didn't speak for three days after they'd rescued me.

I supposed there were few things more traumatic than watching your mother die in the jaws of a dragon.

I leaned back in my seat and gazed out the window. Far, far below, I could see glimmers of light where a few hours ago there had been nothing but darkness. I'd be happy to get on the ground again, to be able to move around instead of sitting in a tiny cramped space surrounded by strangers. The woman beside me had talked nonstop at the beginning of the flight, saying I reminded her of her grandson, showing me pictures of her various family members, lamenting that they never visited anymore. When the pictures had run out, she'd started asking questions about *me*, how old was I, where were my parents, was I traveling overseas all by myself, until I put in earbuds and feigned sleep in self-defense. I'd heard her mutter "poor dear" before she'd dug a crossword book out of her purse and scribbled in silence until she dozed off. I'd been careful not to wake her while she slept and to appear engaged in other things when she was awake, on the long, long flight across the Atlantic.

The plane shuddered as it hit a patch of rough air, and the

woman beside me muttered but didn't open her eyes. Leaning my head against the window, I watched the lights scroll past hundreds of feet below. *Do dragons ever fly this high?* my tired mind wondered.

My thoughts drifted. Another dragon appeared in my head, crimson red instead of black, bright and cheerful instead of murderous. Pain flickered, and I shoved it away, willing myself to forget, to feel nothing. She was no longer part of my life; the girl with the quick smile and brilliant green eyes, who had made me feel things I'd never thought possible... I would never see her again. I didn't hate her; I wasn't even that angry. How could I be, when she had saved my life, when she had showed me so much, including how wrong the Order was? I'd spent my life slaughtering her kind, and she had responded by befriending me, saving me from execution and fighting at my side against Talon and St. George.

But she was a dragon, and when I'd finally confessed my feelings and confronted her about her own, she'd balked. Admitted she wasn't sure if dragons could feel that way, that they weren't *supposed* to feel human emotion. And that her pull toward Riley, a fellow dragon who'd set his sights on her, couldn't be ignored any longer.

I'd realized then, how futile it was. Loving a dragon. It had been easy to overlook her true nature, to just see the girl. I'd never forgotten what she was, especially when she Shifted into her true form and I was reminded of how powerful, savage and dangerous dragons could be. But it was more complicated than that. Hovering in the back of my mind, constantly plaguing me, was the knowledge that, even if Ember could return my feelings, she would outlive me by hundreds of years. We had no future together; we were two different species, and there was a war raging on both sides that would stop at nothing to destroy us. Even if I could love both the girl and the dragon, what kind of life would I—a former soldier of St. George—be able to give her? I didn't even have a future for myself.

Resolve settled over me. It was better that I'd left; now she could be with her own kind, as it should be. She was with Riley and his rogue dragons. Their lives would be dangerous, constantly running from Talon and St. George, but Ember was stubborn and resourceful, and Riley had been outsmarting both Talon and St. George for a long time. They didn't need me. Ember Hill, the dragon I'd fallen in love with, would do just fine.

"Ladies and gentlemen, we are making our final descent into Heathrow Airport," the intercom droned again. "Please put away all laptops and large electronic devices and make sure your seat trays are in the upright and locked position. We'll be landing in about fifteen minutes."

The lady beside me woke with a snort and gazed blearily around. Taking her neck pillow off her shoulders, she turned to me with a smile.

"We made it," she announced, as I smiled stiffly back. "It'll be so nice to get up and walk around, won't it? I swear, these flights get longer and longer. Where in London are you headed after this, dear?"

"Knightsbridge," I lied. "I have friends there. I'll be staying with them for a couple weeks."

She bobbed her gray head. "Well, make sure they take you to see the sights. London is a wonderful city. Are you planning to visit Buckingham Palace or Westminster Abbey?"

"I'm not sure, ma'am."

"Oh, well, you have to go to Buckingham! Can't visit London without seeing the palace." And she launched into a lecture on all the popular tourist places I should go to, the ones I should avoid, the hidden "treasures" around the city, and she didn't stop talking until the plane had landed and we had filed out into the bustle of Heathrow Airport.

★ ★ ★

I watched the city of London roll by under the streetlamps as the cab took me to a small hotel in South Kensington, about a mile from Hyde Park. As we passed an old church, a flutter of white overhead caught my eye. The flag of St. George, a red cross on a background of white, flew prominently in the wind, and the uneasiness that had somewhat faded on the plane returned with a vengeance.

I had arrived. In London. The Order's largest and most influential territory. Though I'd been to the city only once, I could be sure of one thing: I would find no dragons here, or in any of the surrounding towns. St. George's presence in the city was huge and obvious. The Order's symbol, the red cross on a white shield, was everywhere throughout London, on signs and churches and building walls. Though St. George was the patron saint of England itself, and we shared his flag with the rest of the country, the message to Talon was very clear: no dragons allowed.

It was dangerous for me to be here. I knew that. The Order was looking for me, and if I was recognized, I'd never make it out of the city. Thankfully, most of St. George's soldiers and armed forces were housed elsewhere, as England's laws on weapons and firearms were very strict. But the Patriarch, the head of the Order itself, ruled from London with the rest of the council and oversaw all of St. George's activities. If he discovered I was here, I'd have the whole of the Order on my back in a heartbeat.

But he was also the reason I'd come, the reason I was looking for answers. How much did he and the council really know about Talon? Did they truly not know about the rogues, the dragons who wanted nothing to do with the organization and the war? I couldn't believe they were that ignorant, that they had been ignorant for so long. St. George knew something, and if the Order was keeping secrets, I needed to find them. I had killed dozens—dragons and humans alike—because the Order told me I was protecting the world. I owed it to those lives, to all the innocents I might've killed, to discover the truth.

At the hotel, I checked in, tossed my single bag on the bed and, even though I'd been traveling for more than ten hours straight, pulled out my burner phone and called the number I had memorized before I left the States.

As the phone rang, I checked my watch. It was 6:32 a.m. London time; early, but he knew I would be calling once I'd landed. Still, I counted seven rings before there was a click, and a gruff voice sounded on the other end.

"Yeah?"

"I'm here," I said quietly.

He grunted. "No trouble with the Order?"

"None."

"Good. I'd lie low if I were you. Though you really shouldn't be here at all." There was a snort, and I imagined him shaking his head. "Stubborn bastard. I still think you're insane, Sebastian, coming *here* while the Order has a price on your head."

I gave a faint smile. "This is the last place they'll think to look for me."

"Doesn't mean you should push your luck, mate."

"I need your help, Andrew," I went on. "I wouldn't have come if it wasn't important. But if you can't see me, if you think it's too dangerous, you can walk away."

"Oh, piss off," Andrew growled. "Like I'm going to turn in the guy who saved my life." He sighed. "But we do need to be cautious. The Order literally has eyes everywhere. If they see us together, we're both dead."

"When is a good time to meet?"

"Today," was the reply. "This afternoon, twelve o' clock. I'll text you the address now."

"Roger that."

I hung up, double-checked my door to make sure it was locked and finally stretched out on my bed and stared at the ceiling. My eyes felt heavy, but I needed to stay awake, both for the impending meeting and because the jet lag would kill my internal clock. I wished I had a pistol or even a knife, but smuggling either onto a commercial airline wasn't possible. I'd have to get by without a weapon, for now, anyway. There was a bolt and a chain on the door; if anyone was going to break into my room to kill me, at least I'd have a little warning.

All right, St. George. I'm here. What haven't you been telling us? And is it going to destroy the last bit of faith I have in the Order's ideals? Will I discover that you are just as soulless and corrupt as Talon?

I almost didn't want to know the answer.

EMBER

On three, Riley mouthed, gazing at me from the other side of the door frame. I nodded, feeling my muscles tense as we stared at the peeling white door with the gold 14 near the top, hearing sounds of a television through the wood. My dragon growled and stirred, sensing violence, and I narrowed my eyes. Riley took a deep breath and raised the pistol he'd kept hidden under his leather jacket. *One…two…three!*

He drove his boot into the wood, kicking it right beside the brass knob, and the door flew open with a crash. I lunged inside, Riley right behind me, sweeping the pistol around the hotel room. It was small and dirty, an unmade bed in the corner, the television blaring away…but the room itself was empty.

"Dammit!" Riley lowered the gun, glaring around the abandoned space. "Gone again. We probably just missed the slimy bastard." Scowling, he yanked his phone out of his pocket, pressed a button and put it to his ear. "Wes, he's already gone." Pause. "I don't know how he knew—it's Griffin! When was he not a paranoid cockroach?" He sighed. "Right. Heading back now. Call me if there's an emergency."

I exhaled slowly, letting the dragon and her hope for retribution settle back reluctantly. "Now what?" I asked Riley, who snorted.

"Back to square one, unfortunately. Wes will track him down again, see where the bastard has gone to hide next. But it could take time, and we're running out of it. Dammit." He punched the wall, causing a hollow *boom* to echo through the hallway. "So close. Well, come on, Firebrand. Before the cops show up, let's see if he left anything behind. Any hints as to where he's gone now."

We quickly searched the room, but despite it being a dump, Griffin hadn't left anything that could be traced back to him, not even a crumpled receipt.

"He probably paid with cash," Riley growled, after emptying the trash bins, looking under the bed and rummaging through the bathroom yielded nothing. "And covered his tracks really well. Damn him. Looks like he cleared out in a hurry—he knows we're onto him." He scrubbed a hand down his face. "I don't know what's more irritating—that he's being a giant pain in the ass, or that he's so good at it because *I'm* the one who taught him."

"He'll make a mistake," I said. "Just like last time. Wes will catch it when he does. He can't run forever."

"You don't know Griffin," Riley muttered. "But, yeah, I guess you're right." He shook his head. "Anyway, there's nothing here and nothing we can do now. Let's head back."

I followed him out the door, back down the hall to the parking lot. A dented black Mustang with tinted windows sat in a corner space, and Riley wrenched open the door, slid inside and slammed it so hard, the car shook.

I sat down and closed my door with a little less force, then

SOLDIER   19

watched Riley gun the engine to life before squealing out of
the hotel lot. Light from the streetlamps slid over his angry
face, his jaw set, gaze glued to the windshield. Leaning back
in the faux leather seat, I sighed and looked out the window.
Another small Midwestern town, ordinary and indistinctive,
sat beyond the glass. We'd been through so many lately, I didn't
even remember its name.

I understood Riley's frustration. The human we were chasing, Griffin Walker, had been one of Riley's contacts before
we discovered he'd been feeding information to both Talon
and St. George on the sly. Griffin was the traitor, the mole in
the rogue's network. In Las Vegas, he had sold us out to Talon,
and we'd nearly been killed because of it. But worse, because
of him, all of Riley's safe houses, all the hatchlings he'd gotten out of Talon, could be in danger. We had to find him and
discover what he knew and how much he had leaked to the
organization. But catching one human on the run was prov-
ing more difficult than we could have imagined. This was the
second time in nearly a month that we'd gotten close, only to
have our elusive quarry disappear yet again.

It was beyond infuriating, but at the same time, it kept my
mind off...other things. Issues I didn't want to deal with right
now. I was so busy helping Riley track down Griffin, I didn't
have time or the energy to dwell on anything else. And Riley
was determined to save his underground, to keep his network
safe and his hatchlings away from Talon; he was consumed
with finding the traitor that had sold us out to Talon and St.
George. In the days following Las Vegas, we'd barely spoken
to each other about anything non-Griffin or Talon related,
which was both a relief and a disappointment. If we slowed

down at all I would start to remember...certain people, and I wasn't ready to face that, yet.

Back at our own hotel, we went straight to Wes's room and locked the bolt behind us. The human sat hunched over his laptop on the corner desk, the same position we had left him in hours earlier. He gave us a weary look as we came in and shook his head.

"Nothing," he said before Riley could ask. "No phone calls, no new credit card transactions, bloody nothing. Trail's gone cold, mate. Griffin is officially off the radar."

"Dammit," Riley growled, stalking forward. "Slimy, slippery bastard. Keep looking," he ordered, and Wes turned back to the computer with a sigh. "We were *that* close, Wes. We can't let him sneak away now."

Rubbing my eyes, I turned away, knowing Riley and Wes would be working for a couple hours at least. Wes practically lived in front of a screen, and Riley's anger would keep him going, but this constant breakneck pace was starting to get to me. "All right, you two have fun," I said, moving toward the door. "I'm going to crash until you need me."

Riley looked back, gold eyes solemn as they met mine. For a moment, my dragon stirred, her gaze almost challenging as we stared at each other. Daring Riley—no, daring *Cobalt*—to come out and face her. He wouldn't, and we both knew it; Riley certainly would not risk exposure by Shifting into his true form when there was no need. But my dragon instincts still hoped he would. Riley hesitated, as if he was about to say something, but then Wes muttered at him and he turned away.

"Get some rest while you can, Firebrand," he murmured, bending down again. "We'll probably be leaving in a few hours."

Without answering, I retreated to my room across the hall, went to the bathroom and stripped out of my clothes. Including the black Viper suit, which I dropped unceremoniously on the floor. It slithered to the tile in a spill of rippling black fabric, and I wrinkled my nose at it before stepping into the shower.

The near-scalding water hit my skin, and I sighed, closing my eyes as the steam rose around me. We'd come so close tonight. So close to being done with this crazy search, to discovering what information Griffin was leaking to Talon and putting a cap on it for good. I had no doubt we'd find him, sooner or later. No one could hide from Wes for long, and if you dared screw around with Riley's hatchlings and safe houses, well, good luck to you. I wouldn't call Riley *obsessive*, but he was certainly unyielding and determined, and his underground was everything to him. Plus, he could be a teensy bit on the vengeful side.

After shutting off the water, I toweled, dressed quickly and wandered into my empty room, flipping on the television out of habit. Noise was welcome. Silence was depressing and kind of lonely. Worse, in the total silence, my thoughts went places I didn't want them to go. Memories that were still too raw, too painful, to shine a light on. People whose absence was a great yawning emptiness in the pit of my stomach, or whose betrayal made it feel like a mirror had shattered within and the shards were cutting me up from inside.

Flopping onto the bed, I turned to some random action movie and cranked up the volume, trying to drown out my thoughts. *Focus*, I told myself, watching some guy in a sports car speed down narrow streets, knocking over trash cans and barely missing passersby. There were more important things to worry about than my own jumbled emotions. I wasn't a normal hatchling anymore, whose only concerns were having fun, fitting in and doing what the organization told me to do. I was a rogue, part of Riley's underground and probably Talon's most-wanted dragon next to Cobalt himself. Vegas had shown me exactly what the organization was capable of. If I didn't take things seriously, more people, and more dragons, would die.

A soft tap on the door made me look up. "Firebrand," came a familiar voice through the wood, and my dragon perked at the sound. "You still up?"

Pushing her down, I swung off the bed, crossed the room and opened the door. Riley stood on the other side, hands in his jacket pockets, dark hair hanging in his eyes. He looked tired, though his mouth curled into a faint smile when he saw me.

"Hey," he greeted in a quiet voice. "I…uh, wanted to talk to you before you crashed. Okay if I come in for a second?"

I shrugged and moved aside, even as my insides began a crazy swirling dance, sending heat rushing through me. "Did Wes find anything on Griffin?" I asked, reminding myself to stay on topic.

Riley shook his head. "No, nothing yet. But that's not why I'm here." Keeping his hands in his pockets, he leaned against the wall, watching me with solemn gold eyes. I perched on the edge of the mattress, facing him. "I'm worried about you, Firebrand," Riley said. "Ever since we left Vegas, you haven't been yourself."

I forced a grin. "What should I be?" I asked, and he sighed.

"I don't know. More…talkative? Stubborn?" He shrugged, looking frustrated and at a loss. "You haven't really talked to me since we left Vegas. And everything I say, no matter what, you just...agree with. It's disconcerting."

"You *want* me to argue with you?"

"At this point? Yes." Riley frowned, raking his hair back. "Argue with me. Tell me I'm wrong. Say something, anything! I don't know what you're thinking anymore, Ember. I know it hasn't been easy for you, with Dante in Talon and—"

"I'm just trying to pull my weight here," I interrupted, before he could go any further. He blinked, and I pushed back the anger and grief that rose up whenever I heard my brother's name. "I don't want to slow you down. I know what's at stake. How important this is, for all of us." His brows furrowed, and I shrugged, looking over at the television. "I'm a rogue, now," I said. "No more playing around. No more sneaking off, or being distracted by human things. I'm going to have to learn to shoot and fight and...kill, or more of us are going to die." My mind flickered to the image of a small purple dragon, sprawled on the cement floor of a warehouse, gold eyes staring up at nothing, before I shoved the memory down.

"So...yeah." I looked back at Riley. "I'm taking this seriously. Which means following your lead, and concentrating on the mission. Nothing else matters."

"Ember..." Riley sounded even more weary all of a sudden. Pushing himself off the wall, he stepped in front of me, his expression almost sad. "That doesn't mean I want you to lose yourself completely," he said, as I gazed up at him. "Don't let this life break you. You're young. You have a very, very long existence ahead. No, I don't want you sneaking out or throwing crazy parties in the middle of the night, but it can't be war and fighting every second of every day. You'll burn out before you hit Juvenile. Or you'll get so bitter and angry, you might do something *really* crazy." The corner of his mouth twitched into a wry grin, then he sobered once more. I didn't smile back, and he eased closer—close enough for me to smell his leather jacket, to feel the subtle heat that pulsed beneath his skin.

"I don't want you to hate being here, Firebrand," he went on. "I don't want you to regret going rogue. I know I've been distracted, but I want you to know you can come to me for anything. Don't think you have to go through this alone. Trust me, I have been through everything you can imagine." He snorted. "Just ask Wes. He can tell you horror stories."

My heart beat faster. Having him this near made my back itch and my skin feel tight from wanting to Shift so bad. Riley hesitated, as if just realizing how close we were, but he didn't move away. I looked up at him and saw Cobalt's intense, golden gaze peering down at me.

For a moment, we teetered on the edge, both dragons close to the surface, waiting for the other to make a move. But then Riley's gaze darkened and he stepped away, breaking eye contact.

"You should get some sleep," he said, as my dragon growled with frustration and disappointment. "It's been a long day, and we'll want an early start tomorrow. I'll come wake you when we're ready to go."

"Riley!"

A sharp rap made us jump. Riley drew back, looking almost relieved, and strode quickly to the door. Pulling it open, he glared out at Wes. "Did you find him?"

"Not quite, mate." Wes spared me a quick glance and narrowed his eyes, before turning to Riley again. "But you'll want to see this. Griffin contacted *us*. I just got a message from the slimy bastard."

"Where is he?"

"No clue." Wes shrugged. "But he wants to meet us soon, face-to-face. Said he wants to make a deal. That he has information he's willing to trade...for protection."

Riley scowled. "Protection? What makes him think that I would..." He trailed off, shaking his head. "Dammit," he breathed. "Talon. Talon is after him, too. He wouldn't have contacted us if he wasn't freaking out."

"Yeah." Wes nodded, a grim smile crossing his narrow face. "That's what I'd guess. And under normal circumstances I would say to hell with the two-faced cockroach—he can reap what he's sowed. Let a Viper chase *him* around for a change of pace. But..."

"But we need whatever information he might have," Riley growled. "And we can't let Talon learn what he knows." He raked a hand through his hair and glared at Wes. "What does Griffin want us to do?"

"Says he'll contact us with a meeting place if we agree to his terms," Wes replied, making a sour face. "Terms being that we won't kick his ass when we find him, and that we provide him with a safe place to hide for as long as he needs it."

Riley growled again, clenching a fist. "Fine," he said through gritted teeth. "I can't risk losing any more safe houses, and I can't let Talon get their claws on Griffin. He knows too much about us." He gave Wes a brisk nod. "Contact Griffin. Let him know we agree to his terms. Tell him to try not to get himself killed by a Viper before we can reach him."

Wes nodded and ducked out of the room, and Riley looked

back at me. The moment was gone; Cobalt had disappeared, and it was just Riley again.

"Sorry, Firebrand," he said, taking a step toward the door. "I should probably be there when Griffin contacts us again. Will you be all right?"

I nodded. "I'll be here," I said simply, and he went, striding into the hall after Wes and closing the door behind him.

For a moment, I stared after him, a heavy weight settling over me. I knew, logically, that Riley was distracted. Finding Griffin and keeping his underground safe was foremost on his mind, as it should be. Rationally, I accepted that.

But at the same time, I wondered if Riley's feelings toward me had changed. There had been no hints or clues of what he wanted from me, if he even wanted me anymore. Now that I thought about it, whenever we were alone—either in the car or in the hotel room—he was careful to keep his distance. To not get too close. Tonight was a good example. There had been something between us—we'd both felt it…but he had backed off. Had he forgotten his promise of a few short weeks ago? Or had I been a fleeting distraction that he'd gotten over?

I hopped up, threw the lock and returned to the bed. The dragon still writhed and squirmed inside, making it hard to relax. Sleep would probably be impossible tonight, as it had been most nights since we left Vegas. I was exhausted, but my brain just wouldn't shut off. When I did sleep, the dreams were waiting. Being chased through tight quarters by humans with guns, skinned dragon hides hanging on the walls and Lilith appearing every so often to taunt me. Or urging me to turn and slaughter everything in sight. I'd wake up covered in sweat, my blood roaring in my ears, while the echoes of screams and gunfire faded into the darkness.

But those dreams weren't the worst. The worst dreams were the ones when, cornered and trapped, I'd spin around to finally face my pursuers...and it was Dante who appeared from the shadows, green eyes hard as he came into the light. Or sometimes it wasn't Dante, but a human with short blond hair and metallic-gray eyes, staring me down over the muzzle of a gun. Once or twice, it was a girl, delicate and pale, her dark curls tumbling down her shoulders as she stepped forward. Sometimes we spoke, though I could never recall the conversations. Sometimes they ended with an apology, sometimes with a gunshot that jerked me awake and sent my heart racing. But more than a few times, I would find myself in dragon form, wondering what had happened, and there would be a charred, blackened body sprawled on the cement. I wouldn't recognize it at first, didn't know what I was looking at, until its eyes opened—black or green or metallic-gray—and it would whisper a single word.

Why?

Those were the dreams where I'd wake gasping, my eyes blurry and hot. Those were the images that kept me from going back to sleep, where I'd turn on the television and all the lights and try to forget everything until morning.

Riley didn't know about the nightmares. He was too busy with the hunt and keeping his network safe. Sometimes, I thought Wes suspected something, the way he looked at me when I joined them in the mornings, his taciturn face almost worried. But I couldn't break down. It was just the three of us, now: me, Riley and Wes. Riley needed an equal partner, someone he could count on, not some kid he had to worry about. I had to focus on what was important. I couldn't let any more of us die.

My stomach throbbed, a constant, low-grade ache from the stress of not Shifting. I could still feel Riley's touch, the heat in his gaze when our eyes met. My dragon side wanted him; it was obvious now that I couldn't ignore those instincts. But, at the same time, I still thought of *him* constantly. Where was he? What was he doing right now? The more I tried to forget, the more he returned to haunt me, making me realize that I'd made a mistake.

I missed the soldier.

Frowning, I straightened on the pillows. *You can't think like that, Ember,* I scolded myself. *He's gone, and it's better that way. He's human. You're a dragon. It would have never worked. Let him go.*

My throat felt tight, and I breathed deep, banishing the last of the memories, at least for now. Griffin would contact us soon, and Riley would probably want to move out as soon as he did. Not much time for sleep, but I wasn't going to get a lot, anyway.

Grabbing the remote, I turned up the volume of the television and leaned back against the headboard. Who needed sleep when you could watch car chases and random explosions all night? Settling into the pillow nest, I let my eyes unfocus and my mind go blank, as revving engines and Hollywood drama replaced reality for a little while.

RILEY

"Riley," Wes said, sounding impatient. "Did you hear what I just told you, mate?"

"Huh?" I turned back from the door to face my partner's annoyed glare. "Sorry, Wes. What?"

He huffed. "I said that if Griffin is in trouble with Talon, we're going to have to be bloody careful ourselves. For all we know, this could be another brilliant trap we're walking into. I wouldn't put it past the bastard to set us up again."

I nodded. "Yeah, I know." I scratched my chin, frowning. "But we don't have much choice. Who knows what kind of information he has now."

"Bloody hell," Wes growled. "For a computer illiterate, the blighter certainly can get his hands on a lot of intel."

I shrugged. "He's been at this a long time, Wes, almost as long as us. He was a slimy little toad even before we met." Back then, Griffin had worked as a liaison for Talon, infiltrating companies they wanted to acquire, learning everything he could—their policies, financials and dirty laundry—even turning a few of their own employees against them. All to set up Talon's hostile takeover.

But Griffin's talent for acquiring information eventually got him into trouble. As his web of contacts grew and the secrets he uncovered got bigger and bigger, Talon had decided that he knew a little too much. Through his contacts, Griffin had learned of his impending "retirement," and that was when he'd reached out to me. The deal was simple: if I helped him get out of Talon *and* taught him to stay off their radar, he would give me what he knew about the organization. The trade had sounded fair, and the info he'd offered had seemed too good to pass up, so I'd accepted.

"Too bad you didn't know what a two-faced bastard he was before you let him into our operations," Wes muttered. "I never liked him, Riley, have I mentioned that? I thought he was shady from the start."

"You *have* mentioned that one or sixty times, yes." I glanced back at the door, wondering what Ember was doing now. "After Griffin contacts us," I told Wes, "turn off the damn laptop and get some sleep. You're running on Red Bull and Mountain Dew fumes right now, and we could all use a couple hours rest."

Wes leaned away from the laptop with a slight frown. "That's not like you, Riley. I was expecting to be halfway out the door as soon as we heard from him."

"I would be, but Ember needs the break. She's tired, and this constant running around isn't helping. I thought I'd give her at least a few hours' sleep before we start again."

"She's not sleeping, mate," Wes said quietly, still staring at me. I frowned at him.

"What are you talking about?"

Wes's gaze darkened. "You haven't noticed? Bloody hell, Riley. Have you really looked at the girl lately? She's more than tired—she's bloody exhausted. She sleepwalks through half our conversations. I go into the hall at three in the morning, and her light is still on and the television is blaring away." Wes shook his head at me. "I doubt she's getting more than a couple hours of sleep a night, and a tired dragon is a ticking time bomb. She's going to explode, unless you can get to the bottom of what's eating her."

Slightly dazed, I leaned against the bed frame, thinking back over the past couple weeks. I'd noticed Ember had gotten quieter, but hadn't confronted her about it until tonight. She'd been withdrawn for several days, and that worried me, but I'd assumed it was the frantic pace we were setting—the strain of the hunt—that was getting to her. Recently, she'd grown snappish and irritable, snarling at Wes whenever he made one of his "Wes comments." I knew she was tired. I hadn't known she wasn't getting any sleep at all.

This was bad. Exhausted dragons were more than irritable and cranky, we could be downright dangerous as our control slipped and our baser instincts rose to the surface. Poking a tired dragon was an excellent way to get yourself burned.

"What do you think is bothering her?" I asked Wes. "I talked to her tonight, but I didn't get a clear answer. Just that she doesn't want to slow us down, but I know that can't be the whole story."

Wes rolled his eyes. "Oh, I don't know, mate. We haven't been doing anything stressful lately, have we?" Shaking his head, he leaned back and began ticking things off on his fingers. "Let's see. In the past few weeks, she was shot, we were ambushed by St. George, you got kidnapped by Talon, your bloody hatchling had to fight *Lilith's* murderous Viper student…" Wes grimaced. "Take your pick, mate. She's not a soldier. She didn't have years of training like you. Bloody hell, Riley, a couple weeks ago she killed a human for the first time and watched another dragon get murdered in front of her. What do you think that's doing to her head right now?"

"Shit." I stabbed a hand through my hair. What was wrong with me? We had been running and fighting nonstop ever since we left Crescent Beach. Ember had seen nothing but constant battles, blood and death. I was desensitized to it, but she had killed for the very first time in her life. Of course it would be getting to her.

I was about to turn around and stalk back to her room when the laptop chimed. Wes looked down, tapped a few keys and scowled.

"It's Griffin. He's got a meeting place for us."

Rage flickered again, and I swallowed the growl crawling up my throat. For the sake of my underground, I would play nice with the backstabbing traitor and not rip his throat out through his teeth, but I wasn't going to be happy about it. "Where?"

"Tomorrow evening. Louisiana?" Wes squinted at the screen and groaned. "Oh, bloody hell. He's in New Orleans."

DANTE

I finished cleaning out my desk and closed the box, then left it on the corner for a worker to take down to the car. *Not even a month in, and I'm already packing up my office,* I thought, walking to the window for a final view of the Los Angeles cityscape below. *At least I'm moving in the right direction: up. Or, I hope I am, anyway.* Per normal, Mr. Roth hadn't given me any real details. Only that I was being moved to another "project" that would make better use of my talents. I could only imagine what Talon wanted me to do now. Especially after the fiasco with Mist and Faith, and the unsuccessful attempt to return Ember to the organization.

Ember, I thought, staring through the glass. The open sky beckoned enticingly beyond the pane, but it never called to me the way that it did her. *Where are you? Why couldn't you just do what Talon asked? Now you've forced their hand. You've chosen to stay with that rogue, which the organization can't ignore, and I might not be there to protect you this time.*

"Ah, Mr. Hill. Are you ready?"

I turned. Mr. Roth had entered the room, trailed by a skinny, younger human who immediately walked to my desk, picked up the box and left without making eye contact with either of us. The senior dragon didn't spare the human a single glance but smiled brightly at me, though as always, the smile never quite reached his eyes.

"Exciting, isn't it?" Mr. Roth said, clasping his hands in front of him. "New location, new assignment, another opportunity to advance. You must be pleased that the organization is taking such an interest in you, Mr. Hill. Not many are afforded such a privilege."

"Yes, sir," I said, because I *was* pleased. I was happy that Talon had noticed me, that despite the mission to retrieve Ember not having the desired results, the part I had played had proved my worth to the organization. But something still nagged at me, despite my best attempts to quell it. "I did have a question, sir," I ventured, and Mr. Roth arched one slender eyebrow. "What of my sister? She's still out there, with Cobalt. What does Talon intend to do about her?"

Mr. Roth's eyes glittered coldly, though his smile remained in place. "You needn't worry about your sister, Mr. Hill," he said. "Plans are in place to find and return her to Talon, though you must understand, she is a rogue and criminal in the eyes of the organization. We will take every opportunity to detain her without harm, but you saw the lengths to which she was willing to go to evade us. The last time we attempted contact with Ember Hill, an agent died. We cannot afford to have that happen again."

His tone hadn't changed; it was still calm and informative, but an edge had crept into his voice, and I felt a chill slide up my back at the reminder. One of Talon's agents, a young Viper named Faith, had been dispatched to bring Ember back to the organization. Faith's job was to get close to Ember, earn her trust and, when the time was right, persuade her to return to Talon. It had been a good plan; Faith and a second agent named Mist had been able to infiltrate Cobalt's hideout, and neither Ember nor the rogue had suspected anything. But something had gone terribly wrong, for when it was over, Faith was dead, the mission was in shambles and Ember had disappeared again.

Mist, I'd later discovered, was alive, though she had also failed in her mission to extract certain information from Cobalt. She'd returned to Talon quietly and was immediately reassigned, though I had no idea where. I hadn't seen her since the day she'd left for the mission.

"Your sister is no longer your responsibility, Mr. Hill," Mr. Roth continued. "Rest assured, we will find her. Trust that Talon has her best interests at heart, and will take every precaution to return Ms. Hill alive and unharmed. But you have another role now. Another project that requires your skill and talents. We hope you will make it your top priority."

"Yes, sir," I said, hearing the subtle threat beneath the words. "Of course. I was simply confirming that I can put my sister from my mind and focus on what I need to do."

I kept the confident smile on my face in front of Mr. Roth, but guilt gnawed at me. Ember had always been my responsibility. I'd looked after us both for so long, cleaning up Ember's messes, covering for her, getting her out of trouble time and time again. I would never admit it to Talon, but it was partially my fault that she had gone rogue back in Crescent Beach. Maybe if I'd kept a better eye on her, paid more atten-

tion, I could have stopped my sister from falling in with Cobalt and throwing away her future.

I'd tried to help her. I'd done all I could to return her to the
organization, knowing that if she just came back, she would
realize her mistake. But Ember had stubbornly refused, and
now her fate was out of my hands. I could only trust that the
organization would find my twin and bring her back to Talon,
where she belonged.

"Excellent, Mr. Hill." Mr. Roth nodded, the cold smile never
fading. "Exactly what we need to hear. Put your sister from your
mind—her fate is in good hands, I assure you." He raised a
hand to the door. "Shall we go, then? The car is waiting, and
I am sure you are eager to see what we have planned."

I nodded. I was moving up in the organization, as I'd intended. Designs were falling into place, and I couldn't dwell
on the past, even if it meant letting Ember go for now. Without a backward glance, I joined Mr. Roth in the hall, shutting
the door to the office, and that part of my life, behind me.

GARRET

Tourist attractions always made me jumpy.

I didn't like crowds. It was the soldier in me, obviously, responding to potential threats, to having too many people in my personal space. Crowds were a good place to hide, but that meant the enemy could do the same—melt into the throng and remain unseen until it was too late. I didn't like being surrounded, and I really didn't like strangers touching me, something that happened often in these places, as tourists seemed to share a general obliviousness to their surroundings and bumped into each other a lot.

I wove through the crowds along the river Thames, keeping my head down and my cap pulled low. It was a bright fall afternoon, and the river walk teemed with people milling down the sidewalk with no sense of urgency. But I could easily see my destination over the tops of their heads; it soared four hundred feet into the air, the massive white Ferris wheel known as the London Eye, silhouetted against the blue. An even larger crowd had massed at the base of the huge wheel, and an impressive line led up the steps to the clear plastic pods at the bottom. I set my jaw and marched resolutely forward.

"Sebastian."

A man rose from a bench and came toward me, hand out-stretched. He wore plain civilian clothes like me, but I could see the soldier in him, the way his dark eyes scanned the crowds, never still. He walked with a faint limp, favoring his right knee, a memento from a raid that went south and nearly killed us all. I shook his hand, and he jerked his head toward the end of the line waiting to get onto the Ferris wheel.

"I paid off the attendants," he said in a low voice as we started toward the Eye. "We have a capsule all to ourselves for the entire thirty-minute ride. If you can stand me for that long, anyway." He grinned wolfishly, showing a set of crooked white teeth.

"Why here?" I asked. "Seems exposed."

He chuckled. "Think about it, Sebastian. The Order hates crowds and frivolity and...well, *fun*, and they avoid the tour-isty parts of town like the plague. They wouldn't be caught dead here." He waved a hand at the massive wheel. "Plus, we'll have an enclosed glass room all to ourselves, with absolutely no chance of anyone eavesdropping on the conversation. Unless someone snipes us out, there's no way to get to us."

It was vastly improbable, but I scanned the area for snip-ers, anyway, especially the many buildings across the river. My skin prickled. So many dark windows and ledges and perches. If Tristan was here, that's where he would be now, patient and motionless behind the barrel of his rifle.

"So how did that partner of yours take it, anyway?" An-drew asked, seeming to read my mind. "Have you talked to him since the...um..."

"No," I said softly. "I haven't seen him since my trial." I

hoped I would never see my ex-partner again, because if I did, he'd probably be trying to kill me. And truthfully, if Tristan St. Anthony *was* given that order, I'd be dead before I knew he was within a thousand meters. Ironic, if I was shot down by the person I once considered my brother in everything but blood.

Suddenly wary, I glanced at Andrew, wondering how much he really knew. Had the Order shared the details with other chapters? I knew my name was out there: a rogue soldier who'd gone over to the enemy. As far as St. George was concerned, I was to be shot on sight, no questions asked. The Perfect Soldier, now Order Enemy Number One.

If Andrew's plan was to kill me, I couldn't do anything about it now, unless I wanted to take off or overpower him on a crowded riverfront. Since neither choice would help me get what I came for, I waited quietly in line until we reached the front, where the ride attendant nodded to Andrew and pulled open the door to the glass pod, then motioned us both inside. The door shut, and the capsule began to move.

Stepping farther into the pod, I gazed around warily. The oval room was quite spacious, clearly meant for large groups. You could fit a full-size car in the middle and still have room to walk around it. A wooden bench sat in the center, and the walls were clear, showing all of London far below.

Andrew stalked to one side of the room, turned and leaned against a wall, fixing me with a solemn glare. "Relax, Sebastian," he said. "I told you before. I heard what happened back in the States, most of it, anyway. I know what you're accused of. Bullshit or not, you saved my life once. That's something you don't forget. And I don't care what the Order says—anyone who has ever fought with you would know that you wouldn't just betray your brothers like that. Not without reason."

He looked away as the pod climbed slowly higher, sunlight streaming through the glass. I gazed down at Big Ben on the other side of the river, its giant face announcing that it was almost noon.

"Thanks," I said. "I wouldn't blame you for turning me in, Andrew. I'm just glad you're willing to give me the benefit of the doubt."

"I'm not the only one," Andrew replied. "A lot of us weren't happy with the way your trial was handled." He lowered his voice, as if there could be people eavesdropping, even here. "When you 'escaped,' we knew there had to be more to the story than what the Order was telling us. And I suspected I might see you again, sooner or later—I did say you could call on me for anything." He gave a wry grin. "So if you need a favor, Sebastian, as long as it doesn't involve going directly against St. George, you just have to ask. I'm guessing that's why you're here."

I nodded, smiling faintly in return. "There *is* something I wanted to ask you," I said. "You're a scout now, right?"

His brow furrowed, as if that fact was painful. "Yeah," he answered shortly. "After that close encounter with a bullet, I couldn't go on any more raids. They stuck me with intel gathering, rooting out Talon activity in assigned areas."

"And the number of strikes has increased recently, correct?"

Again, he nodded, though there was a wariness to him now, as if he knew where I was going with this.

"How are you getting the information?" I asked.

"Good question. Wish I could answer it." His brow furrowed

as he gazed back down at the city. "The Order hasn't contacted me in several months," he admitted. "I haven't found or given them any information, and I know several others in the same boat as me. St. George isn't using its scouts to find the nests. And yet...the number of strikes is at an all-time high." He made a vague gesture with his hand. "How are they finding these dragons? They're certainly not coming to us."

I frowned. That wasn't what I was expecting. I'd contacted Andrew because I had hoped to learn why Order attacks on dragons had taken such a jump. But if St. George wasn't using its scouts at all...

"That is strange," I muttered.

"I think so, too," Andrew agreed. "And it gets even stranger. I asked around, trying to find where the Order has been getting their information, and you know what I heard?" A dubious look crossed his face. "Rumors are that the Patriarch himself is receiving visions from God, telling him where to find the devils."

My brows rose. The Patriarch was more than the leader of St. George; he was almost a holy figure in the eyes of the Order. Only the most revered, staunchest devotee of St. George could become Patriarch, and once the position was filled, it was his for life. The council chose a new Patriarch only when the old one died, as they had done since the Order was founded. The Patriarch was a symbol of purity, incorruptible and utterly dedicated to the cause. But visions from God? I wasn't sure what to think about that.

"Has he been right?" I wondered.

Andrew barked a laugh.

"Well, I don't know where the man is getting his intel, but

whether it's from God or not, he's been spot-on every time.
Wherever he sends the teams, they find dragons. I guess the
Order doesn't need us anymore."

I fell silent, thinking. The capsule spun lazily, stopping every
so often as the Eye picked up new passengers or let others off.
A gull flapped by, soaring past us toward the river. "Is Order
headquarters in the same spot?" I asked finally.

Andrew nodded. "Same place it's been for the past hundred years," he answered. "Why?" His eyes widened. "You're
not thinking of going in! Sebastian, they'll put a hole in your
head before you get past the front desk."

"Relax, I'm not going inside." There wouldn't be any point.
Headquarters would not leave suspicious files or dealings out
in plain sight, and I wasn't a computer genius like Wes, able
to hack my way through almost anything. I'd never been to
Order HQ, didn't know the layout of the building, its cameras or security systems; if I sneaked in, I'd be going in blind,
something I didn't care for. Besides, I was a wanted man within
the Order; venturing into the heart of St. George's operations
seemed like a bad idea.

Andrew watched me, a suspicious look crossing his face.
"Don't suppose you're going to let me know what you're planning, are you?"

"Sorry, Andrew." I offered a half smile. "No offense, but
if anyone does find out we spoke, I can't risk the Order discovering anything about me. Better for us both if you know
nothing."

"Fair enough." The other gave a brisk nod. "I don't like it,
but fair enough. Just answer me this, Sebastian." He pushed
himself off the wall and stood straight, his gaze intense. "Is

what they say about you true?" he asked in a grim voice. "Did you really throw in with the lizards? To destabilize the Order and everything it stands for?"

I hesitated. The question wasn't angry, or accusing. It was just a question, from someone who wanted a serious answer. For a moment, I didn't know what to say. Andrew might be helping me, but he was still part of the Order, someone who hated dragons and accepted that they were soulless monsters. I could've brushed it off, told him what he wanted to hear, but deep down, he would know I was lying, and that would be a disservice to someone I respected.

"I'm trying to uncover the truth," I said at last. "Too many things happened that don't make sense with what the Order taught us. I can't ignore it anymore. I want to know whether the Order is hiding things from us. If they are who they say they are."

"Damn." Andrew regarded me solemnly. "Dangerous ground, Sebastian. I might have my own questions about the Order, but you're talking treason. No wonder St. George wants your head on a pike." He gave me a look that was both suspicious and resigned. "What is it you're hoping to uncover, exactly?"

"I don't know," I said. "Truthfully, I hope I'm wrong. But with what I've been through... I have to be sure."

"Well, you're right about one thing," Andrew said. "I don't want anything to do with whatever you're planning. If you're determined to go poking around the affairs of the Patriarch himself..." He raised both hands in a distancing gesture. "I won't warn him you're coming, but if you don't watch where you're stepping, you're going get yourself killed. But you know

that better than I do." He sighed. "After this, you're going to
vanish and I won't ever see you again, I suppose."

"Probably not."

Andrew nodded slowly. "Well, good luck to you, Sebastian,"
he muttered, with the expression of someone who thought the
other was going to die. "You're going to need it."

★ ★ ★

After the meeting with Andrew, I tackled my next obstacle:
renting a car at seventeen, on a fake ID, in a foreign country.
The clerk at the rental place gave me dubious looks all through
the transaction but finally handed over the keys. Another barrier cleared. The bigger concern was the dwindling amount
of cash in my wallet. I was loath to draw anything from the
small stipend I'd acquired from my years in the Order, as my
funds were limited and I had no way to get more. But certain things were necessary, and being able to move about the
country without depending on taxis or trains was one of them.
After that was done, I waited a few hours until early evening,
when the sun was just beginning to sink into the west. Time
to seek some answers.

Sliding behind the wheel on the right side of the car, I
headed north across the river, following the map in my head.
I'd never seen nor been inside St. George headquarters, but
Tristan had told me where it was located, so I knew where I
was going. Past St. George's Bloomsbury, St. George's Court
and St. George's Gardens, my heart beating faster with every
mile deeper that I went into Order territory.

Not far from King's Cross station, I pulled to the curb behind a double-decker bus, across the street from a row of un-
marked office buildings, and let the engine run. Around me,

it seemed like a perfectly normal afternoon; vehicles cruised down the road and civilians walked down the sidewalks, going about their business. Everything looked commonplace; there was nothing to indicate that an ancient order of knights waged war from this very spot, invisible to the public.

I leaned back in my seat, pulled my cap low over my eyes and waited.

Thirty seconds after seventeen hundred, a vehicle emerged from the private underground garage across the street. A black sedan with tinted windows rolled smoothly out of the darkness, turned left and cruised away.

Putting the car into Drive, I followed.

SEBASTIAN

Thirteen years ago

"Hello, Garret," a man said in a deep, quiet voice. "My name is Lucas Benedict, and you're going to be living with me for a little while. How does that sound?"

I didn't answer. He was a stranger. Everyone I'd seen so far had been a stranger. Where were my parents? I wanted my mommy. I shrugged and turned away a little when the man crouched down in front of me.

"Your name," the man before me said, "is Garret Xavier Sebastian. Can you repeat that, Garret?"

I frowned. That was wrong. The first part was right; my name was Garret. But the next two I hadn't heard before. "That's not my name," I told the man, who smiled. It was the first thing I'd said since my mommy...went away. But it seemed important, suddenly, to tell him. To let him know I hadn't forgotten who I was. Even if I couldn't remember what happened to Mommy and Daddy. Were they coming to get me? But no... this man said I was going to live with him.

"It is now," the man said. "And you should be proud of it. Many in the Order are named after saints, and yours is a very special one. Saint Sebastian was a great man who helped many people." He put a hand on my head, leaning close. "Did you know that Saint Sebastian was tied to a tree and shot full of arrows, but he didn't die?"

I blinked and peeked up. "Really?"

"Yes," Benedict said. "He was also a centurion, a warrior for God. Which is what you are going to be one day—a warrior. A soldier who protects people from evil and monsters, just like he did." He ruffled my hair and stood, gazing down at me. "So, Garret Xavier Sebastian, do you think you can do that?"

I nodded solemnly.

"Good," said Benedict. "Because you're going to have to work hard to become that soldier. But don't worry." He put a hand on my shoulder and squeezed. His fingers were thick and strong, but not painful. "I'll help you get there. From here on out, you're not just a little boy. You're a warrior in training. And someday, if you work hard, you'll become a soldier who protects people and fights real monsters. Remember that, Garret."

I did.

If I'd had an ordinary life before I came to live with Lucas Benedict, it was long gone. I lived in his small apartment in the middle of an Order chapterhouse and watched the daily lives, practices and routines of St. George soldiers until that was all that I knew. I ate, slept and breathed the Order, adopting its beliefs, viewing the soldiers as family, not knowing any life beyond the Order walls. When I was six, I started private classes at the chapel. It would be a few years until I was old enough to join the Academy of St. George, where all hopeful dragonslayers were trained. My education was overseen

by Brother Gregory, who drilled perfectionism into my head
even more than science or math or history. But my real les-
sons didn't begin in the classroom.

"Garret."

"Yes, sir." Never *Father*, or *Dad*, or even *Uncle*. From the
very beginning, the only title Lucas Benedict ever accepted
from me was *sir*.

"Come here. I have something for you."

Obediently, I slid from my desk, where I'd been doing that
night's homework—an essay about the Order's involvement
in the Salem witch trials—and padded across the room to
stand before my mentor. He regarded me seriously, as he always did, before he knelt and put something hard and cold
into my hands.

I looked down and blinked. A black pistol lay in my six-
year-old palms, cradled between my small fingers. A chill raced
up my back. I remembered gunshots, fire, men screaming, bits
and pieces of that night, and I shivered.

"Don't be afraid of it," Lucas Benedict told me. "It's not
loaded, so it can't hurt you. A gun is only a tool—it can kill,
but the person wielding it has to make that decision." He put
his large hand over both of mine and the weapon. "This is
yours now, Garret. I'll teach you how to hold it, clean it and
handle it safely so that when it is loaded, you'll know what to
do. But I want you to start learning now. This is what you'll
be using to fight monsters someday, so it's important, understand?"

I looked at the gun again. I could kill monsters with this.
Like the horrible black-winged creature that murdered my family. On my own, I was no match for the demons. I was just a

scared little kid who still had nightmares sometimes. But with a weapon like this, I could do my own killing. I wouldn't have to be afraid anymore.

"Yes," I replied, looking back at my mentor. "I understand. When will I get to shoot things?"

He chuckled and ruffled my hair in a rare moment of affection. "When you've proved to me that you know how to clean, handle and take care of it properly when it's unloaded, I'll teach you how to shoot it. But not before. Not until I'm certain you know what you're doing. So...want me to show you how to clean your weapon, soldier?"

"Yes, sir!"

That was the beginning.

EMBER

"Too bad it's not Mardi Gras."

Riley shot me a look from the driver's seat, the hint of a smile playing at his lips as we cruised down the narrow road. "Hoping to catch some beads, Firebrand?"

"No." I wrinkled my nose at him. "But we're here, in New Orleans. On *Bourbon* Street." I looked out the window, at the buildings with their elegant verandas draped with flags and hanging plants. I imagined them filled with people in costume, crazy masks and colorful beads, with streamers of purple and gold flying all around. One huge party, like I'd seen on TV. "I was just wondering what it would be like," I mused.

Riley snorted. "Crowded."

"Noisy," added Wes.

I rolled my eyes at them both.

"Where does Griffin want to meet us, again?" Wes asked, sounding annoyed as he gazed out the window, as if the crowds and pedestrians strolling past the car personally offended him. "And why here, in New Orleans, of all places? Right out in the open."

"Exactly," Riley said, and turned down another road, leaving Bourbon Street behind. I sighed and watched it vanish in the rearview mirror. "Out in the open, where everyone can see you. Where a Talon operative can't walk up and shoot you in the face without causing a panic."

I blinked. "Or where a pissed-off rogue dragon can't kick his ass for selling us out?" I guessed.

"That, too." Riley clenched the steering wheel, his expression promising retribution, even if it wasn't at the moment. "Griffin is a sleazebag, but he knows what it takes to survive. And if you have a Viper breathing down your neck, the last place you want to meet someone is in a dark warehouse in the middle of the night."

"Still." Wes sniffed, gazing out the window in disdain. "He could've picked a less touristy place to meet. At least it's not on Bourbon Street itself. I wouldn't...oh, look there's the blighter now."

I followed Wes's gaze. A figure in a familiar red suit sat at an outdoor table next to one of New Orleans's many bars. His legs were crossed, and a half-full glass of something sat on the table in front of him. Riley's lip curled, his hands clenching on the steering wheel. There were no parking spots anywhere on the street, so we drove past and found a place around the block.

"Wait here," Riley told Wes, as I opened the door and slid out. The day was humid and warm, and the air felt heavy. "Keep the engine running. If Talon or St. George shows up, we'll need to clear out fast. Firebrand..." Riley glanced at me. "Keep your eyes open. If you see anything suspicious, tell me right away. Ready?"

"Yeah." I nodded. "Let's go."

We walked back to the outdoor patio where the human in

the red suit waited for us. I scanned the crowds, the corners, the overhead verandas and the tops of buildings, searching for anyone suspicious. For anyone who might be hiding a gun, or whose gaze lingered too long on us. For just a moment, I remembered the words of a certain human soldier long ago, when I first accused him of paranoia.

It's not being paranoid, if they're really out to get you.

A lump rose to my throat, and angrily I shoved it down. *Not now. Focus, Ember.*

As we approached, the human raised his glass to us in a mocking salute. "Riley!" he said cheerfully, showing a flash of brilliant white teeth. "And his little sidekick herself. Have a seat, won't you? Let me buy you a drink."

"Thanks, but I'll pass." Riley hooked a plastic chair with his boot and pulled it toward him before sliding into it. I took the seat beside him, glaring at the human across from us, as Riley gave a dangerous smile. "I'm still trying to figure out how you think you're going to get out of this without me bashing your head in."

"Now, now. Temper, Riley." Griffin waggled a finger at him. "No eruptions—that will get you into trouble here. There's no need to be unpleasant, is there?"

I growled softly, my dragon seething under my skin. "There are plenty of reasons to be unpleasant," I said, baring my teeth just slightly in the human's direction. "Considering you sold us out to the highest bidder."

Griffin seemed unconcerned. "Oh, come now. That was business. Nothing personal. Thousands like me would do the same. Besides..." He swirled the ice in his drink. "I think you're going to want what I know. It's worth more to you than bashing my head in right now. You wouldn't be here otherwise."

Riley sneered. "Don't try to sell me a line now that the organization is gunning for you," he said in a low voice. "This is what happens when you play both sides. Eventually, they both discover you can't be trusted…except now you know too much."

"No such thing." Griffin sniffed and stared us down over the bridge of his nose. "It's what I know that keeps me alive and makes everyone want what I have. Case in point, you're here because I have information, and you're willing to bargain for it."

"Yeah? Don't be so sure," Riley said. He leaned back in his seat and crossed his arms. "Seems to me you're getting exactly what you deserve. Give me one good reason not to walk away and let a Viper do me the favor of slitting your throat."

"Two words." Griffin put down his drink and laced ringed fingers under his chin. His eyes were hard as he said in a slow, clear voice, "Breeding facilities."

"What?" Riley dropped his arms and leaned forward, his eyes intense. My stomach dropped. The "facilities" were the places where Talon sent female dragons who had either failed assimilation or were deemed unfit in other ways. They became breeder females whose only purpose was to produce fertile eggs for the organization. The breeders and their locations were some of Talon's most jealously guarded secrets. Riley had been looking for the facilities for years, but had never been able to find them.

"You know where a facility is?" Riley asked, not quite able to hide the faint thread of hope in his tone.

A slow smile crept across Griffin's face. "Not just one facility," he said. "All three of them."

"Where?"

Griffin shrugged, and Riley clenched a fist on the table. "Dammit, Griffin," he said. "You have my attention, so stop being an asshole. What do you want already?"

"I'll tell you what I want." The human leaned forward, his jaw set. "I want your promise that you'll protect me from Talon," he said. "I want a new face, a new identity, a new career, the works. I want Wes to help me disappear, and when all of that is taken care of, I want you to forget you ever knew me. I walk away from this whole mess, and you don't darken my doorstep, now or anytime in the future." Griffin leaned back again and picked up his glass. "That's my offer," he said, watching us over the rim. "And you know you're going to take it, Riley. You've been looking for those facilities for how long? Longer than I've known you, right?"

I heard the faint rumble of a growl in the back of Riley's throat. "How do I know you're not lying to me again?" he asked. "Or that you're not still working for *them*, and I'm walking into a trap?"

"You don't," Griffin said easily. He smirked, and I wanted to fly across the table, grab his smug neck and shake him until he either gave us the info, or it snapped. "But you're going to trust me, anyway, because this is too good to pass up. You can't risk me being right and letting the facilities slip through your claws, can you? All those poor breeder females, slaves to Talon forever." He spread his hands, palms up, on the table. "But, the choice is yours, of course. You know what I want. We have a deal or not?"

Riley's jaw tightened, and I could sense the dragon surging in him, too, wanting to spring up and burn the self-satisfied triumph right off the human's face. But his voice was carefully controlled as he answered. "Fine. Tell me where the facilities are, and you have a deal."

"Your word," Griffin replied, his expression serious now. "I want your word, Riley. I give you what you want, you help me disappear, and neither you—" he shot a quick glance in my direction "—nor *anyone* in your network, ever bothers me again."

"Yes," Riley growled. "You have my word. Now give me the damn information before I change my mind and rip that forked tongue out through your teeth."

Griffin nodded. Fishing in his breast pocket, he withdrew a pen and pulled a napkin toward him across the table. After scribbling a few lines, he folded it again and shoved it toward Riley.

"GPS coordinates," Griffin said as Riley grabbed the square and flipped it open. "Give that to Wes. He should be able to find it. Have him confirm that it's there."

Riley frowned. "This is just one location," he said, holding up the napkin. "You told me you knew where the others were."

"I do. And I'm certainly not stupid enough to hand them over all at once. What's to stop you from running off and leaving me high and dry with Talon?"

My temper flared. "Because we're not like *you*?" I challenged, and he gave me a patronizing smile.

"You mean handsome, well-dressed and able to see when the tide is turning? More's the pity."

My dragon raged at him, itching to rend and claw and bite,

but Riley's warning glare stopped me. Griffin pulled a phone out of his suit jacket and glanced at the screen. "Well. I think we're done here, for now, anyway. I do hope you rented rooms at decent hotel, Riley, and not one of those hole-in-the-wall dumps you usually go for."

I curled a lip. "He's coming with us?"

"Of course. How else am I going to avoid the organization? I certainly can't uphold my end of the deal if a Viper sneaks in my window one night and caps me in the head. Then you'd never get the rest of the information, would you?" At my disgusted look, he chuckled. "Don't worry, chickadee, you won't even know I'm there. And once Wes sets me up with a new identity and life, you'll never see m—"

A muffled *pop* rang out, the distant retort echoing behind us, and Griffin jerked in his seat, his eyes going wide. I jumped and stared in shock as a thin stream of blood ran down his face from the hole in his forehead. For a second, he sat motionless, looking stunned. Then he toppled forward and hit the table facedown with a thud. The empty glass fell to the sidewalk and shattered, the crash unnaturally loud in the sudden quiet. For a single heartbeat, everything was frozen.

Then someone close by let out a shriek and pandemonium exploded around us.

Riley leaped up, shoving his seat back, as the restaurant crowd began to flee, overturning tables and chairs, shoving each other aside in their desperation to get away. "Get inside, Firebrand!" he snarled, glaring wildly at the rooftops across the narrow street. "Get out of the open, now!" Dodging humans, we ducked into the tavern, which was in a similar state of chaos. People were either running away, hiding or talking frantically into their cells. I heard the bartender on the restaurant phone, trying to speak into it while two patrons yelled at him over the counter.

Riley pulled out his own phone and spoke briefly to Wes, his golden eyes scanning the crowds and rooftops across the street. The patio was nearly empty now. I could see Griffin's body lying on the table, a pool of crimson spreading over the white cloth. My cheeks felt sticky, and with a start of horror, I realized his blood had spattered over my face when he was shot. Firmly I shoved my stomach down before it could crawl up my throat.

"I don't see anyone," Riley muttered, and a tremor went through his voice. But whether it was fear or rage, I couldn't tell. I shivered, and he looked down at me, his gaze intense. One hand rose, his thumb gently brushing my cheek, as if assuring himself the blood on my face wasn't mine. "You okay, Firebrand?" he whispered.

Shakily, I nodded. "Was this...Talon?" I whispered back, and he gave a grim nod.

"Yeah. It must be. Though this is the first time I've seen a Viper take someone out in broad daylight, in front of a crowd. That's not like them at all."

"Could it have been the Order?"

"I don't think so. They wouldn't have any reason to kill him, especially if he was selling them information, too. Talon is the one who wanted him silenced." His gaze flickered to the patio and the body sprawled on the table, and his brow creased. "They must've really wanted him dead, to take him out like that."

A siren blared in the distance, making us both jerk up, just as a familiar car lurched to a stop in front of the tavern.

"There's Wes," Riley said and brushed my arm. "Let's get out of here. Keep your head down and move fast."

With one last look at the body on the table, I fled the tavern after Riley, my heart pounding wildly as I threw myself into the backseat and slammed the door. Riley dived into the front as Wes hit the gas, honking the horn and weaving through pedestrians, and we sped away into the city.

GARRET

6:22 p.m.

Parked in the shade beneath a gnarled tree, I raised the binoculars and stared at the mansion at the bottom of the rise. This hilly, residential area several miles outside London seemed to be one of the wealthier parts of town, as large houses with an acre or two of land were not uncommon. Through the gated fence, the enormous, redbrick estate loomed at the end of a long carriage driveway. To the untrained eye, it looked like a normal—albeit huge—mansion, with tall windows, a pool out back, and a perfectly landscaped lawn and garden. But normal homes didn't have guards posted around the perimeter, or a pair of trained attack dogs that swept the grounds every so often, searching for intruders. Normal homes didn't have the type of security usually reserved for royalty—the precautions here indicated a man who either was so paranoid, he thought enemies lurked around every corner…or had something to hide.

The first time I followed the Patriarch to this neighborhood just north of London, I'd been surprised, maybe even a little stunned. In the Order, prudence was commended and extravagance was frowned upon. Everyone, from the senior officers to the newest grunt, made do with what he had and did not reach beyond his station. Wealth and physical possessions were unimportant. We served a higher order and anything that could tempt or distract us from our holy mission was to be avoided.

But the Patriarch was certainly doing well for himself, considering the size of his home and the number of guards posted. I knew he also had a small apartment in London, because he'd spent the evening there once, entertaining what looked to be a pair of officers from the Order. Perhaps he kept the apartment to hide the fact that he really lived here, in this enormous mansion. Considering the mansion's isolation, I suspected most of the Order didn't know where their revered leader actually lived. I wondered what they would think if they did know. If the man really was receiving visions from God, it was definitely paying well.

Lowering the binoculars, I leaned back in the seat, trying to get comfortable and knowing that was impossible. This was the fourth evening I'd sat here, lurking around the home of my former leader, the head of the Order itself. So far, I'd seen nothing unusual. No suspicious activity, no strange guests arriving in the middle of the night. The downstairs window, where I assumed the Patriarch's office was located, glowed softly with lamp and computer light, and would for another thirty-eight minutes.

I took a sip of bitter black coffee, trying to curb my restlessness. Stakeouts were not my forte. Sitting around, waiting for something to happen…that was what Tristan had been good at, what made him such a deadly sniper—his ability to wait as long as it took for the target to show itself. I was better at kicking down doors and charging in, guns blazing, to shoot everything that moved. That wasn't an option here, but I was running out of time. If something didn't happen in the next few nights, I was going to forgo the stakeout and try to sneak into the house itself. Given the amount of guards, dogs and security, such a plan would've horrified Tristan.

Tristan. Memories flickered, dark and unwelcome. That was another reason I didn't like sitting around—my mind tended to dredge up things I'd rather forget. I wondered where Tristan was now, if he was still alive, fighting dragons in the never-ending war with Talon. I wondered if he ever told stories about his former partner the Perfect Soldier, before that soldier turned traitor and sided with the enemy.

A vehicle rolled up to the gates. I sat up quickly, grabbing for the binoculars, as it entered the driveway, then pulled to a stop outside the front door. It was the same dark SUV that drove the Patriarch to and from St. George headquarters. Until now, the Patriarch's schedule could be timed to the minute. He left work at seventeen hundred on the dot. Barring traffic, he arrived home exactly twenty minutes later and immediately went to his office, where he remained until 7:00 p.m. At 9:30 p.m., his lights went out and wouldn't click on again until five o'clock the following morning. No one bothered him or interrupted his schedule. Except for the guards, he lived alone—no wife, children, or pets. Everything he did was order, habit and routine.

But not tonight.

Gripping the binoculars, I focused on the front door just as a familiar figure emerged. He wasn't a tall man, and his short brown hair was peppered with silver, but he was still powerful and imposing, and his gait was confident as he walked to the waiting car. This was not a man who sat in meetings or behind a desk all day; this was a warrior and a soldier. Nodding briskly to the man who opened the door for him, the Patriarch slipped into the backseat. The doors slammed, and the SUV began to move.

All right. Time to get some answers.

They didn't go far. Ten minutes after I began discreetly trailing the SUV through a quiet neighborhood, the vehicle slowed and pulled up to the curb. The back door opened, and the Patriarch emerged, followed by two large men. Though they were dressed casually, I could tell they were armed—definitely his security detail. All three gazed calmly up and down the street before they crossed the road and entered the public park on the corner.

I shut off the engine, then grabbed the backpack on the floor and exited the car, watching the Patriarch's vehicle turn the corner and drive away. Shouldering the bag, I hurried across the street and peeked around a tree, catching sight of my quarry as they strode purposefully through the short grass and deeper into the park.

I dug my earbuds out of my pocket, stuck them in my ears, then pulled out my throwaway phone, keeping my head down. I'd never met the Patriarch, but I could only assume he knew what I looked like. My photo had probably been circulated through the Order, and the Patriarch would certainly keep up with current affairs in St. George. Following him was a risk, but if he did happen to glance back, hopefully all he would see was an oblivious teenager listening to music while texting on his phone.

With my eyes glued to the screen, I started walking.

I trailed them as casually as I could while still attempting to keep them in my peripheral vision. Thankfully, this area of the park was wide and open, with sweeping fields and few trees to block lines of sight. A fair amount of civilians wandered the paths; joggers and bikers, parents with children, people walking their dogs. It was easy to mimic them, to pretend I was just a random civilian enjoying the evening.

Finally, the Patriarch and his men made their way toward a large blue-green pond at the end of one field. A man in a gray suit sat on a nearby bench, staring over the water. The Patriarch stopped a few dozen feet from the bench and spoke quietly to his guards. They turned, folded their hands in front of them and scanned the area while the Patriarch continued toward the pond.

Shrugging off my pack, I walked to a tree about a hundred yards from the bench and sat down, leaning against the trunk with my back to the water. Setting my bag on the ground, I unzipped the top just enough to feel around inside. The shotgun microphone sat nestled in the bottom—amazing what you could pick up on the internet. Carefully, I plugged my headphones into the microphone, switched it on and pointed the entire backpack toward the bench, trying to find the right angle. There was a buzz of static in my ear, and snatches of a conversation filtered through the earbuds before resolving into separate voices.

"—llo, Richard," crackled one voice, smooth and confident, making me frown. Richard? Who was on a first name basis with the Patriarch? I held my breath, easing the backpack to a better position. The voice sputtered a moment, then grew stronger. "Lovely evening, isn't it? I heard last week was nothing but rain."

"Let's skip the pleasantries." The deep second voice was clipped, impatient, which surprised me. I'd heard speeches given by the Patriarch, his words inspiring the soldiers of St. George as he reminded them of our holy mission. In all instances, he was poised and confident, never raising his voice to get a point across. He'd sounded nothing like the brusque, almost nervous man across the lawn. "That's not why we're here."

Interesting. I suddenly understood why the Patriarch had chosen to meet in a very public park. If he didn't trust the other man, he wouldn't want to pick a location where the other could do something nefarious with no witnesses. Rules of enemy negotiations: don't meet on the enemy's turf, and don't give him the opportunity to double-cross you.

So, who *was* this other man? And how had he convinced the Patriarch, the leader of St. George, to meet with him like this, when he obviously didn't want to?

"As you say. I suppose we should get down to business, then." By comparison, the other's voice was cool and almost smug. "I trust the operation in China was a success?"

There was a creak, as if the Patriarch had seated himself on the bench and leaned back. His voice was begrudging as he answered. "The squad located the temple in the mountains and found the targets inside, just as you said."

"And?"

"They've been dealt with."

"Excellent. My people will be pleased to hear it." A pause, and then the faint tapping of keys, as if the stranger was typing something on a laptop. "Another successful raid, and your men have done well. The funds should be in your account by the time you get home."

My stomach dropped. *Certainly not the vision from God the Order would have us believe. Who is this person? Is he even part of St. George, or is he something else entirely?*

"You don't look pleased, my friend," the stranger went on. "Are you disappointed with our arrangement? Surely the destruction of another nest is cause for celebration, yet you seem unhappy."

"I am not," the Patriarch said in a cold voice, "nor will I ever be, your friend." His voice faded as static buzzed through the headphones, and I carefully adjusted the backpack until it cleared. "...benefits us now," the Patriarch went on. "But do not think we will ever be allies, and do not think I will change our beliefs. The Order does not bow to the whims of dragons, regardless of loyalties or circumstances."

What?

"Be that as it may," the man returned with a smile in his voice, "I'm afraid it is far too late for you to reconsider our arrangement. What would the rest of the Order say, if they knew their Patriarch had sold himself to the enemy? Do you think they would care that one tiny branch of Talon wants to bring down the whole? Do you think St. George would agree that doing business with a handful of dragons in order to destroy the rest is for the good of us all?" His voice grew faintly threatening. "If certain documents suddenly became known to the rest of the Order, what do you think would happen?" The stranger snorted. "Well, you know your people better than I. What is the punishment for treason—for consorting with dragons?"

I was barely breathing now. This...this was unreal. I sat rigid with my back to the tree, listening to the leader of St. George—the man the Order revered above all others—carry out a secret transaction with a dragon. Accept *money* from a dragon, to eliminate other dragons. And not only that, it sounded like these meetings had been going on for a while. My mind whirled with questions as confusion, disbelief and anger surged to life. How long had the Patriarch been lying to us? How long had he advocated the complete destruction of an entire species, when he himself was in Talon's pocket?

The Patriarch...is in league with Talon, I thought numbly. No one was going to believe this. I was having trouble believing it myself.

"So, I'm afraid our transactions are going to have to continue, my friend," the stranger—the *dragon*—went on in that same cool, smooth voice. "There is too much at stake, for both of us, to stop now. But that's not the end of the world, is it? After all, you're still eliminating your enemies. You're destabilizing the organization. Who cares where the information comes from—as long as dragons are dying, you're still achieving your holy mission, are you not? Protecting humanity and all that."

"You mock me, lizard. But I will see your kind extinct. Even if I must make a deal with the devil to see it come to pass."

"There you go." The dragon didn't seem at all perturbed at the Patriarch's threat. "We have similar goals, you and I. The Order wants dragons dead—we want *some* dragons dead. And if Talon grows weak in the meantime, how is that a bad thing for St. George?"

The Patriarch's voice went coldly polite. "I assume you have another lead."

"I do." I heard the faint rustle of paper. "And another opportunity for your people to redeem themselves, since they cannot seem to pin down this one dragon long enough to eliminate him." The stranger's voice took on a dangerous edge, even though his tone was light. "A pair of dragons waltzes into your chapterhouse, frees a traitor and waltzes out again, right under your noses. I would think finding them would be the Order's top priority."

I jerked up, hitting the back of my head against the tree trunk. My heart pounded as I realized he was talking about us, about Ember and Riley and myself, and the night they'd freed me from St. George. I knew the Order wanted us dead. I'd had no idea that it was Talon itself sending them after us.

"Sebastian will be taken care of," the Patriarch replied, making my blood chill at the sound of my name. "As will the dragons who aided him. We were unaware of how deeply involved he was until they came for him that night. Every chapterhouse in the States is on alert for this traitor and the dragons you described. We will find and eliminate them."

"Well. Now's your chance. We've uncovered one of Cobalt's hideouts, an abandoned industrial park about ten miles north of a small town in West Virginia. I've marked its location on your map. Our intelligence indicates he is heading there now, possibly with several dragons and the soldier in tow, but I would act quickly. Cobalt is intelligent, paranoid and he's slipped through your fingers before. Let's try to avoid that this time." The stranger's voice turned faintly mocking. "We don't want a repeat of Vegas."

"We know what we're up against now." The Patriarch's voice was brittle. "This time, we'll be ready for them." There was a rustle, as if the Patriarch closed the file and rose. "We're done here," he announced. "I will contact you once it's finished."

"Of course." The stranger rose, as well. "Always a pleasure, my friend. We'll be in touch."

I zipped up the backpack and stood, still slightly dazed but knowing I couldn't be spotted now. Shrugging the pack over my shoulders, I put my head down and walked away, keeping my back to the bench where the meeting had taken place. I didn't see the Patriarch, or his mysterious dragon informant, but I wasn't looking for them. My mind was spinning. The Patriarch, the exalted leader of the Order of St. George, the man who condemned dragons and anyone associated with them, was working with Talon. For the second time in my life, my world had been tipped on its head. I didn't know what to think anymore.

I did know one thing. Ember was in danger. She and Riley had no idea that Talon had set St. George on them. Right now, they were walking right into a trap. And though I knew the two dragons were more than capable of handling themselves, I also knew that, this time, the Order would go after them full force. Because they were also looking for me, a traitor who had turned his back on his brothers to side with the enemy. Who knew far too much about the Order of St. George.

Once free of the park, I stood on the sidewalk for a moment, fighting with myself. I knew I should keep digging, discover just how far the Patriarch's involvement with Talon went. This was possibly the largest conspiracy in the history of Talon and St. George, one that would throw everything into chaos. I needed proof; without some kind of hard-core evidence, neither St. George nor Talon would ever listen to me.

But I knew what I was going to do now, and it wasn't follow up on the Patriarch. Not when my mind was consumed with worry for Ember. I had no way of contacting her, Riley, or Wes; the number she'd given me was no longer in service. If I'd been thinking clearly that night, I would have talked with Wes, arranged some way of contacting them if I needed to. But I'd thought I was done with that group. My walking away was supposed to be a clean break; I hadn't thought I would ever see them again. I hadn't thought I would ever see *her* again.

That was foolish of me. This was war. Talon and St. George were still trying to destroy each other, and Ember was in the center of it all. As long as those two organizations existed, her life would be in jeopardy. Taking myself out of the picture wouldn't change that.

And now, St. George was closing in. Across the ocean, Riley, Ember and Wes were walking into a trap, because Talon itself had set them up.

Unless I could get to them first.

I called the airlines on the drive back to the hotel and booked the first available flight back to the States, then returned to my room to grab my belongings. As I slid the key through the slot, my nerves prickled. Warily, I glanced around the hallway, then opened the door and stepped through.

A woman rose from a chair in one corner of the room, a grim smile on her face. She was small and thin, dressed in dark jeans and a jacket, with straight black hair and solemn eyes. "Here you are," she greeted as I stopped short. "You certainly are a hard man to track down."

Before I could back out, the door swung shut, and a shadow moved from behind the wood. I started to turn, to block whatever was coming, but the last thing I felt was a blow beneath my ear, and the world went black.

EMBER

"All right," Riley sighed, flipping on the hotel light. "We made it." Glancing back at the parking lot, he narrowed his eyes, golden and intense. "The Viper could still be out there, so everyone stay alert. Ember, I need you to pack up. We'll be leaving soon."

"Where are we going?" I asked, and my voice shook at the end despite myself. Thankfully, Riley didn't seem to notice.

"I don't know yet. I'll tell you as soon as Wes deciphers the coordinates Griffin gave us. It shouldn't take long, right, Wes?"

"Trust me, mate," Wes replied, stalking past him to the table. "We just survived watching a man's head get exploded—we can't leave soon enough." He glanced up at Riley, eyes shadowed. "What I want to know is why the bloody Viper didn't take either of *your* heads off. It had the shot, you were all sitting there like ducks, nice and lined up in a row. Why didn't it kill you, too?"

Riley scrubbed a hand through his hair. "It's pretty hard to cap three heads at the exact same time with a rifle. Maybe it had to decide between us, and Griffin was its official target. Maybe there was too much commotion, and it had to leave the area before the police arrived. I have no idea why it didn't shoot us." He blew out a shaky breath. "But, it didn't. That's all I care about right now. Looks like we got lucky."

"Unlike Griffin," Wes muttered.

Riley sighed. "Dammit, Griffin," he growled, dropping onto the bed. "He was a traitorous greedy bastard, but I knew him. I've known him for years. Or I thought I did." He rubbed his eyes. "Fucking Talon. No one deserves to go like that."

My stomach curled, and I dug my nails into my palms. "I'm… gonna go pack," I said, backing toward the exit. Riley looked up at me in concern.

"You okay, Firebrand?"

"Yeah." I nodded and forced a grin. "I'm fine. Be right back—it won't take long."

I slipped through the door, feeling Riley's worried gaze on my back, and crossed the hall to my own room.

As the door clicked shut behind me, I began to shake. Not bothering with the lamps, I walked to the bathroom and flipped the switch, meeting my gaze in the mirror.

My insides heaved. My cheeks and forehead were covered in dried red spatters—Griffin's blood. I remembered the human, smug and confident, talking to me across the table. Alive and perfectly fine one second, lying facedown in a pool of his own blood the next.

With shaking hands, I wrenched the faucet to hot, then began scrubbing the sticky dark mist from my face and hands. The water in the basin ran red for a while, then became clear. But no matter how hard I scraped, I could still feel his blood on me, and my movements became harder and faster as my anger grew. Faces filtered through my mind; Griffin, Faith,

Dante, Garret. All gone. All taken away, either by Talon, St. George, or the war itself.

No, I thought, as my thoughts settled on one face in particular. The one that had been plaguing me ever since he left. *That's not entirely true. You drove him away. Don't blame Talon or St. George. He's not here now, because of you.*

With an inner roar, I raised my fist and drove it into the face of the girl in the mirror. She fractured, shattering into pieces, dozens of accusing green eyes glaring at me over the sink. *Gone*, I thought in despair. *They're all gone. Garret, Dante, almost everyone I care about. How many more will I lose? How many more will I watch die right in front of me?*

"Hey! Ember, stop."

Strong hands closed around my wrists, pulling me away from the sink and out of the bathroom. My dragon snarled and surged up, ready to turn her rage and grief on something else, but Riley's piercing gold eyes halted her.

"Stop," he said again, his voice softer. "Firebrand, breathe. It's just me." I sucked in a deep breath, feeling the dragon subside, and Riley relaxed. "What happened?"

"I...don't know. I just..." Biting my lip, I looked down at my hands and saw blood starting to well from my knuckles. Riley looked down, too, and grimaced.

"Come here," he sighed, gently pulling me to the bed. "Sit." I sat, and he retrieved the small first-aid kit I always carried in my bag now. I watched him drag up a stool and take my hand, then dab away the blood. I waited for the exasperation, for the questions as to why I had punched the mirror into oblivion, but he didn't say anything.

"There," he said, tying the last of the gauze around my hand.

"That's done. Try not to punch any more mirrors, Firebrand. You'll jinx my luck." His voice was light, but his eyes were still dark with concern. I slipped off the bed, flexing my fingers to test the range of motion.

"Thanks," I said, forcing a smile. "I...uh...guess you wouldn't believe me if I said there was this really big roach on the mirror, and I didn't have a shoe handy—"

"Ember." His voice was quiet, making my stomach dance. I looked back to find him gazing at me, all amusement gone from his face. "Why didn't you tell me you haven't been sleeping? You didn't think I would want to know about that?"

I swallowed. "They're just stupid nightmares," I said, making him frown. "It's not important. I'm fine, Riley. I can handle it."

Swiftly, Riley rose, grabbed my wrist and held it up, watching me over the bandages. "This is not handling it, Firebrand," he said firmly. "This is the opposite of fine." Scowling, I pulled my arm back, and he narrowed his eyes. "Something is bothering you, and it's been affecting you for a while. I want to know what. You're exhausted and on edge, and if you keep going like this you're going to explode. You nearly lost it with Griffin today, don't think I didn't notice." When I didn't answer, his brow furrowed. "Talk to me, Ember," he urged. "What's going on in that head of yours?"

"Nothing."

I turned away, and he growled. "Dammit, Firebrand. Wait." Fingers took my arm, strong and cool against my skin, and something inside me finally snapped.

I didn't remember Shifting. Didn't remember making that decision. But suddenly, I was in dragon form, my wings brushing the sides of the wall, and Riley was pressed against the bed, eyes wide as he stared at me. The hotel room abruptly felt tiny and cramped; my tail uncoiled, thumping the desk, and my talons dug into the cheap carpet as I leaned forward, crowding Riley and making him sit down on the mattress. Lowering my head, I gave a low, throaty growl that was both an invitation and a challenge, and Riley squeezed his eyes shut.

"Ember." His voice was a rasp, and I saw a tremor go through him as he tried to keep the dragon down. His jaw was clenched, making it difficult to get out the words. "This…is not the time, or the place. Change back."

I lashed my tail and snorted a curl of smoke in his face. I didn't want to Shift back; I wanted Cobalt to come out. I knew he wanted to. I could feel it in the human's ragged breathing, the way his hands clenched in the blankets. The past few weeks had been a mire of chaos and nightmare and emotion, but for once, my thoughts were clear. "Why?" I demanded, hoping the defiance would be enough to force Cobalt into the open. It wasn't, and I bared my fangs at him.

I was tired of the confusion. Tired of the fear and the nightmares, the guilt eating me from within. I didn't want to think, or feel. Being a dragon was so much simpler. I knew exactly what I wanted; I just had to get the human below me to go away. "You once told me you weren't holding back anymore," I reminded him, half opening my wings to drape him in my shadow. "What's stopping you? Or was that just a lie?"

"I know…what I said. And no, it wasn't a lie. But…" Opening his eyes, Riley gave me a look that was both hungry and pleading at the same time. "Not here, Firebrand," he choked out. "Get ahold of yourself. We're in the middle of a city. We can't be seen like this." He took a deep breath, as if strengthening his resolve. "Ember, I… You know I want to. But, this is not the time. You have to Shift back." I curled a lip, and another shiver went through him as his voice became strangled. "Now."

Anger flared. Baring my teeth, I snarled in his face, whirled and willed myself back into human form. The black Viper suit became visible, covering me from neck to ankles as I shrank down, but the remains of my jeans and shirt lay shredded at the foot of the bed. For a second, I was sorry I was wearing the suit; if I hadn't been, being naked would've been a good excuse not to Shift back.

I rubbed my eyes, not looking at Riley, as hurt and anger still simmered in my chest. I didn't know if it was the dragon's frustration or my own tangle of feelings, but I suddenly felt very alone.

I heard him shift off the mattress and take a hesitant step toward me, his voice low. "Ember..."

I stiffened. "Sorry about that," I said in a flat voice, and headed toward the bathroom. Where I could close the door on rogue dragons and not have to face him for a few minutes. Where he wouldn't see me fall apart. "I'm tired," I muttered, swiping a hand across my eyes. "It won't happen again."

"Wait." Riley hurried forward, coming around to face me. "Hold *on* a second, will you?" I stopped as he barred the way to the bathroom, the look on his face frustrated, as well. "Look, I know things have been crazy. I know with all the running around, we've barely had a chance to breathe. But I haven't forgotten about...us, all right?"

Hope flickered inside, though the dragon snarled, unappeased. "You've been busy," I said, shrugging. "I get it."

"That's not it, Firebrand. Dammit, how do I say this?" He sighed, raking a hand through his hair. "It's not that I don't see you, it's just... I'm not good at...human stuff, Ember. I've been on my own a long time, dealing with dragons and hatchlings and Vipers—and Wes isn't what you'd call warm and cuddly. I don't mean to ignore you, but whenever we're close all I can think of is Shifting into my real form, and we *can't* do that in a car, or a hotel room, or anywhere people could see us. And all those human things—hugging, touching, kissing, whatever… it doesn't come natural to me. I'm not the soldier, Firebrand. I'm a *dragon*." He gave a short, frustrated laugh and made a hopeless gesture. "It's just not in my makeup."

"Yeah," I muttered, looking down. "I know." It didn't make me feel much better, knowing we would have to be completely alone and isolated for Cobalt to appear. Being around humans had spoiled me, I supposed. Dragons weren't supposed to love. I couldn't expect Riley to act like Garret.

"But…" A soft brush against my cheek made me glance up. Cobalt was staring down at me, golden eyes solemn and intense as he lowered his head. "That doesn't mean I can't learn," he whispered, making my insides swirl. "I've been around awhile—I've picked up a few things over the years." I blinked at him, and one corner of his mouth twitched in a wry smirk. "I can be more human, Ember," he murmured. "I can't say I'll remember all the time, but if that's what you want… I'll try."

I licked dry lips. "No," I said, making his brows arch. "I don't want you to change for me. It wouldn't be you—"

"No?" Riley's eyes gleamed, and he grabbed my wrist. "You don't think so?"

Pulling me close, he slipped one arm around my waist, pressed the other to the back of my neck and kissed me.

I froze, stunned. My hands went to his chest, flattening over his shirt, not knowing whether to push him off or yank him closer. His lips were warm, firm and confident. I could smell his leather jacket, feel the heat thrumming through us both as he held me against him, his arms like steel bands pressing me close. Through the elation and shock, one thought filtered through my astonished brain.

Riley was...a really good kisser.

Pulling back, Riley gazed down at me, smiling at my stunned expression. "There," he said quietly, brushing a strand of hair from my face. "Is that enough to convince you that I'm still thinking about us? That you are constantly on my mind, even when I'm distracted?"

I swallowed, trying to find my voice. "For a dragon, I'd say you've got this human thing down pretty well," I whispered, and he smirked.

"I haven't lived this long by not being observant." Releasing me, he stepped back, shoving his fingers through his hair and looking faintly embarrassed. "Wes should be done in a few minutes," he said, glancing at the door. "Will you be ready to leave by then?"

"Yeah." I nodded, feeling a lightness in my chest that drove away the fear and anger and frustration, at least for now. "I'll be right out. I just wish I knew where we were going."

As if on cue, Riley's phone chimed. Pulling it out of his jacket, he stared at the screen a moment, then shook his head.

"Well, it looks like you'll get your wish, Firebrand. Wes found the coordinates." He scanned the message, brow furrowing slightly. "Makes sense, I guess. Away from people, out in the middle of nowhere."

"Where?"

He sighed and stuck his phone in his pocket again. "According to Wes, we're going to West Virginia."

DANTE

"How many vessels have you awakened so far, Dr. Olsen?"

The thin, bearded man in a stained lab coat gave Mr. Roth a proud, weary smile as we left the elevator and followed the scientist down the twisting corridors that led deeper underground. "Twenty-two," he announced.

"And how many have survived?"

"Thirteen vessels have lived through the initial adjustment phase and are expected to continue without support."

He said it with satisfaction, but I felt my stomach twist painfully at the number. The project was progressing at an astonishing rate. More than half the replicas had survived, better than predicted, but that was still nine dragons that hadn't made it. Dragons who had died because they hadn't developed properly, or whose minds had been damaged from the programming process. Or, worst of all, had simply never developed that mysterious spark of life that couldn't be replicated by science. Their lungs and hearts functioned, everything seemed to be working fine, but they were empty shells; living pieces of meat that slowly starved to death when the feeding tubes were removed.

It made me sick to think about. In fact, though I would never admit it out loud, the whole thing was making me rather ill. Was this truly the only way we could survive? Making clones of ourselves? Dragons who were grown in a vat, whose memories and personality traits were artificially implanted to make them more compliant? It didn't sit well with me, but at the same time, I trusted that the organization knew what it was doing. This *was* a war, and we were vastly outnumbered. Every year, we lost more of our kind to St. George, and their numbers weren't getting any smaller. Something had to be done to even out the score, or we would find ourselves close to extinction again.

"And how is their training progressing?" Mr. Roth inquired as we continued down the corridor, passing armed guards and other scientists, who bowed their heads or averted their gazes as we went by. Mr. Roth paid them no attention whatsoever. "Have they shown any signs of being able to Shift?"

Dr. Olsen paused at a heavy metal door, punched a code into the keypad beside it and pressed his thumb to the lit screen. It beeped, flashed green and the door unlocked with a soft hiss. The scientist looked back at us and smiled. "Come see for yourself," he replied, and opened the door.

I stepped through the frame onto a metal balcony that overlooked a large room. The walls and floor were cement, and the ceiling rose above us in a steel dome. Several doors of heavy-duty steel were set into the walls every dozen or so feet, individual cells that made me shiver.

A dozen lean, metallic-gray bodies lay on the cold concrete floor, unmoving. They didn't stir or look up, or give any indication that they'd heard us, and my heart gave a violent lurch as, for just a moment, I thought they were dead. But then the scientist stepped to the edge of the railing and raised his arms, as if embracing them all.

"Hello, my darlings!" Dr. Olsen called into the room, his voice echoing in the vast space around us. No response from the dragons below, not even a tail or wing twitch, and the scientist smacked his forehead. "Oh, that's right. I told them to stay." He clapped his hands. "Up here, please! Everyone, look at me!"

As one, the dragons raised their heads and looked up.

My skin crawled, and I clutched the cold railing, repressing a shiver as I stared at them. These were hatchlings, my age, or they would have been if they'd had a normal hatching. They were dragons who should have been like me, but they were all...wrong. There was no spark of personality, no individual that stood out from the rest, no defining features or characteristics. They were carbon copies, perfectly alike, staring up at us with eyes as blank and empty as a statue.

"We're still in the testing phase," Dr. Olsen said, observing the dragons with a faint smile on his face. "There have been a few hiccups here and there—you have to tell them when to eat, and sleep, and...well, let's say they don't follow the call of nature on their own. But we've found them highly responsive to stimuli and able to retain nearly everything they have learned. So far, they are able to follow complex commands without fail, provided you show them what you want them to do first. Observe."

He pulled a silver dog whistle from inside his lab coat, then blew on it sharply, though the only sound I heard was a faint, high-pitched hissing noise. The clones, however, straightened and instantly began to Shift. Scales melted away; wings shrank down and vanished; tails, claws and horns disappeared. Now a dozen barefoot, identical humans stood in two neat rows at the edge of the room. They wore skintight black briefs, their heads were shaved, and I could just make out a line of numbers tattooed above their left ears. Thirteen pairs of blank, silvery eyes stared fixedly at the scientist, unblinking.

A chill crept up my back. Somehow, this was even worse.

"Marvelous," breathed Mr. Roth, gazing down at the replicas with a broad smile on his face. "They *can* Shift, after all. The organization will be very pleased, indeed."

I swallowed the dryness in my throat. "Why do they all look the same, Dr. Olsen?"

"Part of their genetic code," the scientist replied. "They look the same because they share the same genetic makeup. You can't clump them together in public, of course, but they are much easier to hide and transport in human form." Dr. Olsen beamed, as if showing off a winning science project. "The knowledge of Shifting was also part of the encoding," he went on, turning to Mr. Roth. "So these dozen hatchlings managed to learn and reliably perform the skill in a few days, rather than the standard two years."

"Very impressive," Mr. Roth said, a dark gleam in his eyes as he stared down at them. "And how long have they been able to hold a human shape, Doctor?"

"We've been slowly testing to see how long they are able to remain Shifted," the scientist replied, gazing over the clones with an almost fatherly smile on his face. "So far, they can reliably retain human form for eight hours."

"Excellent. So they are very nearly ready." Mr. Roth nodded once, then turned to me. "Soon, Mr. Hill, you will have the opportunity to prove yourself. You will have the chance to show Talon exactly what you, and these vessels, can do." I gave him a puzzled look, and he gestured back to the creatures below us. "We will need the clones ready for battle as soon as possible, able to follow commands and kill without question. We need them to be a fighting force, and *you* will be in charge of overseeing this project, Mr. Hill." His smile widened as I blinked at him in shock. "We realize you are not a Viper or a Basilisk and this is not what you were trained for, but nonetheless, Talon is entrusting you with this task. I hope you surpass all our expectations."

"Sir…" For a moment, I stumbled on what I wanted to say, torn between confusion and horror. Talon was putting *me* in charge of making the vessels battle ready? Why? I wasn't prepared for this. My calling was politics and business, meeting important people and swaying them to our way of thinking. Blending in to the human population. What did I know about preparing things for war?

"You have questions," Mr. Roth said matter-of-factly, still smiling at me. "Don't be afraid to ask, Mr. Hill. Talon wants you to be fully comfortable in the tasks we set for you."

"I only have one question, sir," I said, knowing that statement wasn't entirely true. It didn't matter what I felt or what doubts I had. It didn't matter that just watching the vessels from a hundred yards away made my skin crawl, and that I certainly didn't want to get close to any of them. When Talon gave you a job, you did it, no questions asked. Talon's interest lay in how well you completed your task and whether you succeeded or failed. Nothing else mattered.

"Why me?" I asked. I didn't explain what I meant; Mr. Roth already knew. Loyalty and determination could get you only so far. I was a hatchling, and this was possibly Talon's biggest, most expensive project to date. Yes, I had managed to impress the organization, but they were taking a massive risk by bringing me on. Even I understood that.

Mr. Roth regarded me with cold professionalism. "Because it's in your blood, Mr. Hill," he said, and walked away, leaving me staring after him in utter confusion.

GARRET

When I opened my eyes, the world was still dark. My skull throbbed, and the air was hot, stale, and smelled of burlap and sweat. I raised my head and realized it was covered with a thick black bag. My hands had been tied behind my back, bound with coarse rope, and there was a cloth gag in my mouth. Judging from the rumble of an engine and the vibrations of my seat, I could guess I was in the backseat of a car, heading in an indeterminate direction.

I shifted, and something hard and pointed pressed into my ribs from the side. "Don't try anything," said a voice, the same female who'd been waiting for me at the hotel. "Just relax. It won't be much longer."

Who are you? I wanted to ask. *Are you with St. George, or Talon? If you know who I am, why haven't you killed me yet?*

Maybe they were taking me to the Patriarch. Perhaps the leader of St. George wished to see the traitor in person so he could execute him himself. Grim as it was, that was the best scenario I could hope for. St. George would show me no mercy, but at least it would be over quickly. If this was Talon, they'd probably want to interrogate me for information on Riley's rogue underground and the Order. I could take a lot of pain, and I'd been trained to withstand torture without breaking, but I could only imagine what Talon would do to a former soldier of St. George.

Unfortunately, I could only wait until my captors revealed who they were and what they wanted from me. Meanwhile, across the ocean, Ember was still in danger, unaware that she and Riley were walking into a trap. Helpless, I clenched my fists against my back, well aware that every mile, every minute that ticked by, took me ever farther from getting to them in time and closer to losing the red dragon forever.

We drove on for several more minutes, taking multiple twists and turns, before the car finally shuddered to a halt. Still blindfolded, I was dragged out of the vehicle, led across a cement floor and down a flight of steps. The air was cold and damp, cooling my face a little through the suffocating bag, making it easier to breathe. There was a scraping sound, like a chair was being dragged across the floor behind me. A moment later, I was pushed into it, and the sack was torn from my head.

Blinking, I looked around. I was in a basement, with thick stone walls and a few shelves holding various outdoor tools. There were no windows, and only one dim lightbulb, flickering right above my head. Three people surrounded me; two bald, grave-looking men standing to either side of my chair, and the small Asian woman I'd seen earlier. I hadn't gotten a good look at her before I'd been knocked senseless, but seeing her now, I realized she wasn't very old—though her exact age was impossible to tell, and she was very attractive. She regarded me coolly with her arms crossed over her chest before stepping forward and yanking the gag from my mouth.

"Apologies for the somewhat barbaric treatment." Her voice was soft and had the faintest hint of an accent. "Normally we are not quite so rude, but I couldn't take any chances with the Order being so close. We had to move quickly, and I didn't have time for arguments. I hope you understand."

I didn't answer, though my heart sank at her words. Not from the Order. So, they were part of Talon, after all. I took a furtive breath, steeling myself for what was to come. They'd no doubt brought me here, where screams and cries of pain would go unheard, to interrogate me. But I would not break. I would not give up Ember's location, or Riley's underground. The next few hours might have me wishing I was dead, but I would not betray the girl I loved to the organization. They would have to kill me.

The woman cocked her head at me, dark eyes narrowing, and her voice turned hard. "So. Now that that's out of the way...why are you here? Who sent you? And please," she added, holding up a hand, "don't try to lie and claim you don't know what I'm talking about. We have seen you outside St. George. You've been trailing the Patriarch for days. We know you are involved, and that you're working for the organization. You wouldn't be following the leader of St. George if you weren't."

Still silent, I blinked. Now I was confused. Why accuse me of being from "the organization" if she was from Talon herself? I knew she couldn't be from the Order, but if she wasn't part of Talon, and she wasn't of St. George, who was she?

The woman stepped forward, looming over my chair. Something feral glittered in her dark eyes, and for a moment, the pupils almost appeared green. "So, talk, mortal," she commanded, as with a jolt, I realized what she was. "I don't have time for games, and recently I've been a little short on patience. I really would prefer to be civil, but if you do not cooperate, I will reluctantly have it done the hard way."

"I… Are you from Talon?" I asked instead, and she frowned.

"No." For some reason, the very thought seemed to disgust her. Her lips curled in an expression of loathing that could not be faked. "I am not. Nor will I ever be part of that cursed organization."

"But…you *are* a dragon."

She sighed, and I caught a hint of smoke on her breath, though it was different, somehow. Almost spicy, like incense. "I do loathe that word," she murmured, more to herself than to me. "So clunky and inelegant. It lumps us all into one basket, assumes that we are all one and the same." She scowled at me. "Yes, mortal," she said bluntly. "I am, as you say, a dragon. In my language, I am known as a *shen-lung*, though I don't expect you to remember that. Continue to call me *dragon*, if you like, but you *will* talk and you *will* tell me about Talon and what they are doing here."

An Eastern dragon. For a moment, I could only stare in wonder. We—St. George—knew so little of them. I had never even seen an Eastern dragon before, though I knew they existed. Unlike their Western counterparts, the dragons of the Orient were far more reclusive and difficult to track down. In the Order, not much was known about them, though it was assumed they were still part of Talon, as all dragons were.

I knew better, now. And if this woman, this *shen-lung*, despised Talon as much as she appeared to, maybe I could turn this to my advantage. If I could get her to trust me.

"I'm not from Talon," I said.

She was clearly unconvinced. "Don't make this hard on yourself," she said, though her voice wasn't threatening or ominous, it was just weary. "I truly do not wish to hurt you, especially one so young, but I will have answers. You were clearly following the leader of the Order. Spying on him, as we were. No one from St. George would do such a thing—the only one to benefit from such activities would be Talon. So please." She made a vague gesture with a hand, and the two men flanking me closed in, resting corded hands on my shoulders. I felt the strength in their fingers as they squeezed; my bones started to bend from the pressure. "Dispense with the lies. Talon cannot protect you now. I will ask once more. Who are you, and why are you here?"

"I am not working for Talon," I said again, keeping my voice steady through the growing pain. "And you can have your thugs hit me, break my arms, whatever—I'll still give you the same answer. I can't tell you anything about Talon, because I'm not from the organization."

"Then who *are* you working for?" the woman asked in an overly patient tone. "You know far too much to be an ordinary human. What is your interest in the Patriarch? Who are you, exactly?" When I didn't answer, the dragon's voice became lethally soft. "If you want me to start believing you, mortal, this is your last chance."

I clenched my jaw. If I told her who I really was, what I really was, she might kill me, anyway. I didn't know what Eastern dragons thought of the Order, but I could assume they knew who we were and what we did. St. George was the enemy of *all* dragons, and Talon would show me no mercy. Would their Eastern counterparts do the same?

I hesitated a moment longer, then decided to take the gamble. Even though I knew it was risky and she might immediately have her thugs snap my neck if she knew the truth. But I was out of options and in desperate need of allies. If I could convince this dragon we were on the same side, maybe we could help each other. If she didn't decide to kill me on principle.

"I know about Talon and the Patriarch," I said carefully, feeling my heartbeat pick up, "because…I *was* part of the Order. I was once a soldier of St. George."

Both men straightened, and the dragon drew back, narrowing her eyes. "This is a lie," she stated, her voice hard. "Soldiers of St. George never leave the Order. You are lying again—"

"I'm not," I insisted.

"You must be." She glared down, anger and hatred glittering from her previously calm expression. "If you know about Talon and the Order, you know what St. George does to us."

"Yes," I agreed. "I know. If I'm lying, why would I tell you I've taken part in slaughtering your kind?" She had no answer for that, watching me with hard black eyes. "I was a soldier of the Order," I said again. "If you want the truth, there it is."

She frowned, suspicion and curiosity warring with anger and hate. "Why would you tell me this?" she asked in a soft voice, coming forward again. "You say you were part of the Order that would see us extinct. You have admitted to killing my kind, massacring us wholesale, in the name of your God." She leaned forward, close enough for me to see my reflection in her jet-black eyes. "The only reason I do not kill you where you stand is because you told the truth, and you knew what that would mean. I find myself curious as to why. Why would a soldier of St. George reveal himself to his enemy? What kind of game are you playing?"

"It's not a game," I told her. "I'm not your enemy. And I'm not part of the Order any longer. We can help each other." One of the men snorted, but I ignored him. "I have information on the Patriarch and Talon," I continued, holding her gaze, "and I'm willing to share it with you. But you have to trust me."

"Trust you?" The dragon rose, giving me a look of contempt. "*Trust* you?" Walking to the opposite wall, she stood there a moment, arms crossed, as if trying to compose herself. "Do you know why I'm here, mortal?" she said, whirling around again. "Do you think I want to be in this bizarre country, surrounded by oblivious mortals and their strange customs? I had a temple, in the Hua Shan mountains. A small, isolated temple perched on a cliff, where I lived in peace with the humans for over a hundred years. The temple monks all knew me and revered me. I was the third dragon to make my home there, as my ancestors did before me.

"And then," she continued, narrowing her eyes, "one day, we had a visitor. A dragon, from the Western lands, all fancy and civilized in his expensive suit, always looking at his smartphone. He spoke of his grand organization, Talon, and tried to get me to join. All dragons should be united under one banner, he said. Think of what we could accomplish if all our kind joined together against the mortals. I refused. I didn't want to be part of his massive corporation—I was content living my simple life with no interruptions or demands. I craved peace, isolation. Not power. I'd heard rumors of our Western cousin's sprawling organization, and the Elder Wyrm's constant quest for supremacy. I wanted nothing to do with Talon, and told him so.

"Before he left, he told me this—be careful you are not making a terrible mistake. Without Talon, you are vulnerable. Without Talon, St. George will eventually come for you, and all your desires for peace and simplicity will mean nothing when they are burning your temple to the ground."

My skin prickled, and cold spread through my insides. I knew where was this was going. I remembered the conversation between the Patriarch and the Talon agent, about a temple in China, and suddenly everything became perfectly, sickeningly clear.

"One month later," the dragon continued softly, "that is exactly what happened. The Order of St. George came in the night and began slaughtering everyone in the temple. Unarmed monks, who had never killed so much as a grasshopper in their entire lives, were cut down in a hail of bullets as the soldiers marched through, searching for me. I know the monks tried to talk to the soldiers, reason with them. I know they strove for a peaceful solution and were gunned down without mercy or thought. I wanted to fight—my friends, men I'd known since they were children, infants, were being systematically executed. But the abbot convinced me to flee.

"We are the only ones to survive the massacre at the temple," the dragon finished, glancing at the two men standing like rocks beside me. "Three survivors, out of a dozen souls who wished only to live their lives in peace and isolation. And then, St. George came through, slaughtered them all, and burned the ancient temple to the ground. Nothing remains of my home but cinders and ash. So, tell me, St. George..." She stepped forward, raising her arm, and the cold edge of a knife was pressed against my throat. The dragon's gaze was glassy as she leaned in. "Why should I trust you? Why shouldn't I show you the same amount of mercy your kind showed the monks at my temple?"

I closed my eyes. "You have no reason to trust me," I said. "I've done all the things you've seen St. George do and more. Had circumstances been different, I might have been on that raid." Opening my eyes, I met her furious stare. "I know it means little now, and nothing I say can make up for what you've lost, but…I am sorry for what happened."

The dragon paused, confusion and astonishment battling the anger in her expression. "You are either a very gifted manipulator, or the strangest soldier of St. George I have ever seen," she murmured at last. The blade's edge dropped from my throat, and she stepped back, regarding me intently. "All right, mortal. Let us say, against all my better judgment, I decide to believe you for the moment. You went from butchering every dragon you came across to apologizing to one of them today. What changed?"

"I met someone," I said quietly. "A dragon. A hatchling out of Talon, being sent to live with humans for the first time. The Order knew the organization had sent one of their agents to a small town in California. My mission was to track her down, expose what she really was and kill her."

"Her," the Asian woman said. "A female." I nodded.

"I found who I thought could be the target," I went on, as memories of Crescent Beach rose up again, never far from my mind. "A girl, living with her brother and her guardians on the edge of the beach. If she was a dragon, I was supposed to kill her, but...the more time I spent with her, the more things didn't add up. She made me see things in a different light. She made me realize...that the Order might be wrong about dragons."

All three of my captors were staring at me now. I could feel their disbelief, but all I could think of at that moment was Ember. The ache I had suppressed returned as memories crowded in; everything from surfing to slow dancing to fighting for my life with the red dragon beside me. A kiss, stolen on the rooftop of a Vegas casino, the city glittering beneath us. And the final, devastating blow when she backed out of my arms, and I realized the dragon I would give my life for could never love me back.

"This girl," the Asian woman said at last. "What happened to her?"

"She left," I answered softly. "When she discovered what Talon wanted of her, she went rogue with another dragon and joined his underground. I don't know where she is now. But..." I swallowed, remembering the meeting with the Patriarch, and the shocking truth I'd uncovered. Even that paled in comparison to Ember's life on the line. "I do know she's in danger," I went on, beseeching the dragon with my gaze. "I know she and some others are walking into a trap, and I have to get to them before St. George finds her. Please..." I leaned forward, letting a little desperation slip into my voice. "She saved my life, and I can't let her die. We can help each other—I'm willing to give you whatever information you need on Talon and the Order, but I have to take care of this first."

A very long silence followed. The female dragon was motionless, staring down with hard black eyes, as if trying to decide what to do with me. The men on either side didn't move or say a word, but I could feel the suspicion pulsing between them.

"Why should I believe you?" the dragon said at last. "Even if you are telling the truth, why should I offer to help a stranger when I watched my temple burn to the ground, and not one of my Western cousins was there to help? Why should I trust a human, a soldier of St. George, and a few rogue dragons I know nothing about?" She paused, glancing at the men behind me, and raised her chin. "We've survived this long on our own, with no others to help us," she said, her voice resolved. "We can find what we need without you."

"You can't," I said firmly, "because Talon and St. George are working together."

For the very first time, the woman seemed shaken. The color drained from her face, and she took a step back, staring at me in horror.

"We're on the same side," I told her, taking advantage of the silence. "We're facing the same enemies. Talon is sending St. George after rogues and dragons they want out of the way. That's why your temple was attacked—because you wouldn't conform to Talon. And they'll do it again, send the Order after others, unless we stop them."

The dragon didn't say anything, just continued to watch me in silence. I took that as a hopeful sign and hurried on. "I have a contact in the States," I told her. "A rogue dragon who has defied Talon and St. George for decades. He knows more about fighting both organizations than any dragon out there. But he's with the girl, and Talon has sent the Order after them both. If I don't get back in time, we're going to lose him and any knowledge he has. I know it goes against everything you believe, but we have a chance of surviving both Talon and St. George if we help each other."

"Talon and the Order of St. George are working together," the dragon repeated, as if making sure she had heard correctly. "Are you very certain of this?"

"Yes. I witnessed a meeting between the Patriarch and Talon. I heard the agent tell him where Ember and Cobalt will be going next. St. George will be waiting for them when they show up."

She sighed. "Then, as you Americans say, the shit is about to hit the fan." Still wearing that grave expression, the woman walked around the back of my chair, and a moment later, my hands were free. Shaking off the ropes, I stood, turning to face her. She gave me a tight smile.

"I never thought I would stand here holding a civil conversation with a soldier of St. George," she mused. "What is your name, human?"

"Garret."

"You may call me Jade," the dragon returned with a slight nod. "And it seems we have a lot of work to do."

RILEY

"This is it," Wes muttered.

I slowed the car and pulled off the road, easing to a stop at the edge of an empty, barren stretch of concrete several miles from anywhere. A rusty chain-link fence surrounded the perimeter, and in the distance, I could see the bulky shapes of buildings, run-down and seemingly abandoned. Danger and trespassers-will-be-prosecuted signs hung on the fence every hundred or so feet, and there were no guards, vehicles or anything to indicate that a top secret facility used for housing breeder dragons lay just beyond the barrier.

"Looks abandoned," Wes remarked. "But, if the facility is here, I'm sure that's what they want you to think."

"Yeah," I agreed, gazing out over the long stretch of pavement and concrete. One of Talon's ploys, especially if they wanted to keep something hidden, was to buy all the property surrounding the thing as a buffer zone, then leave it empty and deserted. A common tactic to hide in plain sight, and one that worked well. "The facility itself will probably be underground somewhere," I mused, scanning the cluster of buildings near the center. "We won't know until we get closer."

"Be careful of guards," Wes muttered. "If this *is* the facility, security is going to be tight, even if it is hidden. Though I still don't know what you intend to do once you find it, mate. Waltz in and free all the breeders with no opposition whatsoever? Just you and the bloody hatchling?"

"I told you," I growled at him. "This is just recon. I'm not going to storm the damned gates. But I want to see what we're up against." We'd argued over timing and strategy during the entire fifteen-hour drive from Louisiana to West Virginia, and I still hadn't been able to convince him that I wasn't going to die in a blaze of dragonfire trying to lead the breeders to safety. "I know what I'm doing," I said impatiently. "This isn't any different than when we rescued the soldier, or the countless other times we've gone up against Talon. I'm not going in half-assed and, after all this time, you should know me better."

"I do know you, Riley," Wes returned in a low voice. "Don't you dare throw that in my face." We'd been speaking in near whispers for a couple hours, mostly because of the sleeping Ember in the backseat. She had finally drifted off, and I'd kept a close eye on her in the mirror, watching for any signs of nightmares. But for maybe the first time in weeks, she seemed to be sleeping peacefully, and the last thing I wanted was to wake her up.

"Yes, I am aware we've done this before," Wes went on, still glaring at me. "I will readily admit that, either through skill or bloody dumb luck, you have gotten yourself out of situations most men would die in. But I also know what's at stake here, Riley. I know how long you've been searching for the facilities. If this place had an impenetrable security system and a few hundred guards, that wouldn't deter you at all, would it?"

The human continued to stare me down, defiant. "You're not going to abandon this, no matter what happens. Are you?"

He paused, waiting for an answer, and I sighed. "No."

"That's what I thought," Wes muttered, shaking his head. "This is your personal white whale, mate. I just want you to be careful. To not become so obsessed, you get yourself and everyone around you killed."

A shuffle from the backseat made us pause. Ember stirred and sat up, blinking sleepily as she gazed around. Her hair stuck out at odd angles, almost like horns, as she rubbed her eyes. "Where are we?" she said, yawning. "Are we there yet?"

At the sound of her voice, Cobalt stirred, and I took a deep breath to calm him down. Ever since that night, when it had taken everything in me not to Shift, not to respond like Ember wanted and join her in my real form, consequences be damned, my instincts were on a hair-trigger reaction. That moment we'd shared afterward, that kiss, hadn't made it any easier.

What the hell are you doing, Riley? I'd thought when I had retreated to my room that night. *Did you really just kiss the girl, like a human? What is wrong with you? You're not the damned soldier of St. George. She doesn't want that from us.*

Truthfully, I had no idea what I was doing. This whole situation had turned my life upside down, and I was doing things I never would have considered before. Things I had scoffed at a few months ago. Kissing a girl? Promising to be more human? What *was* wrong with me? I had no idea, just that Ember called to me, but due to circumstance, there were very few times we could both be ourselves. So, for now, anyway, I guess I would give this human thing a try.

Even though I knew full well our dragon sides would never be satisfied with that.

"Hey, Firebrand," I greeted softly as her gaze met mine. "Yeah, we're here. Or, as close as we're going to get in the car." I gestured at the fence and the deserted lot beyond. "The facility is somewhere on this property, according to Wes. You ready for this?"

She nodded eagerly and slid out of the car. I did the same, then turned to Wes, watching grimly from the passenger seat. "You know the drill," I said, as Ember unzipped the duffel lying on the floor and took out a small black pistol. "Keep the engine running. We stay in contact the whole time, and if I say get out, just go."

Wes sighed and adjusted the headset he was wearing. "I have a bad feeling about this, Riley."

"You have a bad feeling about everything." I smirked as he slid into the driver's seat. "Back in a few minutes. Like I said, we're just scouting the area. It shouldn't take long."

"Famous last words," Wes muttered as I closed the door and turned to Ember. She solemnly handed me a gun, and I felt a prickle of both pride and unease at how quickly she was picking this up. A few weeks ago, she'd been reluctant to touch a firearm, much less use it. Now it had become routine, though I knew she still hated actually pulling the trigger.

Not for the first time, I wondered why Talon had her pegged to become a Viper, an assassin for the organization. And why they had chosen Lilith, Talon's best, to train her in the art of killing. Had they seen something in Ember that I didn't? Or were they just hoping she would become as ruthless and practical as her trainer, a killing machine who showed no remorse when ordered to destroy Talon's enemies?

Ember frowned at me, and I realized I'd been staring at her, lost in my own thoughts. "What?" she asked, and I quickly shook myself. "What's that look for?"

"Nothing," I said, looking toward the fence "You know what we're doing, Firebrand?"

She bobbed her head. "Recon."

"Yeah, so be on the lookout for guards, cameras, security, hidden entrances, anything like that. We want to avoid a fight, and we don't want anyone to know we're here."

She frowned. "If there are cameras and alarms all over the place, how will we get through unnoticed?"

"Leave that to me, Firebrand. I've done this before. I know what to look for, enough to keep us from tripping an alarm, anyway. But still, we have to be careful." I gazed through the fence at the distant buildings, narrowing my eyes. "We only get one shot at this. If this is the facility, if there are breeder dragons here, the last thing I want to do is go in blind."

Ember gave a grave nod. "I'm ready."

We hopped the fence and started walking across the barren lot.

★ ★ ★

"It's too quiet," Ember remarked several minutes later, after we'd passed the first set of buildings, all dark and abandoned. Weeds poked through the cracks in the cement, but the buildings themselves were eerily intact. No broken windows, no streaks of graffiti, no signs of break-in or vandalism. Nothing moved in the stillness except us and a couple startled birds.

"How can they hide a bunch of dragons in the middle of nothing? This place seems completely deserted."

"One of the things they do best, Firebrand," I replied, still scanning the grounds for security measures. So far, there had been nothing, which made me even more wary. I guessed it would be more heavily guarded the closer we got to the actual facility, but the complete lack of security was disconcerting. "Talon excels at hiding in plain sight," I went on. "This is just a front, to make sure no one comes poking around. They certainly can't keep their breeders in a hospital, or anywhere close to people for that matter."

"Why not?"

"Because of...you know." I looked at her; she seemed truly baffled, and I winced. "You're kidding. Your tutors didn't teach you Dragon Hatching 101?"

"Not really."

Wes snickered in my ear. "Oh, this should be good," he muttered. "The infamous *breeding* conversation. Hanging on every word here, mate."

"You know, you should really ask Wes," I told Ember. "It would make his day, I'm sure."

"What?" yelped the voice in my ear. "Don't you dare point her at me."

Ember frowned. "Just tell me, Riley."

I groaned. "All right, fine. So, breeding. Not an awkward conversation at all." Wes gave another snicker, enjoying my discomfort far too much. I tried to ignore him. "You know that dragons in Talon don't...uh...mate with whomever they want, right? It's yet another thing that the organization controls. Talon maintains a strict schedule of who gets mated to whom, and once the female has been…impregnated…she can't remain in human form after the first couple months."

Ember cocked her head, looking bewildered. "Why?"

"Well, because…" I raised my hands like I was hefting a watermelon. "The egg inside her gets too big and starts to stretch…certain things—"

"Okay, okay." Ember held up both hands, wrinkling her nose. "I get it. Point taken." She frowned. "So, how long after… breeding…does it take for the egg to come out?"

"Fifteen months. And most of that time will be spent in dragon form. From what I've been able to discern, as soon as the egg is laid, it's taken from the female and sent to the hatchery, where it's put under an incubator. The hatchlings grow up never knowing their parents—they're raised to be loyal to the organization and nothing else, as I'm sure you've experienced. So you can see why Talon maintains such a tight hold on their breeding facilities. And why no one in the organization is allowed to choose their own mates."

"Well, that's…awful, as usual." Ember snorted. "So Talon tells you who you're going to be mated with, as well? Good thing I'm out of the organization, then."

A sudden, awkward silence fell. My stomach danced, and I didn't know if it was me or Cobalt tying himself into a knot. I sneaked a glance at Ember and saw her staring rigidly forward, her cheeks as red as her hair.

We rounded a corner, and I lurched to a halt. About a hundred yards away, another building sat alone and quiet at the end of the lot. It looked the same as the ones surrounding it: deserted and abandoned. No cars, no lights, no people.

But it was the sign near the entrance that caught my attention.

Quickly, I ducked behind the wall, pulling Ember with me. She gave me a puzzled look but didn't say anything as I scanned the area for cameras, guards, security, anything that seemed out of place.

Nothing. This was getting weirder and weirder.

"Did you see anything?" Ember whispered, peering around my arm.

"No," I muttered, drawing back. "But we're in the right place."

"How do you know?"

"Do you see the sign?" I gestured back to the building. New-Tech Industries, it read. Building a Brighter Tomorrow.

I smiled grimly. "NewTech is one of Talon's branches," I said. "They maintain a front as a medical equipment manufacturer, but they're really a genetics research lab working for the organization."

"Do you think this is where they keep the breeders?"

"I don't know. Wes, did you get that?" I continued, speaking into the wire. "There's a NewTech branch here, but it looks deserted. Could this be the facility? Everything we've seen so far has been empty."

"Hang on." There was a pause as Wes turned to his trusty laptop. After a few silent minutes, he muttered, "Well, according to the internet, there *was* a NewTech lab here. But it was shut down five years ago and has been abandoned ever since."

"Dammit." I clenched a fist against the brick wall. It seemed the likelihood that this was the facility I'd been searching for had completely vanished. I'd suspected as much, from the lack of security around the building, but I still held out hope that we might find it. "So this was a waste of time. I knew I shouldn't have trusted Griffin."

Ember put a hand my arm. "We've come all this way, and it *is* a Talon facility," she observed, as Cobalt leaped inside at her touch. "Maybe we should go in, see if they've left anything behind that we can use against the organization. Maybe there's something that will tell us where the real facilities are."

"I doubt it, Firebrand." Even if this had been a facility, there were no dragons here now, and the chance to rescue the breeders was gone. It was back to square one. "But, yeah, we should go in, look around. Any dirty secrets we can dig up, any hints at what Talon is up to will be worth it. Let's just be cautious. We don't know what's really in there."

"I don't like this, Riley," Wes muttered, a worried buzz in my ear. "It's too clean. Something about this whole situation seems wrong."

"We won't be long," I told him, walking around the corner toward the building at the end of the lot. Wes was right; the area was way too clean to be in use anymore, but we still might be able to learn some things about Talon. I wasn't about to give up on the breeding facilities. "It's worth a quick look around," I said. "Fifteen minutes, tops, and then we'll leave. If you see anything strange out there, let me know."

Wes gave a frustrated sigh. "Right. Well, be careful, Riley. If you hear me screaming, you'll know something's up."

Warily, Ember and I made our way across the lot. The New-Tech lab remained eerily silent as we edged up the steps to the main entrance. I scanned every corner and wall of the building for cameras, alarms, motion sensors, anything. But, like the rest of the lot, it was disturbingly empty.

Two large glass doors sat at the top of the steps, unbroken and locked. I reached into my jacket lining for the picks I always carried and easily jimmied the lock open, with Ember watching curiously over my shoulder.

"You're good at that," she remarked as the mechanism clicked under my fingers. "I keep forgetting you have breaking and entering down to an art form." I grinned at her.

"It's what I do, Firebrand. That and blowing up buildings." Carefully, I pulled the door open, and we picked our way into the lobby. I scanned the walls and floors for bullet holes, grenade burns, pools of dried blood, telltale signs of trigger-happy St. George soldiers. But, aside from being dark and abandoned, the place was almost pristine. A large white welcome counter sat against the back wall, dusty models of prosthetic limbs set out on display. I saw Ember shiver and wrinkle her nose at them. Brochures were scattered across the tile floor, rustling underfoot as we walked.

"Everything looks pretty normal," Ember remarked, picking up one of the brochures and flipping it open. "Creepy dismembered limbs aside. No signs of the Order, anyway. Or Talon."

I walked to the welcome counter, taking everything in. "No computer," I mused, seeing the spot where a computer would have rested. Ember followed my gaze and frowned.

"Stolen?"

"Maybe. Given everything we've seen so far, though, not likely. Nothing else has been touched, and prosthetics are damned expensive for thieves to leave behind. Talon probably took it themselves."

"So we won't be able to see what this place really is."

"Not here," I agreed. This was just the front, to keep up appearances. I glanced down a corridor that snaked off into the darkness. "We'll have to go deeper if we want to find what they've really been up to."

As I suspected, the first floor held nothing interesting. Ember and I passed offices filled with desks and chairs and models of prosthetic limbs sitting on display. Like they were trying overly hard to appear legit, that everything here was as it seemed. As we went farther into the building, however, I began to notice the inconsistencies.

There were no computers, anywhere, in the rooms. No security cameras in the halls. No files scattered among the brochures and envelopes on the ground. Anything that would hold any bit of information concerning the building or the business was gone. And I realized why the grounds out front had been completely empty.

"This place has been cleaned," I said.

"Oh?" Wes said in my ear, sounding wary. "Well, that's bloody suspicious. Not surprising, though, considering this is a Talon business."

Ember glanced at me, frowning. "What does that mean?"

"It means that Talon has erased all the information regarding this facility," I replied. "Computers, files, even the security cameras. Anything that showed what went on here has been stripped and taken away or destroyed."

Her eyes gleamed in the dim light, and she gave a thoughtful nod. "Which means they're definitely hiding something."

"Yeah," I growled. "Let's keep searching."

We continued farther into the building, passing more of the

same. Silent, abandoned rooms and darkness. None of the el-
evators worked, but through a pair of doors that read Employees Only Beyond This Point, a flight of metal stairs led down
into the unknown.

Motioning Ember to stop, I stepped back into the hall.
"Wes," I said, "we found the stairs down. Everything still okay
out there?"

"Pretty much," was the terse reply. "I still don't like this,
Riley, have I mentioned that before? Poking around Talon's
territory is always risky, even if this place is abandoned. You
two almost done in there?"

"Almost. Nothing interesting up top, but I want to keep
searching." Opening the door again, I peered down the stairwell, seeing it vanish into the dark. "If Talon is hiding something here, it won't be out in the open," I said, my voice
echoing down the shaft. "We're heading to the lower floors
now. Just keep watching the building."

"Roger that," Wes sighed, and I stepped into the stairwell
and turned on my flashlight.

Ember followed, our footsteps thumping against the metal
steps and reverberating up the shaft. About halfway down,
Wes's voice started to sputter, and by the time we reached the
bottom, it had flickered out entirely.

"Great," I muttered. "Wes, you there? Can you hear me?"
No answer, just the continuous sound of static. I looked over
at Ember and frowned. "Signal cut out," I told her. "I lost Wes.
Looks like it's just us now."

She blinked. "Should we go back?"

"No." I glanced at the door that marked the end of the
stairway. "I want to see what this place is," I said firmly. "If

this *was* the facility at some point, I want to learn as much as I can. Anything to help me find the current one. Come on."

The door at the bottom of the steps was metal and a touch pad hung beside the frame, a final security measure against interlopers. But the screen was dark, and the handle turned easily under my palm as I wrenched it down. Shoving the door back, I stepped through the frame and shone the flashlight beam into the room.

For a moment, as the faint light scuttled over the walls and floor, I could only stare, the pit of my stomach coiling like a frightened snake. I didn't know what I had been expecting, but it wasn't this.

"What the hell?" I whispered.

EMBER

Okay, I was definitely creeped out here.

Too many horror flicks when I was growing up, I supposed. When I was about thirteen, I went through a phase where I was addicted to ghost and monster movies. Freddy, Jason, Chucky, *The Ring*, *The Grudge*, all the *Aliens*, *Predator*, *Poltergeist*; I devoured everything that involved some kind of creature tearing people apart or freaking them out. I drove Dante crazy with the times I would sneak into his room late at night because I was convinced some pale little girl would crawl through the television and flicker her way to my bed. Paranormal movies always got to me, because while I was fairly certain the *Alien* or *Predator* would die from a fireball between the eyes, and even Jason would be no match for a dragon, what could you do to a ghost?

True, this was not your typical poltergeist set, but that didn't mean anything. I'd seen plenty of sci-fi movies where the heroes were sent to investigate a laboratory or compound or spaceship that had abruptly gone dark, and everything was quiet and abandoned when they arrived, but you just knew *something* was still out there, stalking them.

In fact, I think I'd seen this exact setup before: the creepy underground lab, the rows of strange machines, the large glass cylinders stretched to the ceiling. I could feel a shiver run up my spine as Riley's flashlight beam skittered over the tubes, all thankfully empty but no less disturbing. I knew what those tubes were for: growing things. Living things. Either trying to improve upon nature, or to create something new. And it was *always*, as every movie, book and story had shown, a very, very bad idea.

"What the hell?" Riley muttered, echoing my sentiments. Scanning the light around the room, which was large and stretched back into the darkness, he shook his head. Beyond the glass cylinders were seemingly endless rows of countertops, aisles upon aisles of flat surfaces holding glass vials, beakers, strange machines and other lab-y things. "This is a Talon laboratory, all right," Riley said. "I'd heard of these places when I was still with the organization, but I've never seen one before. What were they doing down here?" He pinned the beam on one of the containers, revealing a set of tubes and wires hanging down from the inside. "Those vats look all kinds of ominous, don't they? What do you think was in them?"

I swallowed. All the answers I could think of made my skin crawl. "Maybe Talon was secretly operating a chocolate factory," I joked, "because they discovered that making chocolate is much more rewarding than trying to take over everything."

Riley snorted. "If they put something in the bars that turned all humans into mindless drones, I wouldn't put it past them," he replied. "But I doubt that's what happened here, Firebrand."

"Okay, but if we run into chocolate-fueled zombies, you owe me dinner."

"Always the zombies with you."

Our voices sounded too glib, too light and breezy for the surroundings. Silence fell, and the shadows seemed to press in, as if offended by our flippancy. Riley swept his flashlight beam around, his tone grave once more. "Though they were definitely working on something," he muttered. "I'd give my back teeth to know what Talon was really doing here. And why this place is deserted now."

My skin prickled. In the movies, the answer to that question was always the same: because the specimens, prisoners, or experiments had all escaped and gone on a killing spree before everything was locked down.

Riley sighed. "Come on," he told me, turning from the row of vats, as if he didn't want to stare at them any longer. "Let's see if we can find some answers."

As we went farther into the lab, passing the long rows of countertops, the feeling that I'd seen this all before continued to haunt me. Riley and I were the unsuspecting humans venturing into the monster's lair and, at any moment, some twisted freak of nature was going to come leaping out at us. Of course, those movies never had protagonists who happened to be dragons, and when the raging monstrosity did finally appear, it always sank its claws into a soft, easily-ripped-apart human. I'd always wondered what the monster would do if its prey suddenly turned into a winged, scaly, sharp-toothed monster itself. Probably the reason that there were no dragons starring in horror movies—the real monster wouldn't be quite as scary in comparison.

Will you stop thinking about that? This isn't the movies. Focus, Ember.

"Look at this," Riley muttered, shining his flashlight into the corner of the room. A door stood on the far wall with the words Danger! Authorized Personnel Only in large red letters across the front. "That looks like all kinds of fun."

Riley strode across the room to push open the door. It swung back to reveal another long hallway, with one wall made of thick glass. The room beyond the glass was a mess: shelves tipped over, chairs knocked down, papers and debris strewed everywhere.

"What happened here?" Riley mused as we traversed the hallway and edged through the door. The hinges groaned as we pushed it back, and I wrinkled my nose. The place smelled of bleach and chemicals and sterilizer, but beneath all that, like a stain soaked deep into the carpet, it still reeked faintly of blood and fear. My dragon growled uneasily as the door creaked shut behind us. Something had happened in this room. Something awful. Continuing my movie comparison, this was the place where the aliens or monsters or clones finally escaped and slaughtered every living soul in a violent, bloody massacre. There were no bloodstains, no skeletons or mangled bodies lying on the floor, but judging from the smell, I guessed someone had cleaned up whatever mess was left behind.

I mentioned this to Riley, who snorted.

"Normally I'd say you've been watching too many Alien flicks, Firebrand," he said, his voice echoing weirdly in the absolute silence. "But it's kind of hard to argue when you're staring at that."

He swept his flashlight beam around, and my stomach knotted. In the center of the room, another large holding vat rose up from the tile, but this one had been smashed and broken, glass scattered about the floor in front of the machine.

"Looks like whatever they were trying to do didn't turn out like they expected," he muttered, walking forward. My dragon hissed, reluctant to get closer to that yawning tube, but I strode after him, glass crinkling under my feet as I got close. "What does that look like to you?" Riley asked, shining the beam into the cylinder. A tangle of clear tubes and wires hung from the ceiling, slowly dripping water into the vat, and I shivered.

"Like something broke out."

"Yep." Riley backed up, eyes dark as he gazed around the room. "So, the question is...what were they keeping down here? What kind of twisted experiments were they performing?"

"Maybe we can find something. If Wes could get into the computer system—"

He shook his head. "If I know Talon, they didn't leave any information behind. All data will be wiped, all files removed, everything about this place will be gone. Frankly, I'm surprised we found this much—it's not like the organization to leave a mess like this behind, unless they needed to clear everyone out as quickly as possible."

I caught a glimmer in the glass—four slashes raked lengthwise down the wall—and felt my stomach drop. Whatever made those gashes wasn't huge, probably no larger than a tiger. I knew, because I had seen claw marks like this before, when I had made them. They were the exact size of a Shifted hatchling dragon's.

"Son of a bitch," Riley breathed, sounding horrified. I glanced at him, and even in the minimal illumination from the flashlight, his face was deathly pale. "This is...this must be one of the labs Remy always talked about." He looked at me, his eyes a little wild. "Remember, Firebrand? What he said, about Talon shipping their 'undesirable' dragons to a lab? Dammit, he was right all along."

Remy. Remy was another rogue, a scrawny hatchling Riley had gotten away from Talon because he was "too small," his bloodline "unsuitable" for the breeding pool. I'd briefly met him and another hatchling, Nettle, at Riley's hideout in Crescent Beach, before we all had to flee from St. George. Remy liked to tell stories, and one of the stories he told was that Talon sent undesirable hatchlings to secret laboratories to be—in his own words—sliced up and poked and prodded and turned into something new.

Riley had scoffed at the stories then. Now, it was pretty hard not to believe it.

"Is this...where the hatchlings are going?" Riley whispered. He sounded more than horrified. He sounded sick, and he stared at the glass tube like he'd just witnessed a baby being murdered in front of him. "All my rogues, all the hatchlings taken away by the organization. When Talon finds them again, is this where they end up? As some sick lab experiment?"

He smashed a fist into an unbroken part of the tube, shattering it. I jumped. Glass shards rained to the floor, pinging off the cold tile, as Riley stood there, shaking.

"I promised I would keep them safe," he rasped, mostly to himself now. Blood welled from his cut hand and dripped to the floor, but he didn't seem to notice. "I swore to free as many of my kind as I could before the organization killed me. That's been my mission for so long, getting dragons out, making them see the truth of Talon, even though I knew it was dangerous. Even though I knew some of them might be killed. I hated every single death, but I knew they would be better off free. But this..." His gaze, bright with anguish, slid over the tube. "How can I stand against *this*? How can I justify freeing anyone, convince any hatchling to trust me, when I know they could end up here?"

I stepped forward, gently taking his hand and holding it in both of mine. "This is *why* we can't give up," I whispered as his tortured gaze flicked to me. "This is why we have to keep fighting. We have to show everyone what Talon is really like, that they're willing to sacrifice their own kind for gain. If we don't, even more hatchlings could end up in a place like this."

Riley took a deep breath. "Yeah," he said, nodding. "You're right. We can't stop. We can't let this continue. The organization will do horrible things to their hatchlings and undesirables even if there are no rogues to take the fall. If I don't keep fighting Talon, who will?"

"I will," I said softly.

He chuckled. "I don't know, Firebrand. Think you can handle a dozen hormonal teen dragons if I go down someday?"

"I lived with an obnoxious twin brother for years," I responded. "I think I could manage." He arched a dubious eyebrow, and I sobered. "But that's not going to happen, Riley, because you're not going to die. This work, what you're doing now, is too important. Someone has to stand against Talon, to show our kind what the organization is really like. And you're the only one who has a chance." I raised my chin, my voice firm. "You can't let them win. *We* can't let them win. And I'm going to do whatever it takes for us to succeed." Riley was motionless, watching me with glittering gold eyes, and I held his stare. "I'm not walking away from this," I told him. "Or you. I'll keep fighting, however long it takes."

Riley blinked slowly and when he opened his eyes, it was Cobalt staring out at me with an intense, hungry gaze. My own instincts responded, rising to the surface, making my skin flush. I was suddenly aware of our surroundings—dark, empty, isolated. No one here but us. My skin felt tight against my bones, stretched out and constricting, and the air in my lungs tasted like smoke.

No, I thought, willing the heat inside to die down. *Not now. Focus, Ember. A creepy abandoned laboratory is not the place for...anything, really. Get a hold of yourself.*

"Come on," Riley said after a moment of intense silence. His voice sounded strained, frustrated. "I don't think we're going to learn anything else. Let's get out of here."

Silently, we headed back through the corridor and empty rooms, past the row of glass containers and up the stairs again. Neither of us said anything, but halfway up the stairwell, Riley jerked to a halt, putting out a hand to stop me. Puzzled, I looked up and saw that he had a strange frown on his face, as if he was trying to catch something just out of earshot.

"Wes? Can you hear me?" Putting a hand to his ear, his brow furrowed. "The signal is breaking up, Wes. I can barely understand you. Slow down. What are you shouting about—

"No." He stopped, the blood draining from his face. "You can't be serious." Another second's pause, and he shook his head. "*Shit.* Wes, get out of here now! That's an order!"

Whirling around, he pointed frantically down the stairs.

"Go back!" he snarled at me, as I stared at him, wide-eyed. "Move, Firebrand! St. George is here—"

A *boom* from up top made me jump, and beams of light flooded the stairwell as a squad of armed, masked soldiers burst through the door and started pouring down the steps.

DANTE

"So," I began, staring around at the table of dragons and humans, all older than me. "Tell me where we stand on progress with the vessels."

Vessels. Not *clones.* Both Talon and the scientists refused to call them clones, despite them being exactly that. Genetic replicas, grown in vat from the DNA of their original counterparts. I didn't know the reasoning behind this. Maybe Talon thought the term *clone* too demeaning, as if we as a race would somehow be lessened for creating carbon copies of ourselves. Or maybe it was something else. Personally, I found the term *vessel* even more disturbing, because it implied they were just there to be filled. That they were empty. That something inside was missing.

Regardless, my personal tastes didn't matter. Whatever we called them, I had a job to do, and I wouldn't fail.

I observed the table before me with cool detachment, noting everyone in attendance. Dr. Olsen, the lead scientist, sat on one side looking impatient, as if he would rather be at work. Another human, the one responsible for the care and general well-being of the vessels, sat beside him. Mr. Schulz was a small, severe man, all points and hard angles, with a thin mouth and impassive black eyes. He was, to hear Dr. Olsen speak of him, quite brilliant with the vessels, but I wouldn't put anything small and vulnerable in his care and expect it to live very long. A human female with thick glasses hovered over her tablet on the other side of the table, and seemed quite nervous about being there. Or maybe it was who she was seated next to that was disconcerting.

A massive black man with huge scarred forearms sat in the chair to the woman's left, his elbows resting on the table and his chin on his knuckles. Four pale claw marks were slashed down his right eye, rendering it blind, but by no means decreasing his lethality. He was, of course, a dragon, a young adult who was known simply as Mace. I didn't know much about him, just that he was a higher-ranking dragon who trained young Gilas for combat and protection work. And that he didn't think much of me. I'd seen him curl a lip in my direction the second I walked in, no doubt wondering why he was under the command of some skinny Chameleon hatchling he'd never seen before. That was fine. I didn't need him to like me; I just needed him to follow orders.

"Progress?" Dr. Olsen repeated, sounding faintly insulted. "We have awakened nine more vessels without setbacks or side effects, bringing the total number up to twenty-two. Eighteen of those vessels have been able to Shift and hold a human form for a minimum of forty-eight hours, and could possibly do so for longer if we order it. They are able to learn and retain an enormous amount of information in a short period, and once they have memorized a command, they do not forget. I'd say progress has been extraordinary, Mr. Hill."

"But there was an incident recently," I said, making him frown. "With one of the vessels. Something where you couldn't control it, is that correct?"

"Well...yes, but—"

"One of the vessels attacked a worker," Mr. Schulz said, his nasal voice interrupting the scientist. "We don't know what set it off, but during a normal exercise it turned and savaged one of its handlers, nearly killing him before we could subdue it. After the incident, it became docile and responsive again, but we've had it in isolation since the attack."

"What can we do to prevent such attacks in the future?"

"We don't know," the woman said, looking up from her tablet. "Its programming should have made it impossible for it to attack anyone in the facility." She shook her head and glanced at the screen again, fingers tapping. "We're testing it by itself now to see if we can pinpoint the trigger. But it might just have been a glitch in the brain cells that caused it to act out."

I nodded and finally turned my attention to the other dragon in the room, who met my gaze with cold apathy. "Just Mace, is that correct?" I asked, and he nodded once. "You've seen the vessels in action. How soon can you have them in full fighting force?"

He smirked. "Depends."

"On what?"

"Lots of things. Can they follow orders? How fast do they learn commands? Will they work together, or will it be like training a pack of hounds that hate each other? Because let's face it—those...*things* aren't really dragons." His expression twisted into one of pure contempt. "They're dogs that look like us and can Shift into human form, that's all."

"I beg your pardon!" Dr. Olsen exclaimed, half rising from his chair. "Dogs? You couldn't even begin to understand the complexity of these vessels, sir. Their genetic makeup is nearly identical to your own, perhaps even improved upon. Their growth rate, learning capacity, everything, has been accelerated, and they have been programmed with the highest intelligence possible while still maintaining their tractability. They are a marvel of science, technology and ancient magic, and they certainly are not simply *dogs* that can change their shape at will."

Mace sneered. "You tell them to sit, they sit. You tell them roll over, they roll over. One of them snapped and now needs to be muzzled to be allowed anywhere near humans. Yeah, they're dogs. Scaly, semi-intelligent, flying dogs." He shook his head. "You're never going to convince me that those copies are anything like us."

"Enough," I said, as the scientist rose fully upright, bristling with fury and indignation. "Dr. Olsen, please sit down. Mr. Mace, it doesn't matter what the vessels are, or your personal thoughts on them. You will still train them as you would any new recruit, and you will get them battle ready as soon as you can, because that is what Talon requires. Their success or failure reflects on you—on all of us. The organization has given us this task, and we must see it through." I narrowed my eyes at the other dragon. "Unless, of course, you want to inform Talon that the project they have invested so much time, resources and money into is a waste, and the subjects are nothing but intelligent canines."

Mace glared at me, his face tight, then smirked. "No, we can't have them thinking that, can we?" he muttered, and bowed his head. A short, simple gesture in my direction. "All right, boss," he said, only slightly begrudgingly. "If that's what you want, I'll whip these dragon dogs into shape in no time."

"Good." I smiled as Dr. Olsen sat down again, still glowering. "We're a team," I reminded them. "With a common interest. Our goals are the same, and the organization is watching us. If there is a problem, or if you need anything, please come to me. I will do whatever it takes to ensure that we succeed. Is that understood?"

"Yes, sir," said nearly everyone, including Mace.

"All right." I nodded and looked at Dr. Olsen, the only one who hadn't answered with the rest of them. "One more thing," I told him. "You understand, more than anyone, that this project must succeed. We cannot allow anything to endanger it. There can be no instability, no 'glitches' in the program. Nothing we cannot predict."

"I know that, Mr. Hill," Dr. Olsen said. "And you are obviously leading up to something. So please stop stalling. Whatever you want me to do, out with it already."

"As you say." I hardened my voice and crushed my own doubts. This was necessary, I told myself. I had to prove to the team, to the workers and to Talon, that I had the strength to make this project a success. Even if some things had to be sacrificed. "The vessel that attacked the worker," I said, watching Dr. Olsen's face turn white. "Terminate it."

RILEY

I leaped back, drawing my gun and firing at the first soldiers that came down the stairs. The shots boomed in the dark stairwell, flaring white and sparking off the railing and walls. The soldiers didn't slow down, their heavy combat armor deflecting the pistol rounds as they raised their assault rifles.

There was a ripple of energy, and a small red dragon suddenly appeared, nearly crushing me into the wall, a split second before her jaws opened and a column of flame roared up the steps. It blazed a furious orange in the enclosed space, turning the stairwell into an oven and catching the first soldiers in the blast. They flinched back with cries of alarm and pain, giving us a few seconds to flee down the stairs. Before the roar of assault rifles joined the deafening cacophony as the rest of them opened fire.

I hit the door first and yanked it open to let the red dragon bound through before I darted in behind her. "This way!" I hissed, running past the rows of glass tubes and ducking behind one of the long white counters, kneeling down to stay hidden. Ember followed, pressed close to the floor like a cat, her wings folded tight to her body. Peeking around the corner,

I whispered a curse. Across the floor, on the opposite wall, the stairwell door opened and soldiers spilled into the lab.

"Dammit," I whispered, shrugging out of my jacket and tossing it aside. "There's no way out. We're going to have to fight our way through." The gun holster and 9 mm joined the discarded jacket; it was no use trying to shoot the enemy. That heavy armor would just absorb pistol rounds. Not that claws and teeth would fare much better; if I was close enough to a soldier of St. George to bite him, he and his friends were definitely close enough to shoot me full of holes.

"How many of them?" Ember growled softly.

"Hard to say. At least eight, maybe more."

I shivered, trying to banish the sudden fear, the dark reality of the situation. We were trapped. I tried to tell myself this was no different than the other times St. George had had us surrounded, but I knew better. There was no escape from this floor. No windows, no back doors, no hidden exits. No way out except up the stairs that were now crawling with soldiers and guns. I didn't know how many soldiers were above us or might have surrounded the building, but the chances of even making it to the front entrance seemed pretty bleak.

Ember was watching me, green eyes bright in the shadows of the room. She crouched against the wall with her wings pressed close and her tail curled around herself. Even with her fangs slightly bared and her sides heaving with fear, she was still beautiful, elegant, fiery, everything my dragon wanted. And she was probably going to die here with me.

I gave her a weary smile.

"Well, looks like you got your wish, Firebrand," I whispered, feeling the heat in my veins rise up, growing hotter by the second. "Screw this waiting around. If we survive this, I swear you will have my full attention from now on."

Her eyes flashed, and I released the hold on my true self, letting Cobalt surge to the surface. My wings unfurled, brushing the countertop, and my talons clicked on the tile floor as I sank down and made myself small, folding my wings tight to my body. The soldiers reached the first of the countertops and began filing down the rows, guns and flashlights leading the way.

I nudged Ember's shoulder and we slunk away, staying low like stalking cats, darting behind counters and avoiding the beams of light sliding over the walls and floor. The soldiers fanned out as they moved through the aisles, never far from each other. I glanced back at the exit and saw a pair guarding the door, blocking escape. My heart sank. Too many of them. We could keep pressing farther into the lab, knowing we'd eventually run out of space, or we could go forward and risk running through a bullet storm.

Ember pressed close, brushing my shoulder with hers, and my pulse spiked. I looked over, saw the fierce determination in her gaze and felt a defiant growl rumble in my throat as a hot, vicious rage spread through my veins. Ember was *mine*. The other half of me. And I would fight Talon, St. George and the entire damned world to keep her safe.

I jerked my head toward the back room and we crept toward it, my best hope being to avoid St. George for a few minutes while I figured out a plan to save our hides. Ember followed, perfectly silent, not even her talons clicking on the tile to give us away. But the soldiers were closer than I thought. As we moved from one counter to another, a flashlight beam sliced over us and someone gave a shout.

Gunfire exploded, making me cringe. Ember snarled, hunkering down, as bullets peppered the countertop and shattered the glass vials overhead. The din was deafening, and I hissed a curse, trying to think. I knew the soldiers would be converging on this spot, weaving between aisles and continuing to fire as they advanced, but we couldn't move without risking a few bullets to the back.

"Here!" Ember hissed, darting to the counter opposite us and lashing out with her claws. A pair of cabinet doors slid back, revealing cleaning solutions and aerosol cans, the opening just big enough for a dragon to slip through, and she gestured at me frantically. "Come on!"

I followed her, peeling back doors beneath the countertops as we crossed the room, shattering glass vials and knocking aside plastic bottles as we went. We fled the main floor through the door with the glass wall, and took cover behind the broken glass cylinder, breathing hard. Flashlights scuttled over the door frame, footsteps echoed down the hall and shadows appeared through the frame. I hunkered down, heart pounding, as St. George drew closer to our hiding place.

Dammit. Still no way out.

"We're not going to make it this time, are we?" Ember's voice was eerily calm. The red dragon crouched beside me, observing the soldiers' approach with glittering green eyes. A few entered the room, M4s leading the way, while others formed a line in front of the door, blocking the way out. "There's too many of them. No flying, no back door, nowhere to go but through St. George."

"Ember." I unfurled a wing, draping it over her and pulling her close. She shivered, pressing into my ribs, and heat roared through my insides. "I'm sorry," I whispered. "I never wanted this for you. This life... I knew it was going to kill me in the end. I wish you didn't have to be here when it finally caught up."

Ember's tail coiled with mine. "I wouldn't have changed it."

The soldiers were almost to our hiding spot, flashlight beams crawling on the walls overhead, booted feet stomping against the tile. They were coming slower now, being cautious, knowing we were close. It was dangerous to continue speaking, though I had so much I wanted to say. A white beam sliced past, illuminating the shattered glass, and I ducked my head, heart racing, until it passed.

Ember gave a throaty, defiant growl, and for a moment, I closed my eyes, just feeling her against me. This would be the last time I saw her like this, in her beautiful true form. Unless Wes came charging in with a bazooka—very unlikely—or all of St. George had a sudden, miraculous change of heart, luck wasn't going to help us, not this time. So, that left me. To save my hatchlings and my underground, even if I couldn't be there anymore. "Wait for them to start chasing me," I told Ember, ignoring her frown of confusion. I heard shots outside the door, probably more St. George soldiers on the way, and I tensed for a final, desperate lunge. "I'll take as many of them down as I can. You just go for the door. If you see Wes again, do me a favor and tell him thanks, for everything."

Before she could say anything, I jumped out with a roar, straight into the line of oncoming soldiers, and smoke erupted around me.

EMBER

I realized what the rogue was saying a second too late. With a defiant roar, Cobalt leaped out of cover, straight at the line of St. George soldiers and their guns. Heart seizing, I lunged after him, hoping to get to him in time, knowing it was too late. That I was a heartbeat away from seeing the brave, brash, infuriating rogue gunned down right in front of me.

Time seemed to slow. Just as Cobalt sprang into the open, something tiny sailed through the air and landed between him and the soldiers with a clink. There was a deafening hiss, and white smoke erupted from the object, spraying everywhere and filling the room. Shots rang out from somewhere in the fog, and two of the soldiers I could still see jerked and went down.

"We're under attack! Take cover!"

More shots cracked, the triple tap of burst fire, and another soldier cried out. Utterly bewildered, I looked around for Cobalt and found him crouched nearby, glaring around warily, clearly as shocked as I was.

"Ember! Riley!"

The breath left my lungs in a forceful explosion. *That voice.* No, it couldn't be. He was gone. I'd sent him away myself.

And then, a body emerged from the smoke, M4 in hand, firing into the corners of the room, face grim and determined. For a second, nothing seemed real, as a pair of familiar gun-metal eyes met mine.

"Come on!" Garret Xavier Sebastian snapped, gesturing at us with the gun. "While they're disoriented! Let's go!"

PART II

UNDER ONE BANNER

SEBASTIAN

Six years ago

"Garret, are you listening to me?"

I tore my eyes from the window and the ancient Spanish-style monastery looming at the end of the drive. Surrounded by a high stone wall, red tiled roofs peeking over the top, it was an intriguing sight, especially since the number of times I had been outside the Order chapterhouse where I had lived until today could be counted on my fingers.

"Yes, sir," I said, turning to Benedict, who glared at me from behind the wheel of the Jeep. "I'm listening."

"Really? Repeat what I just said."

"Formal training has already started," I recited. "I'll be joining the classes late."

"And?"

"The Headmaster's name is Robert St. Julian. He fought the dragons until he lost his arm in battle, but he'll still kick my ass in sparring any day of the week. So be respectful when speaking to him."

"And?"

"Work hard, follow commands and don't talk about the Order to outsiders. Sir."

"Hmph." Benedict grunted, reluctantly appeased, and didn't say anything else. Careful not to let any triumph show on my face, I went back to gazing out the window as we pulled to a stop at the huge wooden gate guarding the entrance to the monastery. It creaked open, and we rolled into a large court-yard with a single gnarled banyan tree in the center, out-stretched branches mottling the ground with shade. It was a cold, wintry morning, and no one was around. We parked the Jeep, and I grabbed my duffel bag from the back before follow-ing Benedict across the grounds to the largest stone building at the end of the walk.

Inside, the rooms were dim and cool, the white stucco walls bare of adornments, windows or decorations. We marched down a corridor in silence until we came to a heavy wooden door at the end of the passage. Benedict knocked twice, and a quiet "Enter" drifted through the wood. Pushing the door back, we stepped into a small, equally bare office, where two men waited for us in the dimly lit room.

The first man who rose from behind a desk and came for-ward was dressed in flowing black robes, a simple rope belt tied around his waist and an iron cross hanging at his throat. He was tall, even taller than Benedict, with a long gray beard and a narrow, angular face, eyes peering down at me with the in-tensity of a hawk. The sleeve of his right arm had been folded and pinned to his shoulder, the fabric hanging limply at his side. A string of wooden beads were entwined in the fingers of his left hand, and they clicked softly as he approached and loomed over me like a grim specter of death.

"Ah, Garret Xavier Sebastian." His voice scraped in my ears like a pair of knives. "We meet at last. I am Headmaster St. Julian, and I have been anticipating your arrival for a very long time. Do you know why you are here?"

"Yes, sir," I replied, keeping my voice steady and my eyes glued to a point over his left shoulder. "I'm here to learn how to kill dragons."

St. Julian laughed, a raspy sound in the small room. "Right to the heart of the matter," he said, looking at Benedict, standing behind me. "I see this one has no illusions. Have you told him everything?"

"I told him everything about the war, and what the Order does, sir," Benedict replied. "I've prepared him for this day as best I could. He knows our enemies, and he understands what is at stake. Now, I leave him in your capable hands, to turn into a true soldier for the cause."

A quiet chuckle came from the second man in the room. "If I know you, Lucas, the boy can already outshoot and out-fight every recruit in his class," he mused, gazing at me with piercing black eyes. "I hear he could reliably hit the center of a target at fifty paces when he was eight. How old is he now?"

"Eleven," Benedict replied.

The man shook his head. "He'll already be singled out, coming in late and being younger than everyone by at least a year. You're not doing him any favors."

"That can't be helped," Benedict replied. "I've been assigned to the South America mission and I leave the country in a week. They're not certain how long we'll be gone—better that he's here, learning, and not sitting on his bunk, staring at walls. Sebastian is old enough to begin training, and he knows what he has to do. The Headmaster has agreed to take him a year early. He's learned everything he can with me.

"Besides," he continued ruthlessly, "I've never done the boy any favors. I don't want things to be easy for him—I want him to be the best. So make it hard for him. Push him beyond what everyone else can take." I felt his gaze on the back of my head. "When his training is done, I expect him to be the perfect soldier."

The perfect soldier. I swallowed hard. I had to excel, to be the best. The better I was, the sooner I could go to war and start killing the monsters that slaughtered my family.

"Very well," the Headmaster said, nodding slowly. "If that is what you wish, Benedict. We will see what your recruit can do." He turned to me, and there was a new interest in his expression now; a master sizing up his latest apprentice. "I'll have someone show you to your room," he said. "Dinner is at five thirty in the main hall, and classes begin promptly at eight a.m. I expect you to be early for both, Sebastian."

"Yes, sir."

The door opened, and a monk appeared as if summoned by magic. "Please show our newest recruit to his quarters," the Headmaster told the monk. "I believe there is one room left. The chamber closest to the outer wall. Put him in there." His hard gray eyes fixed on me once more. "You have until dinner to familiarize yourself with the grounds," he told me. "Tomorrow morning, if I don't see you in the correct room on time, your entire class will receive a punishment detail. Succeed or fail together. That is how we do things here, recruit." He gave a humorless smile that was a clear challenge, an invitation to impress. "Welcome to the Academy of St. George."

The monk didn't take my bag or make any gesture to follow. He simply stood just inside the door with his hands clasped before him, waiting. I turned to Benedict, who gave me a short nod.

"Work hard," he told me. "Remember what I taught you. This is what you trained for, what you were always meant to do."

"Yes, sir," I replied simply, and turned away. No goodbyes, no sentimental farewells. I followed the monk into the hall, but paused when my mentor called my name. Lucas Benedict stood in the door frame with a peculiar expression on his face, one that seemed torn between defiance and an almost angry pride. My gut prickled. It wasn't the first time he had looked at me like that. Every so often, when I did extraordinarily well, or when I recited the St. George teachings I knew by heart, he would smile faintly and nod. As if, despite everyone's misgivings, I was coming along just fine.

"Knock 'em dead, soldier," he stated, and shut the door between us.

That was the last thing he ever said to me.

"Hey, Sebastian!"

I looked up warily. It had been three months since my arrival at the academy, and in that time, I'd made as many enemies as I had friends. The school itself was quite small; in my class there were only eight of us. The recruits, I'd learned, were drawn from temples and monasteries around the world. St. George was an ancient order, with ties to the Church and other religious organizations that stretched back for centuries. Every year, a few boys were chosen to serve the Order and were sent to the academy to be raised as soldiers in the holy war against demons. It gave St. George a constant supply of troops while allowing them to control their numbers, as they were still a secret organization and could not afford to draw attention from outsiders. With few exceptions, most of the recruits arrived with little to no training and only the barest knowledge of the war. They knew they had been chosen to battle evil and protect mankind, but didn't truly understand what it meant to be a soldier of St. George, or the truth of what the Order really fought, until they came to the academy.

Peter Matthews was an exception.

He was the son of a lieutenant, part of a family who could trace their ancestry back to the Knights Templars themselves, and he had come to the academy knowing exactly what was expected of him. Much like myself, Matthews had been trained by his father in the ways of St. George. Not only that, he was big for his age, intimidating and a decent shot with a firearm. He had been at the top of his class in nearly every subject.

Until me.

Today at the shooting range, Brother Adam had corrected his form, saying he was pulling left because he was overcompensating for the recoil, and Matthews had argued that his form was fine; it was the sight on the gun that was faulty. Adam had then handed the same weapon to me, and I had proceeded to hit the target on every shot. The look on Peter Matthews's face, as Brother Adam told the rest of the class to follow my example, promised retribution, but I hadn't thought much of it. I was used to his insults by now, and his anger had never progressed to actual violence. Though that was more due to my never letting him catch me alone and unawares. Sometimes he would meet me in the hall with a hard shove and a warning to watch my step, but it never went further than that. Fighting among recruits was severely punished, and Matthews was careful to give the impression of a model recruit when the instructors were around.

Today, however, it seemed the festering anger and resentment had finally reached a boiling point because Matthews didn't look like he was going to be satisfied with a shove and a warning to back off. He stood in the doorway of the bathroom with his palms planted on either side of the frame, blocking the exit. His two friends, Levi Smith and Edwin James, flanked him like attack dogs, but Matthews was bigger than either and was the far greater threat.

"Think you're smart?" he demanded, stepping into the room, out of sight of any monks that might catch him loitering in the hall. "What was that today, Sebastian? You think you're better than me?"

"No," I said calmly. "I don't think I'm better than you. I know I am."

He lunged at me, swinging a fist at my face. I ducked my head and raised my arm, taking it on the shoulder rather than the chin, and lashed out with a punch of my own, striking him in the jaw. He staggered back with a yelp, and then his friends were on me, kicking and flailing. I covered my head and backed up, trying to disengage, but the bathroom was small, and I was soon pressed into a corner. Blows hammered down on me, six hard fists striking wherever they could land, but I kept my guard up and threw back punches when I could, trying to protect my face.

"Enough!"

My assailants were yanked away, and the rain of blows came to an end. Panting, I looked up to see Brother Eli glaring at us, his large frame a barrier between myself and the others. Levi and Edwin had instantly backed off and were huddled together, looking guilty, but Matthews stared at me with murder in his eyes.

"What's going on here?" the monk demanded, as though it wasn't obvious. My head ached, my mouth tasted like copper and I could feel blood trickling from my nose. But my attackers hadn't escaped unscathed, either. Matthews's jaw was already swelling, and Edwin had a split lip that was dripping blood into the collar of his shirt. "Who started this?" Brother Eli asked, eyeing each of us, and our wounds, in turn. "Sebastian? Matthews? I'm waiting." When we didn't answer, his voice grew hard. "One of you had better start talking in the next three seconds, or your entire class will be punished for this transgression."

"I did, sir," I said, and he turned on me with a frown. "Matthews and I were having an argument, and I pushed him to fight. I'm the one who started it."

"Sebastian." The monk raised a bushy eyebrow, looking severely unconvinced. I was the quiet one, the boy who spoke only when spoken to. The student who never questioned orders and did exactly what he was told, every time. Fighting with your fellow recruits was strictly forbidden on monastery grounds, and I hadn't broken a rule since the day I arrived. It was no secret that Matthews hated me; between us, the guilty party should have been perfectly clear.

But I knew Matthews would never own up to it, and if somebody didn't take the fall, the whole squad would suffer. Succeed or fail together, that was part of the Code of St. George, something I took very seriously. I was not here for myself. I was part of something greater, a brotherhood, united under one banner with one purpose. Even at eleven years old, when I didn't fully understand what was happening, I was starting to think like a soldier. The needs of the many outweigh the needs of the one. I was there to kill dragons, but I couldn't do it alone.

Brother Eli didn't say anything for a moment, perhaps waiting for Matthews to step forward as well, accept some of the blame. When he didn't, the monk sighed and gestured to the door.

"You three, get out of here," he ordered, scowling at the trio. "If this happens again, I don't care who started it—you'll be on kitchen duty for the rest of the year. Out!"

They scrambled to leave, but not before Matthews shot a last, triumphant smirk in my direction. Then they were gone, and Brother Eli turned to me again. I braced myself for the lecture, for my punishment, but the monk sighed and shook his head, his expression becoming grim.

"Here," he said quietly, and pressed a handkerchief into my hand. "Clean yourself up, Sebastian, and follow me. The Headmaster wants to see you."

Puzzled, I did as he said, washing the blood from my face before pressing the cloth to my nose. Brother Eli met me in the hall and silently motioned for me to follow. As I trailed him down the corridor, passing students and other classes still in session, apprehension warred with confusion. Why did the Headmaster want to see me? Had I done something wrong, other than the fight? Did he already know about the incident in the bathroom and want to punish me himself?

When we reached the Headmaster's office, Brother Eli simply nodded for me to go in. Stuffing the bloody handkerchief in my pocket, I walked to the door and knocked twice, hearing the familiar "Enter" a moment later. I pushed back the door and saw Headmaster St. Julian standing before his desk with a man I'd seen once before, when I first arrived with Benedict. Like Brother Eli, both looked grave as they stared at me, and my heart started an irregular thud in my chest.

"Recruit Sebastian." The Headmaster motioned me forward with a withered hand. "Please come inside." I did as I was told and stood at attention before the desk, while the door creaked on its hinges and clicked shut behind me.

"At ease," the Headmaster said, and I relaxed my posture, though everything inside me was still tense. The Headmaster nodded to the man beside him. "Sebastian, this is Lieutenant Gabriel Martin, of the Order's Western Chapterhouse. I don't believe you have formally met."

"No, sir," I replied, glancing at the lieutenant. St. George was a small organization and didn't follow the structure of modern armies with tens of thousands of troops, but it was, in fact, an army. The lieutenants commanded the soldiers of the various chapterhouses throughout the country and were responsible for a unit's training and general preparedness. Above them were the captains, and above them, the Patriarch himself.

The lieutenant smiled, but it was a tight, painful smile, as if he would rather be anywhere else. "If you'll excuse us, Headmaster," he murmured, and the other man nodded. Rising from the desk, he gave me a brief, unreadable look and left me alone with Lieutenant Martin.

I waited until the Headmaster had gone and the door had

closed behind him, before turning to the lieutenant. "Am I in trouble, sir?" I asked quietly.

"No." Gabriel Martin shook his head. "No, Garret, you're not in trouble. Lucas Benedict was a good friend of mine. He's the reason I'm here. He made me promise that if anything happened to him…" He paused, and in that moment, I knew what had happened. Why he'd come.

"Garret." I heard Martin sigh. "Lucas Benedict…was killed last week in battle. He was in South America on a mission for the Order, and his squad was ambushed by the enemy. There were no survivors."

My stomach dropped, and for a moment, everything inside me went numb. Benedict had never been a father to me, he'd made that clear himself. My whole life, all of our interactions had been strictly student to teacher, and he'd kept me at arm's length with professional detachment, never getting too close. But he had always been there. And there were times when that mask would slip and he would look at me with pride. Almost with affection. It hadn't been much, but it had been enough.

Now he was gone. For the second time in my life, I was an orphan.

It took several breaths before I could ask, "Was…was it the dragons?"

"Not directly," Martin replied in a solemn voice. "The target they were looking for was not at the location, but it had left servants behind. Lucas was leading the squad when the ambush happened. He was shot and killed instantly."

"So, it *was* Talon."

"Garret." Martin stepped forward, pulled up a chair and sat in it so that we were the same height. "Listen to me. I've known Lucas a long time. He was a good soldier and an excellent leader. When you first came to us and he took you in, I thought he was crazy. But I've watched you through the years, and now, I understand what he saw. You have the potential to become something incredible. Not just a soldier." His dark gaze sharpened. "A leader. A champion for St. George. I know this news comes as a shock and, believe me, I wish I didn't have to deliver it. But Lucas wanted you to continue. Not only that, he wanted you to excel. To be the best there is." Those piercing eyes softened, though his voice remained stern. "Do you understand?"

"Yes, sir," I replied, and my voice was calm. Steady. The soldier Benedict would have wanted. "I understand. Am I dismissed?"

He nodded. "The Headmaster has freed you from the rest of your classes today. I'll be back tomorrow morning to pick you up. I assume you want to attend the funeral." He rose heavily and placed a hand on my shoulder. "The Order has lost a great man," he murmured, regarding me with somber black eyes. "But the war isn't over. And the dragons haven't destroyed him completely. At least, not yet."

And he was gone.

Numb, I returned to my quarters. Monks and teachers saw me in the halls, clearly heading away from my scheduled classes, but no one asked where I was going. Peter Matthews passed me in the courtyard and threw out a jeer, smug and challenging. I ignored him. He was not important, not anymore. I kept walking, head high and expression neutral, until I reached my quarters at the very end of the hall and slipped inside.

Only when I was alone in my tiny chambers and the door had shut firmly behind me did I sink onto the cot, pull my knees to my chest and let the tears come. No one would see me cry, and I knew *he* wouldn't want me to cry, but I couldn't help myself. Even though the shame of my tears burned nearly as bright as the sorrow. Another life the dragons had taken from me, one more they had stolen without a thought. I wouldn't let them get away with it. I'd pay my last respects to my mentor, thank him for everything he'd taught me, and then I would return to my training with renewed purpose. Our enemies— *my* enemies—wouldn't win. The demon lizards had hurt me for the last time. Now, they had a new foe, and I would make sure they remembered my name when I destroyed them on the battlefield.

I would work hard.

I would excel.

I would become the perfect soldier.

GARRET

"Gunfire," Jade murmured beside me.

I clenched my jaw, feeling the tension in my shoulders spread to all parts of my body. We'd been driving all day, setting a frantic, exhausting pace toward our destination, and those were the first words Jade had spoken for several hours. Since departing England, the Asian dragon had been a quiet but efficient travel companion, content to hang back and follow my lead in an unfamiliar country. She had ordered her two monks to stay in London, to keep an eye on the Order and the Patriarch, and inform her if there were any changes. Jade herself was so still and quiet, I'd almost forgotten she was there. Of course, I wasn't in the clearest state of mind, either. Since landing, I had only one thing on my mind: getting to Ember before the Order did. I didn't know how much time I had to warn them, if they were being shot down even as I sped down the highway, helpless to do anything else. I couldn't even call them. Not for the first time, I wished I had Ember's number, or even Riley's. Cutting myself off from my dragon comrades had been a terrible mistake; I would happily call Riley and endure his mockery and disdain if it meant I could warn Ember.

Ember, I thought, staring at the highway through the windshield. *Please be all right. Let me get to you in time.*

A distant report echoed over the buildings, slicing through me like a knife and making my heart skip. Immediately, I slowed and pulled the car to the side of the narrow private road, as several weaker but undeniable *pops* joined the first, coming from the buildings beyond the chain-link fence that surrounded the abandoned industrial park.

"We're too late," Jade murmured, her voice unnaturally calm. "The Order is already here."

No. I jumped from my seat and hurried to the trunk to wrench it open, revealing the duffel bag of personal items I'd hidden away before leaving for England. As Jade stepped up beside me, I reached into the bag and pulled out a Kevlar vest, then slipped it on over my shirt. From behind the duffel I drew out an M4, checked the chamber for rounds and slung the strap over my shoulder.

The Asian dragon's dark eyes burned into the side of my head. "You realize this is very risky," she commented, watching as I slid a Glock into the holster at my side. "We are only two bodies. Even if St. George doesn't expect us, the odds of everyone making it out alive are slim."

"I know," I muttered. "But I'm getting them out. I have to try. Ember would do the same for me." *As a matter of fact, she already did.* "I won't ask you to help me if you're afraid," I told the dragon, who regarded me solemnly, "but I'm going ahead, with or without you. So decide. Are you with me, or not?"

She sighed. "I gave my word that I would help, and a *shenlung* is nothing if she does not keep her promises. Even if it means wading into a war zone full of armed human maniacs."

Shaking her head, she gave a wry smile. "So, lead on. I am right behind you."

I nodded and held up a second handgun. "You'll need one of these, then."

Her nose wrinkled. "Ah, thank you, but no. Even were I not violently opposed to using a gun, I would not know what to do if I had it. No, mortal." She shook her head, and her eyes glinted. "I am more than capable of killing humans, without mechanical help."

"All right." I didn't like it, but I wasn't going to argue. "Then let's go."

We sprinted for the fence and scrambled over, landing warily on the other side. Hugging the many low, darkened buildings, we headed in the direction from which the gunshots had originated. Though the lot was eerily silent now, and the structures deserted. I wondered if Ember and Riley had come this way, down this very path, thinking nothing was wrong. Not knowing that the Order was watching them, lying in wait to spring their trap. If they had come through here, they wouldn't have suspected anything. There were too many places to hide; an army would be able to stay concealed until it was too late.

Peering around a corner, I caught a flash of movement and ducked back, pressing into the wall while Jade flattened herself beside me. I did a quick scan of the area. Rows of long gray warehouse buildings surrounded us and the large white building across the empty lot. NewTech Industries, the sign out front read. Two large delivery trucks sat near the main entrance, and a pair of black SUVs blocked the road to the front.

"Two assault teams," I breathed, ducking back. "And another

out front, holding the exits. They're not taking any chances this time."

Jade watched me, dark eyes somber. "What does that mean?"

I jerked my head in the direction of the building. "St. George would have waited until the targets entered the building before getting the order to move," I said. "If they'd sprung the trap too early, they'd risk the targets flying away. Once inside, they would try to herd them farther in, to lower floors if possible, away from any windows or doors where they could escape. Meanwhile, a third team would be dispatched to block all exits out of the building, and there will be a sniper perched somewhere close by, just in case a target makes it through."

Jade listened to this in silence, deliberating. "So, the first thing we need to do is clear the doors," she said, calm and practical, as if she'd done this many times before. "Perhaps a distraction of some sort, to sow a little chaos in their ranks?" She smiled. "The appearance of another dragon across the lot would certainly cause them to sit up and take notice."

"That might work," I agreed slowly, "but it'll be dangerous for you. Are you sure you want to risk it?"

"I believe, to put it in American terms, that ship has already sailed," Jade said wryly. "I am here. I said I would help. If you need a distraction to reach your friends, I can provide one."

"All right." I nodded. "But I'll need to take out the sniper before I can even think about getting to the front." I peered around the corner again, searching the nearby buildings. A two-story warehouse directly across the road from the target building caught my attention, and I nodded grimly. *If Tristan is here, that will be his spot.* "Wait for my signal," I told Jade, turning back. "Then see if you can draw the soldiers away from the entrance. They'll probably call for backup, so be careful." I shot a quick glance around the corner again, marking the soldier's location, before ducking back again. "Once the soldiers are engaged," I went on, "don't worry about me or the rest of us, just get away from here. If you can make it to the car, drive back to the city and find a crowd. They won't pursue you there."

Jade blinked slowly. "And how will I know you're not dead?" she asked, narrowing her eyes. "I am putting a lot of faith in you, mortal. I trust you are not going to rush in there, guns blazing, as you cowboys put it, and get yourself shot to pieces. And, if you do make it out, how will I know where to find you again? I don't know this country at all. I would not know the first place to search."

"Once we're out and it's safe, I'll call you with our location." She gave me a wary look and I held her gaze. "I promise."

The dragon sighed. "I suppose I have no choice but to trust you," she said. "You have proven yourself to be an honorable human so far, even for one who was part of the Order. I do hope this trend continues." She gave a small nod and drew back a step, preparing to slip away. "I'll wait for your signal, then. Good luck."

I left the corner and circled around the buildings, moving as silently as I could, keeping the walls between myself and the Order. When I reached the back of the warehouse, I slid in through an open window and picked my way across the concrete until I found a flight of metal stairs leading to the second floor. Silently, I ascended the steps, muzzle of the M4 leading the way. The staircase took me to a hall and a row of

ancient doors sitting across from each other. All closed tight…
except for one.

I crept down the hall, praying the floorboards wouldn't creak
and give me away, and peered into the room. There was a soldier kneeling at a boarded-up window, the barrel of a sniper
rifle poking through the cracks, his attention riveted on the
building across from us.

My stomach knotted, but I took a steady breath and raised
my gun, aiming for the back of his head. But as my finger
tightened on the trigger, I shifted my weight and the boards
under me let out a traitorous squeak. The sniper whirled from
the window, hard gaze settling on me, and I was staring into
a pair of familiar blue eyes.

Tristan.

DANTE

I stood on the mezzanine, gazing at the floor below, watching a pair of identical humans kick, punch and pummel each other relentlessly.

"They're getting much better," Dr. Olsen murmured beside me, sounding impressed. I didn't answer, continuing to watch the fight. Or, "sparring," as Mace called it. I wasn't so sure. I'd seen sparring matches before, in boxing or the organized cage fights on television. Yes, they were fairly savage, with both opponents doing their best to beat or choke the other guy into unconsciousness. But there were rules and referees, and though I'd seen some pretty gruesome injuries, no one was in danger of actually dying. If one person conceded, tapped out or was knocked senseless, the other backed off and the fight was over. Everyone understood that.

The vessels, though, didn't get that concept. They stopped only when Mace ordered them to stop. Usually this happened at a clear victory point, when one opponent took a vicious blow that left him reeling, or when the other had him in some kind of hold or lock he couldn't get out of. But I'd never seen a vessel voluntarily back off, and that worried me. How far would they go to follow orders? I felt I had to know, but at the same time, I was afraid of the answer.

Fear is counterproductive, Dante. It's your responsibility to know exactly what your projects are capable of, in every aspect.

Ms. Sutton, the lead programmer for the vessels' behavioral conditioning, suddenly winced. One of the fighters had lashed out with a high roundhouse kick, catching the other in the temple. It staggered back, nearly insensible, and Mace stepped forward to stop the match.

"No!" I called. He looked at me sharply, and I held up a hand. "Let them continue," I ordered. "We need to know how far they'll go before they stop on their own."

Mace's jaw tightened, but he nodded and backed off. Without an order to desist, the first vessel pursued his opponent across the ring and, though the other was clearly injured, slammed a right hook into his jaw, sending him crashing to the cement.

I gritted my teeth, clamping down on the order to stop the fight, forcing myself to keep watching. The injured vessel tried to get to his feet, but his opponent kicked him viciously in the ribs, knocking him onto his back. As I watched, the first vessel pounced on his downed victim, straddled his chest and started raining blows onto his face.

Mace looked at me, clearly asking if he should put an end to this. I shook my head. The injured vessel tried to shield his face at first, but several blows got through, knocking him unconscious. His head fell back, his arms flopping to the side. And still, the savage beating continued unhindered, the other vessel's face blank and emotionless as he smashed his fists into his opponent's unprotected face again and again. Blood appeared on his knuckles, spattered across his face and chest, and my stomach started to heave.

"All right," I finally called, when it was clear the vessel wasn't going to stop on his own. "That's enough!"

Mace strode forward. "Halt!" he barked, his voice booming in the vastness of the room. "Cease-fire, soldier."

The vessel froze instantly. Lowering his arms, he rose and stepped away from the body, his eyes still as blank as ever. Blood covered his face in vivid streaks, and his knuckles were stained red, but it was nothing compared to the mess that was the other dragon. I felt sick and couldn't look directly at its face as Mace walked up and knelt beside the body.

"Is it...all right?" Dr. Olsen called, sounding ill, as well. Mace grunted and stood up.

"It's dead."

"Okay, that is a problem," I said, turning on the scientist. My stomach roiled, and I felt more than slightly nauseous, but I stood tall and glared at the human, who looked pale and horrified himself. "I understand the vessels were programmed for obedience, Dr. Olsen, but having no initiative at all makes them a liability. We need soldiers who can think and act on their own, not robots. Not...whatever that is." I gestured to the blood-soaked vessel, standing motionless and impassive over the mangled mess of his brother. "Can we fix it?" I asked, looking at Ms. Sutton, as well. "Can the process be improved upon?"

"I...don't know." Ms. Sutton ran a hand down her face. "Maybe. The behavior programming is supposed to be foolproof. Trying to change them now could have...unexpected consequences."

"Try." My voice came out flat, nonnegotiable. Dr. Olsen glared at me, and I turned on him, narrowing my eyes. "This is unacceptable, Doctor. They cannot be so empty that they have no independent thoughts of their own."

"Talon told me that obedience is crucial—"

"I'm not saying they should question orders," I snapped. "I'm saying they shouldn't walk off a cliff without blinking an eye because we told them to march forward." I stepped back, preparing to leave because I couldn't stand there any longer knowing the empty, blood-drenched thing that was supposed to be a dragon stood right below us. "Fix it," I told the scientist again. "I don't care how. I don't want more incidents like the one I saw today. Is that understood, Doctor?"

Dr. Olson looked sullen, but nodded. Ms. Sutton gave a tight nod, as well. I whirled and stalked out of the training arena before I could say anything else.

Back in my office, I sank down behind my desk, put my elbows on the wood and ran my hands over my scalp. Well, that was…disturbing. I knew the vessels' programming and behavior modifications had been extensive, but that creature in the training room today wasn't a dragon. It wasn't even a dog, as Mace had so inelegantly commented not long ago. At least dogs had thoughts and feelings of their own. The vessel was a machine. A living, breathing machine.

This can't be what Talon envisioned, I thought, jiggling my computer screen to life, knowing I needed to report today's incident to the organization. *I know these creatures are bred for war. I know they've been created so that we stand a chance against St. George, but how far is too far?* What were we sacrificing to save our race from extinction? If a hundred vessels died so that one "real" dragon would be saved, was it worth it?

Ember wouldn't think so.

I frowned at the thought of my disgraced twin. I'd been keeping myself deliberately busy so that I wouldn't speculate about where she was, what she was doing, but sometimes she crept in all the same. Where was Ember now, I wondered. If Talon found my sister, Mr. Roth had assured me that I would be the first to know. That I hadn't heard anything meant she was probably still causing trouble for the organization with that rogue dragon she'd met in Crescent Beach. Being drawn further into the lies and machinations of Cobalt and his network of criminals. If things continued down this path, I wasn't certain my wayward sibling could be saved. I was even less certain that she would want to be.

Ember made her choice. I shook myself and began composing an email to the organization. Her fate was out of my hands, and I trusted that Talon knew what it was doing. I couldn't worry about my twin now. I had my own problems to deal with.

I finished the email detailing the incident in the training room and hit Send, watching the message vanish from the screen. It was probably a good thing Ember wasn't here now, I reflected, leaning back in the seat. She was too emotional. Too hotheaded. She let feelings get in the way of logic and judgment, and wouldn't have taken that scene in the training room well at all. Whereas I, while I didn't like what had been done to the vessels as a whole, could at least understand Talon's intent. We needed soldiers to bolster our numbers, to fight in the war with St. George. It was necessary for our survival as a race.

Maybe that was why Talon had chosen me for this project.

They knew I would do anything to ensure our survival. Including tasks that would horrify my sibling.

My computer chimed, indicating a new message had come through. It was from Talon headquarters, re: *The incident* in the training room. Surprised at the fast response, I clicked on the email. Per usual, it wasn't very long and got right to the point.

Mr. Hill,
Thank you for the update regarding Project 223590. We understand your concerns. However, the organization is pleased with the behavior of the vessel in question. Your suggestion to modify the subject's future programming has been denied. Continue development as normal. If necessary, modify techniques to better fit the subject's behavior. We appreciate your concern, and we will be happy to send help if you feel it is required.
Irvin Hawkins, Chief of Project Management

My stomach turned. *Continue development as normal.* Talon didn't want the vessels to change. Perhaps they didn't understand the dragon's complete roboticness...but maybe they did. Maybe that *was* what they'd been going for all along. Dragons that wouldn't question orders, that would blindly do whatever they were told, even at the expense of their own lives.

A chill went through me and I shook it off. I didn't like it, but it wasn't my decision, not anymore. The organization had spoken. I was certainly *not* going inform them that I needed help on this project; such an admittance would weaken their trust and label me as incompetent. So be it. If Talon wanted mindless soldiers, I would give them mindless soldiers.

Even if I had to sell my soul to do it.

GARRET

"Garret."

Tristan's voice was stony, his eyes hard as we stared at each other over the barrel of the M4. One hand rested on his rifle, the other crept toward the sidearm at his thigh. I raised my weapon, narrowing my eyes.

"Don't."

The hand froze. Tristan glared at me, icy contempt written across his face, but he dropped his arm. My insides were a conflicted mess, the past warring with what I knew I had to do, but I kept my arm steady, the gun barrel aimed at center mass. At this close range, Tristan's body armor would not protect him. One shot and it would be over.

"I should've known we would find you here," Tristan said, his voice pitched low. "The commander said these could be the same lizards that broke into the chapterhouse that night to free you. Returning the favor, *partner?*" He shook his head, not bothering to hide his disgust. "You really have switched sides, haven't you? Working with the enemy now, Garret? Killing your former brothers to save *them?*"

"The Order didn't give me much choice, did they?" My

voice came out flat, cold. "After everything I did, after all the years I gave them, followed commands, risked my life without a second thought, they would have shot me down for showing mercy to an enemy."

"To a *dragon!*" Tristan's lip curled at the name. "To a soulless lizard, who turned you against everything you once believed in. We don't show mercy to dragons, Garret, you know that! They don't deserve mercy, or understanding, or compassion because they're not capable of it."

"And what if they are?" I asked softly. "What if everything we thought we knew about dragons was a lie? What if they *are* capable of mercy, and compassion, and humanity? Where would the Order be then? How would St. George justify their actions, centuries of slaughter and blood and death, if they knew not all dragons are soulless monsters?"

"Listen to yourself," Tristan returned, his expression now caught between disgust and pity. "You sound like one of their slaves, someone they've manipulated so thoroughly you don't know what's real anymore." He paused, as if weighing his next words, before adding, "And I think your feelings for that girl are making you see things that aren't there. You always believed in what we did, until she came along." His voice hardened. "She's a dragon, Garret. A monster. You're only fooling yourself if you think otherwise."

I ignored that brief stab to the heart, knowing this was useless. Tristan's beliefs would never waver. He was a soldier of St. George; his convictions were ironclad. I knew, because I had thought the same. And there was no time to stand here and argue with my ex-partner. Jade was waiting for my signal, and Ember and Riley were trapped in the building with the soldiers closing in. Maybe it was already too late. Much as I wanted to talk to Tristan, to explain everything I had learned, I had to move on.

Raising the M4, I met Tristan's steely gaze. "Turn around," I ordered, and his eyes went dark.

"Are you going to shoot me now, partner?" he asked softly. "To save the lizards? What's the matter, can't look me in the eye when you pull the trigger?"

I kept my face blank, my voice cold, as I answered. "Now."

Tristan eyed me a moment longer, then spun on his knees and faced the wall. Keeping the gun raised, I walked carefully forward until I stood just a few feet away, the barrel hovering a few inches from the back of his skull.

I wasn't going to shoot him. Despite everything, even knowing that he was my enemy and would take me out if given the command, I couldn't kill him. He would wake up with another throbbing headache, courtesy of a rifle butt to the back of the head, and his treasured sniper rifle would be lost forever, but I wasn't going to stand there and execute my former partner in cold blood. But as I drew back to strike, a flurry of gunfire rang out from the building across from us, followed by excited shouts and barked commands. My attention flickered to the scene outside, just as Tristan whirled on me and lunged.

I jerked up as Tristan slammed into my legs, knocking me off my feet. I hit the floor on my back, and he was on me instantly, grabbing my wrist, keeping the gun pointed away from him. We scrabbled for the weapon, throwing punches when we could, trying to overwhelm the other. I took a couple hard shots to the skull that rocked my head to the side and turned my vision fuzzy, and fought to keep myself protected with one arm.

There was a glint of metal as Tristan suddenly pulled a knife from his vest and sliced it down toward my throat. I threw up my arm, blocking his wrist, feeling the very edge of the blade press against my skin.

Setting his jaw, Tristan leaned his weight into the knife, and my arm started to shake as the blade began slicing into flesh. "I'm sorry, Garret," I heard him mutter, as a thin line of blood ran down my shirt. My other hand was pinned to the floor; I couldn't bring the rifle around to bear. "I wish it didn't have to end like this. I wish we'd never gone to Crescent Beach, and that damn bitch dragon had never gotten her claws into you." Regret flashed across his face, before his expression turned steely. "I never thought I'd see the day when the Perfect Soldier became a slave to the lizards."

"At least I know the truth," I gritted back. "I'm not the one who's being lied to." His brow furrowed, and I spat the truth at him. "The Patriarch works for Talon, Tristan! *All* of St. George is under the rule of the organization, they just don't know it!"

Tristan's eyes widened in shock. The blade at my throat eased the tiniest bit, though it didn't move completely. For a moment, he looked dumbstruck, and I released the grip on my gun. Twisting my arm out of his grip, I shot my hand up to his neck while jerking my head and body to the side, yanking Tristan off balance. The blade scored my neck, slicing another shallow cut across my skin before thunking into the floorboards. Bucking out from under him, I grabbed the rifle, lying forgotten at my side and smashed it into the side of his head. Tristan jerked, falling to his elbows, and I hit him once more, knocking his head to the side. He collapsed to his stomach and didn't get up.

Panting, I rolled to my knees, ignoring the stinging in my neck, and dug my phone out of a pocket. "Jade," I rasped when the dragon picked up. "Go."

"Understood."

I held my breath, waiting. Then, a roar echoed over the buildings, igniting a flurry of shouting among the soldiers stationed outside. Peering out the window, I saw the men across the street climbing into SUVs, while the commander pointed to the other end of the lot. I followed his gaze, just as a long, *long* coiling tail dropped from a rooftop in a flash of green and vanished behind the buildings.

My breath caught at the size. It was at least twice as large as Ember, maybe bigger. How old was Jade, anyway? She definitely wasn't a hatchling, or even a Juvenile like Riley. A dragon that large had to be an Adult, which meant that the Eastern dragon who'd agreed to help me on my mission could be a few hundred years old.

Regardless of her age, she'd certainly accomplished what she'd set out to do. Engines flared, and the two Order vehicles tore off after the Eastern dragon, squealing around a warehouse and out of sight. In seconds, the entrance was clear of cars and only a pair of guards had been left behind.

Silently hoping Jade would be all right, I drew back from the window and slid the Glock into its holster, mentally preparing myself for what came next. The real challenge began now. But I would not falter. I would fight my way through the building, past a horde of my former brothers if necessary, and hope I could reach the fiery red dragon in time. But there was one last thing I had to do.

Turning, I knelt beside Tristan, slung his rifle over my shoulder and relieved him of his sidearm, feeling a sharp pang of guilt for what I had done. Again. After this, we were truly enemies. After this, I didn't think I'd be able to avoid pulling the trigger if we ever crossed paths again. Because he surely wouldn't.

"I'm sorry, Tristan," I muttered and raced out the door without looking back.

Ember, I'm coming. Just hold on.

EMBER

No way. I stared at the human before me, waiting for my startled brain to catch up to reality. This... How was he here? I hadn't seen him in nearly a month, and he suddenly popped in out of nowhere, at the exact moment we needed him most?

"Ember!" The soldier fired twice more and turned to me, metallic-gray eyes piercing through the smoke and darkness, making my heart leap with recognition. If I hadn't been sure this was Garret Xavier Sebastian before, there could be no question now. "We have to move," he snapped, jerking me back to the present. Oh, right. Guns. Bullets. Soldiers. We were kind of surrounded, weren't we? "Where's Riley?"

"Here." The sleek blue dragon appeared out of the smoke, eyes shining gold in the smoke and darkness. Relief shot through me at his arrival, though if we got out of this, I was going to tear into him for that crazy suicide rush. He eyed Garret suspiciously but didn't challenge him as we turned toward the exit. "Never thought I'd be mildly happy to see you, St. George," he growled. "Let's get the hell out of here."

Garret took something from his belt and moved to the door, peering through with narrowed eyes. "When we reach the main room," he said over his shoulder, "go left. There are fewer soldiers on that side. I'll take right and meet you at the exit." He raised his arm, and I tensed to bolt through the door. "On my signal...close your eyes for a second, then go!"

He hurled the grenade into the dark room, where it exploded in a blinding flash of light that flared even through my closed lids. Lunging through the flash, Garret immediately began firing short three-round bursts as he went. Shouts and returning gunfire followed, flaring white in the shadows, and the soldier disappeared into the chaos.

Cobalt and I sprang through the door and quickly banked left, hugging the wall and keeping low as we fled. Tile scraped frantically under my claws as I made a beeline toward the door, ignoring the shots and bullets sparking off the counters and machines around us. A soldier popped out of cover, firing his gun at the other side of the room, and I pounced on him with a snarl, driving him to the ground and slamming his head against the floor until he stopped fighting. Another masked human stepped in front of us, raising his weapon, and Cobalt blasted out a line of flame that engulfed the human and sent him reeling away.

Something hit me in the flank, tearing through scales and muscle and sending a flare of pain up my leg. I staggered, nearly crashing to the floor, and heard Cobalt's enraged snarl behind me. Lunging to my side, he nudged me anxiously, his shoulder brushing mine as he crouched down.

"Come on, Firebrand. Keep going. We're almost there."

Gritting my teeth, I made a last rush for the exit. A soldier stood in front of the door, barring the way out, but gunfire blared, and the human jerked and dropped to the floor a

moment before Garret appeared, his face grim as he slammed
into the door and shoved it open.

"Go!"

We went, scrambling single file up the stairs, our talons
scraping against metal and iron. The soldier followed, covering our escape and firing back down the staircase. The ground
floor was eerily empty, save for a couple motionless soldiers on
the floor near the entrance to the stairwell. I ignored them,
and the blood pooling beneath their bodies, and bounded for
the exit. Lowering my head as I reached the door, I hit the
glass barrier with my horns and it flew open with a crash, spill-
ing us into the open.

Cobalt spun on Garret as he followed us into the empty lot.
"Where to now, St. George?" he snarled.

A deafening honk interrupted him. I looked up to see a semi
barrel through a couple parked vehicles, smashing them aside,
before it came to a skidding halt in front of the building. A
dark-haired woman leaned out the driver's window, gesturing
frantically to Garret.

"Get in! The soldiers are following! Let's go!"

Garret immediately ran for the back of the truck, not stopping to question this strange person who showed up out of
nowhere with a tractor-trailer. I shook off my astonishment
and hurried after him, just as gunshots rang out behind us and
pinged against the side of the truck. The soldier leaped into
the open container and returned fire as Cobalt and I bounded
into the metal box. The long container was musty and hot,
and smelled of rust, but I wasn't going to complain. As soon
as we were inside, the wheels screeched and the truck surged
forward, picking up speed as it moved away from the building.

A trio of soldiers rushed into the lot and raised their guns at the back of the truck a second before Garret reached out and slammed down the door, plunging us into darkness.

★ ★ ★

For a few seconds, nobody moved or said a word. The only sounds were the ragged, gasping breaths of everyone in the container, and the scatter of gunshots fading behind us. Garret still stood at the door, his side braced in the corner and his gun held to his chest, listening to the sounds outside. Cobalt crouched in front of me, sides heaving and fangs bared, glaring at Garret. The semi continued to move, turning corners with the squealing of rubber, making me stumble and clench my jaw, before it finally leveled out and rapidly picked up speed. The sounds of guns and battle faded, and soon the rumble of tires on pavement was all that could be heard.

Garret let out a long breath and lowered his gun. Slumping against the wall, he bowed his head and let the weapon fall to his side. For a moment, he looked exhausted, almost grief stricken. But he quickly raised his head and looked at us. "Is everyone all right?" he asked in a weary voice.

"Still alive, St. George," Cobalt growled, though the words were tight with pain, his movements stiff. "Maybe a little less than when we started, though. Ember was hit in the leg, and there's a chunk missing from my tail that doesn't feel the greatest. Nothing life-threatening, but we'll need a safe place to get patched up." He glanced at me, then turned back, shaking his head. "Also, somewhere along the line, we're going to need clothes, unless you plan to hide two dragons in the back of a semi for a while."

He sounded way too normal, like this was a perfectly ordi-

nary situation: the soldier I'd never thought I'd see again showing up and saving us from St. George. Garret gave a tired nod.
"I can help with at least two of those things," he said, just as
something buzzed in his pocket. Pulling out a phone, he held
it to his ear. "Jade, people have been hurt," he told whoever
was on the other end. "We need to find a safe place now." A
moment of silence, and he nodded once. "Good. Get us there."

Lowering the phone, he winced and slid down until he was
sitting against the wall. I stepped around Cobalt and limped
up to the soldier, trying to keep the weight off my back leg.
He watched me approach until I stood looming over him. Our
gazes met, and he offered a faint smile.

"Hey, you," he murmured, in a voice meant only for me.

There was so much there, so many hidden emotions in that
one short phrase. "Hey," I whispered back. "You're...back."

"I'm back," he repeated. "Surprised to see me?"

I started to answer, but suddenly caught the scent of blood,
soaking his clothes, and snorted in alarm. "Were you hit?"

He nodded once. "Almost impossible to make it through
that without being shot," he answered tiredly. One hand rose
to touch his shoulder, and his brow creased. "I think it's a
graze. Bloody, but not serious. Truthfully, I'm surprised we all
got out. I wasn't expecting to..."

He trailed off. I narrowed my eyes at him. "You weren't expecting to come out of that alive," I finished.

He didn't answer and, at that moment, Cobalt stepped up,
so close that our wings brushed together. I couldn't be sure, but
I thought I felt the echo of a growl in the back of his throat
as he crowded in. Though his voice was perfectly normal as
he gazed down at the soldier.

"What's the plan, St. George?" he asked.

Garret eyed the blue dragon calmly, seemingly unconcerned
with two giant lizards standing a lunge away from him. "Jade
has a place we can go," he answered. "It's a few hours from
here." His gaze flickered to my back leg and darkened with
concern. "How are your injuries? I don't have a first-aid kit on
me. Can you hold up until then?"

"I don't think we have a choice," Cobalt growled, sounding pained. "Not unless there's an emergency room close by
that takes dragons. But don't worry about us—we can take a
lot more punishment than humans, as I'm sure you already
know." He glanced at me then, his gaze softening. "Firebrand?
You going to be okay?"

"Yeah." I wanted to stay, to ask the soldier more questions,
but that was going to be impossible with Cobalt hovering so
close. Besides, my leg was throbbing, and staying on my feet
was feeling more and more like a bad idea. I was sore, confused, overwhelmed and felt I could bite something with very
little provocation. "I'll be fine. I'm going to lie down and growl
at anything that asks me questions."

Turning from them both, I limped to the back of the box
and lowered myself onto the dirty floor with a groan. Craning my neck, I found the hole in my flank left behind by a St.
George bullet. The scales around the puncture were cracked
and broken, and blood oozed slowly down my leg. I was suddenly filled with a primal urge to lick the wound clean, but
figured I'd better wait for disinfectant and painkillers.

Cobalt padded toward me like a cat, curved talons scraping against the floor, his eyes glowing yellow in the dim light.
Puzzled, I watched as he circled around, then abruptly lay

down next to me, curling his lean body around mine. My heart jumped as he pressed close, one wing draped over my back, long tail coiling around us both. Warmth spread through me, soothing and wonderful, and I suddenly felt completely safe.

But my gaze still couldn't help but stray to the soldier, still slumped against the wall with one knee to his chest, watching us with a bleak look of resignation. Part of me resented him being there, watching us; a human who could never fully understand me, not like Cobalt. And part of me longed to Shift, to sit beside him as a human and talk, perhaps ease some of the terrible sorrow in his eyes. To feel the warmth of his skin when we kissed, or that feeling of rightness when his arms slid around me and I pressed close, just listening to his heartbeat.

With an inner growl, I laid my head on my tail and closed my eyes. *I am a dragon*, I reminded myself. Garret left for a reason.

"Dammit," Cobalt muttered. "I left my jacket back at the lab."

RILEY

Well, this sucked donkey balls.

I was grateful to the soldier. I *was*. His timing had been impeccable, and I was trying not to let my baser instincts get in the way of reason. To not give in to the urge to snarl a challenge every time he looked at Ember. Without him, I had no doubt I'd be a holey lump of meat and scales lying on the laboratory floor. A trophy for some St. George bastard to take home and hang above his fireplace. I knew the human had come back for us, that he was the sole reason Ember and I were still alive.

But, at the same time, he *was* back, his very presence making things problematic. And here I thought I'd gotten rid of him for good. Maybe that was shortsighted of me. We had the same enemies; the Order hated him just as much as they hated us now. If he'd known St. George had laid a trap for us—because that *was* a very obvious trap that I'd walked into like a moron, damn Griffin to hell and back—I would expect him to return and help. If for no other reason than to save Ember.

But knowing how he felt about my fiery hatchling, seeing

the way he looked at her, made me want to stalk over and sink my claws into his face.

I bit back a growl. That was instinct talking, my jealous, overprotective male dragon genes coming out, made worse by the fact that I was angry, sickened, confused and sore as hell. Injured, cranky dragons were not known for being reasonable. The base of my tail throbbed from where I'd taken a bullet, and the slug was probably still in there somewhere. Still, better to be shot in the butt than through the heart, and once the slug came out the wound would heal quickly. Though sitting down was going to be obnoxiously painful the next few days.

Dammit. What is Talon up to? I thought back to the laboratory, the glass tubes, the way my skin had crawled when I'd realized they were for living creatures. For dragons. *What are they doing to us? How can they justify experimenting on their own kind?* My stomach turned in rage, and I swallowed the flames wanting to crawl up my throat. *I knew they were corrupt; I never thought they would stoop to this.*

Ember stirred against me, a soft whimper escaping her clenched jaws, though she tried to hide it. My worry and protectiveness spiked, and I lowered my head, laying my chin against her neck.

"Hang in there, Firebrand," I murmured, watching her talons curl, digging into the floor. "I know it sucks, but try not to think about it. You're okay. I'm right here."

She relaxed a bit. "I'm mad at you, you know," she whispered, making me blink in surprise. Her green gaze rose to mine, fierce and indignant, her pupils razor thin with pain and anger. "What was that, back there? Throwing yourself at the soldiers for me? You don't think I would've followed?"

"Ah. I was hoping you might forget that. Not so much, huh?"
I offered a small grin that didn't appease her in the slightest,
and sighed. "I need you to survive, Firebrand," I told her softly.
"If I die, I'm counting on you and Wes to keep going for me.
To take care of my hatchlings and my network, everyone I've
gotten out of Talon. Without some sort of guidance, without
someone fighting for them, the underground will fall apart.
Talon will kill or take them all back, maybe to a laboratory
like the one we saw tonight." She shivered, and I eased closer,
seeing my solemn reflection in those emerald eyes.

"You promised to help me fight," I said. "But I need more
than that, Ember. You can't stop just because I'm gone. Promise me you'll take care of my underground even if I'm not there
anymore. I need to know that my hatchlings will be safe, that
I'm leaving them in good hands."

She blew out a ragged breath. "I can't do what you do, Cobalt," she whispered back. "I don't know the first thing about
your network or how to keep it going, but…I'll try. I'll do my
best to keep everyone safe and away from Talon and the Order,
but *you* have to promise you'll keep fighting, too. Don't you
dare give up and die on me. I think I would kill Wes before
the day was out."

I chuckled. "Fair enough." Though that reminded me, I
needed to call my surly human friend soon, make sure he'd
gotten out okay. I knew Wes; when I gave the order to clear
out, he cleared out. No use in both of us dying, and there
was nothing he could do against an army with guns. Though
he would be insufferable after this; I would have to endure a
few thousand *I told you so*s for the next month at least. Right
now, he was probably having a nervous breakdown. Hopefully

where we were going had a phone, and a place for me to Shift so I could use it.

"Good." Ember sniffed, curled into a ball and laid her head on her tail. "Just remember that."

Smiling, I pressed closer, laying my neck against hers, feeling the rise and fall of her breath. As her tail curled with mine, my gaze went to the soldier, still sitting against the wall. He wasn't looking at us, gazing at the door of the container, but I curled a lip at him, anyway, baring fangs in a silent warning.

Ember is mine, St. George. You can't have her. This time, I'll fight if I have to.

★ ★ ★

The truck finally pulled off the highway, took several measured turns and slowed even more as the tires left pavement and crunched over gravel. We rumbled and bounced along what felt like a winding mountain road for several miles, making Ember growl and dig her claws into my tail, before the truck finally shuddered to a halt.

St. George rose, his posture tense, and we followed his example, Ember letting out a small hiss as she pushed herself upright. Footsteps crunched outside and then the door creaked partway open, letting in a rush of cool night air.

A young Chinese woman peered through the opening, dark eyes solemn as they fell on Ember and me, then sought the soldier by the door. "I've talked to my people here," she told the human as, with a jolt, I realized what she was. "They're expecting us."

"Holy hell," I said, as both of them turned to stare at me. "Where did you find an Eastern dragon, St. George?"

"London," the human replied, a faint smile cracking his

stoic expression. "And you have it backward. She found me."
He nodded to the Asian woman, who regarded me coolly over
the opening. "This is Jade. She's agreed to help us, if we can
aid her in return."

"Oh?" I smirked, staring the Eastern dragon down. "Has
something finally happened, then? Is St. George banging your
doors down now? Because that's the only reason I can think of
for you to come begging for our help. I guess closing your eyes
and pretending the war doesn't exist isn't working anymore."

The soldier blinked at me, surprised, but Jade's mouth
twisted in a bitter smile. "I see our Western cousins' reputa-
tion for rudeness is well-founded," she replied.

"At least we stand and fight," I returned. "Not hide in temples and pretend nothing is wrong, that the war won't ever
touch us."

"It was not our war." Jade slitted her eyes, and I saw the
glimmer of pale green shine through for half a second. "We
wanted nothing to do with your Western ways—the violence,
the killing, the constant scrabble for power. All we desired
was a peaceful existence, a simple life, the way we have lived
for centuries."

"Yeah? And where did that get you?"

"Stop it." The soldier's voice interrupted us, quiet but steely.
I looked at him in surprise. "We are not enemies," he went on.
"We're on the same side, and there's no time for this. Things
are happening that we need to discuss, but first we need everyone healthy again. Standing here arguing about the past
is not going to help."

"Also," a tight, impatient voice at my back chimed in, "I'm
going to start biting things if I don't get this bullet out soon."

The human's expression clouded with worry, but he turned back to the Eastern dragon. "Jade, you said your people are expecting us. Does that mean that they know about…?" He gestured to Ember and me.

"Yes." Jade gave a somber nod. She opened the door farther, revealing a large rectangular building behind her. Wooden pillars lined the veranda, and the roof was tiled in red, giving the structure a distinctly Asian feel. "We are at the Zheng Ji temple," Jade went on. "It's safe for our kind here—there are no visitors or outsiders allowed. The monks who run this temple are aware of our existence and are sworn to secrecy. We can trust them." Her acidic gaze flicked to me again. "So try not to singe or snap at them when they attempt to help you. They're not used to dealing with barbarians."

I would've said something suitably barbaric, but with the shuffle of bare feet on the wooden deck, six humans in orange robes rushed out of the building toward us. All of them stopped to bow deeply to Jade, and one old human spoke to her in Mandarin while the rest peered into the truck with large, curious eyes. I sat down, curling my tail around myself, and resisted the impulse to bare my teeth at them. There was a large difference between knowing dragons existed and actually seeing one, and we were probably the first real dragons these humans had ever laid eyes on, but I still didn't like being stared at like some weird zoo animal.

I was also sore, tired, and feeling unreasonably surly and overprotective, so that probably wasn't helping things. And the thought of a bunch of strange bald men poking and prodding at me set my teeth on edge. I hoped Ember would keep her temper under control. Injured, grumpy dragons did not make the best patients, either.

Finally, the old man stepped forward, rheumy gaze settling on Ember and me, and sank into a deep bow that bent him nearly in half. If he felt any shock or awe about facing two mythological creatures in the back of a semitruck, it didn't show on his face as he rose. "Welcome to the Zheng Ji temple, honored ones," he said in perfect English, and lifted a wrinkled hand. "We have individual rooms set up for all of you. Please, follow us."

"Riley." St. George pushed himself off the wall, stopping me as I went forward. I gave him a wary look, wondering if this was about Ember, but he didn't even look at the red hatchling as she limped past us toward the front of the container. Ember stopped as well, blinking, but the soldier kept his eyes on me. "Where is Wes?" he asked. "Was he with you when the Order attacked?"

I shook my head. "I told him to get the hell out as soon as we knew what was happening. Right now, I assume he's on his way to a random hotel to wait for my call, that's how these things usually work." I bared my teeth in a grimace. "Unfortunately, my burner phone is with the rest of my clothes, back at the lab. I'll need to find a phone and call Wes soon, before he receives a call from the Order, freaks out and disappears."

"What's the number?" The soldier pulled out a phone. "I'll call him for you, explain what's going on and that you're both okay."

You're very helpful all of sudden, I thought, natural suspicion for the former dragonslayer flaring up again. *What's going on here, St. George?* But I did need to contact Wes, and I couldn't do it in my present form. "Yeah," I said, nodding. "That would be helpful. Thanks." I recited the number from memory, watching as he plugged it into the phone. "You might have to call twice," I said when I finished. "If he doesn't recognize the number, he won't pick up on the first try. He's kind of paranoid like that." The soldier nodded absently, and I frowned. "I do have one question, though, St. George."

He paused, his thumb hovering over the screen, and I gave him a scrutinizing look. "Why?" I asked. "Why come back? Why go through all this trouble to find us again?"

Beside me, Ember tensed, as if she, too, was waiting for his answer. The soldier's eyes grew dark. "Because I want all of us together as soon as possible," he said firmly, and something in his voice caused a chill to run down my spine. "Because what I found in London…" He shook his head. "It's bigger than me, than all of us. Possibly bigger than anything we've ever faced. We can't fight each other now. We need everybody and every ally we have to figure out what to do next."

GARRET

"Why?"

Ember's voice was soft, curious. I could sense the flood of questions in the air, ready to burst forth, and racked my brain for something to distract her. It wasn't a good time to reveal what I'd discovered. Everyone was confused and in pain. I hadn't escaped unscathed, either. My shoulder throbbed beneath my vest; it had just been a graze, and I'd stuffed a couple gauze squares under my shirt to stop the bleeding, but I was going to need medical attention, too.

Besides, I didn't know if I could face either dragon right now without my emotions welling to the surface. I could still see Ember, lying on the floor with the blue dragon curled around her, the warning in his eyes perfectly clear. It was my own fault, I knew that. I'd walked away, practically pushed her into his arms. I had no one to blame but myself, and I thought I had been prepared for what that meant.

But seeing them together, remembering when Ember had looked at me like that, I realized I was very much not okay. And a very dark, ugly side of me suddenly wished Riley hadn't made it out.

"I'll explain later," I told Ember, my gaze fixed on the opposite wall. Though I could still see her from the corner of my eye, head slightly cocked, and my insides clenched. "You can trust the monks," I went on. "If Jade says it's safe, I believe her." The red dragon continued to watch me without moving, and I forced myself to speak in that same low, flat voice. "Go, Ember. I'll explain everything soon, but you need to get yourself taken care of. You won't be any use to us injured."

A flash of anger, and she raised her chin, the heat of her gaze searing the side of my face. For a second, I wondered if she would snarl at me or even spit fire. But her tail lashed once and she turned away, hopping stiffly out of the truck. The monks bowed as she hit the ground, then hovered around her, speaking in low, soothing voices as three of them escorted the dragon toward the temple. Even injured, Ember still put weight on her wounded leg as she trailed them across the yard, moving like she was determined not to limp. She did not look back once.

Riley regarded me, his expression unreadable. I knew he wanted to ask questions, too—demand that I tell him what was going on. But all he said was, "Tell Wes we'll need more clothes," and he slid gracefully out of the truck and trotted after Ember, followed by the remaining monks. I watched the procession of two dragons and six monks file up the path, climb the steps to the main building and vanish, one by one, through the door. As soon as Riley's tail slid through the frame, the last monk reached out and shut the door behind him, and the world returned to normal.

Jade walked around the side of the truck, her gaze on the now-closed door and empty veranda. "Your friends are…interesting," she said, making me snort. "I would hate to see your enemies." She looked back at me, black eyes assessing. "You did not mention that one of the 'friends' you risked your life for was desperately hoping he could rip your head off."

"I was a soldier of the Order," I said wearily. "He's the leader of a rogue dragon underground. I'm sure I've killed a few of his dragons in the past." *I'm also stupidly in love with the girl he considers his, and we both know it.*

"Still, you did save their lives. One would assume they would be appreciative, unless there is something going on that I am not aware of?" She gave me a pointed look, raising her eyebrows. I stared back blankly, feigning ignorance, and saw the suspicion in her gaze. I was not good at lying.

"Are you certain we'll be safe here?" I asked to change the subject. "What if the Order followed us?"

A small grin tugged at her mouth. "That would be inexplicitly difficult with all their tires leaking air."

My brows lifted. "How did you manage that, *and* find a tractor-trailer?"

"A *shen-lung* has her ways." She offered a deliberately mysterious smile that made her eyes glimmer green. "In any case," she went on, sobering, "much is at stake, and we have gambled a great deal in coming here. Are you certain your friends will help us when the time comes?"

"I don't know," I answered, suddenly uncertain myself. Her lips thinned, showing her understandable displeasure; she'd come all the way here, put herself at considerable risk to help me, and the help I'd promised her might not pan out. Especially since the blue dragon had seemed to despise the Eastern dragon on sight; I hadn't been expecting that. "Why was

Riley so hostile to you?" I asked, and her lips tightened even further. "I assume the two of you have never met."

She let out a huff, rolling her eyes. "Misconceptions and ancient prejudices," she said, making an exasperated gesture at the building. "The Western dragons accuse us of cowardice and placidity, saying we hide in our temples and mountain retreats to escape the war. They have never understood that it is their own greed, violence and quest for power that brings St. George down upon them." Her voice hardened. "And now, Talon has brought the war to our very doorsteps, forcing us to respond or to be wiped out. They have set the Order on us, for no other reason than we refuse to be like them. How can we not think our Western cousins are anything but corrupt?"

"Jade…" I moved to get down, but at that moment my shoulder sent a sharp jolt of pain up my arm, making me grit my teeth. The Eastern dragon's eyes widened.

"You're injured." She shook her head. "Why are you standing here talking to me? Go tell the monks to take care of that. I did not come all this way, across two oceans, to watch you die of blood loss."

"Point taken." I dropped to the ground, clenching my jaw as my shoulder protested the landing. "What are you going to do?"

She sniffed. "I will need to hide this—oh, what would you Westerners call it?—this *giant-ass truck*, just in case the Order drives up the road and sees it." Her gaze flickered over the semi, then went to the winding, narrow path behind us. "I don't think we were followed, but I will take no chances this time. I will *not* stand by and watch another temple burn to the ground."

I nodded, watching as she headed around the front of the vehicle. "Jade," I said quietly, making her turn back. "Thank you. For what you did today."

She smiled grimly. "Let us hope it was worth it," she said. "Oh, and tell that blue dragon, if he hurts any of my monks, he will see how placid an Eastern dragon can be when I am serenely tearing the heart from his chest."

She turned away, and I started up the path to the building, wondering if the monks had a first-aid kit they could lend me. If they were busy patching up dragons, I could take care of my injuries myself. I'd done it many times before.

Abruptly remembering the phone in my hand, I glanced down at it, the number Riley had given me still displayed across the screen. Wes's number. I hoped he was all right, because we would need him soon. If we were to pull off the huge, crazy, impossible mission lurking in my head, we would need all the help we could get.

I tapped the call button, then put the phone to my ear and waited.

DANTE

I stared at the bank of screens in front of me, each showing a different portion of the warehouse, and waited for the infiltration to begin.

"The vessels have been released," Dr. Olsen said behind me. "They're on their way now."

I gave a short nod, not taking my eyes from the screens. It had been a few weeks since the incident with the vessels, and since then, Mace had stepped up their training, pushing them hard to see what they could do, making them work as a unit. Now, with Talon's unofficial deadline nearly upon us, it was time for a field test. The mission today: reach the command team—myself, Dr. Olsen and Ms. Sutton—in the center of the warehouse without being detected. With all the cameras up top and in the aisles, it was impossible for me not to see them coming, but there were also several "guards" roaming the aisles with paintball guns, on the lookout for intruders. The vessels were under strict orders to deal with threats in a nonlethal manner, and Mace had assured me they understood they were not to permanently harm anyone.

Still, the overall mood was tense. We all knew what they

were capable of. They understood that they weren't to kill anyone only because they had been *ordered* not to. Not because of
any sense of right and wrong. Without that command, without
them being told specifically not to kill, no one would be safe.

Would that programming hold today, in a live simulation?
Guess we'll find out soon enough.

"There they are," Dr. Olsen murmured behind me. "Right
on schedule."

I straightened in my chair, my gaze leaping from screen to
screen until I found them. A group of eight armed, identical
humans creeping through a narrow aisle with guns raised.
They advanced in unison, stealthy and graceful, almost serpentine in their movements. When a guard passed down an
adjacent corridor, the lead vessel held up a fist, and as one the
unit froze. They didn't move, not to change position, lower
their guns, or even blink. They were like rocks until the guard
continued out of sight, and the lead vessel dropped his arm.

I smiled grimly. So far, so good. Like shadows, the unit
continued through the warehouse, weaving down aisles and
blending into the darkness. They were unnaturally efficient,
moving as if they shared one mind, never speaking or making
any noise. When a guard blocked the end of an aisle, facing
away from them, the unit halted, drawing back into the shadows, and one vessel melted from the pack. Sidling up behind
the guard, it snaked one arm around his neck while covering
his mouth with the other. The human jerked, flailed uselessly
for a few seconds, beating at the arm around his neck, before
lapsing into unconsciousness. Without hesitation, the vessel
dragged the body behind a pallet, and the unit continued on
as before.

"This is entirely too easy for them," Dr. Olsen remarked, sounding unabashedly pleased. "Unless something unexpected happens, they'll be here in a few minutes."

"Yes," I agreed, my fingers straying to a bright alarm button near the panels. My heart pounded, but this had to be done. We had to know exactly what the vessels would do in any situation. "So, let's see how they handle the unexpected."

I pressed the button. Instantly, an alarm blared, sirens howling a shrill warning through the warehouse. Spotlights flashed on, circles of light scanning the floors and aisles, and all the guards instantly snapped to alertness.

Leaning forward, I grabbed a microphone and twisted it toward me, my voice broadcasting through the vast room. "Intruders in aisle forty-nine. I repeat, intruders in aisle forty-nine. All stations respond immediately."

The vessels didn't hesitate. My voice had barely died away when the entire unit Shifted, becoming metallic, iron gray dragons in the blink of an eye. Guns clattering to the floor, they scattered in all directions, scaling walls and bounding into the darkness. Within seconds, the entire unit had disappeared.

Surprised, I looked at the screens, trying to follow their movements. All I saw were flashes, a ripple here, the streak of a lean body there. A pair of guards managed to trap one vessel in a corner, shooting it several times with their guns and covering its scales with red paint. The dragon instantly collapsed, flattening itself to the cement, and didn't move.

I jerked in alarm, but Dr. Olsen shook his head with a smile. "Don't worry, Mr. Hill," he told me. "It's not hurt. The vessels were told to play dead if they were shot. It's just following orders."

I relaxed, watching the two guards lower their guns and step back from the "dead" dragon. The vessel didn't move, and stayed so completely motionless, I might have really thought it dead if I didn't know better. Triumphant, the men turned to leave, and a second vessel instantly lunged from its hiding place and pounced on them both.

My stomach dropped as the dragon slammed into the humans from behind, sending them both to the floor. I hoped I was not about to watch the vessel rip them apart with the same detachment it showed its brothers. But after that first hit, the guards didn't move, either, lying motionless on the ground as the dragon hovered over them. Dr. Olsen gave a dark chuckle.

"Our men were also told to play dead and not to move if they were attacked," he said smugly. "As long as they are no longer a threat, the vessels will consider them neutralized and move on. Glad to see that they did not forget themselves and start fighting. It might've been messy, otherwise."

Heart in my throat, I looked back at the screens, catching fleeting glimpses of dragons darting through the shadows. Shouts and the huff of paintball fire sounded over the speakers, followed by the occasional yell of surprise and pain. The vessels didn't make a sound as they swept through with brutal effectiveness. For several minutes, chaos reigned over the speakers, as one by one, the humans fell. The final guard, creeping down an aisle, clearly nervous as he stepped over the bodies of his fallen brethren, barely had time to look up at the ceiling before the dragon hanging upside down by the rafters dropped on him like a monstrous bat. There was one terrified shriek, and then static.

For several heartbeats, we waited. On the screens, nothing

moved. No humans, dragons or even the ripple of a shadow showed up on any of the cameras. Except for the bodies lying on the cement, the warehouse was eerily still.

Then, a thump sounded on the roof overhead, followed by another. I glanced up, as Dr. Olsen and Ms. Sutton did the same, a proud smile curling the scientist's mouth.

"I believe they're here."

Rising from my chair, I walked across the floor, threw the heavy lock and opened the door.

Four dragons stared at me from the other side, pale eyes shining in the darkness. Another two perched on the roof of the security hut like gargoyles, and a third crouched on a stack of crates nearby, wings partially flared for balance. Seven pairs of flat, emotionless eyes fixed solely on me.

"Gentlemen," Ms. Sutton said, sounding triumphant. "I believe we have our answer. What do you think, Mr. Hill?"

I looked around, seeing myself reflected in those flat, alien eyes, and smiled.

"Yes," I said, as the lead dragon watched me with the expression of a statue. "I think they're ready."

EMBER

Annoyingly cheerful birdsong penetrated my comfortable sleep.

Nostrils twitching, I opened my eyes, then squinted at the sunlight coming through an open window. Raising my head, I peered at my surroundings, letting my mind catch up to the present. I was in dragon form, lying in the same small room I'd been shown to last night by men in orange robes. I remembered a flurry of movement, the shuffle of bare feet around me and the babble of voices speaking in a language I didn't know. I recalled one smiling monk kneeling at my head, talking to me throughout the removal of the bullet in my leg. And though I hadn't understand a word he said, his voice had been low and soothing, and the fingers against my brow cool, even through my scales. He was, I reflected, very brave to sit at the head of an injured dragon while his companions dug a bullet out of its leg, with the patient hissing and growling in pain through the whole ordeal.

Carefully, I sat up, bracing myself, but though there was a dull ache at the site of the wound, my leg felt strangely numb, almost tingly. Craning my neck around, I examined my flank.

A gauze square had been taped over the wound, so I couldn't see the injury, but it felt clean and taken care of, certainly better than when I'd had a piece of lead jammed under my scales. Although the bandage gave off a strong herbal smell that made me flinch and pull back.

At least it doesn't hurt much. Yay for painkillers, in whatever form they come. I've really got to stop this whole being-shot thing. I pushed myself upright and stretched, shaking out my neck and wings, and looked around. *Wonder where everyone is?*

Memories of the night before came back to me: gunfire and soldiers, the smell of smoke and fear, being trapped underground with men closing in on all sides. Cobalt's fervent whispers, huddling behind a counter, waiting to die. And then, *his* sudden arrival, and the way my heart stuttered when I realized who it was.

With a sigh, I pushed those thoughts away before the tide of emotion behind the gates could smash through and overwhelm me. Sooner or later, I would have to face him again, and I was both anticipating and dreading that encounter, but I wasn't going to think about it now. Spotting a pile of neatly folded clothes on a cot, I padded over to examine them, finding loose jeans, underwear and a T-shirt. At least someone had been prepared for the eventual Shifting back, though as always, I was reluctant to return to human form after being myself for so long. But on the bright side, I wouldn't have to mince around the temple in a slinky Viper suit or orange robes eight sizes too big.

As I forced myself back to human form, my leg gave a weak throb, making me grit my teeth. But whatever numbing salve had been smeared on the wound did its job. After peeling out of the Viper suit, I changed carefully, sliding the jeans over the bandages, grateful that the denim didn't rub against my skin. After pulling on the shirt, I raked my fingers through my hair, wincing at the snarls. *Ouch. Why in the world is it always so tangled after a Shift? It's not like I'm flying around with my hair blowing in the wind.* Briefly, I wondered if I could borrow a brush from someone, then realized how ridiculous *that* was. *Bald monks, Ember. This place probably hasn't seen a comb since the day it was built.*

When I was convinced I looked at least halfway presentable—harder than it sounded, since the room had no mirrors—I pushed open the door to my room and stepped out into the hall. A monk coming through another doorway instantly stopped and bowed to me, hands pressed under his chin. Slightly uncomfortable—I wasn't used to being bowed to—I offered a weak smile and raised my hand.

"Um. Hi." He nodded pleasantly, but his gaze remained intense, as if waiting for me to ask him something. "I'm looking for my friends," I continued, wondering if he understood a word I was saying. "Do you know where I can find them?"

He silently lifted his arm, pointing behind me. Bemused, I turned around...

...and there was Garret, at the end of the hallway.

My stomach lurched. Garret straightened, as if he hadn't expected to find me there. For a moment, we stared at each other, the silence settling around us like brittle glass. He had changed out of the soldier's uniform; jeans and a white T-shirt had replaced the boots and combat vest, though he still wore a pistol strapped to his waist. I could see a bandage poking out from the sleeve of his left arm, and felt a flicker of guilt.

I hadn't handled last night well. I should've explained what was going on, talked to him more. He had seen Cobalt and me, lying together on the floor of the truck, and would have assumed...

I faltered. He would have assumed Riley and I were together now. Of course he would, there was no reason to think otherwise. And...wasn't that the truth? Hadn't Riley said he wanted to be with me? And I... I wanted him, too. Or at least, my dragon side was very certain.

But if I was so sure, why did the mere presence of the soldier cause my heart to pound wildly? Why had he been on my mind, hovering in my subconscious, since the night he'd walked away? With Cobalt, my dragon felt complete, like he was my other half. As if, through fate or instinct or destiny, we were supposed to be together. But my emotions wouldn't let Garret go.

"Ember." His voice was soft, making my skin flush. Something raw glimmered in his eyes, before he blinked and they turned cold. The mask of the Perfect Soldier.

"Are you all right?" he asked, but it was a polite question. Routine. A soldier wondering whether or not a teammate was battle ready. "How are your injuries?"

I shrugged. "I'll live. I've survived worse." He didn't answer, didn't even smile, and I rubbed my arm self-consciously. "What about you?

"Surface injuries. Just a graze, as I said before." The words were flat. Not harsh or rude, just impassive. It made my insides hurt, hearing him talk like that. Like we were strangers again. "I should go," he went on, before I could ask the million questions floating around my brain. "If you're looking for Riley," he added, pointing behind me, "he and Wes are in the room down the hall. I'll talk to you later this evening."

"Why did you come back?" He stiffened, and I changed tactics before he could shut down completely. "You mentioned something happened. That you found something in England, something big. What's going on?"

"I'll explain everything tonight, when everyone has had a chance to rest. It's something everyone should hear together." He stepped back, eyes shadowed, and gave me a polite nod. "I have things I need to check on," he stated, though he wasn't looking at me anymore. "I'll see you tonight."

"Garret."

He stopped with his back to me, and didn't turn around. Biting my lip, I took a few steps toward him, gazing at the line of his broad shoulders. "Is this how it's going to be with us?" I asked. "Like we never knew each other at all?"

"I don't know." Now his voice sounded flat. He turned, metallic-gray eyes accusing and sorrowful, making my insides curl. "I didn't think I'd see you again. For a while, I wondered if I'd made the right choice, but it looks like I have my answer. It didn't take long for you to make your decision."

"You're the one who left," I reminded him hotly. "You didn't have to go."

"You didn't ask me to stay."

We stared at each other, a thousand emotions simmering below the surface. My thoughts and feelings were a tangled mess, woven around each other until it was impossible to separate them. Garret stood there, wounded and beautiful, the shadow of the boy staring out through the soldier's mask, and guilt settled in my stomach like a lead ball.

The squeak of a door opening interrupted us. My heart sank, even as a rush of heat across my skin told me who had stepped into the corridor. For a second, Riley paused, observing Garret and me in the hall, before striding forward.

"Hey." His voice was perfectly civil; there was no echo of a growl in his tone or evil glint in his eye as he stepped up. But I could feel the tension lining his shoulders, the subtle heat radiating from his skin. As if Cobalt lurked just below the surface and was a breath away from coming out and snarling in Garret's face. He flicked a glance at the soldier, his gaze cool and unruffled and somehow still a threat, before turning to me. "I didn't know you were awake, Firebrand," he said, and one hand rose to brush my cheek, light and caressing. Warmth flooded my skin, as Riley gave me a tentative, crooked smile. "Everything okay?"

No. Everything was not okay. I could feel them both gazing at me. I could feel Riley's protectiveness and Garret's torment pulling at me, tearing me in half. It was too much. I had to get away from them both.

"I need some air," I said, and lurched away from them, backing down the corridor. Both started after me, concerned, and I pointed at them in warning. "Don't!" I said, almost a snarl. "I'm fine. I just…have to think. Alone. Both of you stay right there."

And before they could say anything else, I turned and fled down the hall through the first exit I could find, and out into the sun.

RILEY

I watched Ember leave, nearly tripping over herself to get away from me, and was torn between going after her and risking the hellfire sure to be spat in my direction, or turning around, grabbing the soldier and smashing his head through the wall.

"Okay." I breathed deep, opting for the less violent approach, and shoved Cobalt down. Enough was enough. I could either be a bastard to the human and drive him off for good, or I could accept that something was happening that was bigger than all of us, and having a former soldier of St. George backing us up wasn't a bad idea. "I think we're gonna have to have a talk, St. George."

"It's not necessary." The soldier's voice was flat. "If this is about Ember—"

"No." I narrowed my gaze. "It's not about Ember. I don't have a problem with you being here—let's get that out of the way right now." He blinked in surprise, probably wondering why I wasn't in dragon form already, snarling at him to back off. I twisted my lips in a smirk. "I'm actually a pretty reasonable guy, most of the time."

He raised his brows in a very dubious manner, and I rolled

my eyes. "When I'm not dealing with genocidal maniacs trying to murder all my friends, anyway. Then I get a little bad
tempered."

"Fair enough." St. George seemed to relax a bit. "What do
you want to know, Riley?"

"You knew about that trap with the Order," I continued.
"That's why you came back. But there's more to it, isn't there?
Last I heard, you were in England snooping around St. George
central. And then you suddenly turn up, with an Eastern
dragon, of all things, to save our hides. So I'm guessing you
found something, am I right?"

The soldier didn't answer, and I crossed my arms. "Come
on, St. George," I cajoled. "Spill it. Something is going on,
and I hate being kept in the dark. Wanna fill in the missing
pieces for me?"

The soldier sighed. "I was hoping to tell everyone together,
but that might not be an option now," he said, glancing in the
direction Ember had fled. I suppressed a wince, planning to
talk to her when this was resolved and we had an actual plan.
Human stuff, I reminded myself. *You're trying to be more human
for her. Find her and talk to her, make sure she knows she's yours.
That she doesn't ever need the soldier.*

I would do that, as soon as I knew what the hell was going
on.

"You're right," St. George went on, leaning against the wall.
"The Order *is* after you specifically. Ever since you and Ember
broke me out of the Western Chapterhouse, they've been looking for you. For all of us." His expression darkened. "But Griffin
wasn't sending St. George after you," he went on. "Talon was."

I blinked. "I'm sorry, *what?*" I stared at him, thinking that either he had lost his mind, or I had. "I think I just heard you say that *Talon* was responsible for sending the Order after us. But, that *can't* be what I heard, right, St. George?"

"I met Jade in England," the soldier went on, as if he hadn't just dropped the biggest bombshell ever on my head like it was nothing at all. "Her temple had been destroyed by the Order, right after she got a visit from Talon. We were both following the Patriarch when she found me."

I resisted the urge to curl a lip. The Patriarch. The so-called spiritual leader of St. George. Talon had always kept a close watch on the different Patriarchs over the years, but even with all their power, the leader of St. George was nearly untouchable. It was too costly to go after the Patriarch directly, since he rarely left London and was surrounded by so many of the Order. In my time as a Basilisk I'd learned that, long ago, there had been exactly one attempt on a Patriarch's life, and the resulting backlash from St. George had been immediate and terrible enough for the organization to decide that maybe *that* course of action was a bad idea. As a result, as long as the Patriarch remained in St. George central, the organization was content to leave him alone. After all, if they got rid of one, another would just take his place. And the human life span was so short, even if one Patriarch was giving the organization grief, he wouldn't live long enough to make a real difference.

"I trailed the Patriarch to a secret meeting in a park," St. George continued, unaware of my thoughts. "And I watched him meet with an agent of Talon. The agent knew us—all of us—by name. He knew where you were going to be, and he gave that information to the Patriarch so that St. George could be there when you showed up."

I felt slightly ill. "So, you're telling me…"

"Talon and the Order of St. George are working together," the soldier said. "Not only that, they have been for a while. I heard the agent mention other dragons, other places the Order had taken out. I also learned that the number of strikes against dragons has increased, but no one in Talon seemed affected." He gave me a very serious look. "I think Talon has been sending St. George after your safe houses, Riley. They're using the Order to systematically take out rogues and dragons who refuse to align themselves with Talon. And the rest of St. George has no idea."

"Son of a *bitch*." I raked a hand through my hair, dazed. This was huge, worse than anything I could have imagined. Talon and the Order working together? To eliminate rogues? Yeah, this was bad. Very, very, *very* bad. "Why?" I rasped. "The organization has never gone after rogues full-scale, not like this. Why now? What has changed?"

"I don't know," the soldier replied, his expression grave. "But I am certain of one thing. We can't outrun both Talon and St. George, not if they're working as one. Especially since both factions want us dead. Sooner or later, they're going to find us."

I had to agree with him there. "So, what now?" I said. "What are we going to do? If Talon and the Order are after us, it's only a matter of time before they wipe out my entire network, and any dragon that gets in their way. How can we stop both organizations?"

"By turning them against each other." The soldier's face grew hard. "This alliance cannot be allowed to continue. We're going to have to break it."

EMBER

Neither of the boys was coming after me.

Good. My bare feet crushed grass as I headed away from the building toward a cluster of trees at the edge of the lawn. I couldn't face either of them right now. Too many thoughts and emotions were swirling around my head. I didn't know what I felt, and Riley's appearance had only made it worse. I didn't want to snap something I would regret later.

Dammit, how had this gotten so complicated? How did I not know what—or who—I wanted? You'd think it'd be simple. Human or dragon? The steady, unshakable soldier or the brash, defiant rogue? It shouldn't be this hard, but…when I imagined being with one, my other half shriveled into a ball of misery, longing for the other. I didn't want to lose either of them.

Aargh, what is wrong with me? I am so screwed in the head.

The sound of water trickled across my senses, making me look up. I stood a few feet from the edge of a small pond, where a stone fish spewed a continuous stream of water from the center of a fountain. A half dozen real fish swam lazily below the surface, flashing orange, white and red in the sun. A small pagoda sat to one side, red tiled roof curved elegantly at the corners. I stopped at the edge of the water, watching the fish swarm beneath my feet, and sighed.

"Have you come to clear your thoughts, as well?"

I started. The Eastern dragon—Jade, I thought her name was?—sat in the center of the pagoda, facing the water. Her back was straight, and her ankles rested against her knees in the lotus position, hands cupped in her lap. She was dressed in a loose red robe with a golden sash across her shoulder, and her long black hair shimmered down her back like a spill of ink. She had been so very still, I hadn't even noticed her until she said something. How had I missed a beautiful Asian woman in bright red sitting in the middle of the pagoda?

"Your mind is in turmoil," the Eastern dragon intoned, as if reading my thoughts. "I can feel the chaos from here." She regarded me with piercing black eyes. "You are very young, to be tormented so. It is not healthy."

"Sorry," I told her, taking a step back. "I didn't mean to bother you. I'll leave you alone."

"No." Jade held up a hand, stopping me. "You did not come here by chance," she went on as I paused. "Whether you meant to or not, your mind is seeking solace. Or perhaps answers. There is no shame in admitting weakness, in acknowledging that you need help."

Wow. That's something Talon would never say. Maybe she's right.

She gestured, very subtly, to the mat beside her. And, even though I didn't know this woman, this dragon who was here for reasons of her own, I found myself edging forward and lowering myself to the mat. "Why would you help me?" I asked, settling beside her. "I mean, not to sound rude, but you don't even know me."

"Is that a reason not to offer assistance, especially to one of my own kind?" she asked, tilting her head. "Have you been so influenced by Talon that all help must come with a price?"

"I thought you didn't like Western dragons. Riley said—"

"Riley," Jade interrupted in that same serene voice, "has his own philosophies and prejudices to overcome. He was also, from what I understand, part of Talon far longer than you, and the organization's influence still lingers, regardless of what he believes. But we are not talking about Riley, are we?" She gave me a pointed look. "Or, am I wrong?"

"No. Yes. I don't know." Resting my chin on my knee, I brooded over the water. "I guess you don't see many other dragons out where you live, right?" I murmured. "I mean, not like we did in Talon."

"No," Jade agreed. "But I have traveled the world. I have seen much. And my perceptions have not been corrupted by the organization. I am old. Older than you. Older than Riley. If you have questions concerning our nature, know that I will neither judge nor condemn. I will simply answer, to the best of my ability. What passes between us is for our ears alone. Only the fish and the wind will ever know what two drago-nells spoke about today."

I chewed my bottom lip, watching the fish swirl below me, mouths gaping. Should I tell her? I certainly couldn't talk to the boys about this. At least the Eastern dragon seemed sin-cere in her desire to help.

"It's complicated," I murmured. "I'm not really sure how to start." Jade didn't say anything to that, just continued to wait in accepting silence. I took a deep breath and sighed. Well, what did I have to lose? "Okay," I began. "Have you ever in your travels met another dragon and…you just…um, *knew?*" She gave me a puzzled look, and I swallowed my embarrassment to stammer on. "I mean, you've never seen him before in your life, but you just have this feeling that…well, I can't really explain it. Like, you've always known him, even though you've just met."

"Ah." Jade sat back, nodding sagely, though now her expression was sympathetic. "The *Sallith'tahn.* Interesting that you would experience it so young, but I have heard of cases where it has happened before." She paused a moment, then smiled. "That *would* explain a few things."

"The…what?" I furrowed my brow. "Salla-who? What language is that?"

Jade blinked. "It's Draconic," she said, startling me. "That you do not know the word is deeply troubling, but not unexpected. It is one of the many 'inconvenient' things Talon would rather not exist. So they have attempted to suppress, restrain or erase it from the minds of their dragons altogether."

"But, what is it?"

The Asian dragon frowned. "It is…difficult to explain in human terms," she said. "I don't believe the mortal language has a word that encompasses the *Sallith'tahn* completely. The closest term I can think of would be *life-bond,* or *life-mate,* but that is like calling snow 'frozen water.' It is true, but it is also so much more than that."

My heart seemed to seize up. I stared at the other dragon, as the world around us turned hazy and surreal. "Wait. Life… mate? Then, are you saying Riley and I…"

"When a dragon finds their *Sallith'tahn*, they remain to-gether for life," Jade said simply. "It was not a common oc-currence, even before Talon, but one that was accepted and known to all. There is a reason the dragons of the East rarely venture into this country anymore. I assume the organiza-tion has done its best to strike that term, and all that it im-plies, from your language and memories. This is the control they wield, making it so that dragons are loyal to Talon and nothing else. And in doing so, they have suppressed a part of who you are."

"I think I'm going to faint," I said weakly. Jade cocked her head at me, as if confused, and I gestured wildly back to the building. "So, that's it? If Riley is my…my *Sallith'tahn* or what-ever, we're supposed to be together, end of story? How do these things even happen?"

"How does the goose find its way home year after year? How does the eagle choose its mate?" Jade's voice was infuriatingly calm, the complete opposite of what I was feeling at the mo-ment. "There are no whys or hows when it comes to the nat-ural order of things. It just is."

"Yep, I'm definitely going to faint. Or puke." I took several deep breaths to ward off the light-headedness. What did I do now? If Riley and I were dragon life-mates, how could I fight that? Did I even want to try?

"It is a lot to take in all at once," Jade offered.

Massive understatement of the year, I thought.

"I would suggest meditating on it," she continued. "Clear your mind, let your thoughts settle and the turmoil die down. When you are at peace, you will have a better understanding of what to do. I can help you, if you like."

Meditate? What good would that do? How would it help with something as huge as this? "Here?" I asked, looking up at the Eastern dragon. "Right now?"

"No." She rose gracefully, her robes falling around her. "Not right now. At the moment, I believe we should return to the others. The soldier was waiting for you to awaken so he could gather everyone together. There is something important that must be explained."

"Go back?" I looked up quickly, shaking my head. "No. I can't. I can't face…either of them right now. What am I going to say?"

"You need not say anything." Jade's calm expression didn't change. "Nothing has changed. You simply have a name for what you are feeling. Whatever you choose to do about it, your decision should not be made lightly, or in haste. Put it aside for now. Return to it when you feel you are ready. But we must return to the group." For the first time, a shadow darkened her expression. "There are other issues we must address."

Still in a daze, I rose and followed her back to the building, feeling my stomach twist and writhe with every step I took. *Sallith'tahn.* Life-mate. Well, now I knew why my dragon perked to life every time Riley was around, why Cobalt's presence nearly caused her to erupt out of my skin. She knew we were supposed to be together. She had always known.

But that didn't mean *I* was okay with it. Was I only supposed to be with Riley because of some ancient Draconic instinct? Did that mean I had no choice in the matter? And what about Garret? He was a human, but what I felt toward him wasn't less. Just different.

Except dragons weren't supposed to feel human emotion.

My thoughts continued to spin as we left the gardens and walked up the path to the main building, Jade pausing a moment to speak to a monk in what I assumed was Chinese. He bobbed his bald head, pointed to a corner of the building and pressed his hands together in a bow as we continued on. Inside, Jade walked quietly across the wooden floors, down the hall and opened the last door on the right.

Garret, Riley and Wes looked up from where they were huddled around Wes's computer, squinting as the door swung open. The room was quite small, with only a cot and a tiny writing desk beside it, so Garret and Riley stood side by side as they loomed over Wes, who was hunched over his laptop per usual. Riley nodded as Jade came into the room, but then his gaze fell to me, sending my insides into a sickening swirl. Beside him, Garret also watched me, his expression unreadable.

"There you are." Riley straightened. "Good. Close the door, Firebrand. You might want to sit down for this."

RILEY

"I can't believe the Patriarch would willingly ally himself with Talon," St. George said firmly.

We were all still crowded in Wes's room, myself standing next to the desk and the soldier leaning in the corner with his arms crossed. The Eastern dragon stood at the end of the cot, watching us with that serene, cool expression, her arms hidden in the sleeves of her billowy robe. She rarely glanced my way, but she and Ember had come in together, and I'd seen the look the red hatchling had given me across the room; it was almost terrified. I made a point to find out what had happened between them as soon as we were done here. My gaze went to her again, leaning against the door with her hands behind her back. She seemed a bit dazed, but she might still be processing the information St. George had revealed about the Patriarch and Talon working together. That would shake anyone up.

"Oh? And why is that, St. George?" Wes asked from the desk, bringing my attention back to the important conversation. "Talon offers the Order an easy way to kill dragons *and* get paid for it? Seems like a no-brainer to me."

"The Order isn't like that," the soldier replied. "From the beginning, every member of St. George has been trained to resist corruption and temptation. They don't take bribes, they can't be bought, they don't accept compromise. Talon hasn't been able to infiltrate the Order because its leaders refuse to negotiate anything, and they *never* bargain with dragons. They teach their soldiers to adopt that stance, as well."

"Really?" Wes drawled. "Well, maybe the Patriarch didn't get the memo, because he's so deep in bed with Talon he smells like lizard sweat. And now the organization has its claws in the bloody Order. Fabulous." He shook his head. "Just goes to show you anyone can be bought, if the price tag is high enough."

"No," St. George insisted, his voice hard. "I saw that meeting. I heard what was said. The Patriarch wanted out. He would have never willingly accepted help from dragons. Which means Talon either tricked him, or blackmailed him, or both."

"Yeah," I broke in, making everyone glance at me. "That sounds like them. If they can't buy what they want with money or bribes, they'll get it another way. Threats, blackmail, planting false evidence—whatever they can think of, as long as it gets them what they want. It's how they got so powerful, so fast. They've never been afraid to play dirty."

"So, Talon is blackmailing the leader of St. George to hunt down dragons," Ember repeated, as if making sure she was following along correctly. "That's absolutely terrifying. How do we make them stop?"

St. George sighed. "We don't," he said quietly. "Or, more specifically, we *can't*."

"Talon will never stop what they're doing," I went on. "How long do you think they've tried to gain advantage in this war?

And now they finally have the Order right where they want them, with the Patriarch under their claws." I shook my head. "They'll never give that up. Not for all the money in the world."

"The only way to break this alliance," the soldier continued, his voice reluctant, "is to expose the Patriarch to the rest of St. George. The rest of the Order doesn't know about his involvement with Talon. If they did, it would be seen as a massive betrayal. He would be stripped of his rank, imprisoned and probably executed for high treason. Not even the Patriarch is exempt from the Code of St. George."

"And the alliance would be done for," I finished. "Talon would lose whatever leverage they have on the Patriarch, and all these strikes where they've been able to sic the Order on us would come to an end."

Everyone fell silent, thinking. St. George's expression was dark. He knew we had to break up this partnership, that having Talon in control of the Order was possibly the worst thing that could happen to them, but exposing the Patriarch wasn't sitting well, apparently.

Strangely enough, I could understand that. Even though Talon had been using me for years, it had still been hard to walk away, to start fighting the very organization I'd been a part of for so long. I'd been a lone operative who didn't rely on anyone but myself to get the job done, but the soldier had been part of a team; these were men he'd once fought beside. It must suck, I thought, realizing that your leader, the person who was supposed to be the example of everything you stood for, had been so thoroughly corrupted.

Huh. And when did I start sympathizing with St. George?

Finally, the Asian dragon looked up, her voice still as cool as ever. "Then we know what must be done," she stated quietly. "Now, the question is—how are we going to accomplish it?"

St. George stirred from his corner. "We're going to need proof that the Patriarch is working with Talon," he replied, turning businesslike again. "The Order isn't going to listen to any of us, unless we have hard evidence that shows he's directly involved with the organization. At the meeting, the agent mentioned certain documents that would be damning if they ever came to light. Riley..." His gaze went to me. "You were once a spy for Talon. Do you know where Talon would be keeping that kind of blackmail, and how we could access it?"

I sighed. "Oh, yeah," I said, nodding. "I know where it'll be kept. There's only one place Talon will keep something that important. It'll be in the Vault."

"The vault?" Ember echoed. "What, you mean like a giant bank safe?

"Kinda, Firebrand. Except maybe a thousand times bigger. Remember, Talon has been at this a long time. They have enough dirt, blackmail and dirty laundry to make the NSA green with envy. They were around long before computers and electronic storage became the normal thing, so a lot of their evidence was, and still is, physical. They're kind of old-fashioned that way. All of their important documents are stored in the Vault. If we want proof that the Patriarch is working with Talon, we're going to have to break in and steal it. And trust me when I say a bank robbery would be easier."

"Have you been to this Vault before?" Jade asked quietly. "Do you know what to expect?"

I gave a bitter chuckle. "I was a Basilisk. Collecting dirt and blackmail was sort of my job, when I wasn't blowing up buildings." The Asian dragon's brows pulled together in a slight frown; she probably wasn't familiar with that term and what it entailed. Or, maybe she knew *exactly* what a Basilisk was and what I used to do. "I saw the Vault a couple times," I went on, determined not to care what an Eastern dragon thought of me and my role with the organization. "Continuing Talon's theme of hiding in plain sight, it's underneath this big old library in the middle of Chicago."

"A library?" St. George sounded surprised.

I nodded. "Yeah. Like I said, hidden in plain sight. On the outside, this place is pretty ancient. The librarians still use a card catalog to find the title you're looking for."

"What's a—"

"Never mind, Firebrand. It's not important." I shook my head, grinning. "Believe it or not, there was a time when we didn't have computers or smartphones, and we had to look things up in these primitive things called books."

She raised her head, and I thought she was going to snap something in return, maybe a comment along the lines of my age and maturity level. But then her eyes clouded, and she dropped her gaze, a brief tormented look crossing her face.

My blood boiled. What had the Asian dragon said to her, during that brief period when she had run out? Why was she looking at me like a half guilty, half terrified rabbit?

Anger warred with frustration. I couldn't confront either of them now, and we had other things to worry about. Such as how we were going to get top secret evidence away from an organization that'd had a few hundred years to perfect protecting their hoard.

"Anyway," I continued, banishing those morbid thoughts.

"On the surface, this place is nothing special. Just an old, run-down library that hasn't been updated in years. In reality, there are a half dozen hidden cameras watching every entrance, an elevator that requires a key card and a special code to even use, and a security checkpoint at the bottom. And that's before you even get to the Vault."

St. George turned his attention from Ember back to me. Apparently, he, too, had caught that brief flash of emotion, which meant he had been watching her, as well. Dragon rage stirred, making my lungs hot, and I took a deep breath to cool it off. *Stop it*, I thought irritably. *Stay on target, Cobalt. Talon is controlling the Order of St. George; that's world-ending bad. Your entire damned network could be gone in a few months if you don't put a stop to this now. So focus, dammit.*

"Chicago isn't too far," the soldier mused, eyes narrowed slightly, as if calculating the miles in his head. "About ten hours from here, I believe. We should leave tomorrow, early morning at the latest. That should give us enough time to come up with a plan. Riley…" He glanced at me. "You've been there before. You know what we'll be facing. Can you get us in?"

I smirked. "If I can't, no one else will be able to."

"All right," St. George said, but at that moment, there was a pounding on the door, making Ember jump. When she opened it, the monk on the other side bowed to us quickly before speaking frantically to Jade in Mandarin. The Asian dragon straightened, her voice suddenly hard as she replied. They held a short, clipped conversation, which sounded tense even in another language, before the monk bowed and hurried off, his footsteps thumping rapidly down the hall.

"What's going on?" I asked warily. The Eastern dragon stared out the open door for a moment, her back to us, before taking a deep, steadying breath.

"The abbot just received word from the town below," she replied in a tight voice. "Several black armored vehicles just drove through and turned up the road to the monastery." There was a moment of tense silence as we all realized what that meant, and Jade's voice became a growl. "St. George is coming."

"Goddammit!" I surged upright as everyone else did the same. "*How?* How the hell do they keep finding us? It's really starting to piss me off."

"Jade," the soldier said softly, as if he'd just figured something out. "The truck. Where did you ditch the truck?"

"In the forest," she answered as she turned around. "Near the bottom of the…road." Her face grew pale. "But, I made certain to hide it well. No one would be able to see it unless they were right on top of it."

"Doesn't matter," Wes muttered, rubbing his forehead. "If any of them got the license plate of the truck, they could track it using the GPS. Bloody bastards are getting very tech savvy of late." He gave the Eastern dragon a half angry, half sympathetic look. "Not that you'd have any idea what GPS is, but once they located the semi, finding this place wouldn't be difficult."

"Then…I brought them here." Her voice was full of quiet horror, and she put a hand against the wall to steady herself. "I brought the Order to this monastery. If the monks are slaughtered and the temple is burned, it will be on my head this time."

"We need to get out of here." I started for the exit, mentally calculating how much time we had before the Order arrived. "The town is about an hour down the mountain, right? So that gives us a little time, at least. If we go now—"

"No."

I blinked at the Eastern dragon, stunned. She raised her head, eyes flashing green, and I resisted the urge to take a step back. "You can go, if you want to," she said in a low, intense voice. "But I will not abandon this monastery or its people to St. George. Especially since it is my fault they have come. I will not watch another temple burn." Her eyes shifted completely, a pale icy green, slitted and reptilian. "The time for running is over. Now they will face the fury of a *shen-lung*."

"Shit." I raked a hand through my hair, giving her a desperate look. "You do know it's the Order coming for us, right? Genocidal maniacs who hunt dragons for a living? You stay behind, you're going to get blown to pieces."

"I will not leave this temple defenseless." The Asian dragon fixed me with a level, piercing stare. "These people trust me. They have guarded the secret of our existence for centuries. It is my duty to protect them—they will not defend themselves."

"You can't wait here for St. George," I snarled. "You're going to be killed, along with everyone else in this place. We are outnumbered and outgunned. We have to run."

"No," Ember broke in, sounding determined. "She's right. We can't leave all these people to be slaughtered. And I'm tired of running. Enough is enough." She raised her chin as I turned on her, her jaw set in that stubborn resolve I knew all too well. "It's time to start fighting back."

"Firebrand." I shook my head, forcing my voice to be calm

and reasonable. Every minute we stood here arguing, St. George was drawing closer and closer. I had to convince her, and quickly, that we couldn't stay here and wait for the Order to kill us all. The Eastern dragon's mind was made up, and I didn't think I could dissuade her, but I'd be damned if I let the Order kill my brave, fiery hatchling. "You've seen their numbers," I said, moving closer to her. "You know what we're facing. If we wait for St. George, they'll kill us."

"And what about all the monks here? The people who helped us?"

"They're going to have to run, too," I snapped, and plowed on before she could protest. "Yeah, I know that sounds heartless. And yes, it sucks, Firebrand, but that's war for you. There will be casualties and people caught in the cross fire. I have other responsibilities, and I have to decide what is most important. Right now, that includes my friends, my hatchlings, my underground and you. If we wait for the Order to find us, we're dead, and so is everyone around us. There's no way we'll be able to protect them."

In the corner, St. George sighed.

"Yes, there is," he said, and pushed himself off the wall. His expression was grim as he straightened, his eyes shadowed and dangerous. "We're not going to wait for the Order to come to us," he stated, sealing all our fates. "We're going to take the battle to them."

GARRET

Two black armored vehicles wound their way up the narrow mountain road.

Perched in the branches of a pine tree, my M4 held loosely in both hands, I watched the Order of St. George approach and took a quiet breath, then let it out slowly. Around me, the woods were silent, my companions nowhere to be seen. Wes was the only one of our party to remain behind at the monastery, and he was probably doing the sensible thing and hiding in the deepest, darkest hole he could find. The rest of the monks, when told what was happening, refused to flee or take shelter, and instead filed into the main hall to meditate. They did not fear death, Jade told a frustrated Riley. They would not cower and hide in their own temple. If the Order came for them, they would meet them with dignity and respect, as they did all facets of life.

Which meant, if we failed here, the entire monastery would almost certainly be slaughtered for associating with dragons.

I shivered a little in the warm sun, realizing what I was about to do, what this ambush truly meant. A line had been crossed today. I was no longer killing my former brothers in self-defense. This wasn't me fighting my way through the Order to save the very dragons I'd once hunted. This was a calculated decision; I was going to kill the soldiers of St. George, and I wouldn't stop until the entire strike force was dead or incapacitated.

Abruptly, I remembered Tristan's face, the contempt in his eyes as he'd tried to kill me, and I desperately hoped he wouldn't be with this squad. If he was, I'd have to shoot him. He was far too dangerous to ignore, able to kill any of my companions in a single shot. If I saw Tristan St. Anthony through the scope of my rifle, I'd have no choice but to pull the trigger. If he didn't take me out first.

A heaviness settled over me, and I shook it off, tightening the grip on my weapon. I'd chosen my side. Even if I could return to the Order, I wouldn't. Not with what I knew now.

The trucks drew closer, the sound of the engines rumbling over the trees. I pressed a button on my phone, put it to my ear and murmured, "Now."

For a quiet moment, nothing happened. The forest was deathly still. I hefted the M4 and pointed it down the road, training the muzzle on the front windshield of the first car. Curling my finger around the trigger, I held my breath.

A sudden wind rattled the branches of the pine trees, and lightning flickered in the previously cloudless sky. I spared a quick glance up, and my skin prickled.

A dark wall of clouds was rising over the treetops, sweeping across the blue. Wind blasted my perch, heavy with the scent of rain, and the sun rapidly disappeared, turning everything dark. Below me, the truck's headlights flashed on, as thunder growled menacingly and lightning flickered again, like a strobe light.

With a roar, the skies opened up, and water plunged down in sheets. I was instantly drenched, my clothes plastered to my body, as curtains of rain slammed into the trucks, slowing them to a near crawl. It was suddenly difficult to see anything more than ten feet away, as the storm turned everything into a hazy blur.

There was another blinding flash of lightning, a crack of thunder that shook the trees, as a forty-foot Asian dragon landed on the second vehicle with a roar.

Even though I'd been expecting it, I jumped. And for a moment, I just stared at the dragon that had apparently appeared from a lightning bolt. Jade in her true form was very different from her Western counterparts—long and slender, her body twice the length of Ember or Riley and her tail even longer than that. Her scales were the pale green of her namesake, and a silvery-white mane ran from her horned skull down her coiled neck and back, and past the tip of her tail. She didn't have wings, but moved through the air like water, and almost seemed to hover, weightless, over the ground. Digging her talons into the roof, she screamed and tore at the truck, lashing her tail against the doors. Glass shattered, and the vehicle rocked from side to side under her relentless assault.

Shouts and gunfire echoed over the rain as the doors of the other vehicle opened and soldiers poured out, weapons blazing. Swiftly, I raised my gun and fired, striking several before they knew what was happening. A few of them turned, peering into the storm, trying to determine where the shots were coming from.

With a streak of crimson and leathery wings, Ember swooped in with a howl, blasting a cone of flame down a line of soldiers. She didn't stop, but continued into the trees, vanishing through the branches as shots rang out behind her. At the same time, Cobalt descended from the opposite direction, breathing fire onto another group and winging away out of sight.

Confusion broke out through the ranks. Several soldiers scanned the sky with raised guns, expecting another guerrilla attack from swooping dragons. A few hunkered behind the truck to escape the gunfire coming from the forest. But most of the attention was on the large Eastern dragon still savaging the second vehicle. Shots were fired through the roof, missing or sparking off her chest and belly plates, and Jade snarled in fury. Snaking her head through the shattered glass, she dragged a soldier, shouting and kicking, out the window and hurled him into the forest. The body flew through the air, struck a tree with a sickening crack and dropped motionless to the ground.

The rest of the soldiers converged on her, firing their guns. Raising my own, I put three down in rapid succession, forcing myself to fire on their less protected backs. As they fell, Ember swooped from the trees, pounced on another soldier and blasted two more with flame. I shot the soldiers aiming at her back, just as Cobalt bounded from the trees, leaped onto the hood of the second truck and sent a firestorm roaring through the broken windshield. Screams echoed from within the vehicle, and the stench of charred flesh and armor reached me through the pouring rain.

And then, quite suddenly, there was nothing left to shoot. Rain hammered the trucks, and steam hissed through the air as the storm put out the flickering dragonfires, smothering the flames. Bodies lay everywhere, scattered around the trucks, broken and burned, as the rain slowly washed away the blood and quenched the last of the fire.

Swallowing the bitterness in my throat, I glanced at the trio of dragons surrounding the vehicles. My gaze instantly sought the red dragon standing at the edge of the road. She had taken a few steps back from the soldiers she had killed and was now staring around the battlefield at the bodies surrounding her. It was hard to tell with dragons, but she looked almost sickened. Her wings were pressed tight to her body and her stance was more of a cringe than a crouch. Killing still didn't sit well with her, even if they were soldiers of St. George. Or maybe it was the mass destruction and slaughter we'd caused, and the realization was just now hitting home.

Truthfully, even though I felt sympathy and guilt in equal measures, I was relieved. She was still the same. The Ember I'd known...the girl I'd fallen for, was stubborn, hotheaded and all too willing to fight if push came to shove, but even as a dragon, she had never been a coldhearted killer. It had been her mercy, her refusal to kill a known enemy, that had made me realize the Order was wrong. It was because of her that I was here now, risking my life to protect the creatures I'd once driven toward extinction. Because a dragon had spared the life of a soldier of St. George, and everything had changed.

I climbed down from the tree and made my way toward them, silently asking forgiveness as I passed the bodies in the road, the shells of my former brothers in arms. There were more than a dozen of them sprawled over the pavement, burned, blackened, or shot in the back. The attack had been swift and brutal, and had worked only because we'd taken them completely by surprise. Then, of course, there was the storm, which had helped immensely as it was difficult to track targets in the wind and driving rain, especially if you didn't know where they were coming from. The Order certainly never expected the weather to turn on them out of the blue, but apparently, there was a lot about dragons we still didn't know.

Like Eastern dragons being able to call down a thunderstorm. I shook my head in amazement, remembering the disbelief I'd felt when she'd first told us her plan. *Just like the old legends said. I guess some magic isn't quite as gone as we thought.*

Still atop the truck, Jade regarded me with solemn, pale green eyes as I approached, her mane rippling behind her in the wind. The rain had lessened somewhat, the lightning had ceased and the main fury of the storm had died with the soldiers. "It is done," the Eastern dragon stated, sounding neither happy nor sad about it. "I must return to the temple and inform Abbot Lang that we were victorious. I will meet you there soon."

Lifting her head, the Asian dragon rose off the roof, her serpentine body moving from side to side as she climbed into the air and "swam" away over the trees.

As soon as she was gone, the rain faded to a drizzle and died, the clouds slowly parted and the sun shone through the branches again.

On the hood of the truck, Riley snorted, looking simultaneously pleased and disgusted as he gazed around at the carnage. "Well, that was terrifying," he stated, though he didn't exactly sound broken up about it. "I can't believe we actually pulled it off. And that the Eastern dragon actually summoned a freaking thunderstorm." He craned his neck in the direction Jade had vanished. "St. George is going to crap a brick when they find out."

I moved beside Ember, forcing myself not to reach out and touch her, keeping my hands firmly on my M4. Her scales gleamed metallic red in the light, and spots where the sun hit them directly were almost too bright to look at. But her eyes were dark as she gazed over the bodies, the green shadowed nearly to black.

"Are you all right?" I asked softly, and she let out a gusty sigh.

"No. Not really." Turning, she faced me, her narrow muzzle almost level with my face. "I'm so tired of this, Garret," she said, though the anger in her voice wasn't directed at me. "More death, more killing, more chances that somebody I know could die at any time. I know it's a war, and I know it's either us or them, but...when will it stop?" She glanced back at the bodies, shivered and closed her eyes. "I'm not afraid to fight," she muttered, "but right now, it feels like we're at war with *everyone*."

"We are," I told her, as that emerald gaze shifted to me again. "We might be fighting the Order now, but Talon is the one pulling the strings. Once we sever that connection, things will go back to normal."

"Normal." Ember curled a lip, revealing a flash of razor-sharp fangs. "Normal isn't that hot, either. We'll still be killing each other, battle after battle, running and fighting in an endless circle. It seems so pointless." She sat down, curling her tail around her legs, and sighed. "Even if we survive St. George and Talon, will there ever be an end to it all? Or will I still be doing this exact same thing three hundred years from now?"

My stomach twisted at the last statement. Another reminder that Ember was a completely different species than me, that she saw life in an entirely different way. One that was measured in centuries instead of decades. If nothing happened to her, she would see nations rise and fall, live through several wars and see the world transform around her. Long after I was dead and gone.

"Maybe you'll change it," I told her softly. "You have the time, and a lot can happen in a few hundred years. The way things are going with Talon and the Order, it can't continue like this. Things are going to hit critical mass, and then who knows what the fallout will be after that? Maybe someday, you'll actually see the war come to an end." *One way or another.*

"Maybe." She looked at me, and there was something different in her gaze, now. A glint of realization, of dark promise. "Do you really think it's possible?" she asked. "That we could see the end of this stupid fighting?"

"You might," I told her. "I don't think I will."

She cocked her head, regarding me with curious dragon eyes. "Why not?"

"Because soldiers of St. George don't live very long." I gazed at the bodies of the men surrounding us. "Even if they're on the other side."

She straightened, wings fluttering, as she realized what I meant. "Garret…"

With a metallic screech of claws, Riley leaped off the truck and padded toward us, stepping carefully over bodies and abandoned firearms. His stance wasn't overly hostile as he approached, but it was concerned. Maybe slightly protective, the way his eyes flickered between Ember and me, and the way his nostrils flared, like he was sucking in the breath for a gout of flame.

With a start, I realized how wrong I'd been before. Reading dragon body language, and the nuanced ways they showed emotion or state of mind, was fairly easy. It wasn't that different from discerning human body language, really, once you knew what to look for. Or maybe I was just getting better at it. Back in the Order, we'd studied our foes in battle extensively, learning the subtle shifts that told us when they were going to attack, retreat, fly away and—probably the most important— breathe fire. But no one took it further than that, because dragons weren't supposed to show real emotion. Stay with them for any length of time, however, and the emotions became clear as day. Was I the only member of St. George to notice this? Was the Order so blind that they just didn't see it, or was their ignorance deliberate, because it was easier to accept they were slaughtering monsters and not people?

"We should get out of the open," Riley said as he trotted up. And, I couldn't be certain, but I thought I saw Ember flinch as the blue dragon joined us. "I don't feel comfortable standing here where a random human could see us." He glanced at the sprawl of corpses, and curled a lip. "Any idea how long we have before the Order shows up again, St. George?"

"Not long," I said wearily. "Someone probably radioed headquarters as soon as the attack hit. They'll piece together what happened and be back with even more numbers, maybe as soon as tomorrow. We'll need to leave ASAP, and the monks need to get out of here, too. If we can convince them."

"Yeah, that's what I figured." Riley shook his head with a grimace. "Hopefully our Asian friend can persuade them to run and not sit there getting shot full of holes." With a snort, he nodded to me and stepped away. "Let's go, Firebrand. We should head back, find Wes and the others, and get them ready to move out."

"You two go ahead. I'll clean up here." The two dragons paused, and I gestured at the trucks and the sprawl of bodies in the road. "I need to hide the bodies and the trucks in case a civilian comes by and sees this. If the bodies are discovered, law enforcement will be all over the place."

"We don't have time to bury them, St. George," Riley said impatiently. "We need to move. The Order could be breathing down our necks in a few hours."

"I'm not burying them." I set the M4 aside and moved toward one of the soldiers, lying on his back and staring vacantly at the sky. "I'm putting them in the trucks and driving the trucks to the monastery. They don't have to be hidden well, or for long." My voice sounded strangely flat and methodical as I gazed down at the soldier and saw a familiar face gazing back. Not Tristan, thank God, but someone I knew. Someone I recognized. I ignored the sickness in my gut and bent to grab his wrist. "Once St. George discovers the strike failed, after they search the area for dragons, they'll send a team to make all this disappear. The Order doesn't like attention any more than Talon."

The dragons were silent as I heaved the body over my shoulder, setting my jaw as it flopped limply. I felt them watching as I walked to the back of a truck and laid him gently on his back. His head rolled to the side, staring at me accusingly, a soldier just a couple years older than me. I let out a tired sigh.

"I'm sorry, Edwin," I muttered, and closed his eyes.

"Did you know him?" asked a voice at my back. I looked over my shoulder to see Ember, back in human form and wearing her Viper suit, peering in at me from the edge of the truck. Her irises still glowed green in the shadows as she hopped lightly into the bed. "Did you know any of them?"

"Yes," I answered simply. "A few of them are from other barracks but…" I looked back at the body, remembering a monastery far from here, the stern-eyed monks in brown robes, the faces of my fellow recruits. "His name was Edwin James," I murmured. "I went through basic training with him."

"Oh, Garret." The girl knelt at my side, placing one warm hand on my knee. "That's… I'm so sorry."

"It's all right." I looked away from her, telling myself to be detached, to feel nothing. "It's not him anymore. We…the Order believes that when soldiers die in battle, our souls continue on to our reward. The bodies here aren't the people I used to know. These are just the shells they left behind."

Abruptly, I wondered where the rest of my classmates were. We had been sent to different chapterhouses after graduation, and I'd seen only a couple of them since that time, though never long enough for more than a hello. Peter Matthews, my old tormenter, had been stationed at the St. George Eastern Chapterhouse on the other side of the country, and I hadn't seen or heard him since graduation. I wondered if he was still alive. And if he was, I wondered what he would say to me, if our paths ever crossed again.

A scraping sound interrupted us. Ember and I turned to

see Riley dragging one of the soldiers across the road by the ankle, before tossing him to the foot of the truck. He flopped limply, arms and legs splayed ungracefully on the pavement. The blue dragon curled his lip and turned to stalk after another. I winced, and Ember leaped down with a scowl.

"What are you doing, Cobalt?"

"What does it look like I'm doing?" the blue dragon shot back. Hooking a body by the armor, he clawed it out of the bushes onto the road. "Figured I'd help out, or we'll be here forever. If you're not too squeamish, grab a leg or something, would you? These bastards are deadweight."

EMBER

It took us a half hour to drag the bodies out of the road and load them into the trucks. Garret wouldn't let Riley just toss them inside to land where they would. He carefully laid them out side by side, folding arms and laying their hands over their chests when he could. There were over a dozen of them, and the stench of blood, smoke, and charred flesh and armor burned my nose as I pulled the bodies over to the truck. My stomach churned, but I made myself continue. I had done this. I was responsible for the deaths of these humans. The least I could do was not leave them in the sun to rot.

"Hey." Cobalt brushed alongside me, peering down with worried golden eyes. "You okay, Firebrand?" he asked, nudging my shoulder in concern. "You're looking a little green."

I flinched, even as part of me wanted to lean into him. To curl against him and bury my face in his side and forget the rest of the world. *He's your* Sallith'tahn, something inside me whispered. *You're supposed to be together.*

"I'm okay," I said, and stepped away from him. "Just...lots of dead humans. Trying not to think about it."

"You're the one who wanted us to fight, Firebrand."

"I know!" I scowled at him a moment, then slumped. "I know."

"If we didn't kill them, they would have slaughtered us. And everyone at that temple. Just for associating with dragons."

"Yeah," I agreed. "But..." I glanced at the truck, where Garret was laying out the last of the bodies. "They were his friends once. He was one of them. And now, he's fighting on our side." A thought entered my head, one that had been plaguing me for a while now, but I hesitated in voicing out loud. "Could they...could more of them...be like him?"

Cobalt gave a very dubious snort, so emphatic that smoke curled out of his nose. "Don't go down that road, Ember," he warned, making me scowl at him. "That way lies madness, and you'll very quickly get yourself killed. The soldier is a special, and very rare, exception. I'm still trying to figure out how you actually pulled that off, because getting any of the Order to change their mind is like convincing the Elder Wyrm that money is bad. It just can't be done."

"Maybe we should try."

He growled. "A little late, I'm afraid. After today, do you think any of St. George will want to talk to dragons?" My heart sank, and Cobalt tossed his head, gesturing at the scene before us with his horns. "Look around you, Firebrand. This was a massacre. Granted, *we're* usually the ones on the other end, but the Order won't think of it like that. You saw how they reacted when we dared sneak into their compound to rescue one soldier, and we didn't kill anyone on our way out. What do you think they're going to do after this? How do you think they're going to react?"

I swallowed hard. "There's no right answer, is there?"

"There never is in war."

Garret hopped from the truck and made his way over, his face still dark and shadowed. "That's the last of them," he announced. "The keys are still in the ignition. I'll drive one truck back. Can either of you...?"

Cobalt grimaced. "Well, I'd do it, but I'd probably stick to the leather, if you know what I mean."

I rolled my eyes at him. "I'll drive," I told Garret, who nodded without smiling, his expression still far away. "I can make it back to the monastery, at least. But, the soldiers...are you sure you're okay with us leaving them like that?"

He nodded. "There's no time for anything else," he said. "The Order will take care of them when they get here. But we need to not be here when they arrive."

"That gets my vote," Cobalt said, and began trotting toward the vehicles. "I'll ride in the back, Firebrand," he called over his shoulder. "You probably don't want me in the front, in either form."

I headed to the second truck and opened the driver's door, taking a few seconds to brush glass off the seat before I sat down. For a moment, I wondered if the truck would even start. All the windows had been shattered, the seats blackened and charred from where Cobalt had blasted them with fire, and the hood was crumpled from having a dragon leaping atop it. The roof was completely shredded, claw marks and bullet holes raked through like it was made of aluminum foil instead of metal. There'd be no hiding what had happened here. Anyone with even the smallest knowledge of dragons would take one look at this truck and know it had been attacked by something huge that could breathe fire.

Or multiple somethings that could breathe fire.

Thankfully, despite the damage from talons and fire and sheer scaly weight, the truck started easily. I followed Garret carefully up the mountain road, trying not to see into the back of the vehicle in front of me. At the line of soldiers we had killed.

The monks had gathered outside when we pulled up with the trucks, along with Jade and a very stressed-out-looking Wes. The Eastern dragon had Shifted back to human form, though she wore jeans, a jacket and boots instead of robes, signaling her intent to leave. She strode forward as the trucks pulled to a stop, looking grim and determined as Garret dropped from the front seat to meet her.

"I've convinced the abbot they need to leave this place," she told the soldier, who nodded. "St. George will be coming soon—better that a building suffer the Order's wrath than the people who live there. They have an old van, and almost nothing to take with them, so they're very nearly ready to go." She paused, looking back at the cluster of orange robes, then turned back with a frown. "I am going with them."

Garret didn't look surprised. "Do you plan to come back?"

"Yes." Jade nodded firmly. "When I've found them a new place to stay, when I'm sure they're settled in and safe from any further attacks, I'll contact you. But this is my responsibility. I won't abandon them now, not when it's our fault the Order is coming."

An ancient van, more rust than metal, trundled around the side of the building and lurched to a coughing halt at the edge of the road. The monks began piling into it and, for a moment, I wondered what people passing them on the highway would think, when they glanced over and saw a van full of bald men in orange robes peering back at them. Garret watched them a moment, then turned back to Jade.

"Good luck," he said. "And thanks. We'll meet you again when you're done."

She bowed to him, very slightly. Though I got the impression that small, simple gesture was huge in Eastern dragon terms. Turning, she strode to the now-full van, sagging under the weight of a dozen monks crammed into the seats, opened the passenger door and swung inside. With a cough and a sickly rumble, the vehicle rolled away down the road, the faces of the monks peering back at us through the windows. I lifted a hand, and several of them waved to me, as well. Then the van cruised over a hill, around a bend in the road, and disappeared from sight.

Cobalt leaped gracefully out of the back and trotted up, scales gleaming in the sun, and Wes stalked forward to join us, as well.

"Well, that was bloody exciting," Wes growled, as the four of us stood and stared down the road after the van. Two dragons, a hacker and a soldier of St. George, thrown together once more. "Now, can we please get the hell out of here, or were you blighters planning to stick around and invite the Order to tea?"

PART III

COVENANT

RILEY

"Well, there it is," I said. "Ladies and gentlemen, the Vault."

We'd made it to Chicago without further incident, fleeing the temple and the wrath of St. George that was sure to follow in its wake. For most of the ten-hour drive, we'd gone over the plan about a thousand times, poked holes in it, argued about it, played devil's advocate and finally hammered out something that was only somewhat likely to spectacularly fail when we attempted to pull it off. We'd reached the city, rented a single room at a roach motel and caught a few hours of stressed, exhausted sleep before waking up that evening and going over the plan one more time. And then, here we were, on a street outside the library, getting ready to pull the biggest heist of my existence.

"Everyone ready for this?"

"Do we have a choice?" Wes muttered beside me. "It's either risk certain death here if we're caught, or risk certain death with the Order if we're caught. Must be a Tuesday." Ah, the eternal optimist.

Beside me, Ember scooted forward, peering at the squat, unadorned stone building across the street. Her hand brushed my shoulder as she leaned in, and my blood heated. "Doesn't look like much," she observed, green eyes scanning the sidewalk and corners surrounding it. "But I guess that's what Talon is going for."

"Yeah," I rasped out. "So don't let it fool you. This isn't going to be easy."

"There're only a few minutes until the next shift change," St. George remarked from the back. "We need to move fast."

"Right," I muttered, and shoved the earbuds in my ears, then adjusted the mic on the wire. "Can everyone hear me?" They all nodded or muttered affirmation. "Good. Stick to the plan, and remember, everyone stays in touch at all times. If this all goes horribly wrong—"

"We're probably dead," Wes remarked.

I rolled my eyes. "If things go wrong, get out and meet back at the hotel. If Talon realizes what we're trying to do, they'll send everything they can to stop us." I took a quiet breath, narrowing my eyes at the building. "We only get one shot at this," I murmured. "Let's make it count. Wes, St. George. You're up first."

With a sigh, Wes slung his laptop bag over his shoulder, opened the car door and slipped out, heading for the library across the street. After a moment, the soldier stuck a baseball cap on his head and slid the side door open. Pausing in the frame, he glanced back at Ember and me and gave a small nod.

"Good luck," he said, and he was actually talking to us both. "Be careful in there."

"You, too," Ember replied. "See you on the other side, Garret."

This time, the brief smile was only for her. Stepping out,

he slid the door shut behind him, hunched his shoulders and began walking toward the library with his head down and his hands in his pockets. He followed Wes up the steps and vanished through the door.

"All right," I muttered, leaning back and crossing my arms. "Now we just gotta wait for Wes to hack into the security system. Shouldn't take too long. I hope. So..." I pointed the mic away from me and lowered my voice to a murmur. "Now that we're alone, away from Wes and the soldier, and we have a few minutes to kill...you wanna tell me what's going on, Firebrand?"

I felt her freeze, hesitate and then stammer, "What—what do you mean?"

"Don't give me that." I half turned in the seat to face her. "You've been avoiding me ever since we left the monastery. Whenever I try to talk to you, it's like I have the plague. Don't think I haven't noticed you're never in the same room with me alone." I made a vague gesture at the ceiling. "I mean, hell, Firebrand, you even started a conversation with *Wes*, about *coding*, to avoid having to talk to me." She dropped her gaze, and I frowned. "What did that Asian dragon say to you the day of the attack?" I asked, making her flinch. "Because I'm racking my brain to come up with a reason here. What did she say to make you freak out on me?"

"Riley..." Ember looked out the window, her brow furrowed. "I can't...tell you right now," she murmured. "Besides, don't we have more important things to focus on? I mean, it's not something I can casually throw out there just before we pull off a heist."

"All right, fair enough." She did have a point. "But just remember…" Reaching out, I touched her cheek, making her start and look up at me. "I won't forget. When we're done here, you're going to tell me, Ember. I don't like this keeping-secrets thing. We're supposed to be partners. I need to know I can trust my team completely. Hiding things from each other can easily get one or all of us killed."

For some reason, that made her cheeks turn the color of a tomato. "Yeah," she whispered, pulling back. "I know. I'll tell you soon, Riley, I promise. It's something you need to hear, just…not right now. When we're done, I'll explain everything."

"Riley," Wes's voice buzzed in my ear, quiet and tense. "I'm in."

"Copy that," I said, turning the mic toward me once more. "We're on our way." Glancing at Ember, who looked relieved at the interruption, I smiled grimly. "Ready, Firebrand?"

She nodded and pulled up the hood on her jacket, hiding her flaming hair. Grabbing my backpack, I opened the door, slung the pack to one shoulder and headed across the street with Ember beside me.

"Approaching the front doors now," I muttered into the mic. "We'll pass the entrance and the front camera in about twenty seconds, Wes."

"Got it," Wes replied tersely. "Starting the feedback loop… now. All right, you should be good."

I held my breath as we swept through the front doors, deliberately not looking at the camera I knew was hidden right above us, watching the entrance. Nothing happened, except for an oblivious teenager nearly running into me because his face was glued to his phone. I smoothly stepped around him and headed into the library. It was cool and quiet inside, with bright florescent lights, a high ceiling, and shelves of books lining the walls and marching down the floors.

"We're in," I murmured as Ember and I passed the checkout desk, where a stern, white-haired librarian eyed us from behind her glasses, silently warning us not to cause trouble.

"Wes, can you see the elevator room?"

"I'm hacked into the security system," Wes replied. "I can see the whole bloody library, including...oh, wait. Some bloke just came into the elevator room."

"Now?" I growled. "He's early."

"Yeah, well, you need to get moving, because the blighter just went down the elevator. That means someone will be coming up in a couple minutes."

"Dammit. All right, heading to the back now. Where's St. George?"

"En route," said the soldier quietly through the earbud.

The information desk came into view, a long wooden structure with a pair of computers and one bored-looking human sitting behind it. A little to the side, in plain view of the desk, was the door we needed to get through. A large employees-only sign hung prominently to the side of the frame.

The desk clerk hadn't noticed us yet. Before she could, Ember and I slipped into a nearby aisle, pretending to browse but watching her through the shelves. I eyed the door to the left of the desk, the first barrier between us and the Vault.

"Excuse me."

The soldier's voice buzzed quietly in my ear. I peeked through the shelves to see the human walk up to the desk, a slip of paper in hand. The clerk raised her head and gave him an expectant look.

"Hi," St. George said casually. "I'm trying to find this book for class, but I'm having trouble. It's supposed to be in aisle E-14, but I don't see it there."

"What's the title?" asked the clerk, and when he told her, she clicked her keyboard for a few seconds, staring at the computer. I tapped my foot on the floor and tried not to growl as she studied the screen. "Hmm, it says we have a copy in. Are you sure you were in the right aisle?"

"Yes, ma'am."

She blinked at him, perhaps surprised he'd answered so politely, then smiled. "Well, it might've been shelved incorrectly," she said, and slid off her chair. "Let me see if I can find it for you."

"Thank you, ma'am."

He stepped back and followed her away from the desk, toward the front of the library, where he had deliberately chosen an aisle as far from the information desk as possible. I waited until they had vanished, then stepped away from the shelves.

"Wes. Now."

"Roger that. Starting the playback loop again." A heartbeat of silence, and then, "Live feed is dead. Anyone watching is seeing a recording. You're clear."

"Let's go, Firebrand."

We hurried from the aisle, passed the desk and hit the door without breaking stride, slipping through into the hallway beyond. The door closed behind us with a squeak and a soft click, but we couldn't relax just yet. Our window was closing fast.

Quickly, we moved down the short, plain corridor, passing a break room with a table and a couple vending machines, until we came to the last door at the very end. This one was definitely locked, with a numbered keypad that glowed green as we came up. "Wes," I growled, feeling highly exposed in the short, brightly lit hallway. "Door's locked."

"Working on it," was the terse reply, just as a faint beep sounded from the door handle. "Okay. You're clear."

We entered, and I looked around a small dark room. It was filled with gray totes, wheeled carts and books, some piles stacked halfway to the ceiling. A musty smell lingered in the air.

Across from us, a pair of elevator doors stood against the far wall. They were old and gray, paint peeling off in narrow strips, and they sent a stab of recognition through me. I'd seen them before, many years ago, when I came through this very room. The ancient, faded sign beside the doors read Storage, with an arrow pointing down, which I found as ironic as I had the day I first came through. "Storage" didn't quite cover what was really hidden down there.

I took a deep breath. Here was where things got complicated. We couldn't just press a button and be taken down to the Vault. That would be far too easy, and Talon was way too paranoid for such lax security. The elevator required not only a key card to make it work, but a numeric code to get past the basement and, from what I knew of Talon, it probably changed every couple weeks. I hoped Wes had been watching the last person to use the elevator closely. I also hoped he had hacked the camera that was *inside* the elevator, otherwise this was going to be a very short mission.

"Get out of sight," I whispered to Ember. "Hurry. They're changing shifts now—we don't have a lot of time until the next—"

The elevator dinged.

We had just enough time to dart back and press ourselves into the wall before the elevator doors opened and a man stepped out. Dressed in a sweater-vest and slacks, he yawned, scratched the back of his head and started across the room.

I hit him from behind, striking right below his ear, the "knockout button" in humans. His head jerked, and he collapsed into my arms without a sound. Laying him on his back, I quickly searched his pants and wallet until I found what I was looking for.

"Got it," I said triumphantly, pulling a key card out of a pocket, where it dangled on a stretchy cord clamped to his belt. "We're in business. Wes, St. George, get back here now."

"On our way."

I dragged the unconscious human to the corner and dumped him carefully behind a stack of crates and totes, while Ember watched the doorway and elevator like a hawk. I heard Wes's voice buzz in my ear, though he wasn't speaking to me. A few minutes later, the door opened and Wes slipped quietly into the room, followed by the soldier.

"How'd you guys get past the desk clerk a second time?" Ember wanted to know.

Garret smiled. "I informed her that there were a couple teenagers smoking weed in the bathrooms," he replied. "She didn't seem very happy at the notion, though she did thank me for telling her."

Wes rolled his eyes. "Called him an 'upstanding young man' before she left, which I find hilariously ironic. Considering we're about to break into this place and rob it blind." He eyed the elevator like it was a tiger getting ready to pounce. "Into

the belly of the beast, then?" he said with overstated cheerful-
ness. "Where there's no possible way out if we're discovered?
Fabulous, who wants to go first?"

"We go together," I said, shrugging off the backpack as I
stepped forward. "And from here on, we have to move quickly.
At the bottom of the elevator is a guard station you have to
pass through to get to the Vault, and the guards there are all
Talon loyalists. There'll be no sneaking around, no talking our
way through, nothing like that. Once those doors open, the
guards will know something is wrong. They're not going to
escort us out, inform us that we're trespassing, or call the police. They're going to try to kill us." Reaching into the pack,
I pulled out my gun, shoved it into the waistband of my jeans
and tossed the soldier a pistol. "So you know what you have
to do."

St. George caught the gun and racked the slide with a metallic click. "Lead the way."

"Wes? Cameras?"

"They're all on a playback loop," the human replied. "You
could dance naked in the elevator box and the guards won't
see a thing. Not that I'd recommend it. For all our sakes."

I glanced down at Ember, who looked troubled but determined, and lightly touched her arm. "You ready for this, Firebrand?" I murmured as her gaze flickered to mine. "You know
what you have to do?"

She nodded. "Yeah," she said without hesitation. "I'm ready.
Let's go."

We crowded into the elevator. It wasn't large; St. George and
I pressed into the corners and Ember made herself very small in

the center. Wes stood over the panel, swiped the card through the scanner and pressed a series of numbers once it lit up.

The doors slid shut and the elevator began to move.

I breathed a sigh of relief. We were in. On our way to the Vault, and whatever secrets lurked in the depths of Talon's underground. My heart pounded, and I glanced at Ember, standing quietly in the center of the box. I was putting her in danger, again. The last time we'd ventured underground into a shady facility, we almost didn't make it out. At least this time I knew what to expect, up to a point, but everything beyond that was unpredictable and dangerous as hell.

The elevator continued to descend for several minutes, before it slowed and came to a stop with barely a bump. In the two seconds before the doors opened, I was aware of several things at once. Wes, cringing against the panel, as far away from the door as he could get. St. George, pistol in hand, raising the gun to aim through the opening. And Ember, standing in front of the doors, muscles tensing as her eyes glowed a brilliant emerald green.

Then the doors opened, and a ripple of energy went through the box as Ember roared and lunged through, becoming a bright red dragon as she did and sending a cone of fire roaring down the hallway. Screams rang out, followed immediately by gunfire, and everything dissolved into chaos.

EMBER

The final few seconds before the doors slid open, I was terrified.

This was the part of the plan that I'd been dreading. Not the sneaking into yet another highly secure enemy base. Not having to time everything perfectly to make it through the doors and into the elevator room. Not even the knocking out of a random Talon employee and stealing his key card to get down to the Vault. That was all fine. Everyone, from Garret to Riley to Wes, knew what they were doing. Wes would be able to hack into the security system. Garret would be able to distract the clerk to let Riley and me sneak into the back. Riley would be able to get the key card, and Wes would be able to figure out the code.

But passing the final barrier to get into the Vault—the guard station at the bottom of the elevator—was up to me. Or, at least, I had to cause a big enough distraction for the boys to take out the guards. Armed guards, who would certainly try to kill me as soon as they saw a small red dragon burst through the doorway. More fighting. More killing. I was sick to death of it all, but I knew we had to succeed here, or even more of us could die. The hallway was too narrow for two dragons to be there simultaneously, and being smaller than Cobalt, I could maneuver better in cramped spaces. Plus, Garret and Riley were better shots, and I could easily Shift between human and dragon thanks to the Viper suit. It made sense that I would go in first, but that didn't make it less terrifying. Hopefully, the element of shock would give us enough time to eliminate the threat quickly.

I let out a roar as I lunged through the doorway, blasting the air before me with fire, not even knowing what I was aiming for. I heard a scream, and a body lurched away, flailing wildly as flames engulfed him. Two others at the end of the hall pulled guns as I turned on them, shouting something about intruders and sounding the alarm. Gunfire boomed through the corridor, and something sparked off a chest plate, making me snarl and recoil in pain. At the same time, Garret and Riley stepped out of the elevator, guns raised. Their pistols barked, and the two guards jerked away, collapsing to the tile.

I winced, but then Garret lunged past me, heading toward an open doorway on the side of the corridor. A large window stood beside the frame, looking out on the hall, probably the guard station where they viewed all the security footage. The soldier ducked through the frame, and a second later gunshots rang out from inside, making me wince. Garret emerged, a grim expression on his face as he joined us.

"I don't know if I stopped him from sounding the alarm in time," he said, looking at Riley. "Talon could be on their way. We should move fast."

"Wes!" Riley snapped, glaring back at the elevator. "Get out here. The shooting has stopped so you can stop cringing now."

"Oh, well, pardon me for actually having the sense to get

out of sight when bullets start flying through the bloody air," Wes snarled back, coming out of the elevator tube. "I don't have scales or armor or the testosterone God gave a gorilla, so you're all going to have to calm your tits until it's safe."

Quickly, I Shifted back to human form so I wouldn't be so blatantly noticeable, as a bright red dragon strolling through the room would probably raise some flags. Turning from the three motionless humans on the floor, I looked at the thick metal door at the very end of the hall.

"So, the Vault is through here, right?" I asked, hurrying after Riley as he strode forward. Wes followed reluctantly, and Garret hovered behind us, watching our backs. "All we need to do is go in, find the evidence against the Patriarch and get out again, right?"

Riley smiled grimly. "If only it was that easy, Firebrand," he said, and pushed the door open.

My eyes widened. The Vault wasn't a bank safe or a single room with boxes of documents and filing cabinets lining the walls. It was a massive, sprawling warehouse with a ceiling that soared into darkness and dozens upon dozens of aisles spread out like an enormous maze. Boxes, chests, pallets, even a few safes were crammed together on the shelves, stacked atop each other with no space between them. Ladders were scattered through the corridors, leading up to walkways where even more shelves waited, laden with crates and containers.

"Impressive, isn't it?" Riley asked as I stared around the huge chamber. Between all the aisles and crates and shadows, I couldn't even see the other side. "Welcome to one of Talon's greatest treasure hoards," Riley went on. "Like I said, the organization has been collecting secrets, dirty laundry and blackmail material for a long time."

"Jeez," I muttered, shaking my head as I continued to look around. Talk about a needle in a haystack, in a field of haystacks, on a planet made of haystacks. "How the hell are we going to find anything in this mess?" I wondered. "It'll take us forever."

"And this is why you need me," Wes broke in, with an annoyed glance at Riley. "Though some obnoxious lizards tend to forget that without me, you blighters'd be up shit creek without a paddle. Remember that, next time you're yelling at me to stick my head out in the middle of a bullet storm." Riley rolled his eyes but didn't comment, and Wes continued in a smug voice, "If you didn't have me, finding anything in the Vault would be damn near impossible. Thankfully, Talon has caught on to the wonders of modern technology. There'll be a master list of everything and where it's stored in the main computer. We just have to find it before Talon gets here and all hell breaks loose again."

"The office is this way," Riley said, motioning us forward along the outer wall. "Be careful, though. Those guards aren't the only ones down here. There are at least a couple human flunkies who work in the Vault, organizing the shelves and storing new evidence."

"Who is in charge of this place?" Garret asked. Riley shook his head.

"Don't know. Never met him—he was always 'too busy' to see me in person. The few times I came here, a guard would call for one of his assistants, and they would take care of whatever I brought in. I never made it past the office, really. In here."

He turned down a hallway and ducked into a small room with a desk, a couple filing cabinets and a computer.

"Strange that there are no guards here," Garret mused, as Wes instantly plopped into the computer chair and jiggled the screen to life. "If this is where Talon stores all its blackmail and secret evidence, I would think it would be better protected."

"Not many people know about this place, even in the organization," Riley answered. "The only reason I know about it is because I was a Basilisk. Remember, the Vault isn't supposed to exist—it's masquerading as a normal library. Too many armed guards going in and out can attract unwanted attention, from humans and from St. George. Talon's first priority is secrecy at all costs." He crossed his arms. "Besides, this wasn't exactly a cakewalk to get into. If we didn't have a fire-breathing dragon and a superelite hacker with us, we wouldn't have gotten past the elevator."

"Still." Garret looked out the door, his expression troubled. "This seems too easy. I feel like we're missing something." His eyes narrowed. "Where are the people that are supposed to work here? They must have heard the gunshots."

"I don't know," Riley said impatiently. "But we can either chase humans around a giant-ass warehouse, or we can get what we came here for and get out before Talon arrives. Take your pick. Wes?" He looked at the other human, busily clacking away at the keyboard. "How's it coming?"

"Hold your bloody horses," Wes muttered, not looking up from the screen. "It's not like I have a lot to go on...aha. There we go."

"Did you find anything?" I asked.

A few more taps with the keyboard, and Wes breathed out slowly. "Bloody hell, what *didn't* I find? Someone has been a very, very bad Patriarch."

I felt Garret go perfectly still beside me. Riley didn't notice as he leaned in, peering over Wes's shoulder. "What do we have?"

"Bank statements, photographs, bloody recordings, you name it." Wes shook his head. "Enough dirt to blackmail him for the rest of his life, and possibly his successor's life. According to these dates..." He squinted at the screen. "This has been going on for more than a year."

"Perfect," Riley breathed, though Garret didn't seem to share his enthusiasm. The soldier looked almost ill, brows drawn together and mouth set in a grim line. "Where are they?" Riley continued.

"Aisle 147, section G-36," Wes muttered after a short pause. "That's all it says."

Riley nodded and straightened. "We'll figure it out when we get there," he said, heading toward the door. "Right now, we're looking for aisle 147. Let's find that evidence and get the hell out of here."

"I'll wait here," Wes volunteered, leaning back in the chair as Riley frowned at him. "Someone has to keep an eye on the elevator hallway," he explained. "If Talon comes bursting through those doors, I'll be sure to let you know."

"Uh-huh." Riley raised an eyebrow. "Sure you're not staying behind to look at all the juicy blackmail Talon has on everyone?"

"Of course not, mate." Wes smiled evilly. "Whatever gave you that idea?"

"Fine, anarchist. You have fun with that." The other sighed and turned to us. "Ember, St. George, let's go."

We slipped back into the massive warehouse, following Riley through shadowy aisles and corridors, shelves overflowing with boxes, crates, containers and sometimes weird, random crap. An ancient bicycle sat on one of the shelves, handlebars bent at an odd angle. A suit jacket hung in plastic from a wire hanger, suspicious dark blots staining the collar and sleeves. A huge diamond necklace sat on a mannequin bust, dozens of jewels sparkling in the dim light. I resisted the temptation to take the shiny and kept moving.

Through it all, the warehouse appeared eerily empty. We met no resistance, ran into no one else moving through the aisles and around corners. And maybe I was looking for problems that weren't there, but I started to think that maybe Garret was right. Where *were* the other employees, those assistants that Riley had met before? They had to be here somewhere; we'd knocked out one of them when he was leaving the Vault. For that matter, where was this mysterious boss man, the one in charge of this massive place? Was he out to lunch? Or did he just stay down here forever, living below the library like a real-life Phantom of the Opera?

"Here it is," Riley muttered, turning down one of the long corridors. "Aisle 147. The evidence against the Patriarch should be around here…" He stopped and gazed down the aisle, staring at the boxes and containers looming twenty feet overhead. "Somewhere."

I looked closer at the shelves, seeing letters and numbers stickered along the edges, just like the library. "A-14," I read, and glanced at the boys. "The shelves are numbered, too," I called, making them turn. "That's how we can find the evidence. What are we looking for again, Riley? G...something?"

A low chuckle echoed out of the darkness. "G-36 is the shelf you want," said a voice behind me, as a massive ripple of power washed into the aisle. A figure stepped into view, seeming to come from nowhere: an old man with silver hair, tiny gold glasses and a neatly trimmed beard. He folded his hands and smiled at us like a doting grandfather, as his shadow filled the narrow space and stretched all the way to the ceiling. "The evidence on the Patriarch is all there," the old man said, and though his voice was quiet, it seemed to vibrate through the concrete floor. "How you expect to get it past *me* is the problem."

My dragon recoiled with a hiss of terror, cringing back as two ancient, silvery-blue eyes fixed on me. For a moment, I couldn't move, but Garret had his gun drawn in the space of a blink, bringing his weapon level with the man's face.

The old man smiled.

With frightening speed, he darted in, grabbed the wrist that held the gun and wrenched it behind Garret's back. Stunned, the soldier tried to fight, throwing an elbow back at the old man's skull. It connected solidly with his temple, but his captor simply scowled in annoyance. A thin, wrinkled hand clamped around Garret's throat, wrenching his head back, and the soldier gagged, gasping for air as bony fingers began to close like a vise. I let out a terrified cry and tensed to lunge.

"Don't kill him!"

The old man's gaze flicked to me again, and that massive presence froze me in my tracks. Inside, my dragon was cringing in abject, primal terror, making it hard to even look at him, but the fear that I was going to watch Garret die right in front of me was stronger. "Please," I whispered, shaking. "Let him go. Do whatever you want to me, just let him go."

The old man raised a thin white eyebrow. "My dear, if I wanted to kill you, any of you, I would've done so already. We would not be having this conversation." He glanced at the soldier with a frown. "However, if you keep squirming, human, I will crush your trachea right here. Please be a reasonable hostage so that we may be done with this, and I don't have to dispose of yet another body." Garret slumped, lowering his arm in defeat, and the old man nodded in satisfaction. The knot in my stomach loosened the tiniest bit, but I couldn't relax until those bony fingers were away from Garret's throat.

"Ex-Agent Cobalt," the old said abruptly, making my blood chill. "I would advise that you lower your weapon." From the corner of my eye, I saw that Riley had his gun drawn, but his face was pale. "I'd rather not have to Shift," the old man went on. "It's very cramped, and I would spend days trying to reorganize everything again. My assistants would be quite unhappy. Right now you are in no danger. I only wish to have a conversation, like civilized people. So please, Ember Hill..." He smiled, and I trembled as those ancient eyes flickered back to me. He knew my name. He'd known who we all were, from the start. "Behave yourself in my Vault. You know you are no match for me." He twisted Garret's arm, and the soldier's jaw tightened in pain, though he didn't make a sound. My pulse spiked, and I bit down a gasp. "Don't make me tear out this human's throat and destroy you all."

I shared a desperate glance with Riley. He looked stunned

and grim, but after a moment, lowered his weapon and raised both arms to signal compliance.

"All right," I told the old man as I turned back. "You've made your point. We won't fight you, just let him go."

"A wise decision, hatchling."

He released Garret and shoved him at me. I caught the soldier as he staggered, supporting him as his shoulders heaved with raspy coughs, feeling his heart race. Mine picked up, too, desperate relief flooding me as his hands closed on my arms.

"You okay?" I whispered.

"Yes," he rasped, and straightened slowly. For a moment, our eyes met, and I saw a glimmer of longing in them, making my heart skip. I didn't want to let him go, but Garret drew back, and I dropped my arms as we turned to face our opponent.

The old man calmly regarded the gun in his fingers, then placed it on the shelf beside him. "Now, then." Dusting off his hands, he smiled at us. "Here you all are. I will say, your break in to my Vault was amusing, if ill-advised. And yes, I know about your human hacker friend lurking in my office. Did you really think you could sneak past me?"

"Who are you?" Riley growled, easing closer to Garret and me. His tone was defiant, but I heard the faint tremor below the surface, and knew he was fighting a battle within, too.

The other sighed. "You know who I am, ex-Basilisk Cobalt."

"I know *what* you are," Riley answered. "But I don't believe we've had the pleasure of meeting. And I think I'd remember if I was introduced to a Wyrm."

A *Wyrm.* I shivered. So it was true, then. The Wyrms were the oldest and most powerful entities in Talon, dragons who had lived for over a thousand years. Not counting the Elder

Wyrm itself, there were only three of them living in the world today. To meet a Wyrm…that was like running into a celebrity. An extremely dangerous, powerful celebrity who could swallow you whole with scarcely a thought. Actually, it was more like meeting a fickle, unpredictable demigod and hoping you could sneak away without getting changed into a pile of ashes.

"You don't need to know my name," the Wyrm stated calmly. "I've had several spoken names throughout the centuries, but for now, you may call me by my title—the Archivist. And this—" he gestured around him "—is my lair, my kingdom. Nothing escapes me here. I guard all of Talon's greatest secrets, from the time the organization was founded to now. I know every nook and corner. I have memorized every shelf, and every piece of information sitting upon it. I can recite every document in this place by heart, and tell you the date it was written. And in the long, long years I have been doing this, not so much as a sticky note has been stolen from the Vault." He glanced at Riley, the hint of a smile playing over his thin lips. "Didn't count on me, did you, ex-Agent Cobalt? Frankly, I'm rather disappointed. The Chief Basilisk once said you were his brightest student. You should have known Talon would not leave one of their greatest treasure hoards unguarded."

My heart sank, but I took a deep breath and stepped forward, bringing the ancient dragon's attention to me. "We need that evidence," I said firmly, trying not to cower as those silvery eyes shifted, regarding me without emotion. My dragon shrank back, making me want to do the same, but I took a deep breath and stood firm. "We're not leaving without it, no matter what you say. But you haven't killed us yet, so I'm guessing you need something, too."

The Archivist actually chuckled. "I see you are as defiant and reckless as they say, hatchling," he said, making me frown. "But it appears you do actually have a head on your shoulders, after all. The apple does not fall far from the tree, it seems."

Another stab of shock. Did he know my parents? I wanted to ask, but the Wyrm's next sentence froze the question in my throat.

"I could kill the lot of you," he went on, as both Garret and Riley tensed. "That is what Talon would expect, and none of you could stop me. I could destroy the soldier of St. George, crush the outlaw dragon and his rogue underground, and deliver Ms. Hill safely back to the organization. That would certainly please Talon, and the Elder Wyrm."

He paused, watching our reactions, probably enjoying himself as we held our breaths and waited. If he decided to Shift and kill us, there was zilch we could do to stop him. I wasn't exactly sure how big a legendary Wyrm could get, but I did know our pistol rounds would be as effective as spitballs against a dragon that size. Our only prayer would be to scatter and hope we could lose him in the labyrinth of aisles through the Vault. Maybe he was *so* big, he'd have a hard time navigating the maze, like a human trying to catch a mouse hiding in a woodpile. Though that wasn't a very comforting thought.

"Yes," the Archivist went on, nodding thoughtfully. "That would please the Elder Wyrm indeed." He paused for one more heartbeat, then smiled. "Fortunately for you, I am not that interested in currying favor with our esteemed leader. Especially since it was the Elder Wyrm who trapped me here in the first place."

I blinked. "You're a prisoner?" I asked. That was hard to

accept. Unless I was missing something, I didn't see how an iron door and a handful of guards could stop an ancient Wyrm from walking out if he didn't want to be here. "Why don't you just leave?"

"There are two type of cages, hatchling," the Archivist said, holding up a bony finger. "One is where you have no choice in the matter. The door is locked, and your freedom has been forcibly taken from you. But the other is where you become a willing captive, caging yourself, because the alternative is not acceptable.

"I am the second oldest dragon in Talon," he went on, and I heard an awed exhale of breath from Riley. "Second only to the Elder Wyrm, technically. There is…one…other older than me, but he fled the organization many years ago and never surfaced again. Within the organization, at least, I am the Elder Wyrm's strongest rival. So, I was placed here—" he indicated the walls around us "—to guard Talon's greatest secrets. To possess a wealth of knowledge, yet never be able to use it. If I leave now, I'd declare myself rogue and be cast from the organization, and then the Elder Wyrm would be free to come after me full force." The Archivist gave a rueful, bitter smile. "So you see, it is safer for me here. The Vault is both my kingdom and my prison. It is an honor and a punishment at the same time."

I felt a small flicker of hope, and leaned forward, heart pounding. "Then…does that mean you'll let us take the evidence against the Patriarch?"

"Don't jump to conclusions, hatchling." He sniffed, and his eyes glittered as he speared me with a glare. "Make no mistake, if you had come here for any other reason, we would not be having this conversation. The human would be a pile of ashes on the floor, the rogue would be scattered in little bloody strips through the aisles and *you*, my dear, would be on your way back to the organization."

"But?" I prodded.

He sighed. "But...the Elder Wyrm decided to pursue this disgraceful partnership with St. George, and I find myself vastly annoyed." His lip curled in distaste. "Bad enough that we must hide our true selves from the throngs of human vermin. Now the Elder Wyrm forges an alliance with the very ones who nearly hunted us to extinction? Pah." He made a disgusted gesture. "We are dragons. We do not need the Order's help, for anything. It is shameful that Talon has come to this.

"I cannot strike at the Elder Wyrm directly," the Archivist went on. "Such action would be treasonous to Talon, and I would never do anything to jeopardize the safety of the organization. However..." He eyed us intently, lowering his voice. "If a single small box, one among millions, vanished from the shelves, well..." He smiled without humor. "No one but I would ever know it was missing."

Riley drew in a slow breath. "You'll let us go," he confirmed, sounding like he could hardly believe it. "With the evidence that the Patriarch is working with Talon. You won't try to stop us."

"St. George is a black stain upon our organization," the Archivist responded. "A diseased limb that must be cut off, not strengthened. If we are to rule this world, if dragons are to subjugate the humans as we were always meant to do, we cannot have the Order attached to us in any way."

I shifted uncomfortably, but the Archivist didn't seem to

notice my unease. "Regardless, there are others within Talon who believe as I do," the ancient dragon went on. "Who are not happy with this alliance and believe it is a disgrace to collaborate with the Order, but we dare not speak against the organization or the Elder Wyrm. So be it." His voice took on an almost vindictive tone. "The Elder Wyrm is not the only one who makes deals under the table. If I must turn a blind eye to our transactions with St. George, I can turn a blind eye to other things, as well.

"Now," he continued, again clasping his hands before him. "I believe this conversation is over, and I have a lot of work to do...and several bodies to clean up. My assistants are not going to be pleased." He pointed to a small, plain box stuck between two larger but equally indistinguishable boxes on the bottom shelf. "The information you seek is there. There should be more than enough evidence for you to horrify and outrage the Order of St. George. Oh, and one more thing, Ember Hill."

I'd started to reach for the box, but stopped and glanced back at him when I heard my name. He gave me a chilling, mirthless smile. "Try not to die," he said, to my extreme confusion and shock. "If you manage to survive, it will be vastly amusing to see you take on the Elder Wyrm. If that ever happens, know that the entire dragon world will be watching you."

"What? What are you talking about?"

But he only chuckled and walked away, not looking back. Turning a corner, the ancient Wyrm and the third oldest dragon in existence...disappeared.

GARRET

"Bloody hell," Wes breathed, sifting through various documents. "Talon sure doesn't do things half-assed, do they?"

We had left the library a couple hours ago, fleeing the Vault and the ancient Wyrm dragon without incident. No one tried to stop us as we walked out, though I did see the desk clerk glaring at us, and me in particular, as we left the building. Now back in our hotel room, we were all crowded around the bed, watching as Riley began pulling the contents from the cardboard box and setting them on the mattress one by one.

Bank statements. Store receipts. Printed transcripts of conversations. Pictures of the Patriarch with the man I'd seen in the park, in different locations throughout London. All incriminating. All revealing, beyond any doubt, that the Patriarch was meeting with people outside the Order and getting paid for it.

I clenched my jaw, staring at a picture of him in a crowded restaurant, taking an envelope from the Talon agent across the table. Though I was no longer a soldier of the Order, the anger and feeling of betrayal still stung. He was the Patriarch, the supposedly incorruptible leader of St. George. And yet, here I was, staring at pages upon pages of evidence against him, proof that he was just a man, after all. It wasn't even the fact that he'd taken money from Talon that bothered me. I'd already known the Patriarch was involved. I just wished I knew *why.*

"Garret? You okay?"

I glanced at Ember, who was sitting on the bed with a stack of pictures in hand. Wes and Riley had moved to the desk and were pouring over another sheaf of documents, muttering to each other and shaking their heads. I was the only one not looking at the evidence, the proof that not only had my Order betrayed me but the man I used to respect above all was just as bad as Talon.

With a sigh, I stepped around the bedpost and sat next to Ember, resting my elbows on my knees. Her arm brushed against mine, and my heartbeat quickened. "I've been better," I admitted softly.

"At least we're still all here."

"That is true." I glanced at her and felt an ache bloom in my chest. Her eyes were somber, the shadow of something dark lurking behind them. She was no longer the bright, carefree girl I had met in Crescent Beach; death had changed her, hardened her, as I knew it had to. I could sense the lingering guilt and sorrow for what she had done, and I would guess she suffered from nightmares sometimes, if dragons were able to dream. I had seen that expression before, in soldiers who had been through their first battle and were starting to realize what war was really about.

My throat felt dry, remembering her face when the Wyrm dragon finally let me go. The way she'd looked at me, fearful and relieved… Did she still care? *Could* she care, or was I fooling myself again?

"What about you?" I asked. "I know this hasn't been easy. How are you holding up?"

Ember held my gaze, and for a moment, the world went still. I could see my reflection in her eyes, feel the brush of her arm against mine, making my skin prickle. Then she gave a faint smile and everything unfroze. "There's a massive elder dragon underneath Chicago, Garret," she said in a half teasing, half awed voice. "Kinda makes you wonder what *else* is lurking down there. I might never sleep again."

"It puts the 'gators in the sewers' legend to shame, doesn't it?" Riley said, walking back to the bed. He shot us a glance, and there was the barest hint of a warning in his eyes, before he turned and began sifting through the box again. Ember, I noted, didn't move from her place beside me, but I refused to hope that it could mean anything. I had dared to hope before, and had been crushed like an egg in the jaws of a dragon.

"Well, well," Riley muttered, pulling out an envelope. *Recorded meetings* was scrawled across the front, with a series of dates below. "What do we have here?" With a shake, he turned the envelope upside down, and a thumb drive slid out into his palm.

"Ooh," Wes exclaimed, perking immediately. "I'll take that, thank you."

Plucking the drive from Riley's palm, he hurried to his computer. The rest of us followed, encircling the desk as Wes sat down, opened the laptop and shoved the drive into the side slot.

A black rectangle flickered to life on-screen, accompanied

by the sound of static. Then the sound of footsteps echoed from the computer, and the rustle of fabric as someone sat down.

"Thank you for meeting me like this," said a voice, unfamiliar to me. "I assume you got my message? Was the tip I sent you about...certain targets, correct?"

"Who are you?" replied a second voice, deep and instantly familiar. I straightened quickly, and felt everyone in the room hold their breath, as if they were really there, watching it happen.

"A concerned citizen," replied the first voice. "Who, unfortunately, knows a little too much. A human who wants to save our race from the tyranny of monsters."

"How do you know of us?" the Patriarch asked, his voice suddenly cold. "Do you work for them?" My skin prickled, knowing what would happen if the man said yes. The Order did not bargain with Talon employees, even human ones. Even ones that wanted out. St. George believed that to be in the dragon's employ meant that the human's soul was hopelessly corrupted, and Talon was devious enough to try to send in spies to infiltrate the Order, something they could not afford, for any reason.

"No," the other said quickly, as if he knew this, too. "I've never worked for them. Talon doesn't even know about me. Let's just say I'm a...freelance investigator who had something precious stolen away by monsters. Surely you can understand that. After all, most of your own can relate, am I right?" He paused, as if gauging the other's response, before continuing. "Look, I know you have no reason to trust me. I could be a spy for *them* or whatever. But I'll prove to you I'm not. I happen to know where you can find one of the bastards. And if you can take it out, I'll make a generous donation to your Order."

"I'm sorry," said the Patriarch, "but our Order does not work with outsiders who are simply out for revenge. Nor are we common assassins. I sympathize with your loss, but if you contact me again, I will have to take sterner measures against you."

"It's not assassination if they're not human, Patriarch," the man replied, his voice pitched very low. "And I thought your Order was bound to kill these things wherever and whenever they pop up. Well, I'm telling you where one has popped up." There was a hiss of paper, as if he'd slid an envelope or a folded-up letter across the table. "I can make your war with these things a lot easier," he went on. "Just think about it."

"This conversation is over," said the Patriarch, and he stood. But there was a brief rustle as he picked something up from the tabletop. "Good day to you, sir." We listened to his footsteps walk away, but the recording didn't stop. After about a minute of silence, Wes moved to hit Forward, when the voice came again, low and furtive, as if speaking into a phone.

"This is Walker. The Patriarch has taken the bait. Move on to phase two."

"Bloody hell," Wes remarked as the recording came to an end. "So that's how they did it. Sodding ingenious, that. Offer up the one thing St. George can't ignore, the location of a dragon, and make sure the Patriarch is the only one to know about it."

"Probably one of ours," Riley growled. "And it gives the contact full credibility because St. George doesn't know there's a difference between us and Talon. All dragons are the same to them. So the Order goes to kill a dragon, a rogue is slaughtered and Talon wins all around."

"And the Patriarch is now in league with the organization," I finished softly. There were other recordings on the drive, but I didn't need to listen to them to know how they would play out. Unable to resist, the Patriarch would continue to meet with the mysterious agent, who would continue to provide intelligence about the locations of other dragons. And the Patriarch would send St. George after them, killing off a rogue or another dragon Talon wanted out of the way. Not knowing that with every death, he was entrenching himself further into Talon's machinations. Until one day, the agent would reveal who he really worked for, and the Patriarch would be trapped. St. George would not care that Talon was using the Patriarch to kill more dragons. They wouldn't care that he had been duped by the organization, and he would never have taken the offer had he known. All they would see was the Patriarch's corruption. He was working for Talon, accepting money from the Order's greatest enemy. The highest of betrayals. If this evidence became known to St. George, they would kill him.

And that was exactly what we had to make happen.

"Well," Riley said, and the undertone of satisfied glee in his voice made me wince. "I'd say we have a pretty damning case against the Patriarch, wouldn't you agree, St. George? If the Order *doesn't* flip their shit when they find out, we're all screwed. Only question is, how are we going to get it to them? I doubt they're going to let us stroll up and knock on their front door."

"I might be able to send it to them electronically," Wes offered.

"No." I shook my head. "Within the Order, the Patriarch's word is absolute. And anything that comes in from the outside is subject to immediate suspicion. The Order knows Talon and how they work. We can't take the chance that they might destroy the evidence, or that someone might warn the Patriarch. We have to make sure this is known to *all* of St. George. And that means we're going to need someone on the inside." I paused, knowing Riley wouldn't like this, then added, "We have to meet with the Order, face-to-face, and show them the evidence ourselves. It's the only way to be sure they understand it."

"And how are we supposed to do that, exactly?" Riley demanded. "St. George isn't going to listen to us, much less agree to a meeting where they're not slaughtering everyone there. A group of dragons and the guy on their most-wanted hit list right now? We could be offering them the Ark of the Covenant, and they'd still pump us full of holes the second they see us. Unless you've got a completely insane trick up your sleeve, I don't see how we're going to get any of them to stop murdering us long enough to pay attention."

I sighed. I could think of one person in St. George who might be willing to listen. It would be a gamble; he hated me now, thinking I'd turned on him and the Order to side with the dragons. The fight outside the laboratory certainly hadn't helped. He saw me as the enemy, and I was fairly certain that he would have killed me back there, sliced my throat open, if I'd let him. Even if he'd regretted it later, he was a soldier of St. George, and duty was everything to him. I wasn't entirely certain I wouldn't walk into an ambush and be shot dead before I even laid eyes on my former partner.

But I had few options, and this had to be done. Andrew had said there were those in the Order who were sympathetic to me, but Andrew was oceans away, too far to do anything. And he'd said flat out that he wouldn't touch anything to do with the Patriarch. Tristan was the only one close enough to help. If he decided to help. I only hoped our past friendship, brotherhood and the times we'd saved each other's lives would be enough for him to give me the benefit of the doubt and not shoot me in the head the first chance he got.

"I know someone," I said, feeling a heavy weight settle on me for what I had to do. "It'll be a risk, contacting him, but I don't have a better choice. He's the only one in St. George who might agree to a meeting."

"Might?" Riley echoed, crossing his arms. "What you're really saying is, he might agree to a meeting, but he also might tell everyone in St. George so they can be lying in ambush when we show up."

"Not we," I said. "Me. He'll never agree to it otherwise. I have to meet Tristan alone."

SEBASTIAN

Three years ago.

"Garret Xavier Sebastian, I'd like you to meet your squad mate, Tristan St. Anthony. St. Anthony, say hello to your new partner."

I observed the soldier who stood at the foot of the bed, keeping the practiced blank expression on my face as he looked me up and down. I could see the skepticism in his eyes, in the single raised brow he arched in my direction, and stared coolly back, one hand on the strap of my bag. I was fourteen years old, fresh out of boot and had graduated basic training one week ago. At eighteen, Tristan St. Anthony was lean and tall, with short black hair and cynical blue eyes. He had been on several strikes and was making a name for himself in the ranks, but four months ago, tragedy struck when his last partner was caught in a line of dragonfire and killed. St. Anthony had had to wait until they found him a new partner to get back in the field. I imagined he'd been impatient to return to the war, but from his reaction, I was obviously not what he'd been expecting.

"I expect you to show him the ropes, St. Anthony," Lieutenant Martin said to Tristan, the hint of a smile on his weathered face. "Show him what we stand for. Can you do that?" St. Anthony gave a brisk "Yes, sir!" and Martin clapped me on the shoulder.

"Welcome to the war, soldier," he said and left the barracks, striding away without looking back. I watched him go, then stepped around the cot and swung my pack to the thin mattress.

I could feel St. Anthony's eyes on me as I unzipped the bag and started unpacking, moving everything to the footlocker at the foot of the bed. The container was small, but I didn't have much to begin with.

"So. You're him."

St. Anthony's voice was mocking. I glanced at him, seeing his dark stare as he leaned against the wall and watched me. His lips were now twisted into a faint smirk.

"I've heard of you," the other soldier went on. "The prodigy. Martin's favorite little recruit." I didn't answer, continuing to unpack my things. "So they've decided to let you tag along with the real soldiers, huh? And I'm the lucky guy who gets to babysit."

"Do you have a problem with me?" I asked, looking him in the eye. I was the youngest recruit in recent history to graduate basic training, but only by a year or two. It wasn't that uncommon for soldiers to join the ranks at fifteen. I didn't know what St. Anthony's issue was with me, but it couldn't be just my age.

"Not yet." The other soldier continued to lean against the wall, arms crossed. "I will have one the first time you see a dragon, piss your pants and run in the opposite direction. Or freeze up and get your head bitten off."

"I've been trained for this," I said firmly. "I'm not afraid of dragons."

"That's what they all say, until they see one rip through a man's guts like paper. Or blast a line of soldiers into charcoal. The real war out there?" His eyes narrowed, appraising me. "It's nothing like training. It's bloody and crazy and scary as shit. Underestimate a lizard, and you'll be a pile of ashes on the ground. There won't even be enough left to bury." He pushed himself upright, glaring down at me. "So, I need to know that you will actually back me up when I need it, that you'll do your job when it starts getting hot. My last partner died for this cause. If the Order calls for it, I damn well hope you'll do the same."

"You're not telling me anything new." I straightened, meeting his glare. "I know what's expected. And I know everyone is watching me. They're all waiting to see if I perform as Martin hopes, or if I fail and get myself torn to pieces by a lizard. So why don't you save the lecture until *after* I've screwed up? If I'm still alive." He blinked, and I threw back my own smirk. "Maybe I'll surprise you."

My partner snorted. "We'll see," he replied.

One month later, we did.

I stood with my back against the door frame, on point, watching the soldier across from me prepare to kick in the door. Around us, the woods were eerily silent, a damp mist hanging in the air and creeping along the ground. The cabin was tucked away in a remote section of forest, no roads, no civilization for miles. According to intel, there were two Talon agents living here. A middle-aged, human male servant...and a Sleeper. One of the evil lizards themselves.

My heart beat faster, and I took a furtive breath to calm it. I'd be facing a real dragon soon. The moment I'd trained for my entire life was here. I was ready. I wasn't afraid. Starting today, I would begin to avenge my parents, and anyone else whose life had been ruined by Talon. And I wouldn't stop until every one of the fire-breathing demons was dead, or I was.

The soldier across from me held up three fingers, and I gripped my M4, feeling my muscles tense. Behind me, I felt Tristan do the same. *Three*, he mouthed. *Two...one!*

The door exploded inward, and we lunged inside, sweeping our rifles around the room. My finger tightened on the trigger, ready to shoot anything that moved, dragon or human. We couldn't hesitate to wonder if the person in our sights was a Sleeper or a normal human. If they were found in the target's nest, they were with the enemy. They'd been corrupted, working for Talon, which made them just as guilty as the lizards themselves. If you had to shoot a Talon servant to get to the dragon controlling him, then so be it.

But the room we crashed into was silent and dark, devoid of life. I scanned the walls and the corners with the rest of the squad, ready to fire if anything leaped out at us or bolted for the door. Nothing did, though I saw a half-full beer bottle on the counter and the sink was full of dishes, so the cabin wasn't abandoned. They wouldn't have been able to sneak out, either. One of the Order's snipers, a soldier named Jacobs, was watching the doors and windows a half mile back, so anyone fleeing the cabin would be shot down before they got a dozen feet.

The squad leader, a square-jawed man by the name of Talbot, caught my eye and pointed two fingers down the hall. I nodded, moving up to guard his back. Silently, we checked the rest of the house, sweeping the bedrooms, bathroom and office, on high alert for something to lunge through the doorway at us. All the rooms were dark and still, but my nerves jangled with every door we came to, raising the hairs on the back of my neck. Something was here, and it was close. I didn't know how I knew this; I just did.

"Dammit," Talbot breathed after we had checked all the rooms and had come up empty. "Where are they? They couldn't have flown off, Jacobs would've seen them."

Flown off. I frowned, thinking. The dragon wasn't here, and it couldn't fly away. What if it had used another escape route? What if it had gone *down* instead of up?

"Sir," I ventured, and Talbot glanced at me. "Could there be a basement or a cellar? A place the targets could retreat to without being seen?"

He nodded briskly. "Search the place again," he barked at the rest of us. "Look for stairs or a trapdoor—anything that could lead underground." He gave me an approving nod as I turned away. "Good thinking, Sebastian."

I caught Tristan's gaze as we left the room; he rolled his eyes and headed into the master bedroom.

"What?" I challenged after we'd made certain the room was still empty.

"Nothing," my partner replied. "It's just...this whole storming the house and breaking down doors thing. It's getting kinda old." He paused at the entrance to the closet, one hand on the knob, and gestured me forward. I crept up and pointed my gun at the door. At my nod, Tristan flung the door back, and I tensed, ready to fire if anything came leaping out at us. But the closet, save for a few tattered jackets and shirts, was empty.

Tristan sighed. "See, this isn't my thing," he muttered as we scanned the floor and walls of the closet, searching for latches or hidden doors. "I mean, I'm a decent shot up close, but I don't really like things jumping out of closets and melting my face off."

"You're scared of the lizards?" I asked scornfully.

He sneered. "Damn straight I am. And any soldier who's seen real action will tell you the same, or they're lying through their teeth. So don't get all high-and-mighty on me, rookie. Not when you've yet to fire a single bullet at a live target. Talk to me when you've actually killed something." He glared at me and moved to the bed to lift the covers with the rifle barrel, while I knelt and peered beneath the frame. No dragons lurking under the mattress, and no signs of a trapdoor, either. I straightened and shook my head.

"Besides," Tristan went on, letting the covers drop. "I didn't say I wanted to stop fighting. I hate the lizards as much as anyone, and any day I can put a bullet between their eyes is a good one in my book. I just feel my talents are being wasted on the front line. I'm a much better shot when I have the chance to breathe and actually aim at what I'm trying to hit."

"Apply for sniper training, then," I muttered. "Seems like an easy solution to me, since you don't like being down here with the rest of the grunts."

"Actually," Tristan said smugly, "I already have."

Frowning, I looked back at him. He smirked. "I start at the end of the month," he announced. "But don't worry, rookie—

as long as neither of us gets our head bitten off, we'll still be partners. You can go charging in, guns blazing, with the rest of the grunts, and I'll be watching your back. From about a thousand meters."

"Yeah?" I stepped away from the bed, not knowing how I felt about this announcement. "Well, don't let me stop you," I said, walking across the rug, back toward the bedroom door. "If you want to hide in the back and take potshots, that's your—"

I stopped. Part of the floor beneath my boots had shifted slightly, a faint creak rising from beneath the rug. I stomped down, and heard a hollow, rattling thump, like the boards underneath weren't entirely solid.

We pulled back the rug. Beneath it lay a square section of floor that had obviously been cut out and replaced. Grabbing the rope handle, I yanked it back, revealing a trapdoor with a steel ladder going down into the dark.

"Bingo," Tristan breathed.

A minute later, the whole squad was assembled at the bottom of the ladder, our tactical lights scanning what looked to be a cave tunnel, natural stone walls and rocky floors snaking away into the black.

"All right," Talbot murmured, his voice echoing down the corridor. "Everyone, stay alert. We have them on the run, and the most dangerous lizard is a trapped, cornered lizard. We don't want to be ambushed down here."

He took point, and we followed the escape tunnel, the only sounds the scuffle of our boots on the rock and the drip of water somewhere overhead. Except for our lights, it was pitch-black, and at times the passageway narrowed to spots where we had to proceed single file, our helmets brushing the ceiling as we passed.

"Shit," Talbot breathed from up front. I peered over Tristan's shoulder and saw the tunnel had split, veering off in two different directions.

"Dammit." Talbot shone his light down one passage, then the other. "All right, looks like we have no choice. Sebastian, St. Anthony, take the left tunnel. Clement, you're with me. We can't let the targets escape. Just...be careful, you two," he added as Tristan and I headed toward the leftmost tunnel. "Radio us if you find the target, but do what you have to do. Good hunting, and take care of the greenie, St. Anthony."

"Roger that," Tristan muttered as we passed. "See you on the other side."

We followed the tunnel for several silent minutes, our flashlight beams sliding over rocks and limestone and the occasional puddle. Sometimes we had to duck to avoid the low ceiling, and at one point, the roof dropped so low, we had to proceed in a crouch. I tried not to imagine what would happen if a dragon ambushed us here, in a cramped stone hallway, with nowhere to turn or hide if it was suddenly filled with dragonfire.

I was relieved when the tunnel opened up into a large cavern, stalagmites and rocky outcroppings jutting from the floor. Stalactites hung from the ceiling like stony fangs, dripping icy water into the puddles at our feet. At the far end of the room, a thread of sunlight slanted across the floor from between a large pile of rocks. Tristan nodded, and we approached cautiously, guns at the ready, until we came to the base of the pile. Looking up, I could see the glimmer of light between the stones, flickers of open air and the outside world.

"Huh," my partner murmured, sweeping his light over the rocks. "Looks like there was an opening here at one point, probably the cave entrance. Most likely, the targets were hoping to escape this way, but weren't expecting the cave-in." He shone his light on a pile of rocks that looked like it had been recently disturbed, perhaps frantically cast aside. His voice turned hard. "But, if that's the case…"

He spun, just as a dark shape popped from behind a shadowy crag and fired on us, gunshots flaring white in the near blackness. I felt something slam into my combat armor, rocking me back a step. In the two seconds it took for me to regroup, Tristan had raised his weapon and opened fire. The roar of his assault rifle filled the chamber, a deafening cacophony of light, sparks and chaos, before everything faded into silence once more.

Tristan waited a moment, keeping his gun trained on the shadows, before nodding to me. Carefully, I approached the spot the shots had come from, finger curled around the trigger, ready to fire again if needed. I saw a shape on the ground between two boulders and shone my light between them, revealing a middle-aged human male in civilian clothes, blood streaming from his chest and forehead, his eyes staring out at nothing. A heavy pistol was clutched in one limp hand.

"Dead?" Tristan called from where he stood behind me.

I lowered my gun. "Yeah," I muttered, turning away so that I wouldn't have to see those blank, accusing eyes. Not out of sorrow or guilt; he was a dragon servant and would have killed us if he could. But I hadn't been ready, and that made me furious with myself. I'd been taken off guard, surprised in this dark hole, and that could not *ever* happen again.

"Good." Tristan lowered his gun, as well. "Search the place," he ordered. "There might still be servants lurking around, or the dragon could be nearby. Though if it hasn't shown itself by now—"

There was a ripple above him, a slither of movement in the dark, making my blood chill. I pointed my light toward the ceiling and, for a split second, saw something big and scaly wrapped around a stalactite, leathery wings spread to either side.

"Tristan, above you!" I shouted, just as a gout of flame descended from the ceiling, lighting up the whole cavern. Tristan threw himself aside, barely avoiding being incinerated, and the thing dropped onto him with a scream. It wasn't a large dragon—the size of a cougar—but even hatchlings were deadly if they closed on you. Tristan flipped to his back, managing to get his gun between himself and the dragon as the monstrous lizard snapped and tore at him, beating its wings furiously. I raised my weapon, trying to find a clear shot, but Tristan and the dragon were too entwined. I didn't want to risk hitting my partner, but if I didn't do something, I would watch him get ripped to pieces in front of me.

Dropping the rifle, I snatched the combat knife from my belt and charged the huge lizard. I didn't really know what I was planning to do, but as I drew close to the shrieking, flapping, clawing mass of human and dragon, I raised the blade and slammed it into the monster's side, sinking it between the ribs.

It spun on me with a shriek. I caught a split-second glimpse of its yellow eyes, wide with pain and rage, before it bared its fangs and lunged at me, jaws gaping. I staggered back, instinctively throwing up an arm, and felt a blaze of pain as rows of razor-sharp teeth clamped shut on my forearm. The dragon snarled and savaged the limb, biting and chewing, digging its fangs in deeper. As we tumbled to the ground, I snatched my sidearm from my belt, rammed the muzzle into the dragon's side and emptied the magazine into the scaly body.

The dragon jerked, shuddering. For a second we lay there, me on my back beneath a dragon, its fangs sunk deep into my arm. Then, those jaws slowly loosened, and the dragon made a strangled sound as it collapsed, its head hitting the ground just a few inches from mine. I glanced over and saw its eyes staring at me, bright and glassy, the spark of life slowing fading. For a moment, it didn't look angry or enraged; it looked terrified, confused. It made a faint whimpering sound in the back of its throat, as blood streamed from its nose and jaws. Then the slitted pupil rolled up, staring at the ceiling, and didn't move again.

"Garret!"

Tristan strode up and shoved the scaly green body off me with his boot. It rolled limply into a puddle, jaws open, still gazing at nothing. My partner loomed overhead, peering down with piercing, anxious eyes. His face was bloody, and the front of his combat vest was torn to strips, but he didn't appear seriously hurt.

"Dammit, Sebastian," he snapped as I struggled into a sitting position, which might've been a mistake. My arm blazed with agony, and I gritted my teeth, cradling the injured limb to my chest. A quick glance down made my stomach turn: my wrist and forearm had been shredded, blood soaked my mangled glove and dripped to the ground. Tristan swore again and knelt beside me. Pulling his own knife, he began cutting the sleeve from my arm, peeling back the fabric to reveal the length of ravaged skin. Rows of puncture wounds and several deep gashes oozed blood everywhere, and a patch of skin near my wrist was red and shiny, indicating it had been burned as well, as the gases emanating from a dragon's throat were scalding hot. Tristan swore again and shook his head.

"Jeezus, Garret," he growled, pulling several bandages from a compartment on his belt. "What the hell were you thinking? Didn't anyone tell you that hand-to-hand combat with a dragon is generally a bad idea?"

"You're welcome," I gritted out, clenching my jaw as he began swabbing my arm with a cloth, wiping away the blood. He snorted at that, but didn't comment.

Footsteps announced the arrival of the others, and a moment later Talbot swept up, shining his light at my feet. "What the hell happened?" he demanded, eyeing Tristan and me. "We heard shots fired, and now Sebastian is sitting here in his own blood. I assume to you have a damn good explanation for both. Did you find the targets?"

"Yes, sir," Tristan said coolly, not looking up from his task. "If you'll look behind you, you should see them both. One human servant and one dragon." Talbot's flashlight found the lifeless body of the dragon behind me, drawing a muttered curse from the other soldier. "The lizard was waiting for us when we came in," Tristan added, as the squad leader turned back. "It surprised me, but Sebastian managed to kill it, with a combat knife and a pistol." As Talbot's eyes widened, Tristan's mouth twitched in a rueful smile. "Kid saved my life."

"That so." Talbot's voice was expressionless, but the other soldier stared down at me with grudging appreciation. Normally, if a dragon got close enough to bite you, your chances of surviving that encounter were slim. I was lucky that the dragon was small and too enraged to breathe fire in my face. "Well, regardless," Talbot went on, "the thing's dead. I'll radio headquarters and let them know the raid was a success and to send in the cleanup crew." He glanced at me, frowning. "Can you walk, greenie?"

I nodded as Tristan finished wrapping gauze around my forearm, tying it off with a jerk. My arm was pretty messed up, and the meat of my thumb was in ribbons, but I wouldn't know the real damage until a medic looked at it. Hopefully I hadn't sustained any nerve damage. I needed my fingers to kill dragons and had no intention of stopping now. Tristan held out an arm; I grabbed his wrist with my good hand and let him pull me upright.

"All right, let's move. And Sebastian..." Talbot nodded at me, but it was a gesture of silent approval. "Don't think you're off the hook if your arm falls off," he said. "We can't have our youngest dragonslayer hanging up the gun after his very first kill."

I breathed out slowly. "No, sir."

The squad began to move out. I looked at Tristan, and he held out an arm, indicating the path forward. "After you," he said, the hint of a smirk on his face. "Partner."

EMBER

I found Garret in the hotel's business center a couple hours later.

I'd left Riley and Wes checking the status of their safe houses, slipping out of the room when their attention was diverted. I felt a little guilty, knowing Riley still wanted to talk, but I couldn't face him right now. I could still see the Archivist, the ancient, unstoppable Wyrm, wrapping his fingers around Garret's throat, and there had been nothing I could do to stop it. I could feel the utter terror, thinking I was going to lose him. He was more than a friend, I realized, more than the steady, unshakable soldier I could always count on. I was a dragon, and Cobalt was my *Sallith'tahn*, but I couldn't ignore what I felt toward Garret any longer. Even if I had no idea what it was.

Peering through the door of the business center, my heart pounded as I saw him, sitting in the computer chair with his back to me. I didn't know what I wanted to say, if I should say anything. But I slipped through the frame, walked across the room and slid into the seat beside his. His gray eyes shifted to me, wary and puzzled, and I swallowed hard.

"Hey," I greeted, glancing at the screen in front of him. It was blank, all the windows closed out, leaving no clue of what had been on it. "Did you get in touch with Tristan?" I asked. He nodded shortly.

"I sent him a private message," the soldier answered. "Using an old secure channel. He should see it and know who it's from."

"Do you think he'll agree to meet with you?"

"I don't know." He gestured to a small black phone sitting on the desk beside the computer. "I gave him the number of the burner phone. As soon as he contacts me, for whatever reason, I'll destroy it and we can leave the premises. I'm sure Riley is eager to move out."

"Yeah." I nodded. "We're just waiting for Tristan's answer."

He fell silent, staring at the phone, as if willing his former partner to call him. His eyes were bloodshot, and his normally close-cropped hair was getting kind of shaggy. He looked... tired. More than tired. World-weary. The kind of deep, bone-crushing exhaustion that descends on you when you're out of options and all your choices suck.

I understood. The last few days I'd caught only snatches of sleep here and there. Between crappy hotel beds, taking watch every few hours and being paranoid that the Order would kick down the door at any moment, I'd spent more nights awake than not.

Of course, that assumed I could even sleep anymore without the nightmares. I had killed again; it seemed I would never escape that now. Those men in the Vault, those strangers I'd never met, they had died so easily. One moment they were standing there, shouting at me, the next they were gone. Alive, and then dead. Just like that.

Life was so fragile, I mused, shivering. Anyone could be taken away; gone in the blink of an eye. I was terrified that, very soon, I would watch it happen to someone I cared about. Add to that the continuous stress of being hunted, sharing a room with two people who made my insides dance in different ways *and* the whole future conversation with Riley hanging over my head, and I wasn't in the most cheerful of moods. I was weary of running and weary of being shot at. I missed Crescent Beach, where I'd had friends, a brother, a real home. I wondered if Garret felt the same.

"Do you miss it sometimes?" I asked softly. His metallic eyes flicked to me, and I nodded at the phone. "That life? Being part of St. George. Do you ever wonder what would've happened... if you never came to Crescent Beach?"

"If we'd never met?" Garret's voice was emotionless. "I've always thought about it."

I looked away from him, stunned. That hurt a lot more than I thought it would. Though I didn't know what I was expecting. Garret was an outcast, on the run from the Order he once called family, hunted and hated by Talon and St. George alike. Because he'd met a dragon in a tiny town called Crescent Beach, and his world started to fall apart.

"But I don't have to wonder," Garret continued before I could say anything. "I know exactly what would've happened. I'd still be with St. George, hunting and killing dragons because the Order told me it was right. I'd be out there gunning down rogues, maybe hunting Riley himself, because I wouldn't know there's a difference. I'd still be killing indiscriminately. And I…would have never met you."

Warily, I peeked up. The soldier met my gaze and offered a tired smile. "I wouldn't go back," he said softly, clearly. "Not with what I know now. Don't wonder if this is worth it, Ember. It is. Even after all that's happened, I still wouldn't change it for anything."

My heart turned over. He was giving me *that* look. That steady, soulful, faintly sad look that could melt me into a puddle at his feet. The one that said he didn't care if I was a dragon and he was a soldier of St. George. I'd hurt him so badly, crushed his feelings, driven him away, and he still found it in him to return and help the girl who wasn't sure she could ever love him back.

But he was being cautious now, not moving any closer, giving me the choice of staying put or walking away. A part of me knew I should walk away. Leave now, and make absolutely certain that he knew a dragon couldn't feel the same.

Even though it was a complete, horrible lie.

For a moment, a heavy silence hung between us. Then the soldier let out a breath, like he'd finally come to a decision.

"I wanted to forget you," he murmured, as my heart started thudding in my ears, reacting to his presence. I found myself easing forward, closing the distance between us, as Garret's voice dropped even lower. "I wanted to convince myself that I had been wrong, that there was no way I could feel anything for something that wasn't human." He paused, and I bit the corner of my lip, knowing I had driven him there. To decide that I had been a monster, after all.

"I couldn't," he finally whispered. "You were the one who

taught me to live, to take chances. For a while, I convinced myself that we were too different, and that it was better to let you go. But now, I've come to the realization that my life is probably going to be very short. And I want to spend it doing something that matters. *With* someone that matters. I don't want to regret that I gave up without a fight."

My heart seemed to stop. Garret paused, as if gathering his thoughts, or his courage, then took a deep breath. "I know I've made mistakes," he continued, shaking his head. "But there's still the chance for me to fix them. I shouldn't have walked out that night." His brow creased, a flicker of pain and regret going through his eyes. "Ember, I know you can't feel what I do," he said. "I get that. But...I want to be with you. And if that's not possible, I'll be content just to be close. Fighting Talon with you and Riley, helping people, saving other dragons from the Order—there is nothing I want more. And nowhere else I want to be." His fingertips came to rest against the back of my hand, sending a zip of current through my whole body. "I'm done hiding," he whispered. "Nothing has changed. I know we might not have a lot of time, but what we do have, I want to spend right here."

"Garret..." My stomach was turning cartwheels, and the light touch across my hand was making it hard to think. There was so much I wanted to tell him. So much he needed to know. My dragon side would never accept him, she had already claimed someone else. And that someone else was supposedly my life-mate, only he didn't know it yet.

Nothing has changed, he told me. But that wasn't true. I wasn't the same girl he'd met in Crescent Beach. I had killed. Not just in self-defense; I'd attacked with the full knowledge that I was going to murder people. Riley called it a war, and would say that it was either them or us, but that didn't change the fact that I had entered battle with the intent to burn and savage and slaughter humans. Just like Talon wanted.

No, I realized suddenly. *Not like Talon wanted.* Talon wanted me to be a ruthless, coldhearted killer, a Viper like Lilith. They'd expected me to feel no remorse when it came to murdering humans, deceiving humans, manipulating humans. Even Dante, the twin I'd thought knew better than anyone, expected this. Emotions were a human thing; they had no place in the life of a dragon—that's what Talon had taught us. The same organization that said humans were lesser beings, tools to be used and discarded. The same organization that suppressed any hints of independence and killed—quite literally—any thoughts of disloyalty. I had been struggling so hard with the knowledge that dragons weren't supposed to feel, to love, like humans, but who had taught me that? Who had pounded that notion into my head until it became truth, something I didn't question anymore?

Talon.

"Ember." Garret's voice was low and calm as I sat reeling with the sudden insight. "It's all right. You don't have to say anything. I just…wanted to let you know." He rose smoothly, making no sound as he stood. I glanced up at him and saw his eyes were still kind, though a shadow hovered over his face. "Just think about it," he said softly, drawing back. "I'll still be here, whatever you decide."

"Wait." I caught his hand before he could leave, and he went perfectly still. *Choose, Ember. Right now. Dragon or human? Which side are you? What do you want to be the most?*

"I'm sorry," I told him, and felt every muscle beneath my fingers go rigid. "I've made mistakes, too, and people have been hurt because of it. I need to stop running away, and face them head-on, no matter how painful. In the long run, it'll be better for everyone. It shouldn't have taken me this long to realize that."

"Ember..."

"Back at the hotel in Vegas," I continued, hurrying on before I lost my nerve. "Right before you left for England. When you told me..." I trailed off, not wanting to say it out loud. Garret was barely breathing, as if he feared any movement would cause this moment to shatter. I could no longer look at him and dropped my gaze to the desk. Even then, I'd known what I wanted. I'd just let Talon and my own doubts convince me otherwise.

I'm sorry, Riley. But we do have a choice and, at least in this, I choose to be more human.

"I was wrong," I admitted softly. "Letting you walk out...was the stupidest thing I've ever done. I should have said yes." Garret's hand trembled in mine, and I closed my eyes. "I should have asked you to stay."

For just a heartbeat, we were both frozen. The clock on the wall ticked, a faint sound in the absolute silence.

Then Garret grabbed the hand that still held his own, yanked me to my feet and kissed me. I wrapped my arms around his neck as he pressed forward, backing me against the wall of the tiny room. His kisses were hungry and intense, shocking me with their passion. Like this had been pent up for a long time and was finally free. My dragon howled in protest, shrieking that this was wrong, but the flames within only made me desperate to get closer. I gasped and arched my head back, digging my fingers into his shoulders, shivering as his lips traced my jaw and neck. I didn't care that we were in a semipublic place, that people could walk by and see us, and Garret didn't seem to mind, either. My hands roamed over his back and shoulders, tracing his skin, feeling the hard muscles beneath. He leaned forward, kissing my shoulder, and I nipped the side of his neck, hearing his ragged intake of breath as he nearly fell into me. His mouth found mine again, and I growled as I locked our bodies together, startled by how much I wanted this, too.

It seemed like a long time before we drew back. Both our hearts were thudding wildly, our breaths ragged and erratic. Garret gazed down at me, those metallic-gray eyes so open and trusting it made my chest hurt. "What now, dragon girl?" he whispered.

I swallowed hard. Now came the challenge of telling a possessive, hot-tempered rogue dragon that I had chosen to be with a human. "I'll have to talk to Riley," I muttered. *About a lot of things.* "Probably better that he doesn't...see us together. At least not yet."

Garret's thumb brushed my cheek, making me shiver. "Is he going to try to kill me?" he asked with a faint smile. "Am I going to wind up in the emergency room with third-degree burns and a group of very confused doctors?"

Unbidden, a tiny laugh forced its way past my lips, though I wasn't sure if he was half-joking or being completely serious. "I don't know," I said, while inside, the dragon raged at me, furious and appalled. *What are you doing?* she snarled. *You be-*

long with Cobalt! He's your Sallith'tahn! He just doesn't know it yet because you haven't told him.

I pushed her down. *Stop it,* I told her. *This is my choice. I don't want to be with someone just because it's instinct.* Maybe it was the wrong choice, but my human side couldn't ignore this any longer. Dragons being incapable of love was probably another lie Talon had propagated. And even if it wasn't, whatever I was feeling now, emotion, instinct or otherwise, it sure felt awfully close.

Garret's phone buzzed on the countertop.

Reluctantly, he pulled back. Walking to the desk, the soldier plucked the phone from the counter and looked at the screen. I watched tension creep into his shoulders once more, and held my breath.

"It's Tristan." He turned back, and his gaze was solemn once more. "He's agreed to meet with me, alone."

RILEY

I didn't like this.

Generally speaking, I didn't like *anything* that had to do with the Order of St. George, but this had taken it a step further. Parked outside a coffee shop on a busy downtown street, I scanned the cars and sidewalks around me, looking for anything, anyone, that seemed out of place. As a whole, St. George did not have the same blending-in skills that Talon agents possessed, and I could usually pick the soldiers out of a crowd even when they were bothering to be inconspicuous, rather than charging in guns blazing like they usually did. That I didn't see anything suspicious did not lower my apprehension. I didn't like the fact that we were meeting with St. George. I didn't like that I was out here, scanning for hidden threats or ambushes, in case said representative decided to double-cross us. Garret Sebastian was a special case and had proved himself multiple times over, but I trusted the Order about as far as I could throw them. St. George didn't bargain with dragons; there was no compromise. I gave it a fifty-fifty shot that this soldier would come alone, or show up with a group of friends to snipe us all in the head. And he probably felt the same way about us.

"All clear on this side so far," I growled into the mic. "Ember, Wes? What about you?"

"Nothing here, mate," Wes answered from inside the coffee shop, probably huddled over his computer. Of the three of us, he was the only one this St. Anthony person wouldn't recognize on sight. So despite Ember's stubborn insistence that she wanted to be there when the other soldier showed up, in case it turned into an ambush, Garret told her that meeting him alone was the only way St. Anthony would agree. If he saw them together, he might think *he* was being set up and back out, and we couldn't afford that. So instead, the three of us did the normal paranoid thing and set up watch all around the meeting spot, so that if the Order did decide to crash the party, we would at least see them coming.

"Clear on this side, too," came Ember's voice over the receivers. "Although, this might be…yeah. Garret, Tristan just pulled into the parking lot. He's on his way in now."

"Understood," replied St. George. "Keep an eye out for anyone else."

"Yep," I said. "Good luck in there. Yell if you need us."

"I will."

The four of us fell silent, and I settled back into the seat, still watching the sidewalk while waiting impatiently for the meeting to start. I wanted this whole thing with Talon and St. George over and done with. The sooner we broke this alliance, the sooner things could go back to normal. Where my daily concerns were keeping my underground safe from the Order. Where St. George could go back to fighting Talon, and the rogues could go back to hiding from them both.

Where things could finally calm down enough for me to

focus on a certain red hatchling. The past couple days had been bad for that, with the four of us squeezed into a single hotel room, unwilling to separate for fear Talon or the Order could kick in the door at any moment. It was safer, but it did make for some…trying interactions, with a surly hacker, a restless female dragon and an ex-soldier of St. George in such close proximity to each other, all the time. All of us were exhausted and on edge, and there had been a few outbursts and snarky comebacks, but that was to be expected. We were tired. We all wanted this done. We wanted a point where we could breathe again and not feel St. George always at our backs, while looming over them, smiling at us all, was Talon. Of course, if we did succeed and break up Talon and the Order, none of us had really considered or thought about what was going to happen next.

And lately…Ember had been acting strange. I couldn't really say how; outwardly, she seemed the same—withdrawn and tired, but still always ready to go out and *do* something. Even though I knew she was just as drained and on edge as the rest of us. She was changing, losing the innocence of that sheltered girl in Crescent Beach. This life forced everyone to grow up fast, hatchling and human alike, and Ember was no exception. But there was something else. Something in the way she tensed whenever I got close, in the way she rarely looked me in the eye anymore.

It didn't matter, I told myself. I was a dragon, I could be patient. But when this was over, St. George or no, nothing would keep me from Ember's side. That was a promise to us both. To get to the bottom of whatever had come between us, and show her, once and for all, that she belonged with me.

GARRET

The glass door to the coffee shop opened, and Tristan St. Anthony walked inside.

He saw me immediately, his gaze going directly to the far corner where I had staked out a table. That wasn't surprising. This location was tucked against the wall with no windows, out of sight of any snipers who might try to take a bead on me from across the street. It afforded a clear view of the entire coffee shop and more than one way to get out. It was where *he* would choose to sit.

I waited calmly, both hands on the table in plain sight, my fingers curled lightly around a paper cup. Tristan didn't immediately stride to my table, taking a moment to scan the coffee shop for enemies. He then turned and walked to the front counter, smiling at the girl behind the bar as he placed his order. I scanned him for indications of weapons beneath his clothes, a telltale bump or sharp line at the small of his back. It was strange, seeing him like this. The enemy. A threat. I saw him watching me from the corner of his eye, probably doing the same thing, and wondered if this odd sense of guilt and resignation was plaguing him, too.

Finally, he turned, coffee in hand, and sauntered over to my table, sliding into the chair like this was a perfectly normal meeting. For half a heartbeat, we faced each other down, a storm of memories, words and emotion hovering silently between us.

"Hey, partner." Tristan was the first to break the silence, and his voice was heavy with sarcasm. "Good to see you again, when you're not hitting me in the back of the skull. I hope you're enjoying that shiny rifle you stole. Where are your friends?"

"Around," I replied. No use in lying to him; he knew I would be stupid not to post surveillance where I could. "And the Order?"

"Won't be joining us." Leaning back, he crossed his long legs and stared at me over the table. "Though I did spend the last day and a half debating whether or not to turn you in. But you knew that." His dark eyes narrowed. "You knew the risks when you contacted me, using our old emergency code, I noticed. Which is why I'm here, giving you the last benefit of the doubt and not watching the front door through the crosshairs of my scope." He took a sip of coffee and said, in a perfectly conversational voice, "I assume this is fucking important, Garret. I could be court-martialed if they realize where I've gone."

"I know." This meeting was chancy on many levels. Tristan had taken a massive risk just by coming here. The Order would see talking to me as an act of betrayal and would punish him severely if we were discovered. "This is important," I confirmed. "But...you're not going to like it." His brow furrowed, and I hurried on before he could change his mind and leave. "I

need you to hear me out, Tristan. Before you make any conclusions, listen to what I'm going to tell you. That's all I'm asking."

"If this is about your scaly friends, let me save you the breath
right now—"

"It's not about the dragons," I said. "It's about the Patriarch."

That prompted a wary frown, and he tensed, probably remembering our "conversation" at the facility. Where I had
told him that the Patriarch was working for Talon, right before I knocked him out. "This better not be what I think it
is, Garret."

"The Order has been on a lot of strikes recently, haven't
they?" I asked instead, and the frown deepened, bordering on
impatience. "Far more than normal. Three or four successful
raids a year was considered average for us. Now the number
of strikes has more than doubled, but nothing has changed
within the Order."

"Yeah?" Tristan's expression was cautious. "And? What does
this have to do with the Patriarch?"

"Because he is the one receiving the information of possible dragon locations," I said, lowering my voice. "He's the
one responsible for the increasing number of raids. The info
is coming directly from him."

"Again, and I might be repeating myself...so what?" Tristan
shrugged. "The Patriarch is sending us after dragons. I don't
really see the problem here. What does it matter where we get
the information? As long as more enemies are killed, the Patriarch could be getting hints from fat cherubs in diapers and
I wouldn't give a crap."

"Tristan..." I paused, knowing my next words were going
to decide the fate of this meeting. "The Patriarch's informa-

tion isn't coming from St. George. He's getting the locations from within Talon itself." My former partner gave me a blank stare, and I repeated it again, as clearly as I could, just so there was no doubt. "The Patriarch is working with the dragons."

The empty look instantly transformed into one of outrage. "Okay." Tristan pushed his chair back with an angry scraping sound. "I knew I shouldn't have come here. This was obviously a giant waste of time." He picked up his cup and tensed to shove himself out of the seat. "Goodbye, Garret. And don't worry. Next time I see you, I'll put you out of your misery."

"I have proof," I said quietly, making him pause. "I'm not just throwing around wild accusations. I went to England. I saw the Patriarch meet with Talon. But that's not all." My hand dropped to the chair beside me, brushing the manila envelope resting on the seat. "I have the evidence that shows, beyond any doubt, that he's in the organization's pocket."

Tristan still hovered on the edge of his chair, clearly unsure which direction he would go. If he would settle back or stand and walk out the door. "You know me," I said, meeting his gaze. "I have never lied to you. And you've known, deep down, that something isn't right. That the Order has been hiding things from us." I took the envelope off the chair and placed it on the table between us, keeping my hand on it. "This is proof. The Order has been corrupted, Tristan. Talon has been pulling the strings for a while now, and no one in St. George realizes it. If you can't accept that, walk away now—we won't stop you. And I'm sure down the road I'll meet you again on the field." His jaw tightened, making me hope he found that idea as sickening as I did. That the thought of killing his former partner weighed as heavily on him as it did me.

"But, I know you," I went on. "And this is going to drive you crazy if you walk away now. If you're willing to see the truth, it's right here." And I took my hand off the table.

Tristan hesitated a moment more, staring at the envelope like it was a venomous snake curled up on the counter. Then, with a curse, he leaned forward, snagged the corner of the envelope and slid it toward him.

I watched him as he pulled out the contents and flipped through the stack of documents and photographs, his face growing darker with every page. Even if the name of the Patriarch's "partner" was deliberately missing from every document, the evidence was still pretty damning. This was meant to be used as blackmail, and Talon had left nothing to circumstance. Even someone like Tristan, who was searching for a loophole, a way out, would be hard-pressed to disagree that this was anything less than treason.

"Why?" he finally rasped, putting the stack down with a vaguely ill look on his face. I didn't answer, not knowing if the question was directed at me or the universe in general. Tristan stared at the papers a few seconds more before glancing up at me, his expression tormented.

"I don't get it," he said, making a hopeless gesture. "So… Talon is using the Patriarch to kill dragons? Why would they slaughter their own kind? That doesn't make any sense."

Inside, something that I didn't know had been tense relaxed, and I let out a quiet breath. I knew Tristan was pragmatic and logical, and that he looked at the evidence before making any decision, but even with proof, I wasn't certain if he would believe his Patriarch was corrupt. Not only corrupt, but working with the enemy. Committing treason of the highest order. That would be hard for any soldier to swallow.

"It's complicated." He glared at me, and I sighed. "Not all dragons are associated with Talon," I explained, keeping my voice low in case a civilian was watching us. "There are deserters, rogues, who have broken away. Who have gone underground in order to escape. And since Talon doesn't want any dragons to exist outside their organization, they send assassins to kill any rogues that they find. Usually, they dispatch one of their own—that's what the Vipers do when they're not sent against the Order." Tristan gave a short nod; that, at least, made sense to him. The Vipers were Talon's killers, we knew that much.

"But now..." I motioned to the envelope. "They have an even better method. St. George doesn't suspect the Patriarch's hand in this, because the Order is doing what we have always done, and that is to take out every dragon we come across. Without question. Without wondering how we got there. You said it yourself. What does it matter where the information is coming from, as long as it keeps leading us to the enemy? Only, you're just taking out *Talon's* enemies, and making them more powerful than ever."

"Son of a bitch," Tristan breathed. He'd gone very pale, his blue eyes dark pools against his skin. "And the Order doesn't know," he muttered. "The Patriarch is selling us out to Talon, to the *lizards*, and St. George doesn't suspect a thing."

I waited, watching him. The first two hurdles had been cleared; Tristan believed us, and he hadn't arrived with the rest of St. George to blast us to bits. But the last obstacle loomed, and it was the largest one. Would he help us? Would he choose to side with the enemy, to expose the man the Order revered above all else?

"What are you going to do, Tristan?" I finally asked. He jerked up.

"I… I don't know." Leaning back, he raked a hand over his scalp. "I have to think about this. Gimme a day or two." He eyed the documents once more, as if wishing they would spontaneously burst into flame. "Any way I could take those with me?"

"They're just copies," I told him. "We still have all the original documents. Destroying them won't do anything."

"I wasn't going to destroy them, dammit." Tristan glared at me. "And I'm not so stupid as to show them to anyone in the Order. I just…need to make sure." He made a hopeless gesture that hovered very close to despair. "It's *the Patriarch*, Garret. If I'm going to do anything, I have to be certain."

I hesitated. Letting him walk out with the envelope wasn't a good idea. Even if we did have the originals, St. George discovering that evidence could be disastrous if it reached the wrong people. If it got back to the Patriarch, he could find ways to cover it up, to twist it to his advantage and to put the blame on us rather than on himself. Right now, we had the advantage because the Patriarch didn't know that we knew. If Tristan showed those documents to the Order, there would be an uproar, and a lot of questions the Patriarch would have to deal with, but we could lose all chance of credibility, depending on how well the Patriarch had prepared in case he was exposed.

But we couldn't do this from the outside. We were enemies of St. George, monsters, traitors and dragonlovers. Whatever proof or evidence we claimed we had, they would never hear us. If we were going to break up the alliance between the Patriarch and Talon, we had to do it from inside the Order. And Tristan was our best hope of getting into St. George.

Besides, I knew my ex-partner. I wouldn't go so far as to say I trusted him—whatever the circumstances, he was still a loyal soldier of St. George, and I was still on the wrong side. But he wasn't, as he'd snapped at me earlier, stupid. Showing those documents to anyone in the Order would bring him under fire, too. There would be questions as to where he'd gotten such evidence, who he had been meeting with, and eventually it would point back to either us or Talon. And then Tristan might find *himself* in a cell, before he made the short walk to the execution wall.

I didn't say any of this. He knew the consequences of defying the Order as well as I did. I just nodded and watched him lean forward in his chair to pick up the papers. Stuffing them into the envelope, he pushed the seat back and rose, towering over me.

For a heartbeat, he stood there, his expression tortured as we stared at each other. Twice, he seemed on the verge of saying something, only to fall silent. Abruptly, he turned on a heel, tucked the envelope under an arm and walked away. The door swung violently out as he pushed his way through, strode into the parking lot and was gone.

I took a deep breath and released it slowly, just as Riley's voice crackled in my ear. "What the hell, St. George! Did you just let that bastard walk out with the evidence? What if he goes right to the Patriarch and blows the whistle on this whole operation?"

"He won't," I said tiredly. "Tristan's loyal to St. George—he truly believes in the Order's mission. No one is exempt from the Code, no matter who they are. Even the Patriarch himself." *Or your former partner, who saved your life on multiple occasions.*

Riley let out a sigh. "I hope you know what you're doing," he muttered. "'Cause if this doesn't go the way you think, we are all screwed."

Ember's voice echoed over the line, quiet and thoughtful, making my insides stir. "What do we do now?"

I rose, tossing my half-empty cup in the garbage bin, hoping I'd done the right thing. That Tristan would come through. That I wasn't placing my faith in someone who would betray us all. "Now, all we can do is wait."

DANTE

"We're nearly ready, sir."

I stood at the computer terminal, feeling vaguely sick, while the team of humans bustled around me, preparing to carry out my orders. It was just nerves, I told myself. Nerves and anticipation that were making my skin crawl and my stomach churn like a hurricane at sea. Before me, a satellite image was displayed on the screen over the computers, showing a small town at the base of two mountains. Not even a town. A hamlet. A holler, to use the local term. Some forty or so humans lived there, in ramshackle huts and trailers, as far removed from civilization as anyone could be these days. If the whole place was swallowed by a massive sinkhole and disappeared, it would be days before anyone knew about it.

"Vessels are in position, sir," muttered a human beside me. I swallowed hard. On the other half of the screen, a cluster of tiny red dots had halted at the edge of the town, waiting.

"Communications are now blocked," said another human, huddled over a computer. "Phone lines are down, internet access has been cut off, cellular signals have been jammed. We are ready to begin."

I suddenly felt like puking. I stared at the cluster of red on the map screen, at the twenty-two trained killers who possessed no compassion, no empathy or morals or emotion to slow them down. A test, Talon had said. The final test. To gauge skill, efficiency and the vessels' ability to follow commands. The objective was simple.

No survivors.

"We're just waiting on your order, sir."

My hands shook, and I clenched my fists to stop them. How had I arrived at this point? When had my path turned to this? I'd wanted to build a future in Talon, one for myself and for my sibling, a future where we would be safe. The only way to do that was to become more powerful than our enemies. More powerful than St. George, the humans and even other dragons who threatened our survival. Now, I stood on the brink of something huge and dark. An entire town rested on my decision. I knew this choice would decide my future. What I was willing to sacrifice.

"Sir? We really need that order, now."

I closed my eyes. Ember would have found this situation horrifying. More than that. She would think me a monster. If she knew, if she ever discovered I gave that order, she would never forgive me.

But she didn't understand. She had never been able to see past her own emotional desires. Ember never thought about us, or our future. *I* was the one who'd always bailed her out of trouble. I was the one who'd always planned ahead. I understood that everything Talon did, it was for the good of our race. For our continued existence. We were trying to survive a world full of humans who would see us extinct if they knew of us. Sometimes, hard choices were necessary. Even if the ones you were trying to protect hated you in the end. We couldn't remain ignorant and sheltered any longer. This was a war, and war demanded casualties. It was time to grow up.

"Sir?"

I opened my eyes, seeing the cluster of red on the screen, and smiled.

"Do it."

EMBER

Okay. I have to tell him.

I stood in the shower, letting the scalding water run down my back, steam curling around me, as I tried gathering the courage for what had to be done.

He needs to know. This has gone on long enough. I have to tell him. Shouldn't be too hard, right? Hey, Riley, did you know you're my Sallith'tahn, which is the Draconic equivalent for life-mate, only I don't think I'm ready for something like that even though my instincts say the exact opposite and it's been freaking me out ever since the monastery? Also, two nights ago I kissed Garret, and I want to be with him when I'm in my human form, which is 90 percent of the time, but I still feel this Sallith'tahn connection toward you. So, you see the dilemma, right?

I groaned. This wasn't going to end well. At all. No matter what I said, someone was going to be confused, hurt and pissed as hell. And then what? We still had this thing with Talon and St. George to deal with. We had to work together to have any chance of pulling this off, but how was that going to happen with Riley wanting to kill Garret or vice versa?

No, I couldn't tell him, not yet. Succeeding here, breaking

St. George's unknown partnership with Talon, was more important than my feelings toward either of them right now. I had become a rogue not only to get away from the organization and its crushing, power-hungry tyranny, but to help all my kind be free. From St. George, Talon, the Elder Wyrm, the Patriarch, whoever wanted us extinct or enslaved. I needed to stop agonizing and start doing. If I was going to make a difference in this war, I had to have my priorities straight. And right now, we needed clear heads and the ability to work together.

I'll tell them, I promised all three of us. *Soon. When this is over, as soon as we break the Order away from Talon, I'll tell them everything.*

I toweled, slid into my clothes and opened the door with a billow of steam, ready to tell the boys the bathroom was now free.

Riley, alone in the hotel room, looked up from the corner chair and gave a smile that had no humor in it whatsoever.

"Hey, Firebrand," he said, rising from the seat. "About time you got out. We need to have a talk."

RILEY

Ember blinked, glancing warily around the room. "Where is everyone?"

"Gone," I said simply. "I sent them both on an errand while you were in the shower. Figured that was the only way to get you alone. No Wes. No soldier. No distractions. Just you and me."

She eyed me with suspicion, filling me with both fury and sorrow. Was she afraid? Did she hate being around me that much, that just standing in a room with me alone caused her shields to go up? I'd been as patient as I could, waiting for her to clue me in on what was bothering her, and it was driving me to distraction. Wes and I had been checking the status of my safe houses this morning, making sure they were all still there, that everyone was alive, and I could barely focus long enough to hear him out. This standoff needed to end. Now.

"So, what's going on, Firebrand?" I asked, stepping forward. "And don't think you're going to run away from me this time. I'm done waiting. You've been hiding something ever since the monastery and I want to know what."

Ember swallowed. I could see the wheels turning in her

head, trying to think of ways to stall, to dance around the question, and it only pissed me off more. "This isn't a good time, Riley—"

"Bullshit." She gave me a sharp look, and I met her glare. "When will it be a good time, Ember? When we're not running, or fighting for our lives? When we're not dealing with Talon or St. George?" I made a vague gesture, holding her gaze. "You're a rogue now—there will *never* be a good time. There will never be a moment when we don't have to worry about our enemies. There's always going to be something, be it a hatchling we have to rescue, a traitor we have to hunt down, or a strike force coming for us in the middle of the night. Something will always be there, making things difficult. Trust me on that."

She didn't answer.

"But you were fine with that," I said in a low voice, stepping closer. "We were fine. I know things have been rough, especially in the beginning with Griffin, and it's gotten even crazier since. But I haven't forgotten about us, Firebrand. I made you a promise, and you seemed to believe me." I paused. "*Did you believe me?*"

"Yes," Ember replied. "I believed you. I still do. But, that was before…"

"Before the soldier showed up. With the Eastern dragon."

It was barely noticeable, but Ember flinched. The girl who could stare down a dozen St. George soldiers without fear, cringed a little when I mentioned Jade. And that was all the confirmation I needed. If I wasn't certain before, I sure as hell was now.

"What did she say to you?" I asked, careful not to growl,

though everything inside was painfully tight. "It had to be something epically horrible—you've been looking at me like I'm some kind of freak show. Why are you afraid? What could she possibly tell you about me that's so awful? Did she know about my time in Talon, and what I used to do? Because if she did…" I lifted an arm helplessly, before letting it drop. "I can't change my past, Ember. I know I used to do awful things for Talon, but I'm trying to fix that. I…" I raked a hand through my hair, feeling suddenly tired. "I'm trying to make up for those years. Hell, I would think that what we're doing now is proof of that."

"Riley." Ember shook her head, looking anguished. "It's not that. Jade didn't know anything about you, or what you did before you left Talon."

"What, then?" I asked, narrowing my eyes. "Did she say something about *you*?" Ember shook her head again, but I plowed on, anyway. "Firebrand, listen, whatever she told you, I don't care. You hear me? Nothing you can say or do will scare me off, or make me see you any differently."

"I know."

"But that's not it, either," I guessed. No answer from the girl, and I raked both hands through my hair in frustration. "Dammit, just *tell me* what she said, Ember. I'm not going away until you do."

"It's not… I mean…"

"Spit it out, Firebrand. It's not that hard." Her eyes flashed, and I crossed my arms, knowing I was being a dick, but not backing down. Anger, perhaps, would be the most useful in getting her to talk. I would apologize later. "What did she say?"

"I was going to explain everything later."

"There is no later."

"You're going to flip out."

"Why don't you let me be the judge of that?"

"Riley…"

"We can stand here all night if you want. I have time."

"We're supposed to be life-mates!"

"I… *What?*"

Okay, *that* was not what I was expecting. I stared at her, unable to form words or even a cohesive thought for a moment. She glared back, jaw set, eyes bright with anger, fear and a defiant *I told you so* expression. "It's called *Sallith'tahn*," she went on in a quieter voice. "That's the Draconic word for what we're feeling. Jade explained it. In the old days, the only times dragons got together was to mate, but sometimes a bond would form between two dragons, and then that pair stayed together for the rest of their lives. No one knows how it forms or why, but once a dragon finds its *Sallith'tahn*, its life-mate—" she shivered a little at the word "—that's it. They're supposed to be together. Or, that's what Jade said, anyway."

"I've… I've never *heard* of it," I said, my voice coming out somewhat raspy. "In all my years in Talon, this *Sallith'tahn* thing has never come up."

"Because Talon doesn't want us to know it exists," Ember replied. "We're supposed to be loyal to the organization and nothing else. So they've made sure to erase the *Sallith'tahn* from our language and suppress any knowledge that it exists. If dragons knew about the life-mate bond, they might choose the welfare of another dragon over the good of the organization."

"And that's something Talon wants to avoid at all costs," I finished, feeling a bit dazed. Dammit, here was yet another thing the organization had hidden from us in the name of control. Where did it end? How could they justify suppressing something so inherent, something that made us who we were?

Forget Talon for a second! Ember is your Sallith'tahn, *or whatever that word is. Life-mate, Riley. Ember is your life-mate. Just give that a second to sink in.*

I waited for the shock to hit. For the skepticism and disbelief, even the slight panic and disgust at the notion of a life-mate. Nothing. I felt…relieved. Almost *elated*. Ember was my *Sallith'tahn*. I finally had a word for what I felt, and it wasn't unnatural or strange or perverse in any way. It was something as purely Draconic as flying or breathing fire, something humans, with their twisted, messy emotions, could never understand. Ember was my life-mate. We were supposed to be together, simple as that. Cobalt wasn't the least bit surprised; even when we hadn't known the word, he'd recognized his *Sallith'tahn* from the beginning.

"Why didn't you tell me?" I husked at her. "All this time, ever since the monastery you've known we were life-mates or *Sallith'tahn* or whatever, and you didn't want to mention it? That's not like forgetting that you left the door unlocked, Ember. This is kind of a big deal, maybe *the* most important thing to happen between us, and you kept it from me. Hell, you weren't even going to tell me today until I was a massive dick about it. Why?"

"I couldn't tell you," Ember said. "Not yet."

"Did you think I'd be angry? Or that I couldn't handle it?" I shook my head. "I already told you, Firebrand, I want you with me. This doesn't change anything. If anything, it just proves what we knew from the start, we just didn't have a word for it." She turned away, looking miserable, and I stalked forward with a growl. "Don't run away. Look at me, Ember." I reached out and snagged her elbow, but though she didn't flinch, she didn't turn to face me, either. "Why are you fighting this?" I whispered. "You know I would do anything for you, even before I knew the word. This…life-mate thing, don't let it scare you, Firebrand. It just shows we belong together. Simple."

"It's *not* that simple."

"Why?"

"Because," Ember snarled, whirling around, "I think I'm in love with Garret!"

Silence. I stared at her, hearing the words in my head, not fully comprehending them. I knew the soldier was a lost cause; his feelings for my hatchling were as blatant as dragonfire. Odd as it might sound, he really seemed to care for her, love her even, in the way that humans did. I'd tolerated it because we needed him, and because I thought Ember had finally realized what she was. That what she'd "felt" before was a passing curiosity, the desire to experience a human relationship, and when the novelty faded she'd realize a dragon and a human had no business being together. That the very thought was ridiculous.

It appeared that I was wrong. And Cobalt, rising from the darkness like a vengeful flame, was suddenly hell-bent on finding a certain human and ripping his head off.

I pushed him, and the rising fury, down. "That's impossible," I told Ember in a flat voice. "Dragons don't love, Firebrand. We *can't* love, it's not in our makeup."

"Humans can."

"You're not human!"

"Part of me is." Ember blinked rapidly, like she was holding back tears. Another shock; I'd never known a dragon that could really cry. Several of my former associates could, if pressed, produce some very convincing tears, but they were excellent actors, and few things could lower someone's guard better than turning on the waterworks. The old adage of "beware a crocodile's tears" held true for dragons, as well.

"Part of me...has to be," Ember went on, sounding like she was groping to understand, herself. "It's the only thing I can think of. Otherwise, how could I feel like this?" She swiped a hand over her eyes, frowning. "Maybe that's another thing Talon has hidden from us. Maybe...we've been imitating humans for so long, looking and acting and sounding like them, that it's not imitation anymore. Maybe we've *become* human, after all."

I curled a lip at the idea as anger buzzed through my veins, turning them hot, bringing the dragon even closer to the surface. "That's an excuse, Firebrand, and a pretty flimsy one at that," I sneered, and she turned on me, eyes narrowed. "I think you're just scared of this whole life-mate thing, and you're looking for anything to counter it."

"That's not true! I don't want to hurt you."

"You can't hurt me," I said scornfully. Lying through my teeth. "I'm a *dragon*. Don't try to spare my feelings. I'm not the soldier."

And of course at that moment, the bolt clicked, and the door swung back as the soldier stepped into the room.

I didn't stop to think. I didn't even remember moving. Cobalt surged up with a roar, and the next thing I knew, I had lunged across the room, grabbed the solder by the collar and slammed him into the wall.

He grunted as I shoved him into the plaster, and then those hard gray eyes met mine. He didn't struggle or throw any punches, though I could feel the tension in his arms and back, ready to explode into violence if needed. I dug my fingers into his shirt, feeling talons aching to come out, to rip through cloth and flesh and muscle until this human was nothing but a bloody smear on the floor.

"Riley!" Ember snarled, and I heard the echo of the dragon in her voice, too. I ignored it, glaring at the soldier pinned against the wall, the human who had turned my hatchling away from me. Ember was mine. My life-mate. My *Sallith'tahn*. St. George was a threat, and I'd be perfectly within my rights to drive him off; out of my territory, and away from my mate.

If he was a dragon. And we lived in the Dark Ages.

St. George still hadn't moved. His eyes were still locked with mine as he said in a low, reasonable voice, "I'm not your enemy, Riley. Whatever you think of me, this won't help what we're trying to do."

"Shut up, St. George!" I snarled at him. "Don't pull that 'reasonable' crap with me. I was a Basilisk long before you could wrap your fingers around a gun. I know exactly what you're trying to do, and I am in an extremely unreasonable mood right now. So, go on," I hissed, seeing my reflection in his eyes, my pupils narrowed to vertical, reptilian slits. "Give me one reason I shouldn't rip you into five different pieces right here. Or at least kick your ass back to the Order where you belong."

"I can give you several," the soldier replied carefully, and his gaze flicked to something over my shoulder. "But, the most obvious one is standing right behind you."

Still keeping one fist in the human's collar, I turned…

...to face a furious, growling red dragon.

Ember stared at me, her head and neck low to the ground, wings partially spread, muzzle pulled back from her teeth. Her back spines were fully erect, and her tail stretched out behind her, only the spade tip flicking back and forth. A primal, unconscious and very obvious threat display. If I didn't back off right now, she would attack.

Instinctively, I dropped my fist from the human's collar, but didn't move from there, turning to face Ember directly. "So, you've really decided, Firebrand?" I asked the dragon, who then blinked and raised her head, looking almost dazed at her own reaction. "This is what you want. A human, who will never understand you. Who will never be your equal. Who will be gone in the blink of an eye, no matter how hard you try to hold on."

The red hatchling twitched her tail, her eyes shadowed. "I'm sorry, Riley."

"Don't apologize." I twisted my lips into a bitter smile. "Of the three of us, I'm not the one who needs pity."

The door clicked, a sharp sound in the tense quiet, and Wes stepped into the room, his eyes going wide as he saw us. "Shit!" he exclaimed, and quickly shut the door behind him. "Bloody hell, what is *wrong* with you people?" he went on, throwing the locks and whirling on all of us. "At least close the curtains if you're going to be flapping your wings where everyone can see them!" Before I could answer, he turned to the soldier, not picking up on—or choosing to ignore—the obvious tension in the room. "What is taking so bloody long, St. George? I thought you were going to tell them."

The soldier's voice was dry. "I was somewhat distracted."

"Tell us what?" I asked.

"Tristan contacted me," St. George replied. "In the parking lot, just as we were pulling in. He sent me a time and a meeting place not far from here." His tone was carefully neutral as he looked from me to Ember. "I thought you might want to know his answer."

I ground my teeth. There were so many things I wanted to do, violent, unspeakable things, mostly involving the soldier. I wanted to char the human into a little pile of dust and bones, then scatter it to the winds with one sweep of my tail. I wanted to shake some sense into Ember, to demand why she would choose a short-lived human over her *Sallith'tahn*. I wanted to fly up beyond the clouds, where nothing would hear me but the stars, and roar out my frustration until I was cold and empty and there was nothing left.

I couldn't do any of those things. St. George and Talon were still out there, coming dangerously close to eliminating my underground. My network, my hatchlings and all the dragons I'd freed from the organization were counting on our success. I was Cobalt, leader of the rogue underground, and I could not let personal problems get in the way of the mission.

Afterward, though, there would be hell to pay.

I looked at the soldier, then at Ember, still watching me in dragon form, and smiled coldly.

"All right, then. Guess we should go see what the bastard has decided."

GARRET

Tristan looked awful.

The last time I'd seen my former partner, walking out of the coffee shop with the evidence tucked under one arm, he'd seemed fine. Dazed and a bit shaken, but otherwise normal. Now, striding across a soccer field toward the section of bleachers I'd staked out, the soldier looked haggard. His clothes, normally spotlessly clean and pressed, were wrinkled. His eyes were bloodshot and dark stubble shadowed his jaw.

Truthfully, I wasn't feeling much better. My shoulders ached from where Riley had slammed me into the wall, and from the force the rogue dragon had generated, even in human form, I suspected there were a couple bruises hidden beneath my shirt. At least I'd been able to brace myself for the impact. The second I'd walked into the hotel room and seen their faces, I'd realized what was going on, and I knew what was coming. I was just thankful Riley hadn't Shifted before he attacked; I could tell he'd wanted to and was barely holding himself back. I could take the abuse of a furious human; a furious dragon was a different story. Even with Ember's intervention, I might not have survived.

Uneasiness stirred. And, surprisingly, guilt. Would I have to watch my back around him from now on? Would there always be a dragon lurking in dark corners and lonely places, waiting for the perfect moment to get rid of me? I knew Riley hated the Order, and we hadn't seen eye to eye on a lot of things, but to my surprise, I found that I respected him. He was a good leader—brave, cunning and resourceful. And he cared for those under his watch. Except for his obvious disdain for authority, he would have made an exceptional soldier.

I shook myself. There was no time to worry about Riley now. When the mission was done, if we managed to expose the Patriarch, I was certain I would face the full wrath of a jilted male dragon, but at this moment, the approaching soldier of St. George was the bigger concern.

When Tristan spotted me, sitting near the bottom row, he froze, eyes going wide. I held my breath, waiting for his decision. Ember sat beside me, close enough to touch, and Riley leaned against the side with his arms crossed. Tristan knew Ember, of course, and was smart enough to guess the identity of the other. I hoped, when he realized exactly who was waiting for him, he would not turn around and walk away. But after that first hesitation, he took a breath and came forward again, though his eyes were narrowed and his jaw was clenched as he strode up.

"You look like crap," I offered as he reached us.

"Fuck you, Sebastian," Tristan returned, glancing at Ember. "And your scaly friends."

I ignored that and, thankfully, so did the two dragons, though I felt the girl tense beside me. "I take it you reviewed the evidence thoroughly?"

For a second, I thought he was going to snap at me again. His face darkened, and he looked like he wanted to punch something, before he let out a shuddering sigh and bowed his head.

"Yeah," he rasped, and dropped to the end of the bench, running both hands through his hair. "Yeah, I did. Damn you to hell, Garret, why did you have to drop that in my lap? Do you know what this will mean for the Order? What will happen if this comes out?"

I nodded. "I know."

"It'll ruin St. George," Tristan went on angrily. "The Order will be thrown into chaos. The council will be scrambling to find a new Patriarch, there will be discontents who break away, inquisitions, protests. We might never recover. But why am I even telling you this—that's what you fucking dragons want, isn't it?" He shot a glare at Ember over my shoulder. "This is a dream come true for you. You're probably going to throw a party when I leave."

I felt Ember bristle, but her voice stayed surprisingly calm as she answered. "Would you rather Talon be in control of the Order?"

A shudder went through him. "No," he muttered. "No, this can't be allowed to continue. St. George needs to know that the Patriarch is corrupt and is working for the dragons. Though I'm damning myself to hell and back for helping you expose him." He gave me a look that was both resigned and disgusted. "I assume that's the reason you called me, Garret? You needed someone on the inside."

"Yes," I answered truthfully. "You're the only one I could think of who maybe wouldn't shoot me on sight."

"Really wish you wouldn't have bothered, partner," Tristan said in a weary voice. "But there's nothing for it now. I can't unlearn what I know." He paused once more, taking a breath, as if resigning himself to the inevitable. "Fortunately for you, I already have a plan."

"That was quick," Riley muttered behind us.

Tristan ignored him. "In two days time, the Patriarch will be traveling to the States to meet with the various chapterhouses and leaders of St. George," he said, making me straighten. "He'll be *here* in a week, but he's holding an assembly with all the officers, council members and chapter heads as soon as he lands in Salt Lake City. Every high-ranking official in St. George will be at that meeting. If you want to reveal evidence that the Patriarch is allying with Talon, you'd certainly have everyone's attention."

"Oh, that's a great idea," Riley said, shoving himself off the bleachers. "An entire room filled with the high muckety-mucks of St. George, not to mention the Grand Poobah himself. I'm sure they're going to let two dragons and a known traitor waltz right in and accuse the Patriarch of treason. And I'm sure *I'm* going to be strolling merrily into a building full of St. George soldiers with itchy trigger fingers." He stopped at the bottom seat to glare at Tristan, arms crossed and a smirk twisting his mouth. "I'd accuse you of leading us into a trap if it wasn't so blatantly obvious. How the hell do you expect to get us in there, anyway?"

"I don't," Tristan said flatly. "I'm not taking two lizards anywhere near that building—that would be suicide, for me as well as you." He glanced at me, brows drawn together. "I'm taking Garret, but he has to come alone."

"Garret's a traitor to the Order," Ember broke in, sounding worried. "They know who he is. He won't get any farther than us if someone recognizes him."

"I'm counting on it," Tristan muttered, still looking at me. I suddenly realized what he was getting at, and my insides went cold. He smiled grimly. "The only way for you to get close to the Patriarch," Tristan went on, "is as a prisoner. You won't get anywhere near him otherwise—he's too well guarded. But, like your lizard said, they know who you are. We can use that to our advantage. You turned yourself in to me, and I'm presenting you to the Patriarch and the rest of the council for judgment. Once we get inside, I'll release you, and you can show the evidence to everyone."

"What?" Ember exclaimed, as Riley barked a mocking laugh. "Are you *crazy?*"

"Possibly," Tristan said with a humorless smile. "But I can't think of another way to do this. If you want that evidence to reach the Order, Garret, you're going to have to trust me."

"Trust *you,*" Riley sneered. "Trust you to take your most-wanted criminal and the proof of the Patriarch's involvement with Talon into the heart of enemy territory as your hostage with no way for us to reach him if things go south? While we're at it, why don't we tie a pretty bow around his neck and send him in with a card, as well?"

"Look, *dragon,*" Tristan spat, curling a lip in Riley's direction. "I don't like you any more than you like me. I'd rather stand back and put a sniper round between your eyes than sit here talking with you." He paled a bit, and ran a hand over his scalp. "Shit, if anyone knew what I was doing right now," he breathed, shaking his head, "I'd be executed faster than you could say 'treason.'"

I felt a stab of guilt for dragging Tristan into this. Just by coming here, talking to us, he was risking everything. Even if we reached the Patriarch and convinced St. George of the man's betrayal, Tristan wouldn't be off the hook. He'd still met with me, a traitor of the Order. He'd still conspired against St. George. His future, his very life, would be on the line.

Unless he turned me in.

"But if you want to expose the Patriarch," Tristan went on, unaware of my thoughts, "and break St. George away from Talon, this is the only way. The Patriarch only comes to the States once a year at most. There won't be another meeting like this for a long time. If you want to walk into St. George, accuse the Patriarch of conspiracy with Talon and have the barest hope of being heard without getting shot the instant you open your mouth, this is your best chance."

"And then what?" Ember demanded. "Even if you do convince everyone that the Patriarch is working with Talon, what happens after that? They're not just going to let Garret walk away."

"I'll take care of that," Tristan said. "I'll get him out again, I promise."

"Not that I don't *trust* you, St. George," Riley said, the hint of a growl underlying his words, "but if we let you walk into that room with him and the evidence, I'm pretty damn sure we'll never see either of them again."

"I'll do it," I said softly.

All three stared at me. "Garret, no," Ember said, putting a hand on my knee. "It's too dangerous. We won't be there to help you and..." She glanced warily at Tristan. "What's to stop him from turning you over to the Order once you're there?"

"Nothing," I told her. "I'll be putting myself in his custody. If he wants to turn me in, there'll be nothing I can do to stop it." I caught Tristan's gaze as I said this; he glared back at me, though he didn't look away. "But, he's right," I went on. "We have to do this now. We won't get a better shot at exposing the Patriarch to the rest of St. George."

"We don't even know if the Patriarch is really coming here," Riley said. "What if this is an elaborate setup and you're walking oh so casually into a trap?" When I hesitated, he raised his hands. "Look, I know you two had a great time slaughtering dragons together once, but times have changed. You really trust this dragonkiller not to stab you in the back?"

"It has to start somewhere," I said quietly. Someone had to take that first step, or we'd never accomplish anything. "Tristan has saved my life dozens of times before." I looked him right in the eye as I said this. "If he wants it now, he's welcome to it."

My former partner rose, giving us all a hard look. "I'll meet you in Salt Lake City in forty-eight hours," he told me. "Remember, Garret, come alone if you want this to work. No guns, no wires, no transmitters, nothing. Your dragons stay as far away from this as possible, got it?"

"Understood."

He spun on a heel and strode away without looking back.

"Dammit," Riley sighed, giving the retreating Tristan a disgusted look. "I hate Salt Lake."

EMBER

I watched Garret pull his pistol from his back holster, check the chamber for a round, then carefully place it on the dresser. For a moment he hesitated, fingers curled lightly around the weapon, before he released it and pulled his hand away, empty.

Dread blossomed within, adding to the suffocating feeling that had clung to me ever since the meeting with Tristan. We'd driven straight to Salt Lake City and taken refuge in one of Riley's safe houses, a foreclosed home on the outskirts of the city. Despite his aforementioned hatred of Salt Lake, it being one of St. George's primary cities, Riley kept a safe house within enemy territory, "just in case." Talon wouldn't bother us here. If Riley was on the run from the organization and needed to get them off his back, this was a good spot to lie low and wait for things to blow over. If he didn't attract the Order's attention, too.

It was not the best of neighborhoods, and you could barely get through an hour without hearing a siren wail in the distance, but the house itself was actually fairly roomy, and everyone was relieved not to spend another night in a cramped hotel room. The extra space was definitely a good thing. I'd

been afraid, from the confrontation earlier, that Garret and
Riley would try to kill each other on the way up. But after the
meeting with Tristan, it appeared to be business as usual once
more. Garret, Riley and Wes talked—or argued, mostly—about
the plan, with Riley and Wes insisting that this was probably a trap and Garret would be delivering himself right to the
Order's doorstep. The three of us—Riley, Wes and myself—
tried to come up with a plan that would let us keep tabs on
the soldier, or at least know what was going on within Order
territory. But Garret was adamant he would go alone, and in
the end, nothing we said would deter him.

Not one word had been said about what had happened in
the hotel room right before Tristan contacted us. The boys
seemed content to pretend it never happened. Though Riley
spoke to us all a lot less now. There was a coldness to him
that hadn't been there before; he was still perfectly civil and
businesslike, but he kept all of us, even Wes, at arm's length.
As if this was a job he had to complete, and when it was over,
so were we.

It made my stomach ache with guilt, especially since every
time I looked at him, I could see Cobalt's gold eyes staring
back at me, hurt, angry, betrayed. I wanted to talk to him,
but what could I say? I'd made my choice. Even though my
dragon side still protested. Even though she still insisted that
Cobalt was our other half, and I was making a huge mistake
pretending to be human.

And now, it was forty-six hours later. The time had come.
Garret was going to walk out of the room alone, meet with
a former ally turned enemy and let himself be taken before
the Order of St. George. If something went wrong, I couldn't

be there. If Tristan betrayed Garret... I would never see him again.

I clenched my hands against the wooden frame, terrified, angry and desperate all at once. Garret turned, spotting me in the doorway, and his mouth curved in a gentle smile. "Ember," he said as I took a calming breath and stepped into the room. I searched his face carefully, but saw no signs of fear or hesitation, just quiet resolve. "Come to convince me not to go, one more time?"

"You don't have to do this," I told him, holding his gaze as I walked up. "We can find another way, Garret. There has to be another way."

He smiled and shook his head. "This is the best chance we have," he said. "I won't have another shot at getting this close to the Patriarch, with all the leaders of St. George in attendance. Even if they take me prisoner, they can't ignore the evidence. Someone will listen. We just need to plant the seed."

My throat closed up, and the corners of my eyes stung. Closing the gap, I reached out and slipped my arms around his waist, drawing him close. "I can't lose you now," I whispered, feeling his heart pick up beneath his shirt. "I can't bear the thought that you'll be walking in there, alone, and there's nothing I can do if things go wrong."

His arms wrapped around me, his cheek resting atop my head. "Let me do this," he whispered into my hair. "For everything I've done. For all the lives I've taken, all the dragons I've destroyed. I have...a lot of blood on my hands, Ember." He sighed, bowing his head. "A lot to atone for."

"You don't have to *die* to atone for those years, Garret," I told him. "It was a war. You're not responsible for the entire Order of St. George."

"I don't plan to die," he said, and I heard the faintest of smiles in his voice. "I would like very much to live, actually. Especially now." One hand traced small circles against my back, and I pressed closer to him, listening to his heartbeat. "I used to think that having nothing to live for made you a better fighter," he murmured. "Turns out I was wrong on a lot of fronts."

Tell him. The words hovered on the tip of my tongue, reluctant to take that final leap. Why was I hesitating? I'd already blurted it out once, in front of Riley, no less. Why was it so hard with Garret? I knew what I was feeling. For the very first time, I was certain.

"Garret," I began. "I...uh..."

He pressed a palm to my cheek, stroking with a thumb, making me look up. "Tell me when I come back," he said, his eyes very soft. "It will give me something to look forward to. A reason to walk out of there alive."

I swallowed hard. "You'd better come back," I warned him. "If you don't, I'm going to be very pissed at you, and you don't want a pissed-off dragon on your tail, even if you are a ghost."

Garret smiled and bent forward. "I'll keep that in mind."

Our lips met. I wrapped my arms around his neck and pulled him close, and his tightened against my back, pressing us together. There was something desperate in his embrace, something that hinted at resignation and acceptance. He knew he might not be coming back.

I didn't want to let him go, but he finally pulled away. I

looked into his eyes and saw the words I hadn't been able to voice burning in his gaze, bright and intense.

"I'll be back as soon as I can," he murmured. "Wish me luck."

The words sprang to mind again, warring with the dragon, but I just nodded and gave him a brave smile. "I'll be here," I replied. *Waiting. Hoping this isn't the last time I see you. The last chance to tell you what I should said have a long time ago.* "Be careful, Garret."

One last bright, longing glance, and he turned away, walking out of the room and down the hall. I heard Wes mutter something as he passed, heard the front door open and close, and then he was gone.

GARRET

"You know they're going to try to kill you, right?"

I looked up. Riley was leaning against the wall outside the front door, waiting for me. His expression was cold, and for a second, I tensed, wondering if this was the moment he'd choose to attack. To end what he'd started in the hotel room. Outwardly, he'd been brusque but businesslike, keeping things civil between the three of us, though I could sense the anger roiling beneath the surface.

I paused, one hand on the railing of the stairs, wondering if the statement was more a desperate hope than a question. "I know," I said, anyway. "But, it has to be done."

"I don't get you, St. George." Riley gave me a look that was a cross between contempt and genuine confusion. "You've fought us for years. And now you're suddenly willing to play martyr, to challenge the Patriarch to his face, because of her?"

"No. Not just because of her. It's more than that." I looked away for a second as memories crowded in. The teachings of St. George, the missions of death and slaughter, the rigid Code that could not be broken. "The Order can't go on like this," I said, glancing back at the rogue. "Something has to change.

For hundreds of years, we've waged war and hunted and killed without a thought, when we should have been questioning everything."

"Yeah, well…" Riley shook his head, his expression curling with disgust, not directed at me this time. "Talon isn't exactly the most upstanding and righteous organization, either. And the Order of St. George isn't the only one mired in tradition. If you're talking about change, you've got a massive battle ahead. I've seen Talon, what they're really like. And you know your own Order, better than anyone. They're giants, St. George, and we're insects, just trying to stay alive. What chance do we have of them even seeing us?"

"It has to start somewhere," I replied, knowing I was repeating myself and not caring. One step in the right direction. One conversation between a dragon and a soldier, instead of a massacre. "Ember began this the night she chose to spare a soldier of St. George," I went on. "I have to continue it. Even if I die, it will get the Order thinking. And maybe more will start to question things, see the war in a different light. It won't be all at once, and it might take a long time. But we have to try. Otherwise, this fighting and killing will never be over."

Riley sighed. "You know, it would be so much easier to kill you," he said, and shoved himself off the wall, making me tense. "But then you go spouting that noble crap and actually making sense, and I find myself hoping you don't get yourself shot in the head, after all." He paused, his gaze conflicted as he stared at me. An echo hovered between us, her name on both our minds, but neither of us would mention it. There was nothing to say.

"I still think you're crazy," Riley finally said, stepping back.

"But...good luck in there, St. George. You'll need it. You have far more faith in that human than I ever would." A smirk curled his mouth as he gave a grudging nod. "You're not half-bad to have around, for a soldier and a dragonkiller. If you don't manage to get yourself stabbed in the back, you know where to find us."

I nodded, watching Riley turn away and slip through the door. "Thanks," I murmured as it clicked shut behind him, the echo of the unspoken truce hanging in the air as he left. I wondered why he was extending the olive branch now. Maybe he really thought I wasn't coming back.

I walked down the stairs and found the car Wes had called for me waiting at the sidewalk. It was late evening, the air was cool, and the sun had long since vanished behind the distant mountains. Slipping inside, I gave the driver the address, then stared out the window while my thoughts looped in endless circles. The Order, Talon, Tristan, the Patriarch, Ember.

Strangely enough, though the rest of the night loomed before me like a dark cloud, I was calm. Perhaps it was because I knew I was likely walking to my death. Putting myself in the hands of my former partner and appearing at an assembly of those who'd lived through decades of war with Talon... I didn't see how I would walk away alive, let alone free. Even if Tristan didn't turn me in, even if they couldn't ignore the evidence, I was still their most-wanted criminal, a traitor who had sided with the enemy.

The cab dropped me off on a dark corner, and I followed Tristan's directions down a narrow alley to the back of an abandoned lot. A single black car, its windows dark and tinted, sat beneath a sputtering streetlamp. Its lights flashed once as I entered the lot, and I headed toward it.

The front door opened, and Tristan stepped out wearing his dress uniform, the black jacket with brass buttons marching down the front, the symbol of the Order on the right shoulder. His face was set, eyes narrowed in the flickering light of the streetlamp as he stepped away from the car and aimed a 9 mm at my chest.

I stopped and raised my hands, wondering for a second if he would shoot me right here. Leave my body in a lonely alley and take the evidence himself, never to been seen by anyone in St. George. The shot never came, though Tristan approached cautiously, his gaze flicking to the shadows behind me, searching for dragons.

"I'm alone, Tristan," I said as he stopped a few yards away, the gun still trained on my center. I kept my arms raised as he glanced at me warily, gaze searching my waist, my side, anywhere there could be a weapon.

"Are you armed?"

"No."

He patted me down, anyway, checking for wires or transmitters as well as weapons, making sure no dragons were listening to this conversation, ready to follow or pounce. When he was certain I was clean, he stepped back, motioning me toward the car. I obeyed, though my apprehension was growing.

"Do you have the evidence?" he asked.

"Yes," I answered, feeling the envelope tucked into my jacket. It contained the original documents, bank statements and all of the pictures showing the Patriarch with the Talon agent.

"Okay." Tristan paused, as if steeling himself for what he

had to do. "From here on out, this has to look completely real. You turned yourself in, and I'm bringing you before the Patriarch to decide what to do with you. That's how this lie has to work. Otherwise, we'll both be shot dead before we reach the front doors. Do you understand? Once we get there, we're enemies, you're my prisoner and I have to treat you that way."

"I understand."

"All right." He motioned at me with the gun. "Turn around."

I did as he instructed and felt the bite of plastic restraints around my wrists a moment later. "I'll do the talking to get us past the guards," Tristan muttered, cinching the cuffs behind my back. "Once we reach the Patriarch, I'll cut you loose, and you can shock everyone with your announcement."

Or you'll turn me over to the Patriarch for real, and there'll be nothing I can do to stop it. Experimentally, I tested my restraints, wondering if I could slip free if I had to. There was not an ounce of give; the bands were tight around my wrists, to the point of digging into my flesh. As Tristan had said, this felt completely real.

He stepped back and yanked open the passenger door, gesturing me inside. I slid into the seat, leaning forward to keep the weight off my arms as the door slammed, trapping me within. The windows, I noticed, were very dark, almost opaque. No one on the outside would be able to see anything.

Tristan slipped into the driver's seat a moment later, and the locks clicked into place as he closed the door. I glanced down, saw a dark cloth bag on the seat between us, and felt my stomach drop. My former partner saw what I was looking at and grimaced.

"Sorry, partner," he sighed, picking it up. "Just a precaution, in case any lizards are thinking of showing up in the middle of the assembly. Better that you don't know where we're going. It'll be safer for all of us."

I narrowed my eyes. "Are you going to gag me, too? Make sure I can't accuse anyone while we're there?"

"Hmm, intriguing thought. Keep it up and I might."

The bag slipped over my head, plunging me into complete darkness. A few seconds later, the engine shuddered to life, and the car began to move. I leaned carefully back against the seat, trying to calm my breathing, to focus myself for what lay ahead. If this was a trap, I was caught. I was alone, in enemy hands, and there was no Ember to save me from St. George this time. There was nothing I could do now but trust my former partner and hope that he would keep his word.

But if this was a trap, if I was going straight to my death, I knew a certain red dragon would keep fighting, no matter the cost. I was doing this for her, I reminded myself. Yes, it was for Riley, the rogues and all the dragons I had slaughtered in the past, but mostly it was for Ember. To give her the hope of a world without war, without the threat of St. George constantly breathing down her neck. A world where, just maybe, dragons and humans could understand each other a little better. I would try my hardest to give her that, to at least start things down the right path.

Even if I couldn't be there.

RILEY

I found Ember where I thought I would; in the soldier's room, sitting on his bed. Waiting for him to come back. She looked up when I walked in, a wary expression crossing her face.

"What did you say to him, Riley?"

"Nothing," I growled, glaring at her. She looked dubious, and I rolled my eyes. "I said that I thought he was crazy, I wished him luck and I told him to come back alive if he could. Satisfied?"

"That's it?"

"Yeah, Firebrand," I snapped. "That's it. What did you think I was going to do? Cackle and twirl my mustache? Tell him that I hope he fails and doesn't break up the alliance between Talon and the Patriarch that's killing my underground? Do you really think I'm that vindictively shortsighted?"

"You did slam him against a wall and threaten to tear him in half."

"I did not. I threatened to tear him into *five* pieces, get it right, Firebrand."

She snorted. "Yes, well, I'm glad you restrained yourself." I narrowed my eyes, wondering if she was mocking me, and she held up her hands. "I'm serious, Riley," she said in a quieter voice. "I know I kind of dropped that on you. I didn't mean for it to sound like it did, and I know it was unfair." A pained look crossed her face, and she dropped her gaze to the bed. "I'm sorry it turned out that way."

I sighed, raking my hair back. "Yeah, well, since we're on the subject of apologies," I muttered, "I kind of pushed you to that confession, Firebrand. I didn't give you a chance to explain it on your own terms. Maybe if you had, I would've reacted better. So it might've been my own damn fault things went down the way they did. So, ah…" I glanced at the corner. "I'm sorry for that. I might've overreacted. A little bit."

Ember's green eyes looked cautiously hopeful. "So, we're okay?"

"No," I rasped. "Far from it. You're my *Sallith'tahn*, and there is a human interloper between us. We are definitely not okay."

Her face shut down, becoming anguished again. "Riley…"

"Just hear me out, Firebrand." I walked forward until I was standing at the foot of the bed, gazing down at her. "I've been thinking a lot. About us. And the soldier. And what I should do about this situation. And you know what I've decided?"

She shook her head, extremely wary now. "What?"

I smirked. "Nothing."

Confusion flickered over her face.

"I'm a dragon, Firebrand," I said. "And—here's a news flash—so are you. This life-mate thing, this *Sallith'tahn*, it's not going away. If you feel even half of what I do, I know you can't ignore it." I bent down, gripping the bed frame, leaning forward so that we were eye to eye. I heard her heartbeat pick up, saw her nostrils flare and her eyes dilate, and felt the heat in my veins rise up, reaching out for her.

"We're connected, Ember," I said. "This is meant to be. Fight it all you want—it's going to happen sooner or later. So, you go ahead and pretend to be human, if you like. I won't threaten the soldier, and I won't get in your way." Her eyes widened incredulously, and I gave a small smile. "I won't have to. Human emotions are fickle things, Firebrand, you'll see that soon enough. What we have is stronger than emotion, stronger than the humans' idea of love. Dragons will always outlast humans—all I have to do is wait. But…" I leaned closer, lowering my voice to a near growl. "I *will* be at your side, day in and day out, and I will take every opportunity to remind you that you are a dragon. You can count on that."

Ember swallowed. Her eyes had gone rather glassy, echoes of her own dragon staring out at me. "You're my *Sallith'tahn*," I said quietly, and rose, holding her gaze. "That will never change. No matter what you feel for the soldier, you will always be mine.

"Oh, and one more thing," I added, just as she'd started to relax. "The soldier can only be a human. He can never be a dragon." Ember started to reply, but I leaned down so that our faces were maybe an inch apart. She froze, and I brushed a palm across her cheek.

"I can be both," I whispered, and walked away. She didn't move, didn't answer, but I felt the predatory stare on my back, unrelenting, until I left the room and the door clicked shut behind me.

GARRET

"We've arrived a little late," Tristan muttered as the engine died. He tugged the bag off my head. "The assembly has already begun. Everyone but the guards should be in there." He glanced at me, his mouth pulled into a faint smirk, the hint of the Tristan I knew, once. Who could look a hopeless situation in the eye and make a smart-ass comment about it. "You ready for this?"

I took a short breath. "Yes."

He walked around to my side, opened the door and pointed a gun at my face, his eyes hard and cold again. "Get out."

I obeyed, and he shoved me against the side of the car, the pistol at my back, taking a moment to check the cuffs and pat me down once more. I endured, hoping this was part of the deception, that his fellow soldiers could be watching, that Tristan was just playing his part. Dragging me off the car, he gave me a little shove toward the large cathedral looming above the trees. "Move. Try to run, and I'll shoot you before you take three steps. Let's go."

I marched in front of Tristan, a gun held to my ribs, as the stone wall of the cathedral rose above us, blazing with light against the darkness. The cathedral was old and towering, a giant that was meant to impress as well as intimidate. A pair of guards flanked the front door, brows lowered in wary confusion as Tristan walked up with me.

"The hell is this?" one asked, hand straying toward his sidearm. "Stop right there. Identify yourself, soldier."

"Tristan St. Anthony, of the Western Chapterhouse." Tristan's voice was steady as he faced the guards down. "This prisoner and I are here to see the Patriarch."

"Is that so?" the other broke in, raising a brow my direction. "And what makes you think you can march into the assembly, while the Patriarch is addressing the most important people in St. George, to throw this poor bastard at his feet?" Though the guard's tone was mocking, his expression was hard. "Unless this is the dragonloving traitor himself, I don't think you..."

He stopped. Really looked at me. Tristan waited quietly for the realization to sink in, the smugness practically radiating off him in waves. "Holy shit," the guard said at last. "This *is*..."

"Gentlemen..." Tristan gave a cold smile and dragged me forward a step. "May I present Garret Xavier Sebastian, former soldier of St. George, ally to dragons and the most-wanted criminal the Order has seen in decades." I kept my gaze on the ground, as Tristan continued in a voice of quiet triumph. "My former associate decided he was tired of running and turned himself over to me, hoping that St. George might be merciful. I thought the Patriarch would want to know that Sebastian has finally been caught. But..." Tristan pulled me back a pace. "If you think he's too busy..."

"No." The guards raised their weapons, as if afraid we would both try to bolt. "The Patriarch will want to see the traitor," the first said, giving me a look of black hatred. "He'll want to look him in the eye and pass judgment himself. He'll want to know what kind of man betrays his brothers to side with the soulless lizards." Stepping back, he motioned us through the doors. "Go. Sebastian will stand before the Patriarch, and all of St. George. We'll escort you there ourselves."

I exhaled. Well, we were past the doors. Past the guards, in a sense. I wasn't sure if this was a good or bad development, but in a few minutes, it wouldn't matter. I could hear the Patriarch's strong baritone as we entered the cathedral—its vast ceilings soared fifty feet overhead. Stained-glass windows and images of the saints stared down at us as we marched through the center aisle, Tristan keeping a tight grip on my arm. To either side, the pews were filled with officers and soldiers in uniform, their attention riveted to the man at the front of the room. But as we passed, whispers began following us down the aisle, growing louder and stronger, until it was a low, constant murmur at my back. I heard my name, and the words *the traitor* fall from several lips, felt the anger, shock and outrage building like a storm, and kept my gaze fixed straight ahead. At the man standing behind the pulpit.

He had stopped talking and was watching us approach, brow furrowed, obviously wondering what this was about. Who would dare to interrupt him in the middle of his speech?

Then, our eyes met, and I saw the moment he realized exactly who I was.

Tristan, I thought bleakly, as he pulled me to a halt at the base of the dais. If I said anything now, my voice would carry no weight. I was a prisoner, hurling wild accusations to save his life, and would be silenced or dragged away without a thought. *If you're going to release me, now would be the time.*

"Garret Xavier Sebastian." When the Patriarch spoke, the assembly fell silent. He stepped away from the pulpit, "From among the devils, he returns to us. Our prodigal son has come home."

No one spoke. The Patriarch's voice had a mesmerizing quality, like a snake staring down its prey. Pausing at the top of the steps, the Patriarch watched me a moment, then offered a gentle, forgiving smile. He thought he had won.

He probably had.

The Patriarch took one step forward, pausing at the top of the stage, and then his gaze shifted from me to my former partner, assessing. "Your name, soldier?" he asked quietly.

"Tristan St. Anthony, sir."

"And do we have you to thank for the traitor's capture?"

"My former partner surrendered himself to me, sir." Tristan's voice didn't waver, though the grip on my arm tightened. "It was my duty to bring him here, to await your judgment."

"And you have done your duty admirably. I will remember your service, soldier." The Patriarch nodded at Tristan, then turned his attention to me again. "Tell me, Sebastian," he went on, looming over me with that serene smile in place. "Have you realized your mistake? Have you looked into the heart of the enemy and seen the evil staring back at you? Do you come to confess, to beg forgiveness, because you have betrayed not only your brothers, but every brother that came before and died for our cause?" He leaned forward, his voice soft but commanding. "Confess, Sebastian. Confess your crimes, and I will be merciful. Before this brotherhood, before the men you betrayed, renounce the demon lizards, and let your conscience be clear before we send you to your final judgment."

I met his gaze. "My conscience is clear," I murmured, in a voice meant for only the two of us. "I know which side I'm on, and I've never lied about it. Of the two of us, whose crimes are greater?"

The Patriarch's face went deathly pale. His jaw tightened, eyes going blank, and for a moment, I thought he might kill me then. Snatch the pistol from his guard and shoot me through the heart. But then he blinked, and his face smoothed out again, his expression calm as the mask slid into place.

"No," he said, drawing back. "No, you have not come to plead for mercy. There is no shame in your eyes, no remorse, only defiance. So be it." He straightened, ignoring me and raising his voice for the crowd. "The traitor's soul has been corrupted by the devils," he announced. "He refuses to atone for his crimes against the brotherhood and stands defiant before God and man. He is a blasphemer, a worshipper of the Wyrm, and will not repent of his evil."

Something cold slipped between my wrists; the thin edge of a knife, and my legs nearly buckled with relief.

"Garret Xavier Sebastian," the Patriarch went on, speaking to all of us now. "It pains me to do this. To know that you have willingly turned your back on St. George and everything we have taught you. To know you have sold yourself to evil, and we cannot save you from the damnation that awaits. You will be executed before all of St. George for your crimes against the Order. I pray that when you stand before God tonight, he will have mercy upon your soul." He turned, his steps heavy, to walk back to the pulpit. "Take him away."

The ties binding my hands parted with a jerk. I breathed a silent note of thanks to my former partner and stepped forward, raising my voice to echo through the room.

"Before you do that," I announced, and the Patriarch whirled around, eyes widening when he saw that I was free, "and while we're on the subject of confessions, perhaps there is something you should explain to the rest of the assembly, sir." I reached into my jacket and pulled out the envelope, holding it aloft like a torch. "Perhaps you should explain *your* partnership with Talon, and the dragons, for the past year and a half."

Instant pandemonium. Behind me, the room exploded in a cacophony of noise and outrage. Men were on their feet, shouting, calling for my head, demanding answers. One of the guards who'd escorted us in went for me, raising his gun. But Tristan silently stepped between us, a warning look in his eyes, and the guard stumbled to a halt, unsure what to do.

Through all of this, the Patriarch didn't move. He stared at me, his expression calm. Finally, he raised a hand, and the noise gradually died down.

"They are quite desperate now, aren't they?" he stated, shaking his head, as if this whole thing was ridiculous beyond measure. "Did the dragons put you up to this, soldier? Send one of our own to infiltrate the Order and break it from within? They should know by now, we are far too strong for such deception. St. George will never fall to the machinations of dragons."

"That might be true, sir," I replied, "if not for the fact that I have evidence of your treachery right here." Turning my back on him, I faced the angry room, holding up the envelope. "Proof of the Patriarch's involvement!" I called, as the room began to erupt again. "Bank statements, photos of secret meetings, recordings of conversations between Richard Amitage and an agent of Talon. The Patriarch has been accepting money from the organization for over a year!"

"Shoot the traitor!" came a voice from the back, impossible to see who it was in the chaos. I held my breath, half expecting a gunshot to ring out to end the tirade and my life. But Tristan, shockingly, stepped forward, putting himself between me and the throng starting to push forward.

"He's telling the truth!" Tristan shouted, making the first row pause a moment. "I've seen it with my own eyes! This isn't a lie! The evidence is real." He faltered, taking a breath, as if he couldn't believe what he was saying himself. "Sebastian speaks the truth," he said at last, his voice slightly choked. "The Patriarch...is working with Talon."

"Hold."

The ranks parted, and Lieutenant Gabriel Martin stepped to the edge of the circle, his face grim as he faced us. "I know both these boys," he told the crowd, his steely expression freezing them in place. "St. Anthony is one of mine, as was Sebastian. He is...or rather, *was*...one of the best soldiers I've ever seen. Neither is prone to exaggeration or flights of fancy. Sebastian is a traitor to the Order, and I despise what he has become." I felt an almost physical blow as he said this, my stomach clenching in pain as Martin looked at me, black eyes glinting with contempt.

"But," Martin went on, holding my gaze, "if there's one thing Sebastian is *not*, it's a liar. Even in matters as troubling as this."

"Lieutenant," said the Patriarch, his voice full of quiet menace. "Are you saying you would believe a traitor and a dragon convert over your own Patriarch? This boy who has betrayed us all, who has been helping our enemies slaughter and destroy more of our own?"

"No, Patriarch," Martin replied, bowing his head. "But I am concerned with the truth. In whatever form it comes to me. Given the nature of these claims, we must consider all sides. If the boy is lying, I will put the bullet in him myself. And I will accept whatever discipline you choose to bestow upon me for my doubt." His jaw tightened as he turned, staring me down. "These are serious accusations, soldier," he said, a warning and a threat. "Are you prepared to back them up, knowing the repercussions if you cannot?"

"Yes, sir."

He held out a calloused, burn-scarred hand, and I gave him the envelope without hesitation. The sharp sound of the flap being torn open echoed like a gunshot in the deathly quiet of the room. I backed up with Tristan as several other officers crowded in, gazing over Martin's shoulder as he pulled out the contents of the envelope. It was out of my hands now. I had done everything I could. Now, it was up to St. George itself to decide the fate of its Patriarch.

I glanced at the man before the pulpit. He stood quietly, arms folded before him, watching his men sift through the documents and mutter among themselves. His expression remained calm, even a little amused. He didn't look disturbed in the slightest, and my insides shifted anxiously. What if I was wrong? What if I'd overlooked something, misheard the conversation between the Patriarch and the agent of Talon? What if the Patriarch was the one setting up the organization, and I had just made a huge blunder in exposing it?

No, I told myself. *You know what you saw. The Patriarch is a*

master of swaying men to his side. If he acts guilty now, there'll
be no question. Everyone will know what he's done.

For a split second, the Patriarch's gaze flicked to me, hard
and full of hate. Around Martin, the murmurs were growing
louder, more outraged with every page turned, every photo
changing hands. Finally, the murmurs died down, to be replaced with a shocked, furious anticipation.

"Patriarch." A man stepped forward, one I didn't recognize.
But he was older than Martin, older than the Patriarch, with
cropped silver hair and a patch over one eye. His raspy voice
rang with authority, and the other men fell silent as he spoke.
"You have been accused of conspiring with Talon against the
Order of St. George, and the evidence brought against you is
substantial. Have you anything to say in your defense?"

"I am the Patriarch," was the proud reply. "The chosen shep-
herd of the Order of St. George and the right hand of God.
I do not need a defense. Only He may judge me." He shot a
cold look over the crowd and turned to me again, eyes flashing with hate. "I invoke the ancient rite of Trial by Combat," he announced, and murmurs spread rapidly through the
chamber. The Patriarch raised his voice to be heard over the
tide. "Before God and man, I call Garret Xavier Sebastian a
liar and a traitor. His evidence is false, lies fabricated by the
Wyrm to blind our eyes. As such, and in accordance with our
sacred traditions, I challenge Garret Xavier Sebastian to Trial
by Combat. Let the Lord's blessing uphold the righteous, and
let His judgment fall upon the damned. I call upon the Divine
to hear my plea and to punish the one whose soul is corrupt.
Let God choose His champion. Let Him decide who is guilty!"

A shiver raced up my spine. Trial by Combat. I had first

heard the term at the academy when Peter Matthews, enraged by some imagined slight, had thrown down the challenge. *Trial by Combat*, he'd snarled at me, to the gasps of everyone watching. A duel to prove, once and for all, who was the best. The outcome had not been pleasant for either of us, resulting in a severe lecture from the Headmaster himself, who berated us on the seriousness of the challenge, that it was not to be used for foolish pride. Trial by Combat called for the judgment of God Himself to descend upon the guilty, to bless the righteous and smite the wicked. Such a request was never to be taken lightly.

The Patriarch gave a triumphant smile as he held my gaze, dropping his voice so that only I could hear it. "The Code of St. George demands such a challenge be honored by all," he stated, secure in his knowledge of ancient laws and customs. "No one will defend you now, soldier. No one will step forward. This is between the three of us. You, your Patriarch and God." I caught the grim looks of Martin and the rest of the officers, and knew he was right. Once the challenge had been invoked, they could not interfere without breaking tradition. And that was something the Order clung to at all costs.

"Garret Xavier Sebastian," Martin said, stepping forward. His jaw was tight, his eyes angry, but he spoke in a steady voice, and the murmurs surrounding us died away. "You have been challenged by the accused, in a duel to the death, to discern the guilt or innocence of the parties involved. You may choose to either accept the challenge or decline. But know that if you decline, you mark yourself as guilty in the eyes of everyone here. What is your answer?"

I clenched my jaw. I was trapped, and the Patriarch knew it. If I refused, he would win. All the evidence we'd gathered, all our plans to get me here, they would be for nothing. In the eyes of the Order, refusing to fight would acknowledge my guilt and confirm the Patriarch's innocence. It was illogical, it was absurd, but St. George would follow tradition even if it meant a corrupt man would go free.

If I accepted, I would have to fight him. To the death. I didn't know how skilled a fighter the Patriarch was, but I did know he was a trained warrior. Before he became the Patriarch, he was a soldier of the Order, utterly dedicated to the cause. Of course, St. George would not let him anywhere near the real war now; he was far too important to risk, but he trained for the possibility every day, ready and willing, should he ever be called upon to serve the Order in battle once more. Or so the stories went.

I didn't want to fight him. Not that I was afraid; despite his exalted position and claims of holiness, he was only a man. And it didn't matter who or what you were, be it human, dragon or saint; everything could bleed, and everything could die. But I already had the blood of my former brothers on my hands, staining my conscience. If I killed the Patriarch, the divine, God-chosen leader of St. George, I would be forever marked.

But we had come too far, and it was far too late to turn back now. I thought of Ember and Riley, and the underground of rogue dragons, dragons who just wanted to be free. I thought of Jade, risking her life to protect the monastery, refusing to leave her monks to the mercy of the Order. And of Tristan, who had brought me here despite all his misgivings, who'd upheld his end of the bargain even though it could cost him dearly. Maybe even his life. The Order had to change, that much was certain, but change required more than one voice. It would require action, sacrifice, the stubbornness to see it through to the end. I'd been willing to die tonight, to be the voice that started the questions and the doubts, however small they were. Was I willing to kill for it, as well?

The chamber, I realized, had grown deathly silent. Everyone was watching me, waiting for my answer. Martin stood in front of me, solemn and grave, knowing either choice could change the Order forever. Tristan remained at my side; he hadn't moved the whole time, silently telling everyone where he stood. And looming over us all, the Patriarch watched me with a faint, sinister smile, knowing that, whatever my decision, he could still win the day.

I couldn't let that happen. For the innocent lives I'd taken, for Riley and Jade, and for a fiery red dragon who completely owned my heart, I would not let this man be responsible for any more deaths. And if the Order was destroyed as a result, let that be the beginning of the change. Let it start right here.

I raised my voice, and the room seemed to hold its breath as I made my decision.

"I accept."

EMBER

Nearly midnight, and still no Garret.

I sat on his bed, gazing at the clock on the nightstand and feeling the silence thud in my ears. The rest of the rooms were silent. Wes was huddled over his computer and Riley, after his defiant confession that had made my insides ache with longing and guilt, had left me alone. Waiting for a soldier that might not come back.

The clock flipped to midnight, and my heart twisted with every minute that passed, every moment that went by not knowing where he was, what was happening to him. Was he okay? Had he managed to get to the Patriarch and the rest of the Order? Or had St. George imprisoned him, or even killed him? The worst part was, if Garret was in trouble, if he'd been taken captive or struck down by the Order that raised him, I'd never know.

The door opened and closed quietly, and I looked up, heart pounding. Soft footsteps walked down the hall, and then Garret appeared in the door frame, looking grave and exhausted, but alive. He gave a weary smile as he stepped into the room.

"Hey, dragon girl. I'm back."

I skirted the bed, crossed the room and launched myself

into his open arms. He hugged me tight, desperate relief flaring around us both.

"So, it worked?" I whispered, pulling back to look at him. "The Order actually listened to you?" Of course, they must have, otherwise he wouldn't be here now. I gave a breathless laugh and grinned up at him. "I can hardly believe you pulled it off."

But Garret's eyes clouded, and he shook his head. "Not yet," he murmured. "It's not over yet. There is one more thing that I have to do."

★ ★ ★

Dawn. On the salt flats just outside the city. Stepping out of the car, I gazed around in amazement. The ground beyond the railing was white, like snow, and stretched away before us, so flat and empty it seemed you were looking at the edge of the world. The splash of red against the horizon seemed a million miles away. Lifting a hand to shield my eyes, I stared over the landscape. There was absolutely nothing out there; no grass, no trees, nothing but a cracked, brittle layer of salt, glittering coldly in the predawn light.

"Well," Riley said, exiting the driver's seat and coming to stand beside me, "this is it. Hell of a place for a duel to the death, St. George. I'd make a comment about rubbing salt in the wound if it wasn't so obvious." He turned as Garret's footsteps crunched over the ground, a moment before he appeared on my other side. "You're absolutely sure this isn't an ambush? I don't like the idea of being out here with the Order, in the literal middle of nowhere."

"I'm sure." Garret didn't look at Riley as he said this, his gaze on the barren flats before us. "The Order is bound by honor and tradition. That's why they let me go when the challenge was issued. If I ran, or refused to show up, the Patriarch would automatically be the victor. There would be no question of my guilt. The same is true for St. George. Two parties agree to meet on neutral ground, and no one except the combatants are allowed to attack or harm the other. If the Patriarch breaks the rules, he declares himself guilty in the eyes of the Order. His seconds are there to ensure the fight is fair, and that everyone heeds the rules."

Riley scoffed. "So, you're saying that the Order of St. George is just going to stand there, in sight of two dragons, and once this duel starts, they're not going to doing anything?"

"Yes." He finally glanced at us, his gaze solemn. "And I need you to do the same," he said. "We're allowed up to three witnesses each, and there's no one else I trust. But..." His gaze went to mine. "Just remember, if I fall, you can't help me or attack the Order. No matter what happens, even if the Patriarch kills me, you can't interfere. Doing so will forfeit the battle and mark us all as the guilty party. And the Patriarch will win. So, promise me, Ember. No matter what happens to me, promise you won't interfere. Even if the worst happens." He reached out and squeezed my arm, his eyes soft. "No turning into a dragon and setting the Patriarch on fire," he said with a faint smile. "That would defeat what we're trying to do here."

I glared at him. "All right, but you'd better win," I whispered, wondering how he could be so calm about this. When he first told me what he had to do, I'd been shocked. A duel to the death with the leader of St. George? I knew Garret was a skilled soldier and that he could handle himself better than any human I'd seen, but still...it was a duel to the death! If he screwed up, or if something unexpected happened, I would lose him. "You can't let him beat you," I said, gazing into his eyes. "You have to win."

He nodded once. "I intend to." And in an even softer voice, added, "I finally have something worth living for."

We started across the flats, the brittle, crusty salt crunching beneath our footsteps. The alien landscape stretched on, white and barren, so empty you could see all the way to the distant, hazy mountains. Nothing moved on the flats, no grass, trees, animals or anything. The only sounds were our footsteps in the salt and the occasional mutter from Riley.

After a couple minutes, a group of small black dots appeared in the distance, growing larger and larger, until I could recognize them as people. A man stood in front, tall and striking, waiting for us with his arms loose at his sides. He was dressed in a uniform of brilliant white accented by red, the symbol of the scarlet cross and shield on his shoulder. A sword, straight edged and lethal with a cross-shaped hilt, hung from his waist.

I felt Garret tense, just as I glanced from what had to be the Patriarch to the three men standing behind him. Two I didn't recognize. One was an older man with dark hair and stern eyes, and the other, with his snow-white beard and black eye patch, was older still. But the last, standing a little ways away and not quite meeting my gaze, was Tristan. All three were armed, but then again, so were we.

We came to a stop about twenty feet from each other, Garret slightly out in front, Riley and me to either side. I looked at the Patriarch, saw the instant, venomous hatred the second our eyes met, and swallowed the growl rising to my throat.

"These are your witnesses?" The Patriarch's voice was deep, commanding, yet full of unbridled loathing. His cold blue eyes raked over Riley and me, and it took everything I had not to curl a lip in return. "Dragons," he stated flatly, turning back to Garret. "I should have known you would bring demons as your seconds. Can you control them, traitor? Do they understand they are not to interfere?"

I bristled. "Don't worry about us," I said. "We'll behave, as long as *your* soldiers remember they're not allowed to shoot us in cold blood."

"Do not fear, dragon," the Patriarch replied, making the last word sound like a curse. "*They* understand honor. They know what is at stake." He looked at Garret, a faint smile curling his lips, dismissing the rest of us. "I thought it fitting that your treasonous former partner be here to witness your destruction," he said in a low voice. "The true soldiers of St. George will follow the rules of this challenge and will make certain your witnesses do not interfere." His voice dropped even lower. "But know that when we are finished here St. Anthony will be punished for his role in this treachery, as well. God's judgment will extend to all."

I felt Garret's anger, saw it in the way his jaw tightened and his eyes grew hard. But his voice was calm as he answered. "Judgment has yet to be decided, sir."

"Indeed." The Patriarch nodded, and straightened. "Lieutenant Martin," he called without taking his eyes from us. "Please give Sebastian his weapon."

One of the older men approached and held out his arms. Resting in his palms was the sheath of a long, straight blade, much like the Patriarch's, with a black cross handle poking out of the leather.

Riley snorted. "Longswords?" he stated in disbelief. "I know the Order never got past their medieval glory days, but still. Are we back in the Dark Ages? Why don't you guys just mount a horse and charge each other with lances?"

Both men ignored the rogue, though the man called Martin gave him a black look, obviously not pleased with being so close to his ancient enemy. "Trial by Combat is one of the ancient rites of St. George," the Patriarch told Garret. "Therefore, we will fight as the knights did before us, long ago. No guns, no modern tricks. This shall be between two warriors in the eyes of God." He gestured to the sword. "Take your weapon, Sebastian. And don't worry about balance, or inferiority, or keenness. It is a perfectly efficient blade. I sharpened it myself."

Garret reached out and took the offered sword, then drew it from its sheath. Bared to the light, it glimmered coldly, a simple-looking weapon without color or adornment. Not as fine as the Patriarch's blade, I noticed, but I guessed a sword didn't have to look pretty. It just had to kill.

"We'll begin momentarily," Martin said, looking at Garret as he stepped back. "I suggest you use that time to prepare yourself. Pray, settle any final accounts and say your last goodbyes. The duel starts in five minutes."

Garret nodded. We retreated until we were about fifty feet away, well out of earshot, before Riley let out a breath and shook his head. "Well, isn't he a charming bastard," he muttered with a quick glare back at the Patriarch. "You sure you got this, St. George?"

"I don't know." Garret looked at the sword in his hand. "We've trained with knives and blades in the Order, though not as extensively as everything else. The Patriarch, though… it's said that he collects swords and medieval weapons. I have no idea if he knows how to use them." He, too, glanced at the men behind us, silhouetted against the stark white of the flats. "I guess I'll find out soon enough."

"Yeah, well, try not to get yourself killed, Sebastian." Riley's voice was begrudgingly concerned. "Flipping the Order off is a lot easier when you're around."

"Thanks," Garret said drily.

"No problem. Although, if you do get splattered into eighteen parts, that will make certain things easier for me, as well." Riley gave a slightly evil, almost triumphant grin, and his eyes glittered in the dim light. "So remember that, human, because I plan to be around for a long time. I'm not going anywhere."

I scowled at the rogue, but Garret gave him a wary, almost puzzled look. "If I didn't know better, I'd say you were trying to make certain I win," he said.

"Perish the thought, St. George," Riley said breezily. "This is a win-win situation for me. You kill the Patriarch and deal a devastating blow to the Order, awesome. You get yourself killed, the Order is still in chaos over the scandal, and I can use the confusion to make sure my underground is safe from both them and Talon. No more human, no more agonizing. Win-win."

"Riley," I growled, and the rogue gave me the most unapologetic, shit-eating grin I'd ever seen. He was, I thought in dismay, completely confident about his earlier declaration. I didn't know whether to feel angry, relieved or terrified.

"Sebastian!" the Patriarch called before either of us could respond. He had walked to the center of the field and was standing tall with his sword held at his side. "Two minutes, traitor!" he warned, as my heart jumped up and lodged in my throat. "Two minutes until God's judgment is upon us. I have made my peace with the Almighty. Have you?"

Garret looked at me. In the shadows of his gaze I saw longing and determination, and something so strong it made my stomach dance. I knew Riley was watching, but I didn't care. This was a fight to the death.

Stepping forward, I grabbed the front of his shirt, leaned up and kissed him. His arm wrapped around my waist, pulling me close, crushing me to his body. I heard Riley snort and turn away, and then I forgot about him, Talon, the Patriarch, everyone. I was only aware of this spot, this moment in time and the human in my arms.

"You'll win," I whispered as we drew back. "If there is a just God, He won't let you lose, not with what we're trying to do. But you don't need His help, Garret. You've got this. You're going to beat the Patriarch, and St. George will see him for what he really is. And then we can finally put this whole stupid mess behind us." He blinked, and I gave a wobbly smile. "Until the next catastrophe, anyway."

Garret pressed his forehead to mine. "I love you, Ember," he whispered, making my insides knot. "I never...thought I could feel this way, especially for a dragon. But, if this is the last time we're together, I want you to know. Nothing has changed since Vegas. Since Crescent Beach, really. You're still the most important thing that's ever happened to me, and if I die here trying to protect your kind from St. George, I have no regrets."

"Garret..."

"Don't say anything," he murmured, smiling a little as he pulled back. "It sounds like a goodbye, and I still need something to look forward to. To help me win. Just be waiting for me when I get back."

"I will."

He brushed a thumb across my cheek, turned and walked to the center of the ring, where the Patriarch waited in the bloody red light of the rising sun.

GARRET

I hadn't been entirely truthful.

When Riley asked me if I could handle this, I'd sidestepped the question. I'd told him I didn't know if the Patriarch could fight. That was a lie. Not only did the Patriarch collect swords and ancient weapons, he trained with them extensively. When he invoked the right of Trial by Combat, it wasn't the desperate, last-minute ploy of a man with nothing to lose. It was a strategic gamble that would give him all the advantages. I knew little of swordplay; we'd trained with blades in the Order, but it was only a small part of our education, being seen as mostly impractical and taught more for the sake of tradition than for actual use. The Patriarch probably had this plan in reserve all along, knowing that someday he might have to use it. I knew this wouldn't be an easy fight. I wasn't even certain that I could win.

But I couldn't concede. The Patriarch held the advantage in this duel, but there were too many counting on me to fail now. Including a certain fiery dragon girl who would be waiting for me when this was over. She was the reason I was doing this, the reason my life had changed. If I died here trying to change the Order, if even a few in St. George began to question things, it would be worth it.

In the center of the imaginary circle, the Patriarch waited for me, a bright, motionless statue in white and red. Martin stood to one side like a referee, facing us both, his dark figure silhouetted against the pale ground. There was no breeze, no breath of air that stirred the flats, no sound except my footsteps crunching over the salt. I halted ten feet from where my opponent stood, and for a moment, absolute silence descended over the world.

The Patriarch's cold blue eyes met mine over the arena. "Blasphemer," he said softly, the whisper full of horrified loathing, perfectly clear in the complete stillness. "Demon lover. You're enslaved to the she-devil, aren't you, Sebastian? Your soul is tainted beyond redemption. I don't know whether to hate you or pity you. But don't worry." He raised his sword very slightly, letting the light dance along the razor surface. "I'll set you free."

I almost smiled. The Patriarch's words meant nothing to me. Perhaps a few months ago, when I'd first realized I might be falling for the creature that was supposed to be my enemy, perhaps then I would have cared. But it was far too late now. I'd accepted the truth—I was in love with a dragon—and I wasn't ashamed.

"You both know the conditions." Gabriel Martin's firm, quiet voice carried over the flats. "The duel will continue until one of you concedes or is killed. There will be no interference or intervention, and no weapons except the ones you carry now. Breaching any of these rules means that you forfeit the duel. Do you both understand and accept these terms?"

"Yes," I answered, while the Patriarch simply nodded.

"Very well. The duel will start at twenty feet. When I give the signal, you will begin."

Gripping my sword, I retreated the specified length and turned as the Patriarch did the same. I could feel Ember's and Riley's stares at my back, and saw Tristan several yards away, watching with his arms crossed and a grim look on his face. Martin raised his hand, paused a moment, then clenched his fist and stepped back, getting out of the way. The duel for my life, Tristan's life and the lives of all the dragons I'd sworn to protect had officially begun.

The Patriarch sauntered forward, confident and self-assured, the blade still held at his side. But he moved with a lethal grace I'd seen all too often, in both enemies and friends. There was no question that he knew how to fight, and fight well. Raising my sword, I stepped forward to meet him.

We circled each other a moment, looking for openings, probing defenses and weaknesses. Our feet crushed salt beneath them, the noise rippling over the absolute silence as we circled warily, just studying our opponent. The Patriarch was taller, stronger and had a longer reach than me. I'd have to get well inside his guard to land a blow, while he could keep me at a distance.

"How does it feel, Sebastian?" The Patriarch's voice was barely audible, meant only for my ears. "To be completely enslaved to the lizards? To know your soul is damned, but there is nothing you can do about it?"

I narrowed my eyes, circling just outside his reach. "Who are we speaking about?" I answered in an equally low voice. "Me, or yourself?"

The Patriarch gave a weary chuckle. "I know my soul is damned," he said tiredly. "I am fully aware that I've made a deal with the devil, and the time will come when I must stand before God and answer for my crimes. But I am still the leader of this Order, and I can still eliminate our enemies. One day, I will break free of this contract, but for now, our enemies are dying and will continue to die as long as I am here to oversee it. Every death pushes the devils closer to extinction. That is worth the cost of my soul."

Abruptly, the Patriarch lunged, sweeping his sword at my head. I leaped back, smacking the blade away, the clang of steel on steel ringing out in the silence. The Patriarch swung again, and I brought my sword up to block, but abruptly he twisted it and came in from another direction. I dodged, but the tip scored my face, right below my eye. Scrambling away, I braced for more attacks, but the Patriarch stopped and lowered his blade, smiling at his handiwork.

"First blood to me," he said in satisfaction. "I hope you prayed before you came here, soldier."

I took a steadying breath, weighing my options. That he was playing with me was troubling; he obviously knew more about swordplay than I did and was content to stretch this duel out for as long as he could. Or until I made a fatal mistake. I could feel blood trickling down my face and resisted the urge to wipe it away, keeping my attention on my opponent. I couldn't banter with him. The longer we sparred, the smaller my chances of victory became. If I was going to beat the Patriarch, I had to do it now.

I lunged savagely, cutting at his face, making him blink and step back to avoid it. Quickly, I pressed that small advantage with an upward slice that made him retreat another step. I pursued him across the field with a series of slashes and cuts, intending to overwhelm him and give him no chance to recover.

The Patriarch smiled. Parrying a slash, he sidestepped with the motion, appearing behind me in a blindingly quick move, and brought his weapon slicing across my back. I felt the bite of the sword edge rip through my shirt a second before the pain hit and I stifled a yell of agony. I whirled, barely managing to keep my feet, as the Patriarch stepped forward and casually pointed the tip of his sword at my face.

"Yield, soldier," he said. "The fight is lost. I promise to give you a quick death if you renounce your blasphemous crimes and beg forgiveness of the Order. Put down your sword, and I will end your pain and send you to God with a clean conscience. Your dragon friends would not do the same."

"No," I panted, raising my sword as I backed up a few steps. My back and left shoulder burned like they were on fire, and every motion sent a fresh stab of pain up my spine. It was a long, shallow gash, parting muscle and skin, more painful than deadly. I could still stand, and if I could stand, I could fight. I would not yield. I would see this through to the end, for her.

The Patriarch shook his head. "Why do you continue to protect them, Sebastian?" he asked. "They are not deserving of such loyalty. They are creatures. Monsters. They imitate us in order to infiltrate our world, our loved ones and our way of life. To corrupt it from within."

"You're wrong."

"The world does not belong to them," he continued, as if I hadn't said anything. "The world belongs to man, as God intended it to be." He stabbed the point of his blade at the

edge of the circle, where Ember and Riley watched helplessly
from the side. "They are not human, Sebastian. They don't
have souls, they don't feel like we do. They are born of darkness and can never understand us. The only thing they know
is how to manipulate and kill."

"That isn't true," I gritted out. *"Different* doesn't mean *evil.*
Some of those dragons want nothing to do with the war. Some
of them just want to survive. If you would just talk to one of
them, you would understand that."

"Spoken like a true dragonlover." The Patriarch's mild expression faded, growing hard. "I should have known you would
turn on us. It was only a matter of time. It was in your blood,
after all." He shook his head, his features twisting with hate.
"Like mother, like son."

It felt like he'd punched me. For a moment, I could only
stare at him, reeling, while he stood there with a faint smile
on his face, knowing he'd just destroyed my whole perception
of reality with one casual statement.

"What are you talking about?" I finally asked, and amazingly, my voice came out mostly steady. "My parents...they
were killed by Talon."

"Yes, they were," the Patriarch agreed, stalking forward. "Because they both worked for the dragons. Because, intentional
or not, they chose to serve evil and turn their backs on their
fellow man." He gave me another look of pity and loathing.
"Your parents were dragon servants, soldier. They were employees of Talon."

He came at me hard, lunging across the flats, his sword a
streak of metal through the air. Still dazed from having my
entire world shattered, I barely got my blade up in time to

parry. The Patriarch's sword screeched as it hammered into mine, sending vibrations up my arm. I staggered, and the sword clanged against mine again, knocking it away. And then there was a second fiery pain, as the Patriarch's sword sliced into my leg, cutting through cloth and flesh and biting deep.

Gasping, I reeled away, scrambling to put distance between myself and the Patriarch, but my leg buckled and I fell, rolling several feet before coming to an agonizing stop. Salt shards cut at my bare arms, burning into scrapes and open wounds, but it was nothing compared to what my leg was feeling at the moment. Blood blossomed over my jeans, warm and sluggish, staining the material black.

Gripping my sword, I looked around for the Patriarch, but he hadn't pursued. He watched me stagger upright with a triumphant look in his eyes. One way or another, he knew the fight was nearly done. Clenching my teeth as my torn muscles screamed in protest, I planted my feet and raised my sword, facing the Patriarch again.

"It's over, Sebastian," he stated, walking forward. "Do you have any final words before I send you to hell?"

Something clicked in my head, and for a second, the world seemed to stop. A memory, jarred loose from the shadows of my mind.

The dragon loomed overhead, dark and terrifying, yellow eyes glowing in the smoke and the gloom. It was close enough for me to see every scale on its massive body, smell the sulfur and ash that clung to it, feel the hot breath curling from huge, fang-filled jaws. It gazed down with impassive gold eyes, a nightmare creature regarding the small boy and his mother at

*its feet. It blinked once, rumbled deep in its belly and stepped
aside, dismissing us. And then, everything fragmented.*

A burst of gunfire.

*My mother jerking up with a gasp, then falling on top of
me.*

*The howls and screams of the dragon, mixed with more
chattering gunfire, the shouting of men and the hiss of fire
being extinguished by the rain.*

The memory flared and was gone in an instant, a split second between breaths, but it was enough. I gaped at the man before me, momentarily forgetting the pain of my wounds. "It was you," I rasped, as the aftermath of that scene came back in a flood, finally breaking through the wall that held it at bay. "My parents weren't killed by dragons. They were killed by the Order! And you knew! All this time, St. George has lied to me. My whole life, they let me believe my family was murdered by Talon, when it was the Order all along."

The Patriarch's eyes glittered. "I should have ordered them to shoot you then and there," he said. "The mission was to kill every living soul in that compound, regardless of age or gender. But the commander leading the raid begged me for permission to bring you into the Order, to raise you as a soldier for the cause. He thought you could be saved, or perhaps he was simply reluctant to kill one so young." Very briefly, his gaze flickered to Gabriel Martin and narrowed with contempt. "Only a few knew your true lineage. It was kept a secret in the hopes that you would fully embrace our Code and become a soldier of St. George. That you would rise above your heritage and shake whatever evil lay within your soul." He shook his head. "But once a dragon slave, always a dragon slave, it seems. I should have realized your betrayal was only a matter of time."

Another memory jarred loose. Rain and mud and fire, me huddled beside the motionless body of my mother, hoping she would wake up soon so we could go home. A shadow falling over me, as I gazed into the stern, younger face of Lucas Benedict. And all the confusion, shock, pain and disbelief melted into a sudden blinding, fiery rage.

"So, we come full circle," the Patriarch was saying, raising his sword as he closed in. "Talon's wayward son shows his true colors at last. And now, I will finish what I should have done all those years ago, and send you to your masters where you belong!"

He lunged, bringing that sword down at my neck. I forgot my pain, forgot my mission, forgot everything but the image of my mother's body, lying there in the mud. I reacted on instinct, dodging to the side and turning my body so that the blow missed me by millimeters. For just a moment, the Patriarch was off balance, and I slashed at him with everything I had left.

He turned, managing to block the blade, but the force hammered through his guard, and his own sword struck him in the face. Without a sound, he tumbled backward, hitting the ground on his side, the sword coming free of his grip. Almost immediately, he pushed himself to his knees, but before he got any farther, I staggered forward and put the tip of my blade against his throat.

"Yield."

He froze. The metal point hovered at his neck, resting against his skin. He stared at me almost in shock. Blood streamed down his face from the gash in his forehead, staining the collar of his white uniform. My leg shook, pain hammering through my muscles from the abuse, but I stood tall and kept the sword steady as I locked eyes with the Patriarch.

"Yield," I said again, and his face darkened, his expression twisting with hate.

"I will not."

"Then I'm sorry."

I raised the sword to sweep it down through his neck. It would be quick, I told myself. One more death on my hands. One more unforgivable sin, but perhaps it would be enough to end the slaughter. Or at least, start things in the right direction.

"Stop!" the Patriarch hissed, just as I was about to bring the blade down. I looked at his face and saw it was white with the sudden realization that I had been entirely serious about killing him. "Stop," he said again, slumping in defeat. "I concede. The fight is yours."

Relief swept through me, taking with it the adrenaline that had been keeping me upright through most of the fight. I staggered back from the Patriarch, thankful it was over, feeling my wounds throb and my leg threaten to buckle with every step I took. I saw Tristan and Gabriel Martin walking toward us, neither of them looking particularly happy, though Tristan did manage a tiny nod as our gazes met. Shuddering, I let my sword fall, thumping to the salt. It was over. What happened to the Patriarch now was out of my hands. I would worry about the aftermath, and what it meant for the Order, when I was a little less bloody.

"Garret!"

That voice did bring a smile to my face. I turned, and saw Ember and Riley coming toward me from the opposite end of the arena. Ember was out front, grinning at me, Riley following a few steps behind with a look of reluctant relief.

Still smiling, I took a few steps toward them, then paused as Ember's eyes went wide, her expression shifting to alarm.

"Garret, behind you—!"

I turned as shots rang out in the stillness.

EMBER

He'd won.

The breath rushed out of me, making me kind of giddy with relief. I'd kept telling myself he would win. I mean, it was Garret. The Perfect Soldier. He had saved us from an ambush, led a counterstrike against the Order of St. George and had marched into an entire assembly of those who wanted him dead, only to come out of it triumphant. Even after he'd been wounded, I knew he could still pull it off. He'd done it before. He had to win.

But then the Patriarch started talking, telling him things that made my heart pound with shock and horror. I heard Riley swear in disbelief, saw the blood drain from Garret's face as the Patriarch told him he was once part of Talon. That his parents had been servants of the organization. For just a moment, Garret had faltered. And the Patriarch instantly took advantage of it, lunging in and stabbing the soldier while he was off balance. This time, the wound wasn't a glancing blow, but sank deep into his leg, making me cringe. Garret staggered and fell, crumpling to the unforgiving salt, and the heat flaring through my veins was immediate and intense.

He's going to die. For a moment, it took everything I had not to Shift. Not to burst into dragon form, fly to his side and char the Patriarch into an unrecognizable husk. *No! Stop it, Ember,* I told myself, biting my lip to keep the dragon in check. *You can't help him. You'll forfeit everything we worked for if you interfere now. And you made him a promise.*

My throat felt tight as I watched him climb to his feet, keeping weight off his left leg. Blood had already soaked his jeans, and his bearing was rigid with pain. The Patriarch advanced on him slowly, his expression triumphant, his blade coming up for the final rush. I trembled and clenched my fists, feeling claws start to poke through my skin, the breath in my throat start to burn.

"Ember." Riley's fingers closed on my arms from behind, his voice full of warning. "Steady, Firebrand," he whispered. "Don't do anything reckless. We can't go in there, no matter what happens."

Rage flared, but before I could say anything stupid or accusatory, he added, "And no, I *don't* want him dead, so don't even think of throwing that that in my face. I am fully aware of what is at stake. But if we go in there, we're not only forfeiting the battle, we're showing St. George that dragons can't be trusted. That we're the soulless, evil monsters they believe us to be. And then the war will never be over."

"I know," I choked out, watching the Patriarch taunt Garret one last time, wanting nothing more than to lunge between them and take whatever killing blow was coming. "Dammit. I know I can't help him."

"Don't look," Riley murmured, squeezing my arms. "Turn away if you have to, Firebrand. I'll tell you when it's over."

I shook my head. Though my insides felt like they were being shredded, I wouldn't turn from him now. If the Patriarch killed Garret right in front of me, I wanted to see it. I wanted to remember this moment, because when it was over and we'd all left this arena of slaughter, I was going to hunt the Patriarch down and turn him into a pile of ashes. And no guards, rogue dragons or army of dragonslayers were going to stand in my way.

The Patriarch lunged, swinging his blade at the wounded soldier, and I flinched. But Garret moved with shocking speed, ducking under the blow and cutting at his opponent in return. The Patriarch blocked the sword but, amazingly, was knocked off his feet, sprawling to his side in the dirt and salt, the blade sliding from his grasp. Garret instantly followed his advantage, placing the blade against the man's throat and demanding his surrender.

The Patriarch snarled his refusal. Holding my breath, I watched Garret raise his sword to execute his opponent, but hesitated as the Patriarch's desperate voice broke the silence, yielding the fight at last.

Garret staggered back, lowering his blade, and my heart lurched into motion again. It was over. He was alive, and we had won.

"Son of a bitch," Riley muttered, and I heard the faint smile in his voice. "The bastard pulled it off."

Pulling free, I started across the arena, calling out to Garret. He turned, a smile breaking over his face as he saw me. Behind him, the Patriarch stirred, and I saw the glimmer of raw hatred in his eyes as his arm reached to the small of his back and drew out a pistol. My heart lodged in my throat as he pointed it at the soldier.

"Garret, behind you—!"

A shot rang out as Garret turned, the report echoing over the empty flats. I tensed, ready to Shift and fly at the Patriarch with a roar, but even before the first shot died away, five more boomed into the silence…as Tristan drew his gun with blinding speed and fired, point-blank, into his former Patriarch.

The Patriarch jerked as the bullets tore through him. He swayed and collapsed facedown in the salt, the gun flopping limply in his grip. Blood pooled from beneath his chest, staining his uniform and the ground crimson, as the leader of St. George twitched once, then was still.

Ignoring them all, and what that would mean for everyone, I rushed to Garret. He was still on his feet, gazing at the fallen Patriarch with a slightly dazed look on his face. One leg was covered in blood, and the back of his shirt was completely red, soaked through. He looked a bloody mess, but he was still on his feet.

"Garret." Carefully, I slipped my arms around him, trying to be gentle and take some of his weight, when all I wanted to do was hug him in breathless relief. He gazed down at me, and his eyes were distant and glassy, making my insides clench with alarm. "Hey, you okay—?"

I froze as my hands touched something warm and wet below his ribs. Pulling it back, I saw that my palm and fingers were covered in blood. Heart in my throat, I looked at his side, where a dark red stain was spreading rapidly over his shirt.

Garret shuddered, and collapsed in my arms. Numbly, I lowered him to the ground, cradling his head and shoulders, as blood continued to pool from his side and drip to the salt.

So much. There was so much blood. More than I ever seen in my life.

"Riley!" I howled, and the rogue dragon dropped to the other side of Garret, snarling a curse. Tristan appeared somewhere behind me, looming over my shoulders, but I couldn't take my eyes from the soldier bleeding out in my lap.

"Garret." I pressed a palm to his face, and those glassy, metallic eyes flickered to me. "Hang in there," I whispered, as Riley snarled something at the other soldiers, something about ambulances and first-aid kits. I didn't really hear him. "You're going to be okay," I choked out, feeling my eyes start to burn. Riley grabbed something from Tristan and held it to Garret's side, trying to stop the bleeding. But the soldier's gaze was only for me. "You're going to be fine," I said again, gripping his hand. "Just stay with me, all right?"

Garret gave me that gentle smile...and his eyes started to flicker shut. "No," I growled, squeezing his hand, willing him to stay. "Garret, no. Don't do this. You can't die on me now." My voice broke, and I blinked hard to clear my vision, not caring about the tears streaming down my face and that dragons weren't supposed to be able to cry.

Garret's hand tightened on mine. His eyes opened, steady and clear, gazing up at me, though it was clear he was fighting to keep them open. I swallowed the sob and lowered my head, brushing my lips across his.

"I love you," I whispered, knowing it was too late.

Garret smiled. Then his eyes shut completely, his head fell to the side and he went limp in my arms. I knelt in the cold salt, holding the body of the human I loved, as the sun climbed slowly overhead and painted everything to the horizon in blood.

EPILOGUE

DANTE

I wondered if it was possible to die from nerves.

I had nothing to be anxious about, I told myself for about the hundredth time. The mission had been a rousing success. The vessels had performed flawlessly; in a single night, they had swept through a town, eliminated every target and returned to the rendezvous point exactly as planned. None of the humans living in that place had survived or escaped. The vessels had hit hard and fast, and were able to destroy all targets without alerting a single outside source. A few had sustained minor injuries, and one had been wounded so severely that it had to be put down, but all in all, everything had gone according to plan. Talon couldn't be more pleased. And I was the junior executive who had made it all happen.

I should be ecstatic.

"Mr. Hill? The Elder Wyrm will see you now."

I rose, managing to smile and nod at the secretary as I walked toward the pair of colossal wooden doors at the end of the hall. Nothing adorned the wood, no symbols or emblems, though the flat glare of a security camera caught my attention as I approached the huge frame. I had already passed the biggest, scariest security guard I'd ever seen in my life—a Gila who was possibly half a millennium old, judging by the way my instincts shrank back in terror—before coming into the office. He'd scrutinized my badge long enough to memorize every number on it, then reluctantly let me through. Even now, I thought I could feel his cold stare on my back as I walked steadily toward the looming entrance at the end of the corridor.

My hand shook as I reached out and touched the gold door handles, and I took a moment to catch my breath. *The Elder Wyrm has called for you, Dante. The leader of Talon, the oldest, most powerful dragon in the world is waiting right behind these doors. Think of what that means.*

I couldn't think of the implications for too long. One, it was terrifying; only a handful of dragons ever saw the Elder Wyrm face-to-face. And two, I was expected. It would not do to be late.

With a deep breath, I turned the handle, pushed back the door and stepped into the office of the Elder Wyrm.

Surprisingly, though it was huge and modern with one entire wall made up of windows that showed off the brilliant blue sky, the office was simple and functional without being overly extravagant. The walls were bare and stark, no pictures, photographs, inspirational quotes or anything. The theme of the room was black, gray and white; the only spot of color a red coffee mug on the corner of the enormous black desk. A black leather chair sat behind that desk with its back to me, the leather so glossy, I could see my distorted reflection in the seat.

Heart pounding, I walked across the room, my shoes making no sound on the gray carpet, until I stood at the edge of the desk, gazing at the back of the huge chair. I thought I could just make out a few silvery strands of hair drifting over the top, when the leather seat abruptly swung around to face me, revealing what was behind it.

My mouth went dry, and I was sure I turned as pale as a sheet, as the massive aura of power hit me like a tidal wave, nearly knocking me down. Draconic instincts shrieked in utter primal terror, telling me to run, that the woman sitting calmly behind the desk could squash me like an insect and not even realize it.

"Hello, Dante," the Elder Wyrm said in a low, cool voice, regarding me with appraising green eyes. In her human form, she was a striking older woman with bright silver hair cut into a simple, no-nonsense bob. She wore an elegant gray business suit, a thin gold necklace with a tiny emerald at its heart and her perfectly manicured nails were as red as blood. "I've been wanting to meet you for quite some time."

My mind had gone blank. It was all I could do not to flee that tremendous presence, or drop to my knees and press my face to the floor. Fortunately, my training kicked in even when my brain had stupidly frozen. I felt a smile cross my face, and I gave a slight bow.

"It's a tremendous honor to be here, ma'am. I only hope I don't disappoint."

The Elder Wyrm chuckled. "Quite the opposite," she murmured, as that piercing gaze speared through me, like she was seeing all the way to my soul. "I have heard of your success with the vessels, Dante. And your attempts to retrieve your sister, though they did not turn out as we'd hoped, have proven your loyalty. Many in the organization speak highly of you. They say you are charming, resourceful, intelligent." Her eyes gleamed, and the bloodred smile turned sharp as a blade. "Exactly how the son of the Elder Wyrm, and the heir to the Talon empire, should behave. I am quite proud indeed."

I suddenly couldn't catch my breath. The world had gone hazy and surreal, and I was very aware of my heartbeat, thundering in my ears. The Elder Wyrm observed me a second more, then rose and walked to the huge windows on the opposite wall. I followed numbly, my whole world turned upside down. But through the shock, I could feel a savage, growing excitement. I understood now. Why I was special. Why I had been chosen. This changed everything.

Beside me, the Elder Wyrm observed the city spread below us, and smiled.

"Our enemies are in chaos. Now is the time to strike."

Thank you for reading SOLDIER!

*What do you do when you've
sacrificed all you have for what you believe in—
and it wasn't enough?
There are dark days ahead
as dragons' wings black out the sun.*

Don't miss book 4 *of* THE TALON SAGA

LEGION

only from Julie Kagawa and Harlequin TEEN!

ML   4/2016